To
[signature]

[signature]

JACK

AND THE NEW YORK

DEATH MASK

A number of very wonderful people helped me prepare this book
for publication. Each of them contributed significantly.
I have no doubt that errors have slipped through in spite of their
fine efforts, because I constantly revised the content after they
did their work.
For this I apologize.
Thank you Evie, Meredith and Aimee.
And special thanks to George and Gay.

JACK

AND THE NEW YORK
DEATH MASK

MICHAEL CARRIER

GREENWICH VILLAGE INK

An imprint of Alistair Rapids Publishing
Grand Rapids, MI

JACK

JACK and the New York Death Mask. Copyright 2011 by Michael Carrier.

Published 2011 by Greenwich Village Ink, an imprint of Alistair Rapids Publishing, Grand Rapids, MI.

Permission to use the special font on the cover was obtained from the artist.

Visit the JACK website at http:/www.greenwichvillage.com

For upcoming books by the same author visit www.greenwichvillage-ink.com.

Author can be emailed at mike.jon.carrier@gmail.com.

ISBN: 978-1-936092-79-6 (trade pbk) 1-936092-79-4
Printed in the United States of America

Library of Congress Cataloging-in-Publication Data

Carrier, Michael.
JACK and the New York Death Mask / by Michael Carrier. 1st ed.
ISBN: 978-1-936092-79-6 (trade pbk. : alk. paper)
1. Political Intrigue 2. Novel 3.Assassination 4. Plot 5. New York.

Notes

Puzzles and More: There are several Alan Turing type cryptograms contained in this book—particularly in the early chapters. However, the most notable of the puzzles is the one known as the "Inscrutable Puzzle." While introduced at the end of chapter eighty-nine, unlike the earlier puzzles, the Inscrutable Puzzle defies solution throughout the pages of this book. Perhaps you can beat Jack to the solution.

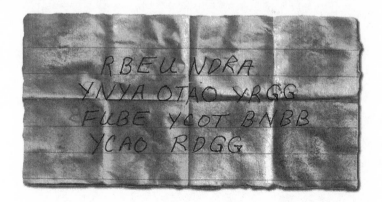

Check out Jack's webpage at: http://www.greenwichvillageink.com
—Michael Carrier

Prologue—Allison and Bernadette

After finding herself bristling every time she had to present her daily plans to the Secret Service, Allison Fulbright, first lady to former President Bob Fulbright, decided to defy the restrictions they imposed upon her. To accomplish this, Allison conjured up an alternate persona—Bernadette Lowery.

At first she would make the transformation into Bernadette in much the same way as Clark Kent donned his Superman identity. However, instead of a telephone booth, Allison would enter her walk-in closet, lock the door, and there slip on a black wig, sunglasses, and a different style of clothes. Once satisfied with Bernadette's appearance, she would then sneak out of her apartment through a private rear door.

Allison had heard that Roger Minsk, the agent who headed up her security detail, suspected that she was up to something, but he never interfered with her clandestine activities. Minsk knew his place, and he also knew what Allison was capable of. He was very much aware that she could get him replaced or even killed with one word whispered into the ear of her husband.

Initially, the Bernadette persona served Allison mostly as an element of convenience—it allowed her to get out on her own without all the trappings of a former first lady. However, as her life progressed in a more self-actuating direction the Bernadette disguise took on a heightened level of significance. In fact, it became so dominant that many lives—even that of a sitting president—were dramatically affected by it.

* * *

If you would like to learn more about the Bernadette persona, and all the technical details involved in developing it, please reference the Appendix (The plotting of Allison's lair) at the end of this book.

Chapter 1—Christmas morn
on the bank of the Chicago River
4:58 a.m., Sunday, December 25

The sun had not yet attempted to peek over Lake Michigan. And it was snowing. While winter storms surprise no one in Chicago, this was a particularly frigid snow, driven by an incredibly stiff westerly—the sort generally reserved for late January or February.

The wind-fractured flakes jetted past Jack Handler more horizontal than vertical, then bounced along the concrete Riverwalk like miniature snowballs.

The inclement weather did not, however, present a problem to Jack. In fact, he embraced it. The fierce storm suggested he would have no company as he wound up this job.

What could be better? he thought.

Carrying an oversized and plastic-lined leather briefcase, he briskly made his way east along the north side of the Chicago River, less than a mile from Lake Michigan.

Just as he reached a preselected point along the water's edge, he turned toward the river. Gripping a support post with his right hand, he swung the heavy case up and rested it on the railing. Then, with a single motion, he unlatched the case and dumped out of it a solid block of ice. Using his thumb, he retained the brown plastic bag that he had wrapped around the ice so that it would not stick to the case.

Once the bag had separated from the ice, he quickly gathered it up and tucked it back into the case.

The water was several feet below the walkway, so the heavy chunk made a loud splashing sound when it landed. Initially, disappearing beneath the surface, the little iceberg bobbed up to the surface almost immediately. Only an inch or so showed above the water, but it was enough to reflect the snow-muted lights of the city as it began floating downstream.

Jack hesitated a moment, took a deep breath, snapped the large brown case closed, and then resumed his walk eastward.

He had chosen this specific spot nearly a week earlier. In fact, he had barely checked into a nearby hotel when he took this exact trek along the river, searching out camera and light locations. He knew that while he could not totally avoid scrutiny, he did need to find the most appropriate place to discard the package—a point that would pose minimal threat from surveillance or excessive lighting.

On his earlier trip, he had also verified that the usually slow-moving current at this specific location was relatively swift. That would ensure his deposit would be swept steadily along.

Initially, he questioned whether the Chicago River would work for him. Theoretically, it might seem that a better choice would have been a river that flowed into a large body of water, as opposed to away from one. But such was not the case with this river—at least not anymore.

Thanks to a series of man-made canals, the Chicago River's course was altered back in the late 1800s so that it flowed westward, away from Lake Michigan. The project had been undertaken to block the flow of industrial waste into Lake Michigan, because the big lake served as the city's water supply.

When Jack initially developed his plan, he painstakingly considered all the ramifications associated with the river's slow westward flow. He finally concluded that convenient accessibility, and size, outweighed any negative factors. Then, when he found a spot on the river where the current was relatively fast, he knew that the Chicago River would work perfectly.

Too bad they all don't go this well, he thought as he glanced backward, checking to be sure that the ice had successfully begun its journey downstream. He had some concern that the hard west wind might actually blow the ice eastward, against the current. But that did not happen. Jack then smiled slightly, turned his face away from the river, and continued walking. *That's a cool one hundred and fifty grand.*

Jack walked a little farther and then stopped abruptly. He extended his left arm, exposing a vintage gold Rolex—a gift from his wife on their third anniversary. He held it up to a dim light he encountered about one hundred and fifty feet upriver. He then turned around quickly (as though remembering something he had forgotten) and headed back toward Michigan Avenue. He had worked through the night, and he was spent—perhaps too tired, he thought, to rest well. Nevertheless, he knew that he had to try to get some sleep. He did, after all, have a plane to catch out of O'Hare at one p.m.

It was not until he had nearly reached Michigan Avenue that he realized just how cold he was. His thinly lined tan windbreaker did not block the sub-zero wind-chill gusts. Perhaps he was just too exhausted, and his body had begun to shut down. Or maybe it was because he now walked directly into the teeth of the wind. Whatever the case, Jack lowered his head, pulled the brim of his Cubs baseball cap down so it would not fly off, and held it there with his left hand to block the pelting snow from his squinting eyes. Lengthening his Asics' stride just a bit, he forced a glance up to the stairs that led to the bridge over the river, then pointed himself in the direction of his hotel, which was on the south bank.

Just as he approached the revolving door leading into the lobby, Jack was startled when his phone began to vibrate. *Who could be calling me this early in the morning?* he wondered. Very few people knew his cell number.

Chapter 2—The unexpected phone call
5:13 a.m., Sunday, December 25

Stopping just outside the hotel entrance, Jack removed his phone from its holder and checked to see who was calling him. When he saw the name "Kitty" on the display, a large smile swept over his tired face. He then continued on into the warmness of the hotel lobby, answering the phone as he walked.

"Kitty, this is awful early to be calling your old man. What's up?"

"You're coming to my town today, right?"

"Yes I am," he answered. "Are you going to let me buy you lunch?"

"I thought you could take me out for dinner while you're here," Katherine (who really preferred to be called Kate) replied.

"Dinner?" Jack said, looking for a place to sit down while he talked to his daughter. "Let's see, I don't think it's your birthday. And I sure know it's not mine—I stopped having them. Must be some other special occasion."

"No special occasion," Kate replied. "I just miss my dad, and I was hoping to spend some time with him. What does he think about it?"

"He thinks that you have an ulterior motive," Jack answered. "Is he right?"

"Of course he's right," she retorted. "Isn't he always right?"

"Not always, but sometimes. I know my daughter real well, and I just don't think you normally get up this early—not on a Sunday morning. So, there must be something on your mind."

"Where you staying? Down by Penn Station?"

"That's right," Jack answered. "I'm due in about three in the after-noon. Give me a call around five, and we'll set something up for Mon-day. Is everything okay?"

"Sure, everything's fine. I just need to pick your brain a little. You always have an answer for me when I have a tough question."

"Kitty, I hope this isn't about sex or anything like that."

Kate chuckled, and said, "Trust me, Dad, you're not the one I go to for matters of the heart, or anything related to it."

"I didn't think so," Jack said. "I can't wait to see what you've got your-self into this time."

"You're gonna love it," Kate said. "It is right up your alley. And, Dad, if you're up to it, maybe we can get together yet today. If you're not too tired."

"Sure, I'd love to," he said. "Call me about five."

"I will," she said. "And I can't wait to see you as well. Love ya, Dad."

"Back at you, Kitty."

This was a perfect diversion for Jack. His daughter was the most important person left in his life. He and Kate's mother (Beth) had been married for only three years, five months, and four days, when a bullet intended for him fatally wounded her. Kate was two years old at the time. After Beth's death, Jack never even dated, much less remarried. In-stead, he devoted all of his energy to the raising of his precious daughter.

It had been tough. As a Chicago detective, his hours were very un-predictable, and the pay was not the greatest. He knew that he was going to need some help, so he hired a wonderful Polish immigrant as a live-in. Her name was Val, which was short for something, but Jack couldn't remember what. He immediately took a liking to the middle-aged wom-an and insisted on paying her nearly twice as much as the typical live-in nanny was making at the time.

Jack slipped his cell phone back into its holder and just sat there for few moments, relishing his memories. He replayed walking into his modest Northeast Chicago home after work and being greeted by Val. She would be cleaning something when he walked in—the house always smelled clean. As soon as she saw him, she would stop what she was doing, take a couple steps toward him, wiping her hands on her tiny-print loose-fitting housedress. It was almost a ritual. He would walk in and say, "Hi, Val. Don't you look nice today." To which she would always respond, "Oh, Mr. Handler." Then, as her round face flushed, she would momentarily break eye contact with him.

"You should be so proud of Katherine," she would say. "She got another 'A.' That daughter of yours is so smart." Then, pointing down the hall with her eyes, Val would say, "Kate's in her room studying right now." She knew that her boss was eager to greet his daughter, so she would immediately direct the conversation toward Kate.

It pleased Jack that Val was always upbeat. He often recalled when he first interviewed her. He noted that she never quit smiling. In fact, that smile was the reason Jack hired her. He wanted his daughter to be surrounded by laughter, and he knew of no better way to do that than to hire a nanny who loved life and loved to make the people around her happy.

Beth was like that. She laughed and joked all the time. Of course, she could be appropriately serious when the situation called for it. But she knew how to fill a home with joy. In that respect, Val reminded him of Kate's mother.

That was the only resemblance, however. While Val was stocky, with brown hair, blue eyes, and thick strong hands, Beth was just the opposite. Grecian ancestry had given Kate's mother the look of a bronze goddess.

Beth had captured Jack's heart the first moment he saw her. He had met her on the job. She was the first-chair violinist for the Chicago Symphony Orchestra while he was a young cop who had found himself assigned to one of her performances for crowd control. After the concert, he spotted her leaving the theater and edged his way close to her. Their eyes met, and she smiled.

"Can I hail a cab for you?" Jack asked, smiling back.

That's all it took. Jack spent the next year winning the heart of this beautiful woman, and they were married exactly fourteen months after their first encounter.

Then it happened. The moment he feared. No matter how hard he tried to block out the events of that awful night, sometimes, especially when he was exhausted, those visions of terror fought their way through his defenses.

Beth had just performed at a concert. Afterward, he took her out for a drink. When the taxi dropped them off at their house, gunmen were waiting. Jack never saw it coming. Two casually dressed men got out of a parked car, approached them, and started firing point blank with 9mm semi-automatic pistols. Jack took four rounds before he could draw his "Service Six" to return fire. Beth was hit only once—but that was in the face, and it was fatal. It was clear that the men were after Jack and that his unfortunate wife was collateral. But she was the one they killed.

Even though seriously wounded, Jack got off six rounds from his Smith and Wesson revolver. Two of Jack's bullets struck one attacker—one in the chest and one in the neck. Either wound would have been fatal. He hit the second with a single round to the heart—also fatal. His other three rounds missed both attackers and were never found.

None of Jack's wounds were life threatening. In fact, he lost consciousness only after the volley was finished, and then just momentarily.

He took a round to his left hand when he reached out trying to deflect his attacker's pistol while he drew his own. A second round glanced off his left shoulder, and one lodged in his left leg after it had ricocheted off the sidewalk.

The fourth round would have hit him squarely in the head had the shooter not been hit in the chest as he fired. Instead, it merely glanced off Jack's forehead, knocking him to the sidewalk. That shot was the last round fired, because by that time both of the attackers had received fatal wounds, and were falling to the ground. They died on the sidewalk only inches apart. That was fortunate for Jack, as he was also face down on the concrete, stunned, immobile, and with an empty revolver locked in his right hand.

Jack never really knew how long he lay there on the sidewalk. For months, the only thing he recalled about the event was waking up with his cheek on the cold, hard concrete. It was not clear if the bullet had knocked him out or if it was the concussion caused by the sidewalk when he struck his head.

On this night, sitting in the lobby of that Chicago hotel, in his mind he could still smell the odor of burned gunpowder. And, of course, the horrible ferrous smell of blood—lots of blood. He recalled slowly regaining consciousness and struggling to comfort his fallen wife. But his hand fell short, reaching only to the warm, sticky moistness that had pooled around her face. In shock, he pushed himself up enough to see death in her dilated eyes.

At that point, Jack wished death for himself, but it did not come.

He remembered trying and failing to stand. He saw the two dead attackers but had no idea how they got there. He then started vomiting.

He surmised that he must have passed out again, because his next recollection was waking up in a hospital, with tubes in both of his arms and doctors and nurses hovering over him.

Jack had not wanted the memory of Beth's murder to captivate his thoughts on this night. But he knew that sooner or later it would crash down on him. It always happened on Christmas. And even though he had kept himself preoccupied with his work, Kate's call triggered the old memories. He removed a paper towel he had stuck in his jacket pocket to wipe off any excess moisture from the case he used to transport the ice. And, using that paper towel, he blotted the tears from his eyes.

Jack took six months off after the attack. He even thought about quitting the force altogether. Instead, at his lieutenant's suggestion, he returned to Northwestern University. There he earned a master's degree in criminal justice and eventually became a Chicago detective.

One of the most significant contacts he made in college was that of a captivating professor. This fellow had retired after twenty years on the force. He and Jack became good friends—probably because the professor had also been shot in the line of duty. When he heard Jack's story and learned that raising a daughter alone was exacting an overwhelming financial burden on Jack, he helped his protégé find part-time work in the private sector.

Jack liked that. In fact, by the time Kate was five years old, Jack was earning more moonlighting than he was at his job with the city. Within a few more years, he had built up such a nice business that he took an early retirement from the department and turned his avocation into his full-time job.

What could be so important to Kitty, Jack wondered, *that she would wake up this early, on Christmas Day, just to call me?*

On other occasions, when Kate would call him to get his opinion on something, it always had to do with a case she was working on. Kate had followed in her father's footsteps. Except, instead of working in Chicago,

Kate was a detective based out of a Manhattan precinct.

"I'll bet she is on a case that has her stumped," Jack muttered aloud. "Damn, it's nice to be wanted … or, at least needed."

Chapter 3—Jack prepares for New York
5:25 a.m., Sunday, December 25

Jack's mind was racing as though he had just tossed down two double espressos. He was wide awake. Not only was he excited about going back to New York; now he was doubly wired at the prospect of spending time with his daughter—especially since she was requesting to see him.

I need something to put me to sleep, he thought, eyeing the hotel coffee shop. Jack had a sugar issue. He did not fully understand it, but he knew that if he ate a doughnut or two, with a glass of milk, within thirty minutes he would fall asleep. Usually, he would wake back up after a few hours. But that would be just fine this time. All he really wanted was to fall asleep. He knew his mind and body would recover enough to function the rest of the day, even with only a limited amount of good rest.

Jack never gloried in past achievements. And he never wallowed in his failures. He simply did not engage in second-guessing. From the moment the ice had hit the water less than an hour earlier, he was on a new mission. This one called him to New York. And from what he could surmise, it was a big job, offering a much larger payday.

As he walked through the lobby, Jack was relieved to see that the coffee shop was open, even on Christmas morning. He was going to need his "doughnut and milk fix" to relax.

Whenever Jack ate in a restaurant, he always sought out a corner booth or table—one that afforded him a clear view of the entrance. He was pleased that on this occasion he was able to seat himself. He found a booth near the rear, one from which he could monitor those entering the coffee shop, as well as keep an eye on Riverwalk activity. He knew that a person in his line of work would stay alive only if he remained keenly aware of his surroundings.

"Sure, honey, we have milk," the waitress said, with more than a friendly smile. "Would you like it warmed? With a nipple perhaps?"

Jack looked up at her and smiled. "No, cold and in a glass will do just fine. Two percent, if you've got it. And how about one of those large frosted cinnamon buns? Could you warm one of those up for me?"

"Darlin', I can warm up more than that for you." She set a glass of water in front of Jack. She then placed both hands on the table and leaned toward him, exposing more than ample cleavage. "Would you like anything else?"

Jack did appreciate the attention—and the view—but he chose not to acknowledge the flirt. He merely smiled again and replied, "Thanks, one of those large rolls, warmed up, would be great."

The waitress smiled again. "I'll be right back, hon," she said, as she turned and walked toward the kitchen. Jack's eyes locked on her shapely form until she disappeared behind double swinging doors. *Youth Dew,* he thought. *That's what she was wearing—Estee Lauder Youth Dew.*

That was the fragrance that Beth had always worn.

He slowly ate half of the white-frosted cinnamon bun and drank most of his two percent. After about twenty minutes, he caught himself staring wide-eyed and unfocused through the window out into the Chicago darkness. The sugar had kicked in. Sensing his heart significantly slowing, he glanced down at his watch. *Five forty-five. Time to head up to my room,* he thought, snatching the bill as he stood to leave.

Just then he heard his cell phone ring. He had turned it on audible after Kate's call. He recognized this ringtone. "Reg," he said, "what are you doing up this time of the morning? ... Christmas morning, no less?"

Jack's face grew somber, as he detected his caller's extreme agitation.

He stood motionless, gripping the bill in his left hand, and holding his cell with his right. "Reg, we can't discuss this on the phone. I'm catching a one o'clock out of O'Hare. I'll be in the city by three. Why don't you meet me at LaGuardia? … Sure. No problem. I am whipped right now, but I'm going to get some rest before the flight. See you there. I'll only have a few minutes though—gotta meet with my daughter, Kitty. You remember Kate—right? But we'll have time to cover the basics … great. See you then."

"I've had enough of this," Jack mumbled. Looking down at his phone, he found and pushed the "off" button with his very large right thumb. "I have *got* to get some rest."

He then slid his phone into the holder and slapped a ten on the table as a tip for the overly friendly waitress. Almost immediately he picked it back up and swapped it for a five. *Can't have her getting the wrong idea,* he reasoned.

"Time for this guy to get a little shut-eye," he mumbled to himself. He paid his bill and headed to his room.

On his way up, Jack could not help but wonder what had made his friend so nervous. The contract in New York had been set up by a very close friend of his, Reginald Black. Up until this call, Jack had not given the job a second thought. *Just another day at the office,* he figured. Through the years, he had worked many jobs with his friend, and never before had he ever heard Reginald sound so worked up.

Jack felt his heart start to race. *Can't let this happen,* he thought. *Got to get some rest. I'll deal with Reg's problems when I get to New York.*

Chapter 4—If we play this right ...

3:15 a.m., Friday, December 30

Allison looked up at James and asked, "What time is it?"

"Three-fifteen," James replied without looking at his watch.

James Colson and Allison Fulbright had spent the whole late evening and early morning drinking and spilling Scotch in a fourth-floor Central Park East apartment. Allison was doing most of the drinking and all of the spilling.

She had gathered up every pillow and bed covering from the entire apartment and piled them on the floor in Bernadette's office. She sat in the middle of the pile, with a half-full glass. James sat at Bernadette's desk, logged on to her computer. The only light in the whole room emanated from a small florescent reading light above where he was working, and from the monitor.

"How in hell did we get to this place?" Allison muttered, miserably slurring her words. She was drunk.

James swiveled around to face her. "We'll survive this, Al. But we have to act quickly. And decisively."

When that word "survive" bounced around and through Allison's neurons, it disrupted her whole being. Her bloodshot hazel eyes immediately opened widely, accenting an uncharacteristically pathetic frown on her sixty-year-old face. For just a moment it appeared that she might burst into tears, but she quickly resisted the urge.

There was nothing attractive about Allison's appearance on this early New York morning. Her bobbed dishwater-blonde hair was a mess. Whatever minimal makeup she might have started with was gone. And the Ralph Lauren robe did nothing to mask her thick calves and hefty thighs. At virtually every other time during any given day, her patented designer beige pantsuits did that job as well as could be hoped for. But she was trying to relax, and she was drunk—always a bad combination when it comes to one's appearance.

But even though she did have too much to drink, she was not sufficiently intoxicated to insulate her feelings from that horrible word James tossed in her direction.

"Survive! What the hell do you mean by that? Survive? I don't want to *survive*. I want to be president. Damn it, James, I'm *supposed* to be president. Surviving doesn't mean anything to me. If you don't get that by now you're no damn use to me. If I'm not sitting in the Oval Office in two years, I might as well be dead. Don't you get it? That's all that matters. That is absolutely *all* that matters."

Allison had already spent eight years in the White House as the wife of a popular president, and she had designs on the office for herself. This driving desire dated back to her days as a law student at Yale. After her husband's second term had ended, Allison spent every moment planning her return to Pennsylvania Avenue, but this time as the first female president of the United States.

Most political analysts predicted she would win the nomination eight years after her husband left office. However, even though she made a powerful attempt, she lost too many primaries and was forced to pull out of the race. She felt she was cheated—she was convinced that she had deserved to be the candidate.

"You're not looking at this from the right perspective."

"What other perspective is there? That bastard printed every word we said. Verbatim! Every damn word that came out of our mouths. It's all right there in your hands, James."

With that, Allison threw up in the large bowl James had placed at her side. It was not the first time. She had been pouring Scotch for several hours, and much of it had made its way between her lips twice. With a slow mechanical swiping motion, she wiped her mouth off with a towel he had placed alongside the bowl. Then, as very drunk people are prone to do, she examined the towel to see what she might have deposited on it, her head weaving a little as she did.

Allison was dressed comfortably. Before she even knew that she was going to meet with James, she had already finished one glass of Scotch, started another, and traded her heels and favorite pantsuit for the robe and more comfortable footwear. As she sat swaying on the floor, she suddenly realized that she was wearing only one slipper. For some reason, the whereabouts of the missing slipper began to preoccupy her. She did not try to stand, but she did raise her head enough to peer around the office in search of it.

"But you're not seeing the larger picture, Al. Mossad does not *want* you destroyed. I can't believe they seek that. They are simply trying to prevent an assassination. They distrust this guy as much as we do, but they fear a power vacuum more than his screwed up Mid-East policies.

"This is how I see it. They recorded our meetings all right, but they're holding onto the recordings. And they'll keep holding them—but only if we give them what they want. They are very good at what they do. If we play ball, there is no way that they will ever release those recordings, at least not in our lifetime. I am sure we can win this thing."

With that, Allison propped herself up against a large pillow that was leaning against the wall. She had, for a moment, fallen on her side and was lying in a quasi-fetal position. She had found that posture quite pleasant—so comfortable, in fact, that for a moment she considered just falling asleep for a while. But James's words had roused her attention, and now she intently listened to what he was saying.

"What exactly do you mean, my dear James? They have already released the damn tapes ... to that bastard reporter—"

She had not finished her sentence before James started shaking his
head. "No, I doubt that very much," he interrupted. "In fact, I'm virtually positive they did not give him the recordings. It's obvious that all
this guy had to work with were transcriptions. And transcriptions don't
mean diddly-squat if you don't have the actual recordings or a good witness to corroborate."

James was from the South. In every respect, he was a true Southern
Gentleman—an African-American Southern Gentleman. Because of his
good Southern upbringing, he always had an aversion to using strong
language in front of a lady. And, even though Allison often sounded
more like a truck driver than a former first lady, James always tried to
avoid profanity in her presence.

Allison appreciated the fact that James was always attentive to her
and that he was polite—two attributes totally absent in her relationship
with her husband.

James had no obvious flaws. He was ruggedly handsome. It was said
about him that he had a voice for radio and a face for TV. His six-foot-
two-inch frame carried his one hundred and eighty-seven pounds well.
It was obvious to all that he worked out regularly. And not just cardio-
vascular exercises—he lifted major weights twice a week.

But beyond his good looks, James was liked and respected by all
who knew him. He never opened his mouth unless he already knew how
his words would affect the people to whom he was speaking. Not that he
engaged in nuance. He did not. He simply thought his words through
carefully. And he never lied.

He could often be seen sitting quietly, even in a conference meeting, not saying a thing. Then, at the appropriate time, he would interject something profound—concise and profound. No matter who was talking at the time, everyone stopped and paid attention to what James had to say.

For all the same reasons, both Bob and Allison totally trusted James.

"Okay, I'm listening," Allison said.

Rolling his chair closer to where Allison was sitting, James leaned forward, placing his elbows on his knees.

Allison had observed that posture a hundred times before. She knew this meant that James was really on to something. Even though Allison was drunk, her mind was clear enough to critically process James's words.

Suddenly he jumped up from his chair and briskly walked out to the kitchen. James never did anything slowly, especially when his mind was so magically engaged. He opened the refrigerator and grabbed two bottles of water and then returned to where Allison was sitting. He opened both. Handing one to Allison, he said, "Drink this. We've got to flush your system. We've both got work to do."

Allison took a small sip of the water. She was not feeling well and suspected that she would not be able to hold it down.

"Don't worry about it. Just drink it. Drink as much as you can. If you toss it, that's fine. That'll just flush some of that expensive Scotch out of your system."

Allison hated to be told what to do. But she knew James was right. So she took several large swallows.

She then looked James in the eye and asked: "Okay. What makes you think this idiot writer does *not* have the tapes?"

"It just figures. If he had the actual recordings, he would be using them right now. Writers, even hack writers like this jerk, they hate to be questioned, much less doubted. If he had the recordings, he would have sent something along with this to prove credibility—something substantial, irrefutable. He would be trying to establish a strong bargaining position."

James paused for a moment and then continued: "He sent only this transcript. Considering all the allegations that can be inferred from it, it is beyond curious for him to send it without any corroborating evidence. That tells us one thing—he has no proof. He wants us to *think* he has, but I'm convinced that he's either bluffing, or ... perhaps he's not even a real journalist."

"Keep going," Allison said, taking another long drink of water.

"Look. I've tickled every friendly news outlet. Nothing suggests that anyone else has specific knowledge about this. The only thing I ran into were rumors, and I think I might have started all of them. ... And the thing about rumors is, they don't mean a thing. If anyone in the media, and I do mean anyone, had recordings, or had even heard the real thing—or if anyone had anything else whatsoever to substantiate this story, somebody would know about it."

James paused again to gather his thoughts and to get Allison's attention. He then continued, "Mossad has them. Mossad created them, and they continue to hold them. And, knowing the way Mossad works, they're not about to give them up, not to anyone. Especially not to anyone in the media."

Allison belched in the most unladylike fashion and then threw up again in the bowl.

"That's great, get rid of it. We've got to get you cleaned out. You're gonna hold the most important press conference of your life. And it has to be today."

"I can't do that. Just look at me. I'm a mess."

"Has to be today. And you can do it. It's Friday. Whatever we get out there today, if it is early enough, it will still carry the weekend. It couldn't be more perfect. ... Well, that's an overstatement. It certainly could be better. But given what we have to work with, I am sure we can turn this whole thing around, if we do it right. ... And right away. At the very least, we'll buy some time."

"Okay, James, let's go over this," Allison said, struggling to sober up. Her words were becoming noticeably less slurred.

"That a girl, Al."

James grew quiet for a moment, organizing his thoughts in a way that he knew Allison would appreciate. "If we're going to pull this off, you have to be up to speed and totally on board," he said. "Here's the deal. Mossad did a great job. They went to a lot of effort. Now listen carefully here. This next part is very important."

James again rested his elbows on his knees, and looked deeply into Allison's slowly sobering eyes. "Okay. If Mossad had wanted to destroy you, and your potential presidency, they would have released the recordings to the FBI—not had this fellow give transcripts to us. All they really wanted to accomplish was to avoid a power vacuum. And that's exactly what they feared would happen if President Butler were to be assassinated."

"So, then, is it off? Is our plan dead?"

"Don't know for sure. Can't know for sure, at least not for right now. At the very least, it has been changed. Our job, right now, is to turn this story, or nonstory, on its head. We have to deflect whatever comes out, and prevent it from grabbing the headlines. Because, if it is released now, without our doing something to direct public attention away from it, potentially it could be very damaging. ... No, that's an understatement. This story, if allowed to take root, will destroy us all. We have to give the press a bigger fish.

"I don't think this guy, or anyone else, is about to run this story. But if a story about these meetings were to get out, it could be all that gets talked about for a very long time.

"And that's what we need—a little time. We need to figure out what Mossad is really after and how they plan to use what they've got for the short term. We need a little breathing room. But, I can promise you that we do not have to worry about the actual recordings ever being released to the media. You can trust me on this one, Allison."

"But, James, they do have physical evidence of a conspiracy. And not just *any* conspiracy. They've got proof that we plotted to assassinate the president of the United States." As those words escaped her lips, she finally started to cry.

"That's right, Mossad does have recordings. And for sure they are incriminating. But that's not the end of the world. … And, as I said before, we can work through this. In fact, I think this whole matter can end up being a positive thing—if we manage it well."

"Are you out of your mind? How in hell can conspiracy tapes work *for* us?"

"They can—I promise you. We just have to handle it properly," James said, in his most reassuring voice.

Allison was not sure she believed him yet, but she wanted to.

"Now, if the Russians had the recordings, it would be a totally different story. But Mossad does not want this country, or you, destroyed. Without us, where would they be? And you have always been a supporter. So, okay, they've got some very embarrassing recordings of us conspiring. Thus far they have used what they've got brilliantly. Like a warning shot across our bow. …The bottom line is this, I think. While they may have blocked us here, temporarily, we must keep in mind that we're playing chess, not checkers. It could be that they just want to be a player. Maybe they think they have a better idea."

James paused a moment and then continued. "Al, you still can be president. Only the when and the how remain to be worked out. Perhaps all they need is to be assured that the transition will be a smooth one. It might not be this next election cycle, but it will happen. The very fact that Mossad holds those recordings can be beneficial to your cause."

"I heard you say that before. I don't see how that can happen."

"Once you are in office, and it is quite possible that they may very well help us get you there, they will use what they have—but not to *destroy* you. ...They will expect favors—maybe missiles, missile defense, fighter jets. So, you give them some B-1s. Big deal. Provide them a base of operations. They're not going to use them to bomb DC.

"If we let them help us get you into the Oval Office, they will be willing to support your every move, as long as you consult with them occasionally—particularly on Mid-East matters. They will think they have you in their pocket, but you will own *them*. If we play this right, that's exactly how it will be."

Just then there was a loud pounding on the door.

"FBI, open up."

Chapter 5—Kate's mystery unfolds
5:15 p.m., Sunday, December 25

Jack's flight arrived on time at LaGuardia, but Reginald was not there to meet him. When he called to see where his friend was, his call went directly to voicemail. That did not trouble Jack because in their line of work there were many times when calls simply could not be answered. The unexpected became the norm. Jack left a message that he was checking into his hotel and that Reginald could contact him later if he wished.

Jack was pleased that he was able to get some rest before and during the flight and that the cab ride to his hotel was uneventful.

"Kitty, it's your old man," Jack said to his daughter. He had called her as he was unpacking his suitcase.

"Dad," Kate answered. "You've landed. Where are you staying? … Wait, let me guess. One of those hotels down by Penn Station. Am I right?"

"Kitty, you're always right," Jack teased his daughter. "Even when you're wrong, you're right. … Right?"

"Dad," Kate said, drawing out the vowel.

"What time is it?" Jack asked, looking down at his watch. "Five-sixteen. Are you in town yet, or are you out on the Island?"

"I'm in town. I'm getting together with you—remember? I thought I would hang around in case you weren't too tired. Maybe we could grab a cup of coffee yet today? What do you think?" Kate asked.

"Love to, Kitty," Jack replied, quickly accepting his daughter's offer. "I would like to jump in the shower first. How about you grab a taxi to

Penn Station. We'll meet up and figure stuff out from there? Will that work for you? Can't wait to see you."

Kate knew her father well. She had anticipated what he would suggest, and he did not disappoint her.

"I'll call you at six-ten. Does that sound about right?" she asked.

"Perfect," Jack said. "I should be there by then. It's only a few blocks."

While Jack and his daughter were close, neither of them actually went out of their way to get together. But, whenever Jack was in New York, he would always give Kate a call. If she had time (and she always had time for him), she would meet her father at a restaurant—or, as was the case this time, at a coffee shop. But seldom at the same place twice.

The lone exception to that rule was Kate's favorite steak house. Jack had taken his daughter there three times. It had become one of their favorite haunts. This time, Jack detected a sense of urgency in his daughter's voice. He had no idea what was prompting it, but he knew she needed something that she was convinced he alone could supply.

Jack checked his watch again as he stripped down. He knew this shower would take three minutes—no longer. Perhaps a bit less, given his desire to see his daughter. He had learned self-discipline from his time as an Army Ranger. Three minutes for a shower, two to shave, three to five to get dressed. It was not as though he were on a stopwatch, but he maintained that schedule just the same.

He was even a disciplined sleeper. He always tried to go to bed at nine p.m. But, regardless of what time he retired, he seemed to wake up promptly at five a.m. He did not need an alarm, but he still set a reminder on his watch anyway. From five a.m. until six, he worked out.

Sometimes his workout regimen interfered with an appointment. When it did, he merely shifted the routine enough to accommodate it. But he always found time to exercise.

As soon as Jack emerged from his shower, he quickly shaved and got dressed.

Just as he was ready to leave, he opened up a zippered section of his luggage and removed a heavy Velcro sealed bag. From it he removed an electronic device that he had devised. It was a transportable magnetic lock. He took it out and carried it over to the door of his hotel room. Carefully he positioned it on the door. A permanent magnet held it in place. He then activated the mechanism by turning on a mechanical switch. Instantly, he could hear one side of the magnetic lock attach itself to the steel door jamb, and the other to the steel door.

He then disengaged the mechanical lock on the door and tried to open it. The magnetic lock held it securely. It was rated at fifteen hundred pounds when the battery was fully charged. That was enough locking power to discourage the largest sumo wrestler.

Jack reached into his pocket and pulled out an RF remote, like the one he used to unlock his car. He had programmed the magnetic lock to the same frequency. So, when he hit the button, his door released electronically, and he opened it up. After fifteen seconds, it relocked.

He wanted to test it from outside, so he unlocked his magnetic lock, and went out the door to the corridor. He listened for his lock to engage. After fifteen seconds, he heard the familiar "click" of the magnet attaching to the door jamb. He then slid his hotel card into the lock and turned the door handle. He pushed on the door heavily, but it would not budge. He then looked down the corridor to be sure no one was observing him, and he lowered his shoulder and hit the door with substantial force. Still, the lock held.

That'll be just fine, Jack thought, as he headed to the elevator.

He knew the battery was fully charged and would, therefore, secure his door for the maximum four hours. When he returned, he would attach it to a charger. He never left the charger on the lock when he was outside the room. His concern was that he might lose the remote, or, for some unknown reason, his invention might stop working. Were that to happen, he would only have to wait out the battery. After five hours, he knew that it would have discharged sufficiently, allowing him to force open the lock. Jack always had a contingency plan.

When he was inside the room, however, he would activate the lock with the charger engaged. That way he could be quite comfortable that he was untouchable against any attack through the door—at least, any conventional attack. He was well aware that the preferred method for forcing a locked hotel room door was a hydraulic spreader. The way that device worked was to spread the jamb of the door away from the lock. Once the standard lock was free, the door could be opened enough to cut any standard hotel secondary lock, thus allowing entry. He also knew that this whole attack could be accomplished with virtually no sound and would take only a few seconds.

His magnetic lock was not susceptible to this entry method. He had engineered the portion that attached to the door jamb on a sliding pivot—that way it could travel the inch or so that the jamb spreader might create and still hold the door securely.

He was very happy with the way his lock worked and often considered obtaining a patent. But he thought better of it because he knew that should he do that, those interested in attacking hotel rooms would merely upgrade their methods.

Besides, he knew that once the drawings were filed with the patent office, offshore manufacturers would start mass-producing it for a fraction of what he could. He thought it sufficient that the lock served *him* well.

Sometimes he wore a disguise when he was traveling—even in New

York. But this time, because he was meeting with Kate, he thought it best to be himself. He figured there would be a fair chance that they might run into someone who recognized Kate and that she would want to introduce the friend to her father. He needed to be himself this time, and he was okay with that.

Besides, never in all the times he visited (or worked in) New York had anyone ever recognized him. He did always make it a point to stay at smaller, out-of-the-way hotels. While the hotel he had chosen this time was not particularly small, it suited Jack well because it always appeared to be fully booked—probably due to the fact that the rooms were very small and relatively inexpensive. It was a favorite of foreign and domestic tourists who wanted to save money.

Not only did Jack like the fact that this particular hotel provided a good level of anonymity, he also appreciated that it was very conveniently located across Eighth Avenue from Penn Station—only a five-minute walk from Madison Square Garden and a five-minute taxi ride from Jacob Javits.

While it did not hurt that the price was right and that the hotel was conveniently positioned, it was that aura of privacy that won his patronage for this trip.

Today, however, Jack's privacy was going to be violated. Just as he prepared to exit the hotel on his way to meet Kate, he sensed a person sliding up from the rear much more quickly than suited him. He then saw the man's reflection in the glass next to the revolving door. He was right. Someone was approaching him quickly.

So, instead of entering the large revolving door, he suddenly stepped aside and turned toward the man. For just a moment their eyes met. Then, as his training kicked in, Jack checked out both of the man's hands. He immediately spotted a six-inch long ice pick extending out of the man's right hand, so Jack took a full step backward to prepare for battle.

But, instead of facing off with Jack, the would-be attacker simply slid the weapon into the pocket of his long wool coat and proceeded to leave the hotel through the revolving door. Jack chose not to pursue the man. Instead, he remained off to the side and watched the man squeeze out of the door as quickly as possible.

The man glanced back to see if Jack was following. Their eyes met briefly once again.

Chapter 6—More questions than answers

6:03 p.m., Sunday, December 25

Jack carefully closed a razor-sharp combat knife with his thumb and slid it back into his jacket pocket. He had pulled out and flipped open the blade at the first sign of danger. Now that he was certain he had thwarted the attack and that Ice Pick Man did not have a partner with him, Jack began to wind down. *What the hell is this all about?* he wondered.

"Damn it!" Jack muttered under his breath. "That was just too close. I've got to be more careful."

There would be no point in pursuing the man—his attacker sought to kill him; he had no reason to return that favor, at least not for right now. Instead, he just stepped outside the hotel to get a better look at the stranger who had wanted to pierce his heart and lungs.

Amazingly young and fit, Jack observed. Especially to be wielding such an unusual weapon. While an ice pick can be a very deadly weapon, Jack did not view it as a popular instrument of choice by professionals. Generally speaking, Jack believed that only women and old men used ice picks for anything other than chilling mixed drinks.

"Really strange—*really* strange," he continued to mutter, taking an additional few steps toward the street to get a better view of the man as he turned west on 34th Street.

Just before Ice Pick Man disappeared behind the corner of the hotel, he glanced back to see if Jack was following.

Jack sensed his heart racing. "This is a bunch of garbage," he said, again to himself.

Here I am running around with this damn knife. Even a can of mace would work better than this two-inch piece of steel.

Jack waited in front of the hotel long enough for Ice Pick Man to get safely away. *What the hell could this be about?* he wondered. *That guy must be working for someone. But who could that possibly be? And why would someone want to kill me badly enough to hire a professional—and with an ice pick, of all things? And what idiot would try to pull off something like this, right out in the open? Someone must be pretty damn desperate.*

Only two people should have known that he was coming to New York—his friend Reginald and his daughter. Jack had worked with his buddy Reginald before, on several projects. He knew Reginald to be the consummate professional—someone who would not allow any sensitive information to pass his lips. The success of jobs such as this depended on total secrecy, and Jack was sure Reginald respected that concept.

Must be Kate has been talking, Jack surmised.

Let me think about this. That fellow was too young to be a typical contract killer. Must be he works for an organization. Now, I would guess that it could be the Russians, or maybe Mossad. … I've got to see what that girl of mine has got herself into.

So, at a brisker than normal pace and with a newfound intensity, Jack took the first walk light at 34th Street, crossing over Eighth Avenue. As he got to the middle of Eighth Avenue, he could not resist the urge to glance west down 34th Street, just to be sure Ice Pick Man was not lurking around the corner, seeking to complete the job.

Just as Jack had expected, the man was long gone. He then continued crossing 34th and headed toward Penn Station. After only a few moments, he heard the familiar voice of his daughter.

"Dad!" Kate called out. "Over here."

Chapter 7—Kate's puzzle, and her old friend Kurt

6:10 p.m., Sunday, December 25

The two hugged each other closely, as only a dad and his loving daughter can hug. "And how's my favorite daughter?" Jack asked.

"I'm your *only* daughter, silly," Kate chuckled.

Still gripping his daughter's arms, Jack pushed her back to get a good look at her. "Man, you just get better looking every day. How can a beautiful young girl like you still be single … and in New York City, no less? Aren't there any red-blooded males in this town?"

"Thanks for the compliment, Dad, but you know I'm not interested in getting married—at least not right now. You're the only man in my life."

They'd had similar discussions before. Jack would like to see his only daughter find a man, a worthy man. He and Kate's mother had something really special, and he wanted to see Kate find a love like that.

"I know, I know," Jack said. "I'm just messing with you. Where're we headed? Isn't there a coffee shop around here?"

"Sure is," Kate replied. "Follow me."

Kate then grabbed her father's hand and pulled him toward the steps leading down into Penn Station. Being that it was Christmas, there were not many other people to deal with. She tightly gripped his hand while they walked. This reminded Jack of the times he and his wife would hold hands just like that. Beth's hands would be cold, much like Kate's hand was cold on this night, and he would warm his wife simply by holding her hand.

"Right around this corner," Kate said. "Here. This is an okay place. At least they have great espressos. I think you will like it."

As the two of them walked in, Kate pointed to a table in the corner and told her dad to go capture it. "Still like double espressos?" she asked, as she headed toward the counter.

"That would be great," Jack said, squeezing into a chair in the corner. This gave him a panoramic view of the mostly empty coffee shop. Kate knew many of her dad's idiosyncrasies, including his desire to always be in a position to size up his surroundings.

Just a few minutes later, Kate carried two double espressos over to the table. "I'll grab a couple waters," she said, setting both of the cups down in front of her father. She returned quickly with two small plastic glasses of water.

"I can't believe this place is open on Christmas," Jack marveled.

"Three hundred and sixty-five," Kate said, as she sat down in front of her father.

"Okay, kitten, what's going on in your life that's got you so troubled?" Jack asked his daughter.

Her countenance immediately changed, as though a somber cloud descended over her. He knew something major was up. She just silently stared down at her coffee for a few moments. Finally, Kate looked up at him. The expression on her face puzzled him. He had never before seen her this unsettled.

"Dad, I've got myself into something that I do not know how to deal with," Kate said. "I've had tough cases before. I've had my life threatened before. But always I felt like I had a handle on what was going on. Gang killings—I can handle them okay. Domestic crime, I can deal with that too. But I do not know what to do with one of my new cases."

"What can you tell me about it?" Jack asked, making sure not to lead his daughter where she should not go.

"It's a murder," Kate said. "That's obvious, after all, I am a homicide detective," Kate looked down at her espresso again and forced a strained chuckle. "But this one has a different feel to it, Dad. It feels like something bigger—something a little strange."

"Strange in what way?" Jack asked.

"Dad, how many people get murdered with an ice pick, in public, during rush hour, waiting for a train? Doesn't that alone sound strange to you?"

"With an ice pick?" Jack asked rhetorically. It was obvious that his daughter now had his undivided attention. "I always thought that only old men and crazy women killed with ice picks. And then only on trains, not waiting for them."

"Right. Exactly," Kate said. "But this murder was committed in a train tunnel. The victim was on his regular evening commute from DC back to Penn Station. Someone walked up behind him, slid an ice pick right through his left lung, puncturing his heart, pulled it out, and pushed it into him again, piercing his right lung. Death was almost instantaneous. And it wasn't an old man or a crazy woman. Witnesses say that they saw a young man walk up to the vic and talk to him. Several describe the man as in his mid-thirties, white, well-dressed, powerfully built, and wearing glasses."

"The glasses might have been to throw you off," Jack said.

"That's what we thought, too."

"Sounds like an episode of Sherlock Holmes to me," Jack said, trying to lighten up the conversation. "Anyone able to come up with a tentative ID for this guy? Or a motive?"

"No. All they saw was the victim being shoved against one of the vertical support beams. He held himself up for a few moments and then just slid down it. It was during the busy rush hour, and he did not bleed out much. Most thought he had suffered a heart attack."

"What about the ice pick? Did the killer leave it in the victim or pull it out?" Jack inquired.

"Strange that you should ask. He broke the handle off, leaving the pick part in the victim," Kate answered. "But you already knew that didn't you?"

"Yeah, that's what I suspected. It sounds almost like a prison hit. They usually break the shiv off inside the victim and take only the handle. Much more effective when carried out like that. If it is broken off inside, the vic can't pull it out. So he just bleeds internally. Plus, it leaves no fingerprints."

"So, you think that the killer has done hard time? Is that what you are thinking?" Kate asked.

"Not necessarily. Obviously, an ice pick is not a sharpened toothbrush. But the same principle might apply. A breakaway tip on an ice pick could suggest a professional hit. In fact, that's exactly what my initial observation would be."

"That's what I was thinking," Kate replied, quite contented to see that her father agreed with her line of thinking. "What makes this even more interesting," she continued, "is what turned up inside the lining of the vic's jacket. That's really why I called you. I want you to take a look at it," Kate said, reaching into her purse and pulling out an envelope.

"Maybe you can make something of this," Kate said, as she slid the contents out of the envelope and pushed it toward her father.

"This is a copy," she said, "the original is still in forensics."

Jack received a folded, handwritten sheet of paper from his daughter and studied it. After a minute he said, "this is a simple cryptogram. Couldn't this guy afford a computer?"

SGCN JNRE SDHC SDCJ MHVW

CECP DCQJ MRPP NCNG TNTQW

CRVR DDPKS CDJR DJADA PXZZ

FQOPO PJKA TFGJS

"Oh, he could afford one all right," Kate replied.

"What sort of work did he do?" Jack asked.

"State Department, mid-level," She said.

"State Department," Jack repeated.

"Did you say this was a simple cryptogram?" Kate asked. "Can you decipher it?"

"I did *say* that," Jack answered. "But simple does not necessarily mean easy. By simple I mean basic. It's not a complicated encryption. But it is probably not easy at all to decipher. And it would be inscrutable to any encryption software. In fact, without the key, or keys, short cryptograms such as these are virtually impossible to decipher."

"What do you mean by 'keys?'" Kate asked.

"Think like this," Jack said. "All a cryptogram does is substitute one letter for another, in some orderly fashion. If conceived correctly, a cryptogram virtually *requires* that the recipient of the code have the key, which merely explains the method of letter substitution employed by the creator of the code. Knowing the key is critical. Especially if there might be multiple keys. Which I suspect is the case here."

Jack then laid the paper down on the table so he could explain it to Kate. But before he commented on it, he momentarily flipped it over to take a look at the back. "This is a copy, right?" Jack asked.

"Yes, it is a copy," Kate told him. "The original is stored as evidence."

"Take a look at how the message is divided into four lines of characters. That suggests there are probably four keys—a separate key for each line. There's no software out there that I know of that could crack this without the keys. The lines are too short to develop patterns or to apply methods involving order and frequency. These things can be created on the fly and are very effective."

"So, there's nothing you can do with it without a key?" Kate asked.

"I didn't say that," Jack said. "This guy was with the State Department, you say. Just what was his area of expertise? Do you know that?"

"East European and Asian, primarily," Kate answered.

"Russia, China, Poland?" Jack asked.

"Russia and China—mostly Russian affairs," she said.

"I'll show you how simple this can be," Jack said. "It probably won't work, but I think it's a reasonable place to start. Who knows, we might get lucky. Let's assume that one of the keys is 'Russia.' Let's apply it to the first line. If Russia is a key for one of the lines, then 'r' will take the place of the first letter in the alphabet, 'a.' Then 'u' is 'b,' 's' is 'c,' and 's' might also 'd,' 'i' is 'e,' and 'a' is 'f.' From there you basically start the alphabet over, plugging in the unused characters in order.

"It is possible that one 's' in Russia might get dropped, making the keyword 'Rusia.' We would have to try it both ways."

"You lost me."

"Okay, just follow this," Jack said, pulling out a tablet from his pocket and writing as he talked. "'B' wasn't part of the key, so that will stand for the next letter, 'g'; 'c' is 'h,' 'd' is 'i,' 'e' is 'j,' 'f' is 'k,' 'g' is 'l,' 'h' is 'm.' 'I' was used in the key, so we would move on to 'j,' which would be 'n'; 'k' is 'o,' 'l' is 'p,' 'm' is 'q,' 'n' is 'r,' 'o' is 's,' 'p' is 't,' 'q' is 'u.' 'R' was used, and so was 's.' In fact, 's' was used twice. That moves us to 't,' which would be 'v.' 'U' was used, so 'v' would be 'w.' 'W' is 'x' and 'x' is 'y' and 'y' is 'z.'

"Now, because 's' was used for two letters, then 'z' wasn't used at all, so we can assume your puzzler used 'z' as a null. That means he could just throw a 'z' in as a place filler wherever he wished. For instance, to fill out a line, or just to throw people off—like a 'monkey wrench.'

"The likelihood of 'z' being used as a null is tipped by its being used for the final two characters of the third puzzle. That suggests that the puzzler employed all the characters in his key, even when duplicated. That produces nulls. It is common practice with short puzzles."

"Dad, you're amazing," Kate said.

"Let's not get ahead of ourselves, Kitty. We don't know if this will work. To this point this is still mere conjecture—what we came up with is just one way of looking at it," Jack said, even though he already saw that the third line ended with two 'z's', which strongly suggested he was on to something.

"Take a look at the third line. It looks like it might have two nulls at the end. If we're right, then this guy of yours was no genius. That would have been too simple. ... Anyway, let's plug it in and see if it works."

Kate slid her chair around a little so she could look over her father's shoulder.

"Here we go," Jack said, as he applied his potential solution to the puzzle. "'Hawaii to China in fifty.' That's it, for the third line. But you can be sure that the other three lines employ different keywords. We just got lucky with that one line."

"You've got to be kidding me, Dad. You figured it out *that* fast? Our best computer guys spent days on it without any success. ... But they were using code-cracking software. And you say that approach might not work so well for a puzzle like this. That's amazing. But if that's right, 'Hawaii to China in fifty,' what would it mean?" Kate asked. "'Hawaii to China in fifty' sounds like a fast plane."

"Beats me, but I doubt that this guy was planning a vacation—and certainly not to Beijing," Jack said, shrugging his shoulders and chuckling slightly. "This thing sounds to me like something for the FBI. This was definitely not a gang-related killing. ... How did *you* get this case?"

"Do you think you can do anything with the other three lines?" Kate asked, disregarding her father's last question.

"I'm gonna need some time with this. Can I take it with me?" Jack asked.

"Sure—not a problem," Kate replied, folding it up. She tucked it back into the envelope and handed it to her father.

"Kate," a man said as he walked up to the table where she and her father were sitting. "Is that really you?"

Kate's head snapped around. The voice was somewhat familiar, but she could not place it.

"The academy," he said. "What's it been, ten or twelve years? I'm Kurt, Kurt Jefferies. Don't you remember me?"

"Yes, sure I do. How are you doing? ... You left the force, didn't you?"

"I did," Jefferies said. "The private sector pays better."

"Private sector—exactly what does that mean?" Kate asked.

Jack observed that the man was sizing him up more than should be expected, particularly when there was a beautiful woman present.

"I do investigations for some attorneys. You know, following rich cheating husbands around. It's nasty work, but it pays well. And you, you're still with the department?"

"I am. I'm a homicide detective," Kate replied, just a little uncomfortable about being questioned.

The man then turned to Jack and asked. "Do you work with Kate?"

"Kate's my daughter. We're just enjoying a cup of espresso."

Jack now was growing a little tense about the encounter—he was fairly certain that it did not happen by chance. And, he was not pleased to be sitting down with this questionable stranger standing over him.

Jack examined the man closely to be sure that he had not seen this

Jefferies fellow before. Convinced that he had not, Jack rose to his feet and squared himself off in front of the visitor. As he stood, he again opened the knife inside his pocket and made certain that he would be able to wield it quickly and effectively should he need to. "We were just leaving, Mr. Jefferies, hope you will excuse us," Jack said, not taking his eyes off the man standing beside his daughter.

Kate took the cue from her father and arose from her chair as well.

"Good to see you, Kurt, but we really have to be going," Kate said, pushing her chair under the table.

"Sure, it was good to see you again too. Can't imagine bumping into you like this," Jefferies said, taking half a step backward, as he sensed his space was about to be violated by Jack.

"And you," Jefferies said, reaching out to shake hands with Jack, "it was nice meeting you." Jefferies had observed that Jack was gripping something in his right hand, and he wanted to see if Jack would release it to shake his hand.

But Jack was not ready to take his hand off the knife in his pocket, so he acted as though he did not see the gesture. Feigning indigestion, Jack placed his left hand over his stomach and said, "Kate, that espresso did not set well with me. How about you? Don't you think it was a little bitter?"

"Yeah, I know what you mean," she said, playing along with her dad. "It is Christmas, after all. Business is slow and maybe it sat out too long."

"That's probably the case," Jack replied, steering his chair with his left hand as he pushed it under the table with his foot. He still had not acknowledged Jefferies's gesture. Then, noticing that the stranger had ceased trying to shake his hand, Jack looked over at him and said, "You will excuse us?"

"Sure, it was good to meet you," Jefferies said. "What did you say your name was?"

"Kate's dad," Jack said, flashing an icy stare, causing Jefferies to take a full step back. "I'm Kate's dad."

"Now, if you will excuse us," Jack said, brushing the man back with his right elbow and taking his daughter's arm in his left hand. "Have a good day," Jack added as he walked away with his daughter, still not taking his hand off the opened combat knife in his pocket.

"What was *that* all about?" Jack asked his daughter, as they walked away. "That guy was no private dick. He was built like a rock. When I brushed against him, he did not budge. And I don't think that husband chasers pack Glock 20s, at least not in Manhattan."

The 10mm round is more powerful than either the .45 ACP or the .357 Magnum. While the 10mm handguns were initially regarded by law enforcement as a superlative size for their application, beginning in the late 1980s it was generally replaced by the smaller .40 S&W cartridge for police use.

The reason the smaller firearm won out over the 10mm had to do with the type of officers being recruited at that time. Because the 10mm round was considerably longer than both the 9mm and the .40 S&W, it caused the handgrip of the firearm that fired it also to be larger. That was because the magazine holding the rounds had to fit inside it.

Beginning in the mid-to-late 1980s, a concerted effort to recruit more women into law enforcement led agencies to abandon the 10mm in favor of the .40 S&W, and to the even smaller 9mm. Both of these semi-automatic handguns had measurably smaller handgrips and also a more manageable recoil.

However, the raw knockdown power of the 10mm won the hearts of private professionals, such as Jack Handler. And the Austrian made Glock 20 10mm was deemed the best. Not only was it reliable and accurate, but it reputedly absorbed and distributed the recoil better than other 10mm handguns.

When Jack observed the bulge of a firearm, he could determine whether it was a semi-auto or a revolver on the basis of its shape and dimension. And if it *was* a semi-auto, he could further tell if it was a 9mm, .40 S&W, or a 10mm. He knew this on the basis of the lump caused by the size of its handgrip.

Of course, it was always possible that a large semi-auto could have been a .45 APC, but the odds were great that a professional would be not carrying that piece.

So, if it was a 10mm, Jack thought it a safe assumption that Jefferies's weapon of choice would be the Glock 20.

"Who do you think he *really* was? And what's this about the espresso setting out too long?"

"You caught that slip-up? ...Well, I knew you were ready to go, and I had to say something.

"But that *was* weird—the business with Jefferies," Kate replied. "I do remember him from the academy. I don't recall much about him, though, except that he was a little older than the rest of us. ... And some of the other girls thought he was cute. I think he had been in the service. Maybe the Marines."

"That figures. Probably some sort of Special Services," Jack said. "He's definitely a formidable dude. And our encounter was *not* by chance. He sought you out. Must have been tailing one of us. ... I'm thinking FBI."

Jack wanted to alert his daughter to the danger he sensed. Yet, he did not want to alarm her.

"You, my dear, need to watch your step," Jack said, carefully choosing his words. "I think you might be in some danger." Jack and his daughter continued walking until they emerged from Penn Station. Jack kept a tight grip on her arm, and an equally tight grip on his knife, as he led her out of the terminal—east, away from his hotel. For a moment Jack considered telling her about his earlier encounter with Ice Pick Man, but he thought better of it. *No need to worry her*, he concluded.

"Where're we headed, Dad?" Kate asked as they walked along.

Jack was so intensely preoccupied with their surroundings that he failed to respond to her.

As the two of them approached Sixth Avenue and Broadway, Handler pulled his daughter off the sidewalk and into a small delivery alcove off 34th Street. The smell of urine was powerful, suggesting that it was a favorite spot for the homeless at night. Kate scrunched up her face, placing her forefinger under her nose. "Dad, this stinks," she complained.

"I know, but we need to make some plans. We'll have no competition for this spot, at least not until later."

Jack took a long and careful look around, making sure that they had not been followed. "Kate, I'll take a closer look at that puzzle tonight. I don't have business until tomorrow. I'll call you, and maybe we can get together then. Do you have plans for lunch, or perhaps dinner?"

"Only you, Dad. I'd love to spend as much time with you as possible," she said. "Just tell me what works."

"That sounds good," Jack said. "But you had better watch your back. I do not trust that Jefferies. And we do not have any idea who he works for or who else might be involved. You can be sure that he is not working alone."

"What do you suggest?" she asked.

"Take a cab home," Jack said.

"All the way to the Island?" she asked.

"All the way to your door. I'll hail it for you," Jack said, signaling his daughter to wait while he went out on the street. He walked right out in front of the first cab and forced the driver to stop.

"Get the hell out of my way, you ignorant bastard!" the driver yelled at him after he had opened his window.

Jack flashed two one hundred dollar bills and walked over to talk to the mouthy driver.

"My daughter needs to go to Long Island. Will this cover it?"

"Yeah, I think it might."

Jack signaled his daughter to get into the cab, and he walked around to the rear passenger door to open it for her. Before she got in, he gave her a hug and kissed her on the top of her head.

"Love ya, Dad," she said, getting into the cab.

"Love ya back, kitten," Handler said, closing the door after her.

He then signaled the driver to lower the front passenger window as he reached in and handed the driver the money. "You take good care of this woman," he said, with his usual level of intimidation.

"I will take good care of her," the driver said, checking out the bills to be sure they were not counterfeit. "You can be sure, I'll take *very* good care of her."

Jack waved to his daughter as she rode east on 34th. She then turned and gestured through the rear window for him to give her a phone call. He smiled broadly and waved one last time.

Still blocking one lane of traffic, Jack remained in the street, taking care to make sure no one was following his daughter's cab. Finally, one of the cars he was hindering started honking at him. Not acknowledging the irritation, he remained in place for another few seconds and then casually walked over to the curb.

He totally ignored one cab driver who had rolled down the front passenger window to share his thoughts with Jack. "What's wrong with ya, buddy, you got some kinda death wish? Stand in front of me a little longer and I'll grant that wish for ya! Ya stupid fool!"

Smiling slightly, but not looking in the direction of traffic, Jack checked his watch and headed back to his hotel. He had the evening free, and he was eager to tackle Kate's puzzle. *Perhaps,* he thought, *I can help her get to the bottom of this case before someone else gets hurt.*

Chapter 8—Jack worries as Kate heads home

6:40 p.m., Thursday, December 25

Jack and his daughter continued walking until they emerged from Penn Station. Jack kept a tight grip on her arm, and an equally tight grip on his knife, as he led her out of the terminal—east, away from his hotel. For a moment, Jack considered telling her about his earlier encounter with Ice Pick Man, but he thought better of it. *No need to worry her*, he concluded.

"Where're we headed, Dad?" Kate asked as they walked along.

Jack was so intensely preoccupied with their surroundings that he failed to respond to her.

As the two of them approached Sixth Avenue and Broadway, Handler pulled his daughter off the sidewalk and into a small delivery alcove off 34th Street. The smell of urine was powerful, suggesting that it was a favorite spot for the homeless at night. Kate scrunched up her face, placing her forefinger under her nose. "Dad, this stinks," she complained.

"I know, but we need to make some plans. We'll have no competition for this spot, at least not until later."

Jack took a long and careful look around, making sure that they had not been followed. "Kate, I'll take a closer look at that puzzle tonight. I don't have business until tomorrow. I'll call you, and maybe we can get together then. Do you have plans for lunch, or perhaps dinner?"

"Only you, Dad. I'd love to spend as much time with you as possible," she said. "Just tell me what works."

"That sounds good," Jack said. "But you had better watch your back.

I do not trust that Jefferies. And we do not have any idea who he works for or who else might be involved. You can be sure that he is not working alone."

"What do you suggest?" she asked.

"Take a cab home," Jack said.

"All the way to the Island?" she asked.

"All the way to your door. I'll hail it for you," Jack said, signaling his daughter to wait while he went out on the street. He walked right out in front of the first cab and forced the driver to stop.

"Get the hell out of my way, you ignorant bastard!" The driver yelled at him after he had opened his window.

Jack flashed two one hundred dollar bills and walked over to talk to the mouthy driver.

"My daughter needs to go to Long Island. Will this cover it?"

"Yeah, I think it might."

Jack signaled his daughter to get into the cab, and he walked around to the rear passenger door to open it for her. Before she got in, he gave her a hug and kissed her on the top of her head.

"Love ya, Dad," she said, getting into the cab.

"Love ya back, Kitten," Handler said, closing the door after her.

He then signaled the driver to lower the front passenger window as he reached in and handed the driver the money. "You take good care of this woman," he said, with his usual level of intimidation.

"I will take good care of her," the driver said, checking out the bills to be sure they were not counterfeit. "You can be sure, I'll take *very* good care of her."

Jack waved to his daughter as she rode east on 34th. She then turned and gestured through the rear window for him to give her a phone call. He smiled broadly and waved one last time.

Still blocking one lane of traffic, Jack remained in the street, taking care to make sure no one was following his daughter's cab. Finally, one of the cars he was hindering started honking at him. Not acknowledging the irritation, he remained in place for another few seconds and then casually walked over to the curb.

He totally ignored one cab driver who had rolled down the front passenger window to share his thoughts with Jack. "What's wrong with ya, Buddy, you got some kinda death wish? Stand in front of me a little longer and I'll grant that wish for ya! Ya stupid fool!"

Smiling slightly, but not looking in the direction of traffic, Jack checked his watch and headed back to his hotel. He had the evening free, and he was eager to tackle Kate's puzzle. *Perhaps*, he thought, *I can help her get to the bottom of this case before someone else gets hurt*

Chapter 9—Jack attacks Kate's puzzle

7:10 p.m., Sunday, December 25

The trek back to the hotel took less than ten minutes. As he walked, he scrutinized every aspect of his surroundings. In particular, he kept an eye out for the fellow he had run into earlier—Ice Pick Man. And for Jefferies.

During that short time, he revisited his thoughts about procuring a handgun for protection instead of the knife. But he decided against it. He was, after all, in the city to do a job. It would be a mistake to jeopardize the whole project for something he should be able to deal with without gambling on an illegal weapon. Of course, he realized that he could get busted for the knife he did carry. New York law often interprets that if a knife looks like a weapon—it's a weapon. But Jack felt more comfortable justifying his possessing a folding knife than trying to explain a loaded, illegal firearm.

Besides, a gun would have served no purpose earlier, because even had he been carrying a piece, he would not have brandished it in the lobby of a hotel. He simply had to be more careful.

He did consider that a walking stick might suit the situation well. He always traveled with one—just in case. But, he would worry about that later.

As he approached his room, he inserted his card and tested his magnetic lock. The door would not budge. That meant that the lock was operating properly. He then employed his remote to deactivate it. He could feel the lock release the door. Once inside, he plugged the adapter in to recharge the battery. He then re-engaged the magnetic lock.

Twisting off the top of a bottle of water he had purchased in the lobby when he checked in, he immediately tackled the puzzle Kate had given him. While he did feel the need to solve the puzzles—as it might help keep Kate safe—he actually considered the challenge quite enjoyable.

The first thing he did was to copy the entire code text, starting with the third line. Even though he had downplayed the initial success, he was pretty certain that he had solved it correctly. And, just as he had suspected, he quickly became certain that each line did have its own key. While "RUSSIA" worked for the third line, he could see immediately that it did not help for the other three. Given the great likelihood that he had line three right, he started out with that line, followed by its plaintext solution. He wrote:

Line 3: CRVR DDPKS CDJR DJADA PXZZ = Hawaii to China in fifty (Key: RUSSIA).

He then copied the other three lines, each on a separate sheet of paper.

Line 1: SGCN JNRE SDHC SDCJ MHVW=

Line 2: CECP DCQJ MRPP NCNG TNTQW =

Line 4: FQOPO PJKA TFGJS =

"Let's see what we can do with these," he muttered aloud. When Jack was by himself (which seemed to be most of the time), he tended to use self-talk to help him think—and generally employed the first person plural when doing it. "What was this poor sucker trying to tell us before he ran into that ice pick? Whatever it was, it got him killed. Let's see if I can think like him for a while.

"Okay, the guy worked for the State Department—in Russian and Chinese relations. And the first key was 'Russia.' One of the other keys could be 'China,' except that might be too short. Wouldn't make a good key. Could be 'China something.' ... Maybe 'Chinatown'? Could it really be that simple?"

Initially, Jack doubted himself, but then he recalled just how simple the keyword was for the third line. So, he attacked the ciphertext using "Chinatown" as the key.

He applied this potential keyword to line one. At first he tried it starting from the left. When that yielded nothing, he tried working from the right. Still nothing. So, he moved to the second line.

Immediately he found the name of another state beginning to appear: "ALAS—"

"That looks like ALASKA ... very interesting."

Continuing with "Chinatown" as the key, he developed the plaintext for the rest of the second line: "ALASKA TO RUSSIA IN FIFTY."

"So, we've got 'Hawaii to China in fifty' and 'Alaska to Russia in fifty.' What could that mean?" he wondered aloud. "That can have nothing to do with fast planes," he chuckled, recalling what his daughter had said. "You can practically drive a golf ball from Alaska to Russia. Has to have another meaning. And it has to be important—important enough to get a man killed. Hell, important enough to almost get *me* killed."

Not anticipating any success using the new keyword on the remaining lines, Jack still tried plugging it in—with, of course, the anticipated failure.

He then tried to come up with other keywords. For the next hour he applied every possibility that came to mind. With such short cryptograms, he knew that the keyword would not be terribly long, nor would it be functional if it were too short.

Suddenly he had another thought. *I wonder what the original code was written on?* he asked himself, rapidly calling Kate's number.

"Kitten, I have a quick question for you. Please do not go into detail or ask me questions. Okay?"

"Sure, Dad."

"I'm looking for short answers—one word, if possible. Okay?"

"Got ya."

Jack carefully chose the correct words to make his request. "What was the original written on?"

Kate thought for just a moment, also carefully weighing her words. "On the back of a ticket for a Knicks–Lakers game—one of those computer printouts. I know that's more than one word, but it's the best I could do. Do you think that is important?"

"Don't know. But your info is wonderful—just perfect," Jack replied. "I'll give you a call tomorrow, and we'll try to get together. Check your schedule. I'm going to be tied up for a while but will have most of the day and evening free. Just don't know for sure right now exactly when I'll be available. Talk to you tomorrow?"

"Sounds good, talk to you later."

"Got a call coming in, love ya," Jack said to his daughter, as he received his other call.

"Reg. How are you?" Jack said.

" … Sure, what *time* tomorrow?

" … How about ten? … No, let's avoid meeting there. How about men's neckties, in Macy's? We'll figure something out from there. … That works? … Great, see you then."

Jack directed his attention back to the puzzle. Suddenly he realized the significance of the two deciphered lines.

"Oh my God!" Jack exclaimed, grabbing his worksheets. "Hawaii to China in fifty—Alaska to Russia in fifty. We are *selling* those states! We are selling Hawaii to China, possession to be taken fully in fifty years. And virtually the same thing with Alaska, except we are selling Alaska to Russia—same terms. That's how the president intends to finance all this deficit spending. Talk about a reverse mortgage! He has worked out a deal with those two countries. They will fund our notes, with the guarantee of receiving those two states in return. Oh my God, Kate, you are in *grave* danger!"

Jack grabbed his cell and quickly dialed his daughter. "Kate!"

"Just a minute, Dad. Someone's at the door," Kate said, answering her father's call and setting the phone down in the same motion.

"Kate! Kate! Don't go to the door!" Jack implored her. But it was too late. Jack could hear a scuffle and a muffled scream.

Then all went silent.

Chapter 10—Kate's abduction
8:35 p.m., Sunday, December 25

Jack kept his ear to his phone. When he finally heard at least two men talking, he began to shout: "Kate! Kate! Can you hear me?"

He strained to monitor the muffled sounds of the men, while they seemed to be ransacking Kate's apartment.

"Kate!" he shouted once more.

Jack then heard one of the men pick up Kate's cell phone. "Put my daughter on, right now," Jack said.

There was no response, but Jack could hear a man breathing.

"Do you hear me, you sonofabitch. I want to talk to my daughter. If you know what you're doing, you'll put her on this phone."

The man who had picked up Kate's phone responded to Jack. "You're Kate's father—right?"

"You're damn right I am. You put her on that phone right now," Jack commanded.

"You're Jack Handler. We'll be talking to you, and soon," the man said.

"Look, you, whoever you are, I—"

"You are in no position to be giving orders," the man calmly interrupted. "If you ever want to see your daughter alive, in fact, if you even want to be able to recognize her body, you listen to me right now, and do exactly what I say. Do you understand me?"

"Let me explain something to you. Obviously you know who I am. Then you must also know what I'm capable of. You release my daughter right now, unharmed. Or I will hunt you down and kill you. I'll kill everyone close to you. I'll find your mother, if she is still alive, and I will *torture* her to death. God forbid you have a wife or children, but if you do I will make them suffer untold agonies. If anything, if even a hair on my daughter's head, is harmed—"

"*You* look," the man said. "Your daughter is still alive, for right now. And we haven't hurt her, yet. You should be happy about that. But, if we don't get everything we are after, and I mean everything, I will personally kill her. Then I will come after you, and I will kill you. Now, the only thing you can do is wait for my call. I will use your daughter's phone. I will tell you where to go and what to do. And you *will* obey."

With that, the man unceremoniously hung up. Jack tried to call the number back, but it was obvious to him that the man who held his daughter had popped the battery out of her cell phone to prevent Jack from calling back, or trying to trace the cell.

Jack had never felt so helpless. "I should have warned her. I knew the man with the ice pick was somehow connected with her victim. Why didn't I warn her when I had the chance?" That was all the second-guessing Jack would allow himself.

Jack was used to being in total control. The events of the past couple hours took him out of his element. Now he had to find a way to go pro-active—to get back on top of the situation. He had to develop a plan to get his daughter back. But he had no idea who held her, nor could he begin to guess where. He sat down on the small overstuffed chair, leaned his head back, and stared at the ceiling. Immediately his eyes went out of focus. He then closed them, and entered deeply into thought.

His self-talk was sometimes audible, sometimes not. "I'm dealing with an organization—could be private—more than likely it has political connections. Perhaps *not*. Perhaps strictly money. Possibly both. But I do think that it is closely tied to the commuter train murder of that

State Department guy—and to this, these puzzles."

Jack opened his eyes, leaned forward, and scooped up the sheets of paper he had been working on. "Hawaii to China in fifty, and Alaska to Russia in fifty," he read aloud.

Jack then looked into the ceiling and said, "Political. The guys who have my daughter are political operatives. CIA, Mossad, Russian. I don't know. Can't even rule out an MI6 connection. They want these puzzles. She is probably safe until they get them. Kate's friend at the coffee shop— he is probably involved, in some way. Jeff, Jefferies—Kurt Jefferies."

For a short moment, he considered calling one of his contacts in the FBI. He looked down at his cell for a moment, and then he thought better of it. *This thing goes much too deep for that. Who knows who can be trusted?*

Jack did have one friend in New York whom he knew he could always count on—Reginald. So he dialed him.

"Reg, it's me again. Change of plan. I have to see you tonight. Can you come over here? ... I'm at the New York State Regency. Call me when you get close, and I'll meet you in the lobby. ... Yes, it is an emergency. Thanks. ... Oh, and grab us some coffee—this could be a long night. ... See you in a few."

Jack began writing down in earnest all he knew regarding the puzzles.

Line 1: SGCN JNRE SDHC SDCJ MHVW =

Line 2: CECP DCQJ MRPP NCNG TNTQW = Alaska to Russia in fifty (Key: CHINATOWN).

Line 3: CRVR DDPKS CDJR DJADA PXZZ = Hawaii to China in fifty (Key: RUSSIA).

Line 4: FQOPO PJKA TFGJS =

Jack determined that he was pretty sure he had lines two and three correctly deciphered. At any rate, he was sufficiently confident that there was nothing to be gained by reworking them anymore. So he concentrated his energies on lines one and four.

However, the longer he stared at those two lines, the more convinced he was that he needed keys to decipher them. And he was at a loss as to where to look for them.

Chapter 11—Reginald has a clue

9:40 p.m., Sunday, December 25

Once he had written down all that he knew about the puzzles, Jack sat back in his chair and stared straight ahead. Even though Kate's abductor did not articulate it, Jack could not help but think that the puzzles had something significant to do with Kate's current situation. He then stood and began pacing around his tiny room. A cloud of helpless frustration had settled over him, and he sensed his need to shake it off.

"I've got to get to the bottom of those remaining lines. ... I've got to decipher them. But what can I do without the keyword ... or key*words*?"

Even though he had concluded that the only proactive thing he could do right now would be to crack the remaining two lines of ciphertext, he was at a loss as to how to move forward with it. Something significant was missing. He needed more information. What exactly that was, he didn't know.

He then checked the battery and reception on his cell to be certain that he would be able to take a call from Kate's abductors.

Confident that his cell was functioning properly, he sat back down and continued to scrutinize the remaining two lines of the puzzle. "I could sure use a cup of coffee," he muttered.

Half an hour later Jack's phone rang. He looked at the calling number to see if was from his daughter's phone. Immediately he recognized that it was Reginald calling him.

"I'll be at your hotel in ten," Reginald said.

"Thanks," Jack replied. "I'll meet you in the lobby. ... And you did remember the coffee, right?"

Jack knew that he would have to escort Reginald past hotel security to the elevators, so he unplugged the charger from his door lock and tested it again to be certain it was functioning properly. Confident he would be able to get back in, he locked up his room and headed down to meet Reginald. He slid his right hand into his jacket pocket and tightly gripped his knife.

"This is a bunch of bull," he said out loud as he stood alone in an elevator. Jack was not used to being on the defensive. And he did not like his dependence on a combat knife.

He had timed it perfectly. Just as he reached the lobby, his friend appeared through the revolving door.

"Hey, buddy," Jack said, reaching out to shake Reginald's hand. "Thanks for coming so quickly. I'll explain what it's all about when we get up to my room." He noticed that his friend was carrying a brown paper bag, just the right size for two large coffees.

"Good to see you too," Reginald replied as the two men headed toward the elevator. Jack did not want to waste time, but he was unable to discuss the matter with his friend on the elevator because an elderly couple had joined them. When the elevator reached Jack's floor, they exchanged pleasantries with the strangers, got off the elevator, and continued on to Jack's room.

Just as they approached the door, Jack hit his remote, unlocking the mag lock.

"What's that all about?" Reginald inquired.

"Just a lock I put on my door when I'm traveling. That way I know my room's secure."

As the two old friends closed and secured the door behind them, Reginald inquired: "Jack, is everything okay?"

"No, far from it," Jack answered. "Kate's been kidnaped."

"What are you talking about?" Reginald asked in disbelief.

Looking down at his watch, Jack replied. "I was on the phone with her less than an hour ago—maybe forty-five minutes. I heard two or more men enter her apartment and abduct her. I talked to one of them."

"That's unbelievable. Do you know who it is that has her, and what they are after? Have they made any demands?"

"Not yet. But I sense that they will not harm her, at least not right now," Jack said.

"Okay, Reg," Jack said. "I want you to listen carefully. This is what I know. See if you can think of anything I might be missing. First of all, when I was about to leave the hotel earlier this evening, on my way to meet Kate, a young muscular fellow approached me from behind. With bad intentions. I had a feeling, so I turned to check him out. And it was this guy. Reg, you're not gonna believe this. He had pulled an ice pick and was about to stick the business end of it through my heart. I side-stepped him, and he kept going."

"An *ice pick*, you say?" Reginald said. "That is a bit unusual."

"That's what I thought," Jack responded. "But when I met up with Kate, right after that, she told me about a murder at a commuter train station, and the weapon used was an ice pick. I suspect it might have been the same fellow I encountered in the hotel. Perhaps not, but the ice pick does make it plausible."

Reginald's countenance abruptly turned very somber. "I've got to tell you right off the top," he said, "the fellow who got hit in the tunnel sounds like a guy who was working with me, Jack. He had information for me that he thought critical. He worked at the State Department. That's what I was hinting at earlier, when I called you while you were still in Chicago."

"Oh yeah? Working for you? Well, Kate's got that case, and she was deeply troubled about it," Jack said.

"I hate to say it, but your daughter is in over her head, Jack," Reginald said. "This is a matter of national security. It goes all the way to the top. Those are very treacherous men she's dealing with."

"What do you mean by 'all the way to the top'? ... The top of what?" Jack asked.

"I am not sure what my man had for me, but I've never heard him so agitated," Reginald said.

"So, when you say this goes to the top, what do you mean? Are you suggesting what I think you are?"

"Yes," Reginald answered, "this could go all the way to the president."

Jack paused for a moment to gather his thoughts. "What sort of transmission device did you use to communicate with your contact?"

"It varied," Reginald said. "But this time we were going to exchange coats at a restaurant. We've done that before. He would put his information in the lining of the coat, always encrypted."

Jack walked over to the bed and retrieved the large envelope into which he had earlier slid the coded messages Kate had given him. Handing them to Reginald, he asked, "Do your messages ever look anything like this?"

"Where did you get this?" Reginald asked, flipping the sheet over to see if there was anything on the underside. "This looks very much like the message I was expecting him to give me. ... Actually, this a copy. Do you know who has the original?"

"I got this from Kate," Jack said. "She did say it was a copy. From what I can tell, it is a cryptogram. Actually, it is four separate cryptograms."

"That's typically how we communicated, all right," Reginald said.

"But it would be very helpful to have the original. Do you know who has it?"

Jack did not immediately respond to the question, instead he pursued the logic of using cryptograms for this purpose. "That's a bit archaic, don't you think?" Jack commented. "Why would you use something so analog in this digital age?"

"It's safer," Reginald replied. "Almost any standard encryption can be cracked if you have the right software, or if you rip off a guy's laptop. But the cryptograms we use are so short, without the keys they are virtually indecipherable. Take these four lines, for instance, typically I would expect each of them to have a different key."

"I'm pretty sure I got two of the four," Jack said. "I plugged 'Russia' into one of them, and 'Chinatown' into another. I got 'Hawaii to China in fifty' and 'Alaska to Russia in fifty.' Does that make any sense to you?"

"Yes it does," Reginald said. "This is all indirectly related to the business I called you in to help me with."

"What, exactly, are you saying?" Jack asked.

"Look, Jack, I am really sorry that your daughter is stuck in the middle of this, and I will do anything and everything I can to help you get her out. ... But I won't kid you about it, these guys are very dangerous."

"Okay, Reg, start talking to me. What the hell is this all about? And what is it these guys are looking for?"

"Well, for starters, I think it safe to say that they want this message," Reginald said. "I think you might negotiate her release with it. At least you can use it to get the process moving. How and when are you supposed to talk to them again?"

"They said they would call me, using Kate's phone," Jack answered. "But I don't know when. Explain to me what this message is all about and why it is so important to these guys. ... And who are they? They're spooks, right? But whose spooks?"

"Mossad. At least I know Mossad is a major player. The Russians are involved as well, but to what extent here, I don't know. … Take your pick. I'm suspecting the guys you are dealing with are either Mossad or the Russians, you know, the GRU. But my guess is Mossad."

"Why are they so interested in this State Department stuff?" Jack asked.

"Here's the deal," Reginald said. "We have known for some time that there have been high-level talks between the president himself and the Russian leader. Recently we learned that he has been talking with China as well. On the highest level. My friend at the State Department got wind of what the talks were about. That was the gist of this message. Apparently our speculation was correct. From the looks of what you have deciphered already, the president is negotiating the sale of Hawaii and Alaska. We surmised that before. It looks like he is planning to use the sale of those two states to finance the debt.

"He has exhausted all the credit available to him, and now they are calling in the chips. The deal he has apparently worked out in both cases is to give the residents of those states fifty years to relocate back in the 48, if they wish to. Fifty years is considered two generations. We've heard that he intends to give each person who relocates during the first year one hundred thousand dollars. Otherwise, if they choose to stay beyond a year, there will be no payoff."

"And that information got your man killed?" Jack asked.

"Sure did. Israel is worried. Even though they have virtually no vested interest in either of those states, they fear that should such a deal be struck, it would cause civil unrest in the US, perhaps even start a revolution. And that could be devastating for them."

"That's who's got my daughter? The Israelis?"

"Could be," Reginald replied. "*Probably* is. We're not totally convinced that's who hit our operative in the State Department. Because, the crazy thing is, the Russians are now actively involving themselves in this thing, but for different reasons than is Mossad. They do have an iron in this fire, and they are hell-bent on making sure this deal happens—that they get Alaska. The natural resources there are worth trillions, plus it would provide them with a base in North America. It is really a sweet deal for them, at any price. I'm sure you know that the Russians have no national debt. So that puts them in a position of strength. They are intent on seeing this deal go through.

"And virtually the same can be said for the Chinese. They would love to take possession of Hawaii. It would fit right into their imperialistic design for world domination."

"Who, exactly, are you working for this time?" Jack asked.

"Freelancing," Reginald replied. "You know how that goes."

"Freelancing. But for who?"

Reginald paused a moment before answering. "Ostensibly I'm working with a group of concerned parties—people both you and I have worked with before."

"And who might they be?"

"Allison is heading it up," Reginald answered after a thoughtful pause. "There are three others, and you know some of them ... maybe all of them."

"Allison is in charge? What is the ultimate goal of this group?" Jack asked. He felt comfortable grilling his friend about this because it had already been established that Reginald had called him in to work with them.

"The five of us have been meeting for a couple of weeks," Reginald replied. "Al put the group together to lay the groundwork for her presidency."

"Is Bob part of this group?"

"No, Al did not think he should be a part of it."

"That scares me more than a little," Jack said. "Bob was always the glue that held everything together."

"I know what you mean," Reginald agreed, "but Al has done a good job so far. That having been said, I can't help but agree with you that I would be a lot more comfortable if Bob were running the show. He invokes an aura of fear that Al is not capable of. I suspect that's what you mean by 'glue.'"

"I'm going to need to know who the other parties are, in your little group, and what their roles are, but right now I'm interested in what you and your buddies are talking about, what decisions have been made. And what sort of work has been contemplated that would elicit so violent a reaction by Mossad or the Russians. Talk to me about *that*, Reg, I need to understand what is going on here. ... My daughter's life is at stake."

"Initially, we started out reviewing what our options might be heading into the general election. Al was concerned that even though she might successfully challenge Butler in the primary, she would likely lose in the general—that, given this president's growing unpopularity and the state of the economy. ... And if Butler were to consummate a deal for the sale of even one of the states, members of his political party would be lucky if their own families voted for them.

"We discussed every possible tactic but could not find one that provided a scenario where she would likely win. In fact, one of our major concerns was that Butler would invoke executive powers and put off the election altogether. Given his penchant for power, it seems a real possibility."

"I've heard that suggested before," Jack said, "but coming from the right. I've not heard any on the left talking like that—not until just now."

"And you won't. But, trust me, it's in the back of everyone's mind. With this president, the unthinkable has become plausible."

"Okay, Reg, given that scenario, what did you guys come up with as a viable option?" Jack asked, already sensing what he was about to hear. "Did you get that far?"

"I'm sure you've got this all figured out, right?" Reginald asked, not wanting to utter the words.

"Maybe," Jack said, "but I want to hear the words come from your mouth."

"It was the consensus of the group," Reginald said, "that ... . " He hesitated for a long moment, obviously looking for the right way to articulate it. "We decided that there was not a way for Al to win against the libertarian coalition," Reginald finally said. "She possibly could wrest the nomination away from Butler, if there were actually to be a convention and a nomination. But, when it came to the general election, she would lose. And we would lose even more seats in both the House and the Senate."

"You're skirting the question," Jack said. "What did you guys decide to do about it?"

"It was decided," Reginald said, again hesitating, "that the only way to deal with this would be to see this president leave office before the end of his term. That having been accomplished, he would be replaced by the VP, who would appoint Al to take his place, as VP.

"We agreed that John was too old to want to run for a full term. So, of course, Al would run. And she would have a great chance to win.

"The critical factor here would be to convince the country that the right was to blame for Butler's departure. The backlash would carry

Al into office, and quite possibly we would make sizeable gains in the House and Senate on her coattails. It was our only viable solution. Or so the group concluded."

"That's what I thought you were going to say," Jack responded. "Of course, you know just how insane this whole thing is, don't you? How the hell could you possibly think I would ever agree to something this nuts? The whole thing is insane. Now you've got my daughter kidnaped."

Jack paused for a moment. He looked over at Reginald, who now sat silently, not able to make eye contact with his old friend.

"Reg, you know me better than any other human being on earth knows me," Jack said. His voice had assumed a very somber tone. "You fully understand what I'm capable of. … I swear to God, if I did not need you to get my daughter back, I just might kill you on the spot. How could you *ever* think I would be willing to help with something this stupid? What were you thinking?"

"Look, Jack," Reginald said, now looking directly into Jack's eyes. "I had no idea that your daughter would be involved in this. I am truly sorry for that. And I will help you get her back. Then, if you still feel you need to, go ahead and kill me. This thing has got so out of hand, the way things are going, I'm a dead man anyway. And I mean that. I would rather have a friend put a bullet in my brain than suffer the indignities of a trial."

"Make me feel better about this," Jack commanded. "You are my friend, but I am not liking what you have been telling me. What am I missing?"

"Jack, I called you in because you are the only person I trust. I would trust my life, and the life of my family, in your hands. … I am looking for a way out of this, and I figured you would be the only person who could help me pull it off. There is just no way in hell that I could allow this assassination to take place. I knew something had to be done. It could mean the end of the free world. I do not mean to sound melodramatic, but it is that serious. I don't think the others in the group appreciate the gravity of what they are planning—what *we* are planning. As a member of the group, I'm virtually helpless. That's why I called you in. If I buck the consensus, I'm dead. And this lunacy moves ahead. I'm trying to find an acceptable way out of this."

"Damn it, Reg, you know I'm *not* a politically motivated person. You know that. Why would you ever drag me into something like this?"

"Jack, if you can help me here, there's several million in it for you. You name your price," Reginald said. "I know that money means nothing to you in light of your daughter's kidnapping. But once we get her back, you help me pull this off, you will be set for the rest of your life. No more penny-ante stuff. ... We just might be able to save the country and get rich at the same time."

Reginald paused for a moment, and then continued. "Jack, I am truly sorry that your daughter got dragged into it. I would never have put Kate in harm's way, any more than I would have done it to my own daughter. But this whole thing is still salvageable, if we work together, like we have before."

"Forget the money, I need to get my daughter back," Jack said. "You help me get her back, unharmed, I might be willing to help you. But she comes first."

Just then, Jack's phone rang. He looked down at it, and then back up at Reginald. "It's them."

Chapter 12—*The call Jack was waiting for*
11:05 p.m., Sunday December 25

Jack held out his hand to Reginald, requesting silence. "Handler here," he said.

"You've got something we want," the man said.

"Put my daughter on," Jack calmly commanded. "I'm not talking to you until my daughter tells me she is okay. Put her on the phone."

"You will do what I say," the man said.

"Look, you deaf sonofabitch. I told you to put my daughter on this phone. I've got nothing to say to you until I talk to her. Put her the hell on. Right now!"

Jack listened intently, as he detected the man muffling the phone against his chest. "Go bring the bitch up here," Jack heard him telling someone who was with him. "Handler won't talk to me until he hears from her. Go get her."

For the first time since the ordeal began Jack was starting to think that he just might be able to gain the upper hand. The information Reginald provided filled in some of the blanks. Now he knew what the kidnappers were after, and how he might bargain for Kate's safety. Then, when the men holding Kate obeyed his command, Jack further sensed a slight shift. He was, however, still far from confident.

Jack also gleaned an important bit of information from the caller when he told his buddy to bring Kate "up." That meant Kate was most likely being held in the basement, because it was unlikely that the kidnappers would base their operation on any level but the main level, as that would make it too hard to defend. That info would be valuable when it came time to rescue Kate.

Jack continued to listen intently. The only sound he could hear for nearly a full minute was that of the man's breathing and the beating of his heart. *Amazingly steady—about sixty beats per second,* Jack thought. *This guy is relaxed and confident. I must appear more relaxed and more confident.*

Jack had learned to extrapolate heart rate from a man's breathing pattern—the slower and more steady the breathing, the slower the heart rate.

Finally, Jack heard the man giving orders to someone he assumed to be Kate. "Tell your dad that you are fine and that he should give us what we want if he ever expects to see you again."

After a few more seconds, the weak voice of his daughter squeaked out of the phone. "Dad, you there?"

"Hi, kitten, you okay?" Jack made certain to exude an aura of confidence when he talked to his daughter. If he allowed her to think he was at all panicked, it would weaken her resolve.

"I'm okay. But they said that you—"

"I heard what they told you to say," Jack interrupted. "I want to know if they've hurt you."

"Not really," Kate answered. "It got a little rough in the beginning, but I'll heal up okay—"

With that, the man holding Kate grabbed the phone away from her.

As soon as Jack knew his daughter's abductor was back on the phone, he returned to his original posture. "You listen to me, you bastard, if you know what's good for you, you will open the door and release my daughter. Right now. Let her walk outta there. The longer you hold her, the worse I'm gonna make it for you and your family. I promise you that I'll track you down and kill you. You need to cut your losses now and take my advice."

"Cut the chatter, Handler. I've got what you want, and you've got what I want."

That was what Jack was waiting for. Now the negotiations could begin. It had all been rhetoric up to this point.

After pausing a few seconds, Jack inquired, "What the hell do you think I've got?"

"You've got the message—the puzzle. Kate gave it to you. We saw her hand it to you in the coffee shop, so don't mess with me. Now, Handler, my friend, you must understand that we're not animals. We're just businessmen, like you. We are not interested in hurting your daughter. We just want the message. Your daughter is blindfolded—she can't identify us. We are protecting your interests. We can release her if we choose to do so. And we will do just that, once you have given us everything she gave you. You know what I'm talking about."

"How will I know my daughter is safe?" Jack asked, beginning to think that there might be a solution to the problem. He noted that the kidnapper had a solid mastery of slang and idioms. *He's grown up in the States. He might be Mossad, but he's been in the states most of his life*, Jack surmised.

"We do not need to hurt her, if you do what I say," the man declared. "All we want is the piece of paper she gave you earlier today—the one with the puzzle on it."

"Then this is what you do," Jack said. "The two of you—Kate and you—take a cab to my hotel. You already know where I'm staying. When the two of you get here, I will come down to the lobby and meet you. I will give you what you want, and you give me my daughter. That's pretty simple. You do that, you get what you want, and I let you live."

Again Jack heard the caller attempting to muffle the phone. "Put her back in the … *bedroom*, and tie her up."

Jack was relieved that Kate's abductor did not deny that he knew what hotel Jack was staying at. That strongly suggested that he was associated with Ice Pick Man. That pleased Jack because it meant that he might be dealing with a single entity.

Jack also caught the hesitation when he ordered Kate to be returned to the bedroom. *He started to say "basement,"* Jack reasoned, *but thought better of it.*

After a few moments, the man again talked to Jack. "Jack, it's okay if I call you by your first name, right? Jack, can you imagine what your daughter's hands will look like in an hour, or two hours? It's pretty amazing what a wire tie will do to blood flow, if it's tight enough. I'll bet by morning, her hands will be cold and purple. How long does it take for gangrene to set in? Do you know anything about that?"

"I hope you're not that stupid," Jack interrupted. "You know better than to harm her. You'd better pay attention to what I'm telling you."

"No, Jack, you listen to me. You need to hear this," the kidnapper said. "Sometimes amputation can save a person who has gangrene. So maybe she will live, if someone finds her soon enough. But I've heard that it's a very painful death. Now, Jack, is that what you want for her? To die up here alone? She's brave now, but that will change. Once she starts to feel the pain in her hands and arms, once the fever of infection sets in. Then delirium. Then more pain—more pain than she can handle. More pain than *anyone* could handle—even more than the great Jack Handler could handle. Finally, merciful death. And she will welcome it. She will pray for death. Is that what you want for your daughter? For your beloved Kate? You will find her curled up in a ball in a cold room. You will see the pain in her dead eyes—"

"I hope you're too smart to hurt her," Jack told him. "I don't give a damn about you. But I do have pity for your family. Some of them are probably nice innocent people. They don't even know what a miserable failure you are, do they? I will take no joy in whacking them. There'll be nothing in it for me, except revenge. Just know that if my daughter is hurt in any way, I will invest the rest of my life hunting down your entire family, and destroying them in the most vicious way I can imagine. I have a hunch you know more than a little about me. If you do, you know what I'm capable of."

"You can say what you want," the abductor interrupted. "I don't care. I'm not worried. But you need to think about what you do. I'm giving you the best opportunity you will ever have to save your daughter. You need to be smart." He paused for a second before pushing the button that he knew would trigger a reaction in Jack. "You killed Kate's mother … Beth, your wife. Isn't that right? You didn't actually pull the trigger, but it was your fault. Well, now I'm giving you a chance to be smarter. Kate does not have to die. You can save her life—if you want to. This is what you need to do. And I really hope you do it. I would like nothing better than to see you and your very beautiful daughter reunited. And unharmed. Isn't that what you want?"

"What the hell is it that you want?" Jack demanded of his daughter's kidnapper.

"I told you, I want the information the detectives removed from your friend's contact at the State Department. That's it. Bring that to me, all of it, everything she gave you, and you get your daughter back. How simple can I make it?"

"Tell me exactly how we make the exchange," Jack said. "Nothing happens without my daughter coming back first."

"Of course," the abductor told Jack. "I would have it no other way. This is what you do. Bring everything Kate gave you down to the lobby

of your hotel at exactly twelve forty-five a.m. Don't come down any earlier. I will walk in with your daughter. There will be another man with
us. Your daughter and my friend will wait in the lobby, just inside the
doors, and I will approach you by myself. Hand me the envelope. I will
examine it, and if it is what I am expecting, I will leave. My friend will
go with me. And Kate will stay."

Jack realized that the kidnapper had the stronger hand, so he decided to take a different approach. "You won't hurt her. You know that she
won't be able to recall the whole puzzle. And certainly not the solutions.
But I have the entire puzzle, and I have the solutions."

There followed dead silence, for an uncomfortable length of time.
For just a moment, Jack considered giving the kidnapper more to think
about. He had just revealed a pair of aces, no need to show his whole
hand—not right now. *The next person who blinks, loses,* Jack was thinking. So, he remained silent.

Finally, Kate's kidnapper broke the uneasy silence. "You've deciphered it? The whole thing?"

"Damn right, I've cracked it—all four lines."

"Then tell me what they are, and I'll release your daughter right
now."

Jack pretended he did not hear what Kate's abductor had just said.
"I suspect you've already got the third line," Jack said. "The third line is,
Hawaii to China in fifty."

The voice at the other end remained silent for a moment. "Your
daughter gave us that line. What else you got? Give me the rest and we've
got a deal."

"Alaska to Russia in fifty," Jack said. "That's one of the other lines.
Now, that's all you get until I get my daughter."

For the first time since this conversation began, Jack felt like he was making substantial progress. It was obvious to him that the kidnapper was getting some information from Kate. But Jack knew she had only that one line to give up. When he provided the solution to the other line, suddenly the kidnapper was more cooperative. Besides, Jack knew that even the most callous among killers did not want to see his own family harmed. He felt that Kate's kidnapper must know enough about his reputation to take the threat seriously. Jack figured the kidnapper was at least to some degree concerned about that.

"I'll be there," Jack said. "And my daughter had better be there too—and smiling."

With that, the kidnapper hung up.

Jack sat back in his seat and stared at his phone. "Reg, we've got our hands full with this. We've got to decipher the other two lines, without keys. … Unless you know what the keys are. How about it? What exactly *do* you know?"

"Not much more than I've already given you," Reginald said. "Tell me all you know. Tell me everything Kate told you about it. Maybe there's a clue in it somewhere."

"Kate said the original was on a computer ticket, for a Knicks game," Jack said.

"A Knicks game," Reginald repeated.

"Right, the code was written on the blank side of the ticket," Jack said. "But she didn't say anything was highlighted or underlined, and there was no additional writing."

"I think the clue to the remaining keys would have something to do with the fact that it was on a ticket, an NBA ticket," Reginald responded, deep in thought. "Do you know who they were playing?"

"Lakers," Jack said. "Kate said it was a Knicks-Lakers game."

"How much time do we have?" Reginald said, checking his watch.

"We're going to have to get awfully lucky to solve this in time."

"What the hell do you normally do?" Jack asked, his impatience growing more obvious.

"Usually, he would leave a voice mail for me, and it would alert me to a coded message," Reginald answered. "And we shared access to a Google account—a Gmail account. He would compose an email containing the keys, but he would not send it. He would just leave it as a 'draft.' Nothing would get sent, so there would be nothing intercepted. And then I would pull the keys off the draft. No emails would be sent.

"But, as a precaution, he would always put his messages on a piece of printed matter containing the keys, or at least something that would allow me to figure out what the keys were. That's where I would look now, if I had a chance. Without more information, I'm not so sure if we have long enough info to figure it out."

"The first two were pretty simple," Jack said. "Why would the rest of it not be just as simple?"

"Because the meat of the message will be contained in the other two lines," Reginald said. "It's *all* important, but if there is some particularly sensitive information, it would be in one or both of the two lines you have not yet deciphered. Sometimes the keys for the remaining lines would be buried in the plaintext of the easier cryptograms. Not so sure that will be the case this time."

"What are our chances of solving this in the next hour?" Jack asked.

"We would have to be very lucky," Reginald said.

"Can't count on *that*," Jack answered. "This is what we do. I will come up with some bogus plaintext solutions for the two remaining lines—something that these fellows will hopefully buy. It will have to make sense. These guys do not know whether or not we have the keys. They may or may not have all four lines of the puzzle. Kate may have a second copy with her, but it doesn't sound like she gave them anything substantive regarding the solution—only what she could recall. But they are not going to do any more work on a solution, not if they think they are going to get it from us. So, if I can give them something that looks legit, they just might accept it."

"And, in the meantime, I will see what I can do to decipher it," Reginald said.

"Exactly," Jack answered. "It's our best shot."

Chapter 13—*The NBA connection*

12:02 a.m., Monday, December 26

Jack quickly set about writing down two sets of the un-deciphered lines of the cryptogram—lines one and four:

Line 1: SGCN JNRE SDHC SDCJ MHVW

Line 4: FQOPO PJKA TFGJS

"No chance these two lines would have the same key?" Jack asked.

"No chance at all," Reginald replied. "One thing to keep in mind, the key would *not* be obvious on the ticket. For instance, because it is a Lakers-Knicks game, you can assume *that* will not be the key.

"However, because the code was written on an NBA ticket, you can be sure that the key, in fact, most likely both of the remaining keys, relates to professional basketball—but not necessarily to the game on the ticket. For instance, I'm going to test 'Lakers World Champs.' That because they beat Boston in the 2010 finals. ... You see where I'm going with this?"

"I do," Jack said. "But I'm not going to take a chance going down that road. You do what you can do to solve one or both of the lines, I'm going to come up with some convincing bogus solutions. Please don't talk to me until we're done."

The two men tore into the cryptograms—Reginald attempting to decipher them, Jack inventing sham solutions.

Jack decided to start with the fourth line. He assumed that Reginald would attack the first line, because it was longer. Generally speaking, the longer a line of code, the easier to crack. He thought his efforts would be best directed with the last line.

Jack suddenly realized that he had never before tried to bogus up a puzzle. There was something about it that ran counter to his ethical makeup. *That OPOP is very curious,* he concluded. *That would suggest we are dealing with a group of shorter words, not a couple longer ones. And, the fact that there were only fourteen letters used also suggests a group of shorter words.*

He knew that if he did not get this solved or phonied up, and quickly, he would probably just have to attack and kill the kidnapper in the hotel lobby, and that would be very dangerous for Kate.

As quickly as he could he started plugging in potential NBA phrases—most of them involving the Lakers. None of them worked.

"Could a key involve an NBA team *not* on the ticket?" Jack asked, violating his own code of silence. "I think you suggested it could."

"Sure," Reginald answered. "In fact, that would be likely."

Jack then remembered the player acquisition of the decade during the summer of 2010, bringing LeBron James and Chris Bosh to the Miami Heat. He first attempted to plug "LeBron James" into the code as the key. He quickly realized it would not work. So he then tried "Miami Heat." He made up the grid, and started to plug in the letters. He was pleased to see that the 'OPOP' that initially captured his interest stood for 'STST.' That, he thought, was significant, because those two letters were two of the most frequently used consonants in the English language, and were commonly used in juxtaposition.

As soon as he looked at it as a whole, he knew he had it right. "Must stop him now," he said, almost shouting. "Line four is 'must stop him now.' Holy hell, Reg—could that possibly be right? Is he suggesting that the president of the United States should be assassinated? Damn, Reg, that is what got your man killed. And it could get us all killed!"

Reginald looked up at Jack, and then back down at his work. It was obvious to Jack that his friend was not really surprised at the plaintext.

Jack decided that he should now attack the first line—the one Reginald was working on. But before he could plug in a potential key, Reginald sat back in his chair and breathed a sigh of relief. "I've got it. The key is 'Lakers in seven,' and the plaintext is 'from the lips of POTUS.' Jack, I do believe we have deciphered this whole code. This is just about what I expected. My man in the State Department knew what the group was looking for, and he concluded that he had found it. With the president signing off on the sale of Hawaii and Alaska, he knew that this would divide the country and possibly spark a revolution. He is stating that the group should implement the plan—and expeditiously."

"Was he in a position to have this information?" Jack asked.

"Yes, he was," Reginald replied. "If he said that these words were from the lips of the president, then he heard the president say them. My man was legit."

"How about the fourth line, the one that authorizes the assassination—how could he make that determination?"

"He was my operative in the State Department," Reginald said. "He was totally aware of what we were looking into and was a valued advisor. In fact, I think that it was he who instigated the plot to begin with. It is unlikely that Al or Jerry would have come up with it without this sort of input."

"Jerry, who the hell is Jerry?" Jack asked.

"You know him, he's Al's and Steve's very close friend," Reginald said.

"And Steve—is that who I think it is?" Jack followed.

"Right."

"Good God, what sort of unholy group of misfits have you guys assembled? I wouldn't trust either one of them in matters this important."

"I know what you are saying, and I agree," Reginald said. "We'll deal with that later. Right now we have a decision to make. Should we or should we not give the correct message to Kate's kidnapper?"

"Look, Reg, we are going to do everything we can to get Kate back," Jack said, "even if it means giving up secrets. The bastard gets the whole plaintext, just the way we deciphered it. He will know immediately that what he is looking at is accurate, and he will be satisfied. At least, if *anything* is going to make him satisfied, this will. We will watch him. As soon as he has had a chance to go through all four lines, if I get a bad feeling, I will kill him on the spot, and you take out whoever is holding Kate. She will be just inside the lobby door. We won't have any extra time. It has to happen quickly if anything goes south."

Reginald nodded in agreement and left the room ahead of his friend to take up a strategic position in the lobby. Jack waited five minutes, and then he headed down as well.

Just then Jack's cell phone rang.

"Yeah," Jack said. "What the hell do you mean by *a change of plan*?"

Chapter 14—The art of misdirection

12:45 a.m., Monday, December 26

Jack stopped in his tracks. "What are you now suggesting? You said you would have my daughter with you, in the lobby of my hotel. Now you're changing the plan?"

"That's right," the kidnapper said. "It's back to Penn Station. Bring the material in the envelope to that same place you had coffee with your daughter earlier. Wait until that same table gets empty, sit down, and tape it to the bottom. Pretty simple, huh? Sit there for only a minute. Call me. Then leave."

"And my daughter?"

"She'll be there with us. And we'll be watching."

"She needs to be with me before I do anything."

"You're not calling the shots here, chief," the kidnapper told Jack. "You do what I just told you to do. Tape the message to the bottom of the table. And by the time you get back to your hotel, you will have your daughter. Got it?"

"Doesn't work that way," Jack countered. "I'll meet you in the lobby of my hotel as we originally planned. You send my daughter in ahead of you. When I have her in my possession, safe and sound, I will pass the envelope off to you. Everybody gets what they want, no one has to die."

"Looks like we've reached an impasse," the kidnapper said. "Fortunately for me, your daughter remembers much of the puzzle. I suspect that with a little coaxing, she will remember more." The kidnapper paused for a moment to let his words sink into Jack's mind. Then he continued. "Look, Handler, if you don't mind what happens to your daughter, then neither do I. I will get what I need, one way or the other.

"Meet me at Penn Station, like I told you, give me the rest of the solutions, taped to the bottom of the table. Be there just before one a.m. Your daughter will be with me. All you have to do is leave the envelope, with all the solutions, all of them, under the table just as I said. You then call me on your daughter's phone, and leave. I don't want to be able to see you. You need to walk away from that table at exactly one a.m. I will arrive at that time, and your daughter will be with me. I will remove the message from under the table and examine it. If I am satisfied, I will leave. And you can have your daughter back. She knows where you are staying, right?"

Jack sensed that arrangement could work—with some adaptation. The kidnapper would still be in a position of strength, because if he was not satisfied with the solution of the code, he would kill Kate on the spot.

The fact that it would not be feasible for the kidnapper to bring Kate into Penn Station blindfolded was significant. It meant that his daughter most likely would be able to identify her kidnappers. If that were the case, it would suggest that the men holding Kate were now willing to sacrifice themselves for this mission.

Or, it was possible that they were intending to kill Kate? Jack did not like to think about that.

In either case, Jack knew that there would be more than one person involved with the transfer—so that if anything went awry, there would be a gun aimed at his daughter, and probably at him. But he also knew that this would be the best deal he could possibly get out of this kidnapper. And, because it now seemed to be rapidly unfolding, Jack sensed (or at least hoped) Kate's chances were improving.

"And when you come, come alone," the abductor said. "If your buddy follows you out, your daughter's dead. You come alone, to the coffee shop. If you're a good boy, you will be able to tell your grandchildren this story. Pull anything, and she dies. Do you understand?"

Jack did not respond; he merely hung up and dialed up Reginald. "Plan's changed," he told Reginald, who had left the room moments before and had found a good seat in the lobby.

"Yeah, Jack, what's up?"

"I'll be walking out in a few minutes," Jack said. "I'm just getting on the elevator right now."

"You got another call?"

"I did, and the meeting is back at Penn Station," Jack said.

"Shall I head down there now?"

"They made you," Jack said. "You had better stay put. I'll handle this on my own."

"How about I follow you after a few?"

"Won't work," Jack admonished. "They'll be watching for you. In fact, you should stay right where you're at. If I need you, I'll call. … It's gonna be the only safe place for you right now. They know you, but you don't know them. It could get very dicey for you. Might as well meet me at the elevator, and I will give you my key. Someone might fall on you with an ice pick. … I'm on the elevator." Jack disconnected and headed down to the lobby.

When the door opened, he looked around for Reginald and found him standing and talking with the security guard assigned to check guests' cards before allowing them on the elevators. Jack did not say a word to Reginald as he passed him, but he slid his card and remote into Reginald's pocket. Reginald then reached into his pocket for the card, showed it to the guard, and took a couple steps toward the elevator. But before getting on the elevator, Reginald turned to watch Jack as he headed out of the hotel.

Jack did not bother to look around for the kidnapper's friend. He simply walked quickly out of the hotel and headed toward the rendez-vous.

As soon as he was outside, Jack immediately proceeded to walk right out onto Eighth Avenue, as though he were planning to cross over before the traffic light. But instead of crossing Eighth Avenue, he remained in the traffic lane and walked toward the intersection, making sure to avoid oncoming traffic. He knew that by doing this, he would discourage anyone who might be following him.

Usually, this practice worked. But not this time. Just as he reached the crosswalk, he spotted a young, very muscular man following him, even though he had taken precautions. "Damn it," Jack silently mouthed. Spinning around, Jack grabbed the man's right wrist, just as he had started to pull an ice pick out of his pocket. In the same motion, Jack pulled his knife out of his jacket pocket and shoved it firmly through the man's jacket, and then slightly downward. Jack did not wish to kill his attacker. He merely wanted to force his blade through the man's clothes, and to cut him a little.

"Are you sure you want to dance with me, you sonofabitch?" Jack asked. He kept his blade where it was, even though he could think of nothing he would enjoy more than running the knife through to the man's spine, piercing his lower intestine. "This is gonna be one slow agonizing death. Are you sure you're ready for this?"

With that, the man tried to step back, but it was too late. Reginald had spotted the man leaving the hotel right after Jack, and he suspected his friend could be in danger. Just as the man attempted to pull his wrist free from Jack's grasp, Reginald slid an ice pick into the attacker's back, piercing his left lung and his heart. He immediately pulled the weapon out and rammed it into his right lung, this time wrenching the handle to the right, snapping the ice pick off inside the attacker. Death was not only certain, but quick.

Reginald eased the man to the street and in an affected, effeminate voice, screamed over to a bellman, "Call an ambulance, this man is having a heart attack! Oh my God, somebody help him!"

As onlookers pushed in, Reginald spoke loudly to the man he had just killed. "I'll be right back, I'm going for help." He then disappeared into the darkness.

Jack had already moved on toward his meeting with his daughter's kidnapper. "That's one less problem I got to deal with," Jack muttered as he picked up his pace.

Reginald's move on his behalf did not surprise Jack. The two of them always had each other's back. Jack did think it a bit curious that Reginald used an ice pick. In fact, all the way across Eighth Avenue, that was all that Jack could think about. He finally concluded that Reginald was making a point—his State Department man had been killed by this man, or one of his buddies, with an ice pick. *Simple justice,* Jack thought. *It's fitting as hell. Get the bastard with the same weapon he used to get your man.*

Besides, Jack liked the use of an ice pick in just such a situation. For starters, an ice pick is an amazingly efficient weapon for an aggressive attack. It is easy to push into a man. In fact, most of the time it will pierce even the best body armor if enough thrust is exerted behind it. It is more effective than a .357, because it will separate the fibers and slide through. A round from a .357 will flatten and most often be stopped by the vest.

And if the ice pick hits a rib, it will redirect itself to softer tissue. A bone will stop most knives.

The greatest advantage is that if the shaft of the pick is ground nearly in two, about three inches from the tip, it can be easily broken off inside the victim. The handle is then removed, leaving the business end below the surface of the skin.

The heart is always the first target. And when the heart is pierced, it immediately ceases to pump blood to the brain, and unconsciousness rapidly ensues, followed by death. It has the appearance of a heart attack. Because the entry wound is so small, any bleeding takes place internally, usually into the lungs. That's why it is always good to puncture both lungs.

Jack took one last glance behind him and continued on toward the meeting. He now could hope that he would surprise the kidnapper. After all, it appeared as though the plan was for him to be killed on the street and the envelope removed from his body.

But, thanks to Reginald, the kidnapper did not know he had survived the attempt.

Jack was fairly confident, however, that the kidnapper would be at the coffee shop, as a backup plan. And, he thought that he might even have brought Kate with him.

At any rate, Jack calculated that his chances of saving his daughter had improved with Reginald's elimination of one of the kidnapper's buddies. Experience told him that there would be a trap.

As Jack entered the coffee shop in Penn Station, his optimism was rewarded. Standing off to the side was a large, powerfully built man, wearing a New York Giants cap and a Giants jacket. He had his arm around Kate's waist. Jack noted that, as he suspected, Kate was not wearing a blindfold. Instead, she had on a pair of very dark Jackie-O sunglasses.

Jack wasted no time. The table he and Kate had shared earlier was vacant, so he walked over to it and sat down. He then taped the envelope containing the puzzle to the underside, and then walked up to the counter as though to order a cup of coffee. There was no need to make any calls—the kidnapper had observed his obedience. Jack's question was whether or not he would reward it.

Glancing back toward the table as he waited at the end of a short line, Jack saw the man guiding Kate into the chair across the table where he had taped the envelope. His first impulse was to walk right up to the two of them, but he then thought it better to let the scene play out.

Kate could get hurt if I act prematurely, Jack reasoned.

Just then, he felt a heavy hand clutch his shoulder. Startled, he shoved his hand under his jacket and started to pull out his knife.

"Take it easy," Reginald advised. He had circled around and entered Penn Station right on Jack's heels.

"Damn," Jack muttered, "you startled the hell out of me. What are you doing here?"

"I figured you could use some help," Reginald said, glancing over his friend's shoulder. "That's your daughter, isn't it?"

"Yeah, they're both here," Jack said. "I wasn't expecting you to make it back so soon."

"How do you want to handle this?" Reginald asked.

"Here's what we do," Jack said, developing his plan on the fly. "Get a good look at this guy. Then position yourself outside the coffee shop. Ideally he will leave alone. Follow him. If he takes the subway, or hits the street, try not to lose him. If Kate is still with him, then take him out. Got it? Giants cap and jacket. You can't miss him."

Just as Reginald left, the abductor sat down at the table with Kate. As he did, he reached for and removed the envelope. Jack watched as the man opened and read the contents. A smile crept across the kidnapper's face when he realized he had the real thing. The man then turned and smiled at Jack, who was still standing nearly thirty feet away. Jack took the smile as a signal that he was satisfied with what Jack had left for him.

"May I help you?" the attendant at the counter asked Jack.

Jack turned to respond, "Yes, a double espresso, please."

"Will that be all?"

"Yes," Jack replied, as he turned back to check on his daughter.

During that few seconds when Jack was placing his order, the abductor looked back at Kate, smiled at her, and then double popped her with a gun he had concealed under his jacket on the table. Because he was using a suppressor, Jack heard nothing.

The first round struck Kate squarely in the forehead, slightly dislodging the sunglasses. The second round struck Kate in the middle of her upper chest, with the bullet lodging in her spine. Both wounds were fatal.

Just as Jack turned back around, he observed that as the abductor stood from the table to leave, he adjusted Kate's sunglasses and then left.

Not realizing that Kate had been shot, Jack immediately made his way over to her. As he approached Kate, he did sneak one quick glance at the fleeing abductor. He observed the man dispose of some items in the trash container at the door, just as he disappeared.

"Kate," Jack said. "Are you okay?"

By the time Jack had reached the girl, he realized that she had been shot. Blood was trickling down the left side of her cheek and off her chin. Because the entry wound was that of a small-caliber revolver, there was not a great deal of blood.

"Kate!" Jack yelled, as he removed the sunglasses to get a better look at his daughter.

The instant he got a look at her face he realized that the girl he had thought was Kate was actually not his daughter. Rather it was a woman about the same age, size, and appearance as Kate. And she was wearing his daughter's coat and scarf.

"My God, child," he cried, "what have they done to you?"

Even though his instincts told him to pursue the killer, he chose instead to remain with the girl. Jack knew that the process of dying was not instantaneous. Even though this beautiful young girl was technically dead, there was a good chance that her mind might still be processing what was happening to her. Jack was not about to let her pass alone.

"Darling," Jack said, gently taking the girl's head in his hands. "I am so sorry this has happened to you." He looked into her eyes one last time. They were the eyes of a dead girl, but her lower lip still moved, as though she were trying to talk.

Jack then placed his lips firmly on the top of the girl's head and tenderly grasped her shoulders. "I will talk to your parents. I will tell them what a beautiful child you are. I will stay with you."

Jack knew that he was lying to her when he said he would talk to her parents—contacting her parents would raise more questions than he could answer. But he did remain with her until he felt her body stop trembling, and life slip away.

Realizing that there was nothing more he could do for her, he turned his attention back in the direction the abductor had fled. Jack hurried over to the trash receptacle to check on what the man had tossed into it on his way out.

Pushing the hinged door on the trash bin in far enough to get a look, Jack saw the Giants jacket lying on top of the trash. *The cap is certainly in there too,* he surmised. *That means Reg most likely missed him.*

Walking out of the coffee shop and over to where he had asked Reginald to wait, Jack knew immediately when he saw his friend standing there that the abductor-turned-murderer had escaped.

Just then Jack's cell rang. "Kitty" appeared on the display.

"Where's my daughter, you murdering sonofabitch? I want—" Jack started to say.

"She's fine, and you'll get her back. Go back to your room at the hotel and wait for instructions," the voice on the other end said. "I have one more job for you to do."

With that the phone went dead.

Jack stood there for a few brief moments contemplating his options. He looked over at Reginald as he returned his phone to its holder, and then he walked out to the street.

Reginald followed at a safe distance.

Chapter 15—Allison recruits Reginald
11:15 a.m., Tuesday, December 13

Bernadette was sitting at a table next to the small fence that separated the eating area from museum exhibits, when Reginald Black walked by on his way to the sandwich counter. She had chosen a seat right there so she could catch him as he passed. "Reg. How are you?"

"I'm well," Reginald said, quite obviously caught by surprise. "I'm sorry, but do I know you?"

"My name is Bernadette. I am a very good friend of Allison's."

"Okay," Reginald responded, suddenly aware that the handsome woman he was talking to was actually Allison. "And you? How are you?"

"I'm pleased to say," Bernadette answered, "I'm always great."

"Well, Bernadette, I'll just grab a sandwich and join you."

"No need, I bought one for you, and a soda. Just hop over the fence and sit down."

Reginald had no problem stepping over the low fence—he was in excellent shape. Even though pushing sixty from the wrong side, he ran several miles every morning before breakfast. But he never boasted about it. He let his trim physique tell the story.

"So, Bernadette, tell me. What's on your mind?"

Reginald never questioned Bob or Allison about anything. If asked, he gave his opinion—but never unsolicited. While he was caught off guard by Allison's disguise, he didn't question it. However, sitting across the table from Allison's altered appearance, Reginald found it a struggle to demonstrate the same level of respect he was accustomed to showing Allison.

"Here's the deal," Bernadette said. "A few of my closest associates share a concern with me. I'm sure you've heard the chatter. ... Namely, the seats that have been lost, and those that are about to be lost. And, it's not just the fact that they've been lost—it's which ones that have been lost, and how badly. It has a number of us very concerned."

"I understand the problem," Reginald said.

"Well, my three associates, my friends, and I, have agreed that we would like you to join us for a private discussion or two, regarding our options."

"Okay."

"Reg, somehow we've got to stop the bleeding."

"It might not be that easy. The public is running scared," Reginald said. He paused for a couple seconds to gather his thoughts, then continued. "Actually, Al, I mean Bernadette, it's not they're so much running scared, they're flat panicked."

"Exactly right. And they are angry. The midterms were the worst ever, and who knows what to expect with the next presidential election. Even if I challenged and won the nomination, I might not win. Hell, I probably wouldn't win. I've never seen it like this before—you can cut the anger and mistrust with a knife."

"What did you have in mind?"

"We can't discuss it here, or anywhere in public."

"I understand."

"What I want you to do is this: I want you to put your fine mind to this. Our group will attack the problem from every conceivable angle. But do not write anything down. There must never be a handwritten note or a computer entry. We will simply think about it first, and then we will talk about it."

"Makes sense."

"One of the reasons we want you to consider this project is that we all know you can be discreet. And that you can make things happen."

"Who are the other three?"

"I can't reveal them to you at this time. You need to take a little time to digest this whole notion, and if you decide you want to be a part of our group, you can let me know when I contact you the next time."

"How and when will you contact me?"

"Don't worry about that. I'll be in touch."

"Okay."

"Here's the deal, Reg. Bob has his own thing going. He will not be a part of these discussions. So, if his absence is a deal-breaker for you, then don't get involved."

"Is Bob aware of any of this?"

"He is not. … Now, I know that the two of you were very tight. Bob thought, rather he still thinks, that you are one of the best minds in the country. He trusts you completely."

Allison felt that by appealing to Reginald's ego he would be more likely to acquiesce to her wishes. But not only did Reginald not respond to her comments, he was visibly unmoved.

"If there is one thing I know about my husband, it is this—if he feels he can trust a person, that person is pretty damn straight. Bob is a great judge of people."

"Bob is a friend of mine. And I have always admired his talents," Reginald finally said.

"That's why we decided to approach you. We believe you can be trusted."

"I would still like to know who the other parties are."

"Can't tell you right now. Suffice it to say you know them all. And if you made a short list, they would all be on it. Nobody new."

"If I change my mind once I find out, or after the first meeting, is that a problem?"

"Damn right it is. Once you're in, that's it. Just like with Bob. Once you're in, the only way you get out is on a gurney."

"That sounds very ominous. I'm not sure I can accept those terms."

"That's why Bernadette and not Allison is meeting with you here and now. There is not a way to know what we will end up with if we do nothing." Bernadette then slid in closer to Reginald, bringing her nose to within a few inches of his. She had seen Bob do this many times to make a point. Besides, she did not want anyone to overhear her next words. "Reg, this country is on the verge of a revolution. People are angry. More angry than ever before—at least in recent history. ... And they have no jobs, and no prospects. This guy just keeps spending money like there's no end to it. We cannot possibly survive this fiasco without rampant inflation, or worse. And when people start spending ten dollars for a loaf of bread or a gallon of gas, they're going to revolt. Now, my fear is that this just might result in a real civil war, not a simple political turf battle."

"I know what you're saying. It's the worst I can recall. At least when Newt rode into town on his white horse, we had someone we could attack—and we did. But this time, it's our own guy."

"Newt will look like a damn white knight, compared to what we're about to see. Every idiot conservative thinks he's going to win next time. All our friends are gonna be sent packin'. It's gonna to be a damn blood bath, if we don't stop it."

"Well, Al, uh, you've given me a lot to think about. I'll wait to hear from you. Give me a few days."

"You've got two hours. I'll call you in two hours. If you want in, you will respond with this: 'I would love to come to dinner.' If you decide to take a pass on it, say, 'Sorry, I can't make it.' Not a word more, and not a word less. It is strictly hardball from this point on. No hard feelings if you opt out. Do you understand me?"

"Yes, I understand. I'll be waiting to hear from you."

With that, Bernadette stood and reached out to shake Reginald's hand, "It was really great seeing you again, Reg. We must do this more often."

Reginald then stood, smiled and returned the gesture. "It was great to see you too, Bernadette."

Bernadette briskly walked away as Reginald scooped up the remains of their lunch and tossed it into the appropriate receptacles. True to form, he stayed behind to clean up the mess. That was one of the other characteristics that had endeared him to Bob.

As Reginald finished cleaning up and prepared to walk away, he took a look around him at some of the thousands of statues and other artifacts housed at the Metropolitan Museum of Art. So much of it re-volved around the public figures of past centuries.

Leaders would rise to power, develop an overinflated view of their significance, and then die. And all too often their demise would be ig-nominious. Many, if not most, were summarily dismissed by someone younger and envious.

Reginald took his time leaving, because he did not want to follow too closely on "Bernadette's" heels. Instead, he took a little side trip, through the magnificent new Greek and Roman Galleries. Reginald did not like to visit The Met without at least taking a quick walk through the thousands of displays.

One of his favorites was the "Black Bedroom," originally built by Agrippa for Emperor Augustus. *I wonder how many leaders were mur-dered in beds like that,* he was thinking, *while they slept peacefully, con-vinced that they would rule forever.*

Reginald had an uneasy feeling about his meeting with Allison. There was just something different about this one. He wondered what his outcome would be if he accepted her offer ... or, if he rejected it.

Chapter 16—The quorum completed

1 p.m., Tuesday, December 13

Bernadette always wore glasses. They were part of the disguise. Allison, on the other hand, was dependent on contact lenses. She thought it would enhance the persona if Bernadette wore glasses (primarily because Allison did not). The glasses that Bernadette should wear, Allison concluded, ought to be photochromic—the type that self-adjust to sunlight, becoming sunglasses outside and clear in the absence of ultraviolet radiation. That meant one less thing Allison had to keep straight.

As Bernadette walked down the numerous steps leading out of the Metropolitan Museum of Art, heading toward Fifth Avenue, she began to admire her accomplishment, regarding her creation of Bernadette. She had pulled this whole thing off without Bob's help. She did not even enlist the help of her top aides. It was totally Allison's idea and Allison's design—from the secret apartment (with its multiple elevators and spiral staircase), to the Bernadette persona. She smiled slyly as she replayed the way she fooled Reginald with the disguise. If she could make it work with Reginald, she could make it work with almost anyone, anywhere.

As she reached the first landing, she realized just how critical it was to consider details. For instance, if she were to take a spill down the steps, it would most likely result in injury and an unexpected trip to an emergency room—perhaps worse. The shoes she was wearing were Bernadette's kitten heel shoes. *I have to watch my step here,* she thought, before descending the rest of the way to the sidewalk.

I just might keep this apartment even after I'm back in the White House, she was thinking as she turned up Fifth Avenue and began her trek home. *It might be a little tricky to get out of the White House and get up here without the Secret Service sticking to me like glue. But I think I could make it work. I would simply slip down and out, just as I do now, while the agents watch TV.*

She loved the freedom and the anonymity. She saw no reason to give it up—not ever.

How many former first ladies get to hail their own cab? she pondered, sensing a little smile creep across her face. Well-dressed middle-aged ladies did not have much trouble hailing cabs, and Bernadette was very good at it. Raising a gloved hand and virtually stepping out into Manhattan traffic, she captured the first on-duty taxi she went after, just as she did every time.

"Fifth Avenue and 94th," she told the driver, as she opened the cab door and slid in.

Sometimes, when she was at the MET or the Guggenheim, she would simply walk back to her apartment; it would only have amounted to an additional twenty minutes or so. But this time, she did not want anyone to know where she had been. Not that anyone would be concerned about the activity of Bernadette, but she still wanted to be prudent. After all, she had just met with Allison's friend Reginald. Someone could be tailing him.

Five minutes later the driver pulled up and stopped at the corner. When he turned around to collect, Bernadette handed him a twenty-dollar bill and thanked him. She knew that it was just as bad to over-tip as it was to stiff. Twenty dollars covered the fare and a reasonable tip. The driver was pleased but not overly so.

Bernadette greeted the doorman with a smile. She never spoke to him, however—she concluded that there was no point for him to hear her voice. He might recognize it. As Allison, she would not be expected even to acknowledge the doorman—that was the job of the Service.

Bernadette got on her elevator and off at her floor. *Smooth, as always*, she thought.

Once in the apartment she quickly found her favorite chair, sat down, kicked off her shoes, and began rubbing her feet. "Damn these things," she said aloud. "I don't know if I will ever get used to Bernadette's shoes." She loved the rest of Bernadette's wardrobe, but preferred Allison's comfortable flats.

She slipped off Bernadette's glasses, leaving them on the dresser, and opened up the small refrigerator she had in the bedroom. Taking a bottle of water, she walked stocking-footed back to her chair and tucked her feet up under her. That chair, Bernadette's favorite chair, a blue leather recliner, had become Allison's happy place. As she sat there, she began to ponder her meeting with Reginald and wondered whether he would come on board.

Bernadette opened her bag, pulled out a throwaway cell, and dialed her friend.

"This is Bernie, can you make it for dinner on Sunday?"

"I didn't expect you to call so soon."

"Well, I'm calling now. Can you make it or not?"

"Yes, but—"

"That's great, I'll be in touch." With that Bernadette clicked off.

Bernadette breathed a sigh of relief. The group was complete. Now the heavy lifting must begin.

Chapter 17—First meeting scheduled

8 p.m., Tuesday, December 13

The thought crossed Allison's mind to have her group of notables meet in Bernadette's apartment. It was, after all, one of the most secure places in the free world. But then she thought better of it. Even though it would have been possible to maintain privacy there better than any other place she could think of, once the meetings were finished, the hideaway would be rendered virtually useless. So, she had to come up with someplace else.

Not only would she not hold the meetings in Bernadette's apartment, she thought it would be less of a distraction if she ran the meetings as Allison, not Bernadette—at least to start out.

She was sure that Reginald and the other three members of the group questioned how she eluded the Secret Service as Bernadette, yet they did not know about the apartment. She continued to sit in Bernadette's favorite chair as she considered her options.

She recalled that sometimes Bob would have a friend rent a car and he would hold private conversations in it. He always felt pretty safe doing that. She thought that she might give his approach a try for at least one of the meetings—perhaps the first. She could have James pick up a full-size car, perhaps a Suburban. Anything but an Expedition—that's what everyone drove, or used to drive, in DC.

She thought about it a bit more, and then concluded that even a Suburban would stand out too much in New York. The perfect car, she reasoned, would be a Cadillac Escalade. No government workers would ever want to be seen in one of those. But Allison felt she could pull it off.

Actors, lawyers, lobbyists, and rich businessmen drove Escalades—no one paid much attention to people riding around in a black Escalade with heavily tinted glass.

"That's it!" Bernadette becoming Allison exclaimed as she sprang out of the Bernadette's chair. She was not quite ready to return to Allison's apartment, but she was beginning the metamorphosis.

She had one more call to make. She had to call James and tell him to rent the Escalade. For this call she used a different cell phone—one given to her by her husband. He told her that it could not be traced or recorded. James, along with the other members of her group, all had similar devices.

"I don't care what color, as long as it's black and clean, with tinted glass. It should be new—at least no more than ten thousand miles."

The request caught James a little off guard. Generally James would meet Allison in a restaurant or at a bar. And when he did, he would usually drive his own Escalade or take a cab. He knew immediately what Allison intended to accomplish with the rented car. He had been the one who frequently would rent a car for Bob, during the Fulbright presidency.

On those occasions, he would meet the president after the "escape" from the White House had already taken place. Bob would sometimes be under a blanket in the back of a car or SUV, and sometimes he would actually be hiding in the trunk. Usually, it was a "special" member of the president's detail who had spirited him out. And then that same agent would meet James and the president later for the return trip.

So, James knew what Allison was up to with the rental—it was an excellent method to accomplish anonymity. She did not have to explain anything to him.

"Should I already have the other two with me when I meet you?"

"There will be three others; Reg is joining us."

"He is? I didn't think he still had it in him. Did you give him any details?"

"What's there to give him? We haven't developed any yet. All I told him was that three or four of my closest friends were going to meet to discuss future events—future events in light of recent elections and what the upcoming weeks and months might hold for us. No specifics."

"And he's in on that basis?"

"Yes he is. I think you underestimate his resolve."

"It's just that he always seems like he's got a ... like he's got a bad case of constipation. The thing is, with Reg, you just never really know what he's thinking. He's always so proper. Being around Reg is like being around your dad. That is, if your dad packed a Glock."

Allison chuckled. "We can use that. He will balance *you* out."

"Don't get me wrong. I really like and respect Reg. I'm the one who recommended you talk to him. He is a good addition. I'm just shocked that you got him."

"Me too. But Reg has always thought for himself. That's why Bob liked him. He constantly bitched about Reg, but when he had a tough decision, or a tough job, he always came back to him. Reg has an amazing ability to see the big picture and get things done. I'm glad you suggested we bring him in."

"Does he know that once he meets with the group, there's no turning back?"

"I told him. He's good with it."

"But he doesn't know who he's getting married to, does he?"

"He will tomorrow."

"Man! I can't wait to see Reg's reaction when he gets in that Escalade with Steve," James said with a smile.

"He might not be constipated any longer," Allison added. "That just might solve his condition."

"He just never liked Steve. Don't get me wrong. A lot of people have issues with Steve. But I don't know anyone who detests him like Reg does. I really think he hates Steve."

"I wouldn't say he *hated* Steve. I think it's more a case of generation gap. Steve is a true metro-sexual—if there even is such a thing. And Reg … Bob suspected he might have doubts about himself. I don't know— I'm no damn psychologist. All I know for sure is that it's gonna be interesting."

"But Reg is a big boy. He knows what Steve brings to the table. And he knows he can trust him. Reg'll just have to get past his hang-ups."

"I would agree with that—Reg has hang-ups," James said, not able to get the smile off his face.

"But, I do have some other reservations," Allison said. "One of the reasons we were able to have those great meetings back during the White House days was that Bob took charge. I'm fully aware of that. He rode all of us like ten-dollar whores. Pardon my sexism, but you know what I mean. Remember the time he beat the hell out of Roger? I always wondered if he did it just to make a point. He never talked to me about that. Whatever the reason, Bob had a way of expressing himself clearly. No one doubted who was in charge when he was around, and no one really ever knew just what he was capable of. Not even me."

"I'm pretty sure none of us ever wanted to know the answer to that one," James said.

"That's what I'm getting at," Allison said. "Bob could pull it off. He could take all those different personalities, scare the hell out of them, and get them to work together."

"Are you suggesting that you might not be able to do that?" James asked.

"That's not what I'm saying."

"I do think that you need to be aware of the potential problems, especially with Reg and Steve. We both understand the genuine animus they hold for each other. But we still have to get them to work toward a common goal."

"I know that. Trust me, if you think Bob was a tough bastard, I am going to be worse than he ever dreamed of being. I'm just hoping I can pull this off, James. And it is not like these meetings are going to be open-ended. We will have no more than four meetings of the whole group. That's it. There will be assignments and responsibilities. And the individual members will report back to me, and only me. But, if you see something growing, particularly between Reg and Steve, be ready to jump in. Nip it. You might catch something that I miss."

"I understand. But I still would pay to see Reg's face when he gets in the car with Steve."

"You're not gonna have to pay for it. Pick me up at the regular place, ten a.m. Bring Jerry and Steve with you. I will have Reg with me. You will drive. I will give you directions when I get in. We will meet for no longer than sixty minutes. Then you will drop Reg off where I tell you, then me. ... Oh, and I'm not sure if I am going to be Allison or Bernadette. Be prepared."

"You got it, boss."

Chapter 18—The first meeting
8:54 a.m., Thursday, December 15

James was on time. That wasn't terribly significant, in that James was always on time. In fact, throughout all his years working with Bob and Allison, with numerous meetings every day, no one could recall James ever having been late. It would, of course, have been difficult to know that for certain, because no meeting ever started without Bob, and he was never on time. Suffice it to say, James always showed up before Bob did—so, whether he was actually on time would be moot.

It was now nine a.m. James was stopping in front of the designated midtown coffee shop to pick up Jerry and Steve. As he hugged the Escalade up close to a parked car, he lowered the tinted passenger window so that he could be recognized. With that, the two men exited the coffee shop and briskly trotted between two parked cars. James pulled up a few feet, allowing them to open the back door and jump in.

"What's with the Escalade, James?"

"Not allowed to talk about anything other than the weather right now—boss's orders. I'll let you know when it's okay."

"You should tickle your ass with a feather, old boy."

"What'd you say?"

"I said it's particularly nasty weather, don't you think?" Jerry blurted out.

"Just get in and be quiet. Okay, boys?" James told them. "And don't think you're fooling me with that 'Little Murders' line. You're not the only one who spent time in the Village."

Jerry's eyebrows arched. "Are you sure about that? The bit about 'Little Murders.' Maybe you should tell us about your time in the Village. When exactly was that?"

They both had a lot of admiration for James. They had all worked closely together during the eight years of Bob's presidency. They knew that when James said something, he meant it. So, after Jerry's failed attempt at conversing, they just sat silently until they arrived at the parking garage, where they were to pick up Allison and Reg.

James knew why Allison had told him to keep the guys silent until she joined them. For one thing, she wanted to establish her leadership over the group. She wanted them to view her as the tough guy.

Another reason for them to remain silent was once they were all in the Escalade, he was going to wand them all for recording and transmission devices. He had already discussed this with Allison. When she and Reg got in, she would give the order and he would go to work.

"Who's the fourth fool?" Jerry blurted out, forgetting what James had just said.

"Silence, please."

"Sorry, James."

James expected his command to be obeyed. He said nothing more, as he stared at Jerry through the rearview mirror.

Jerry immediately realized what he had done wrong. He was beginning to get the picture.

James pulled over to the side and stopped. When he did, Allison and Reginald approached the car. Reginald and Jerry were old friends, but when Jerry spotted Reginald, a small smile crept across his face. He realized that the fireworks were about to start, as soon as Reginald got a look at Steve. He, too, was well aware that those two definitely did not like each other.

While Jerry smiled at the sight of Reginald, Steve's expression was vastly different. When he spotted who was walking with Allison, he audibly groaned and rolled his eyes back in his head. "Oh, hell, I do not believe this."

"You can be quiet as well," James commanded.

James had a way of dressing people down without actually insulting them or raising his voice. His firm tone was expected and even applauded by those who worked with him. No one really minded his taking charge. Perhaps if he were ever to make eye contact with someone while he was scolding, it might have been a different matter. But James had a way of sticking his very large face in your face and almost yelling at you, but at the same time he never actually looked you in the eye while he was doing it. He might be scrutinizing the second button on your shirt or glancing out the window, but his face would be in yours to the point that you would smell the cigar he had smoked an hour earlier. But he did not make eye contact—not when he was scolding.

James knew Allison would recognize the vehicle, so he did not roll the window down. Besides, he was probably sadistic enough to make sure he got a good look at Reginald's face when his friend first realized that he would be working with Steve.

As they approached the car, Reginald reached out to open the front door for Allison. Their hands met at the handle, and she prevailed. "Damn it, Reg, just get in the back," she commanded. "And do not say a word—not one damn word. Not yet."

With that, Reginald opened the back door and got his first glimpse of Jerry and Steve. He knew that James would be part of the group. But he did not know specifically about the other two.

Now, Reginald had no problem whatsoever with Jerry. In many ways, the two of them were a lot alike. They were about the same age— roughly early sixties. And they came up the same way. They were both intellectual ideologues. And, as much as possible, they both avoided the limelight. Neither one of them made it a practice to engage the media unless forced to do so.

Steve, on the other hand, was much younger than the rest. And he loved the cameras. It had frequently been said that the most dangerous place in DC was between Steve and a camera. While that was a common cliché, it was thought that it might have been used first when alluding to Steve's penchant for publicity.

Jerry tolerated Steve, but he did not did not really like him. Reginald, however, loathed the younger man.

When Reginald's eyes met Steve's, it was totally obvious that he was not happy about what he was getting into. However, Reginald was very much aware of protocol. Allison had told him to get in and shut up, and that is exactly what he was going to do. His face got purple, but he never opened his mouth.

"Okay, James now has a job to do," Allison commanded. "I do not expect to hear a damn word out of any of you until James gives the okay. So sit still and shut up."

Chapter 19—The wand

9:56 a.m., Thursday, December 15

The first meeting was just about to begin. But before Allison would allow it to proceed, she had the matter of security to deal with. "James, go ahead and do your thing," she commanded.

"Okay. Let's start with cell phones. Everyone open your cells and remove the batteries. Then do the same with your notebooks, laptops, and any other gadget you might be carrying. Remove the batteries from any electronic device that has one." No one had a problem with that. They all started popping open their electronics and removing batteries.

"I suppose that means that Reg needs to pop the one out of his Glock?" Jerry quipped. "It does have a laser sight, right, Reg?"

No one even smiled.

"James," Steve said. "I need a screwdriver to remove the battery from my notebook. What do you want me to do?"

"For this meeting, make sure it's turned off. And from now on, don't bring anything you can't get open."

Then James got out of the Escalade and walked around to the rear hatch. He hit the release button and retrieved a small black case, not unlike what high school students might use to transport a saxophone. He then closed the hatch and returned to the driver's seat. Opening the case between himself and Allison, he removed from it a very expensive looking stainless steel and black plastic piece of electronic equipment. "This will tell us if we've got company," he said as he turned it on and adjusted the settings.

"Al, you can be first," James said. "Just set your purse on the floor."

He then swiped the wand across her seated torso. The device was emitting a low-volume tone, but he did not seem alarmed about it. He then passed the wand over Allison's purse. Still there was no change in the tone.

"Okay, now you check me out," he said, handing the wand to Allison. She seemed very comfortable, wielding the wand like a weapon. Again, the tone did not change—it remained steady at a low volume. Allison asked, "Should it be making a noise like this? Maybe it needs to be adjusted."

"I just calibrated it, and it is on the right settings. Maybe there is some ambient interference in the area. It's not sounding an alarm, so we need not be concerned."

When she finished wanding James, she handed the device back to him so he could proceed to check the three sitting behind him. As he reached the wand back to Jerry, it went nuts.

"What's the deal, here?" James asked, as he "frisked" Jerry with the wand. "*You're* the reason this thing is acting up. It doesn't like something about you. … What's up with *you?*"

James then made a startling discovery—the wand went into full alarm as it moved past Jerry's head. "I'll be damned!" Jerry exclaimed. "It's my implant. It doesn't like my implant."

"What're you talking about?" James asked, as he pulled the wand back to silence it.

"I have a cochlear implant. I have ninety percent loss in my left, and seventy in my right. With the implant I can hear almost normal. It's great, but your wand wouldn't agree."

"What can we do about this?" James asked, looking over at Allison.

"Yeah, I have known about his implant for months. It shouldn't be a problem. Just wand the rest of his body and see what you get. Is there some setting to accommodate something like that?"

"There's nothing I can do to compensate. Fortunately it's only his head. Mr. Bionic Brain here." James then paused for a moment and thought about what he was doing. "Allison, I am not going to be able to check out the other two with him in the car. He's going to have to get out for a few minutes."

"No problem," Jerry said. "Slide out, Reg, and let me get some fresh air."

Reginald opened the door and let his friend out and then got back in. James quickly scanned Steve and Reginald. "That is weird—this thing goes totally silent with Jerry outside. Maybe we should leave him out there."

"I don't think so," Allison said, lowering her window and inviting Jerry back.

Jerry opened the back door, expecting Reginald to slide over to the middle to allow him back in. But Reginald would have no part of that. He pushed past Jerry, exiting the Escalade altogether. He then motioned for Jerry to get back in first.

"You guys are like a couple high-schoolers," Allison chuckled.

"Reg doesn't want to sit next to Steve—afraid he might catch something," James observed.

"I've got long legs, that's all," Reginald explained. "The outside just works best for me."

"Okay," Allison said. "We all passed James's wand. We will do this every time we meet. We will assume nothing. That means no one will say a word until we have all been thoroughly checked out."

"May I ask a question, now?" Reginald asked.

"Sure," Allison answered.

"The wand that James used, I've never seen anything like it. It doesn't look like the ones we used in the White House. Where did that come from? CIA?"

"No, not CIA. Mossad. I got it from one of my buddies. It's better than anything we've got. In fact, the CIA is now buying them from Israel."

"But it didn't seem very sensitive with Jerry. You had to put it right up against his head before it went nuts."

"Right. But that's a good thing. It has to see a powered microphone, or some sort of transmission device, before it will sound. When I first powered it up, I did question the tone, but I knew we would get to the bottom of it." Reginald started to interrupt with another question, but James was not finished. "Had there been a hot transmitter anywhere within fifty feet, any kind of transmitter, wired or wireless, it would have set off a major alarm. That's why you powered down your cells and notebooks."

"So we're good?" Reginald asked.

"We are. I checked out the vehicle thoroughly before I picked anyone up. So, right now, we're good."

Allison then jumped in. "This is how it is going to work. We will have a total of four meetings—no more, perhaps less. Each of them will be one hour long—no longer. No one will take notes. In fact, no one will ever write anything down. No one will discuss anything about the meetings with another human being. Ever. You will not even discuss the meetings or the content of the meetings with other members of this group, should you have occasion to get together outside this forum. Is all this clear, so far?"

No one said a word, but all four of the men did acknowledge their compliance, in one way or another. It was obvious to them all that Allison was taking charge. She had learned a great deal from Bob through the years.

"Now, one more thing before we begin discussing the issues at hand," Allison added in a very somber tone. "The five of us are now committed to this group. No one will be permitted to quit, not until we have ended our fourth meeting and arrived at a decision. Am I perfectly clear about this?"

They all heard what she said and knew what she meant—the only way out of this quorum was in a box.

Reginald then recalled his thoughts as he had walked through the Greek and Roman Galleries earlier, and he wondered what his life might have been like had he never become involved with the Fulbrights.

Chapter 20—Initial decision

10:21 a.m., Thursday, December 15

Allison opened with her first directive. "As I said, the meetings will be no longer than one hour in length. And there will be no more than four of them. If we find we can't get done what we need to get done under those constraints, that would indicate a lack of consensus, then we'll simply dissolve the group. Unless we are on the same page, unless we all view the problem in a similar fashion, it wouldn't matter how many meetings we held, or how long they were."

The four men had heard all this before. When Allison originally approached them individually, she had made this clear.

"All of you probably already know why we are having these meetings. But just in case you're not sure about it, I'll tell you."

She was on a roll, and the guys knew it. There would be no interruptions.

"Virtually every contested seat in the House went south—we lost them all. Same is likely to happen in the Senate next election. It seems likely that whatever we did not lose in the midterm will be lost in the presidential. Unless things change—and I mean radically change. This guy is about to run the country into the ground, and the people know it. They don't believe a word he says, and he can't sell anything. … That is, even if he had something to sell."

"Do you size him up as a one-termer?" Steve asked. Everyone knew that was a question that did not need asking. Steve was simply tossing Allison some raw meat.

"Definitely. And even if I were the nominee instead, if the libertarian coalition puts up a strong candidate, I might not win. The direction we're going, and the speed we're traveling, who knows what will be left in two years. If they take control of both houses *and* the White House, they will consider it a mandate, and overturn all the gains we have made over the past twenty-five years."

"What are you looking for from us?" Jerry asked.

"Next week we're going to have our second meeting. I will contact each of you separately to let you know the exact time and place. In the meantime, I want each of you to be thinking of different approaches we might consider. Brainstorm it. But, as I said before, do not commit anything to writing—not in any form. Do not record anything. Just think it through, and be prepared to talk about it."

"Are we going to continue meeting in this truck?" Jerry asked. "Because, if we are, I think we ought to put it in some mud and see how it does. I've always wanted to see an Escalade covered so thick that you can't read the plate."

"I'll let you know what to expect," Allison replied, almost cracking a smile. She respected the intellect and creativity of each member of the group. But she really liked only Jerry and James. She had learned to tolerate Reginald and Steve during her years as first lady. Bob leaned heavily on Steve for public relations. Bob believed that Steve could put a happy face on a dead pig. It just seemed as though Steve had a unique gift for viewing everything through the eyes of the public and always knew just how to spin an issue.

Still, Allison knew that Bob did not really like Steve very much either. In fact, in private (and sometimes among friends) Bob referred to Steve as "My Little Gay Buddy." That is where Reginald got the notion that Steve was gay. And Reginald was more than a little homophobic.

Even though Allison knew that there was no one better at what he did than Steve, like her husband, she only forced herself to tolerate him. But she did trust his loyalty. The element that kept Steve loyal to Bob and Allison was not his character. He was loyal to them because he was scared of them. He knew, as did all those who ever worked closely with the couple, that to cross them in any fashion was to commit suicide—figuratively at least, if not always literally.

And this time, and these meetings, were as heavy as any of these men had experienced. They knew that Allison was stone cold serious, and that they had better not only obey her every word, but her every wish as well.

As far as Reginald was concerned, Allison did not really dislike him. She trusted him implicitly, and she greatly respected his judgment. But he had too many hang-ups for her liking. For instance, Reginald would frequently excuse himself from a meeting, ostensibly to use the rest room. But she knew that all he was going to do was wash his hands. He washed them so many times during the day that he constantly had to squeeze on some hand lotion. That bugged her—not only was she irritated by the constant interruptions, but she hated the smell. The hand lotion that he used came in a pink tube, and smelled like cheap perfume. She even gave him a box of lotions that she thought more masculine, but he never used them. When she asked why, he told her that they all irritated his skin.

However, Reginald was not a member of the group because of his soft hands. He was the master of dirty tricks. He was totally ruthless—perhaps brilliantly so.

Others might choose the target and determine the appropriate level of punishment. But when it came to facilitating retribution, that was always left to Reginald.

Even though Allison loved what Reginald was capable of doing, she still found it hard to like him.

No, Allison liked only James and Jerry. Of course, it helped that both of them went out of their way never to offend her.

After only twenty minutes into it, Allison was satisfied that the meeting was over. The brains trust she had assembled needed no nursing. They were all big boys, and she knew that when they got together the next time, each of them would bring their particular talents to bear on the problem. Her only goal for this first meeting was to make sure they all agreed as to what the problem was and were prepared to attack it.

"We're finished. I'll be in touch with each of you and give you the specifics for our next meeting. James, drop Reg off so he can catch a cab, then take care of the other two."

With that, Allison got out of the Escalade and left by herself. No more was said—the first meeting was over. As soon as Allison got out, Reginald did as well. Opening the front passenger door, he said, "Hope you don't mind my sitting up here with you, James. I need a little room to stretch out."

"Not a problem," James replied, as he entered traffic on his way to dropping off the rest of the group.

As he pulled out he did not notice a black Ford Expedition with very tinted windows pull out behind them. It followed at a safe distance.

Chapter 21—Allison prepares for meeting two

11:16 a.m., Thursday, December 15

As Allison, who was actually dressed as Bernadette for the first meeting, headed back to her apartment, she contemplated what had transpired during the previous forty minutes. As she walked along, she repeated audibly what each person had said, as best she could recall.

Ever since her days at Yale she had done that when she wanted to commit something to memory. She would repeat lists, dates, facts of any type, and court rulings. She had become a walking encyclopedia. To a large extent, she credited her academic success to this ability. Unfortunately, over the course of the past few years she found this ability to be diminishing.

When it came to the content of these meetings, Allison was adamant about creating a clear recollection of everything that was said and who said it.

"Then Reg complained about sitting in the middle. His legs were too long. So he had Jerry slide into the middle. I am pretty sure it was because he did not want to sit next to Steve. Of course, when he closed the door, he gripped the handle with a sanitized towel. He has always had such a powerful aversion to germs. That was Reg."

And so she went on, repeating everything that occurred during that meeting, and in the order it had occurred. Even though she might not have been as good at this as she once was, it is likely that no one could have done a better job at making the most of self-talk. As she walked along, she fired off a nonstop regurgitation of the events of the past hour.

She did not miss a point or a nuance.

She recalled how this practice used to garner negative attention on the Yale campus. She would start repeating what she had read as she walked down the steps of the law library. As she passed other students, she sensed their glares. She assumed most thought she was just a little eccentric, talking out loud to herself as she turned up York Street. Now, however, such behavior did not warrant a glance. Passersby simply assumed she was talking on her cell.

Once she had satisfied herself that she had verbalized the entire meeting, she ceased speaking aloud. She then contemplated the best time and location for the next meeting. "We need to get back together within a couple days; I do not want to waste this momentum. Tuesday, we'll meet Tuesday. And we have to find a better venue. The Escalade was okay, but it was altogether too close."

She was confident that no one would recognize her if she were alone. But when the other four were present, it could put her disguise in jeopardy. Anyone who watched cable news would easily recognize James and Steve—especially Steve. Then, once those two were identified, it was only a matter of time until someone concluded who she was. "I have to find a better, more private venue. And it should not be in a car, not even an Escalade. And it must not be totally as Bernadette. We must meet in a place where I can be Allison, at least in part. The Bernadette disguise is just too distracting for the others."

Bernadette had reached her building. She smiled at the doorman as she passed him, and she took the "Bernadette elevator" up to her apartment.

She wondered if Jerry still had that cottage in the Catskills. *That would be perfect, at least for one of the meetings. I could pick up a key from Jerry and have James go up early and do a sweep. If I remember correctly, cells don't work there, and he has no telephone line. Still uses a generator for power, I bet.*

That was it. She would break the news to Jerry later that evening. He liked Allison as much as she liked him, perhaps more. During all their years working together, he never denied any request she had ever made of him. *He will be happy to comply,* she concluded.

And he was. He told her later that evening that he would gladly permit the group to use his little cottage. "Al, of course I don't mind. What's mine is yours—you know that. But keep in mind no one has been up there in nearly a year. My new bride is not fond of roughing it. It can't be very clean, and it probably doesn't even smell very good right now. Shall I run up there and clean it up?" he asked her.

"Definitely not! You simply pick up Reg and Steve. I will have James go up a few hours early and make sure there are no active bugs. If he detects anything, we will postpone the meeting. But if all is well, and I strongly suspect it will be, then I will drive up there by myself. I still remember where it is. And so does James. He never forgets anything."

"That works for me. When is the next meeting?"

"Tuesday at six p.m."

"Next Tuesday? Why so soon?"

"Jerry, don't give me lip. It will be Tuesday, without an argument, and that's it. If I said we were meeting yet tonight, you would be ready. And so would everyone else. You know that."

"Tuesday it is. Should I call the other two to set up a pickup?"

"No, I'll call and let them know where and when."

"Sounds fine. I'll tell you where the key is. There is a large oak tree on the south side of the cottage—less than fifteen feet from the cottage itself. At the trunk, there is a rotten plank. Under the plank is a Ziploc bag. It has the key to the front door."

"I'll pass that information on to James."

"That's not all. I have an alarm system. The code is 7-6-8-9-1. The 7689 is the combo, and the 1 is the off key."

"7689, followed by the number 1."

"That's right. There is a thirty-second delay on the front door."

"What the hell do you have an alarm system for? You don't have a telephone or power? What good can that do?"

"I guess it just makes me feel better. I have a big battery and a solar cell. I should probably put up a wind driven generator. But the solar cell works well enough to power the alarm."

"I will pass that information on to James."

"Al, can I ask you one question relating to the meeting tonight?"

"Hell no. We're not going to get that started. What goes on during our meetings, stays there. There will be *no* conversation relating to it outside everyone being present."

"I understand that, but did you see the way Steve and Reg glared at each other? I don't think—"

"No Jerry, sometimes you don't think. And sometimes you think too much. And right now you're *talking* too much. Did I not make myself clear? There will be no conversation about any of this. None. Do you understand me? I really like you, Jerry, and I know you respect me. But you're gonna do what I tell you to do. I am in charge here. Do you understand me?"

"I sure do. It won't happen again."

"That's right."

As soon as she ended the call to Jerry, she retrieved a small electronic recording device from her bedroom, along with a thumb drive, and verbalized into the microphone all the events of the first meeting as she had remembered them earlier on her walk back to her apartment.

She kept the thumb drive in a small jewelry safe behind the thermostat in her (Bernadette's) bedroom.

She was pleased with herself about that safe, because she had installed it herself. After she had the apartment renovated, she requested a functioning wireless thermostat in her bedroom. After some objections from the contractor, he complied with her wishes. She then procured the small wall safe, removed the thermostat from the wall, and attached it to the cover of the safe. It was just large enough to accommodate a few pieces of jewelry and half a dozen thumb drives.

Once she had finished the recording, she removed the thumb drive and put it in the secret safe. She felt secure leaving the recording device simply lying on her dresser, because it had no hard drive, so no information would be stored on it—therefore, if found, it could not compromise her or her plans.

Bernadette then reassumed the identity of Allison, double-checking every aspect of her metamorphosis until she was confident that all was perfect before opening the door to the secret closet and beginning the descent to her other identity.

Chapter 22—Meeting two (the trip)

4:18 p.m., Tuesday, December 20

Even though she did not use it very much, Bernadette did own a car. She kept it at a parking garage within walking distance of her apartment. That car was another monument to Allison's thoroughness. When she set about establishing the new persona, she knew she wanted Bernadette to have the ability to own and drive her own car. The challenge was getting the appropriate license and registration set up.

For that she took a few trips back to her "beloved" New Orleans. Actually, Allison loathed almost everything about Louisiana. She had a dim view of most of the residents of the state, and she was not particularly fond of her memories as its first lady.

But there was one thing she really liked about this southern state. She had a lot of connections there, many of whom were viewed as shady. But to her, shady meant useful.

On one of her early trips to Louisiana after leaving the White House, she contacted a man who was able to create virtually authentic identities. He had worked closely with her and Bob (mostly for Bob) on many occasions, creating people out of thin air, secret bank accounts, both in the US and abroad, and false identities for foreign nationals involved in various types of smuggling. Allison knew this man to be the best at what he did and to be able to keep secrets. Had he not been able to perform the latter with ultimate determination, he would not still be breathing sweet Louisiana air. She knew she could trust him.

He was happy to help her, and he was equally happy to keep the secret from her husband. He had a great working relationship with the former president. But as far as he was concerned, Bob was just another client—no more or no less important to him than a member of organized crime.

For obvious reasons, Allison had no idea what his real name was, only that he could be contacted via a post office box in New Orleans. That anonymity was fine with her, and obviously fine with his other clients. He had no interest in setting up an email account. "Keep it simple" was his motto.

So, with the help of her "PO Box Buddy," she set up the Bernadette identity and procured a social security number, even paying a small amount of federal and state taxes. For a reasonable fee, this PO Box Buddy handled all the filings. The one thing she needed most of all was the driver's license. That he was also able to obtain for her, through the Louisiana Office of Motor Vehicles.

Initially, she inquired about a passport under Bernadette, but he quickly talked her out of that.

So, on Tuesday afternoon, as Allison/Bernadette made her way to the parking garage, she could not wipe the smile off her face.

The drive to Jerry's cottage could take two hours—perhaps a little more, depending on traffic. She knew it would have been impossible to make any sort of time on a Friday afternoon, as half the city would be trying to make it up to their cottages for the weekend. Tuesday, she thought, would be ideal.

By the time the attendant handed the keys to her, it was about two-thirty p.m. She handed him her customary twenty-dollar tip, and they both smiled. Of course, as was her practice, Bernadette did not utter a word.

The drive was uneventful. Even though traffic was extraordinary for a Tuesday afternoon, she still was able to arrive in the vicinity before five p.m. With about a half an hour to kill, she considered paying a visit to a nearby bar, one she and Bob had frequently stopped at when they went up to Jerry's cottage.

She did, however, quickly change her mind about that. *These folks are so nosy, they're going to be asking me questions I do not want to respond to,* she thought.

So, instead she just drove through a fast food restaurant and bought a burger and a soda. She received the white bag of food and pulled into a parking place at the restaurant to eat. This, she thought, was an experience very alien to her, but one she totally enjoyed. She glanced at her watch several times, trying to gauge her completing the meal with the time she needed to leave for the cottage. She did not want to arrive too early, and she knew she could not be late.

When finished, she opened the car door, got out, and tossed the remains in the trashcan. Once back in the driver's seat, she glanced in her rearview mirror, backed up, and was on her way.

She realized that same smile consumed her face—the one she had worn as she initially picked up the car earlier that day. "I really like being able to do this," she said aloud. And with that, she belched. The sound of her own voice, and that of her extraordinarily loud belch, brought more than a smile to her face. Now she found herself loudly chuckling at what she had just done.

"God, do I love this!"

Chapter 23—Arriving at the cottage

5:55 p.m., Tuesday, December 20

Allison did arrive on time—only James got there before she did. He had found the key in the place described by Jerry and had completed the sweep for bugs.

As Allison drove up, James motioned for her to park beside his car, which was nearly fifty yards from the cottage. She had no notion as to why he would make that request, but she complied.

But before she had even gotten out of her car, concluding that she could conduct the meeting best as Allison, she removed Bernadette's wig and glasses.

As she approached, James explained.

"If we keep the vehicles a reasonable distance from the cottage, I will not have to wand them for pickup devices. It will save time and trouble. Hope that's okay?"

"No problem. You're in charge of security. Do what you think best."

Before James allowed Allison to enter the cottage, he had her stop and remove the battery from her cell, and then he scanned her entire body, just as he had done at the first meeting.

"Now you scan me," he said, holding the wand out for Allison to take.

She then proceeded to pass the wand over his body, head to toe.

"Looks like you're clean."

The two old friends smiled at each other and walked into the cottage.

"Jerry said he had not been up here in some time," Allison said.

"Looks pretty lived-in to me. I had expected it to smell musty. I hate that. It messes with my allergies."

"It wasn't bad when I arrived. I did find some cleaning stuff and tidied up a bit. I've got allergies too. And we all know Jerry. He's a walking sneeze machine. Get him going and he's useless."

"What time did you get here?"

"Around one."

"Damn. You've been cleaning up that whole time?"

"Pretty much."

"God, James, is there anything you don't do?"

James grinned, a little embarrassed.

Just then, a pulsing sounder went off, startling Allison. "What the hell's that?" she asked.

Jumping to his feet, James moved quickly to the door, picking up the wand on the way. "Jerry's got this rigged with a driveway alert. I'll bet that's Jerry, and probably Steve," he said as he exited the cottage and headed out to meet the two arriving members of their group.

Jerry, seeing where Allison and James had parked, pulled his car in beside them.

"What the hell is this all about?" Jerry yelled out to James, as he and Steve started walking toward the cottage.

"Steve," James called out, "you wait by the car for a few minutes, please."

Jerry was beginning to remember the drill. As he approached James he slipped his cell out of its holder, popped the back off, and removed the battery. "There, I'm clean as a newborn baby."

Just as before, as Jerry approached the wand, it began to sound a warning tone.

"Hang on, Mr. Bionics," James said, stopping Jerry a good twenty feet from the cottage. James then carefully passed the wand from each of Jerry's shoes, on up his legs, and finally along his chest. As he reached Jerry's head, the machine again sounded loudly.

"Leave it to you, Jerry, to make my life really difficult," James complained. "I suppose I should be glad you don't have one of those electronic penis implants. You know, like the one you've been checking out."

"Go to hell! I don't need any help with that. If anything, I need a reduction."

"That's not what I heard. Those interns have been saying something else. By the way, what's in that box, Jerry?" James asked, pointing to a box Jerry was carrying in a plastic shopping bag.

"Sandwiches," Jerry answered. "And some bottled water. Can't really drink the water up here."

"Hope you've got a raw hamburger in there for Reg," Steve quipped, taking a few quick steps toward the door, wanting to enter the cottage before Reginald reached it. He had caught a glimpse of Reginald's car coming up the drive, and he did not want to get caught up trying to make small talk with his nemesis. Steve flashed a smile in James's direction and started trotting toward him.

"No special orders," Jerry said, "not even for Reg."

"Steve, I'm ready for you, boy," James said, lifting his wand in Steve's direction. "Jerry, you'd better get in there, Buddy. Allison is locked and loaded. Flash her your disarming smile, before the rest of us come in."

Jerry just flashed James the finger and entered the cottage.

"Hey, James, how ya doin'?" Steve said as he approached. He had already removed the battery from his cell and had left his notepad in the car. He was ready for the wand. James checked him out and motioned for him to enter the building. He then focused his attention on Reginald, who had already walked up to where James was standing.

"Evening, Reg. How are you? Have any trouble finding the cottage?"

"I'm doing well, thank you. And Jerry's directions were clear. Had no problem finding it. I take it everyone's here?"

"You're the last one. Don't forget the cell battery," James said as his wand began to tweet as it approached Reginald's pocket where he kept his smartphone.

Reginald reached into his jacket pocket, retrieved his phone, and removed the battery. Reginald had not forgotten to remove the battery. He just wanted to test James's thoroughness, and the effectiveness of the Mossad wand.

Once finished with Reginald, the last two members of the group entered the cottage.

Chapter 24—All present and accounted for
6:07 p.m., Tuesday, December 20

Allison announced, "We're all here, and on time," again immediately taking charge of the meeting. "I hope all of you gave this matter some serious thought." She paused for a moment, then said, "Jerry, first of all, thank you letting us use your cottage. And for the refreshments. That was very kind of you."

Jerry did not say a word. He smiled broadly and nodded. He knew Allison had an agenda and was not looking for him to verbalize.

"Okay, Jerry, let's start with you. In as few words a possible, and to the point, what are the three biggest problems that you see?"

Jerry was prepared. Even so, he sat silently for a few moments for effect, as though organizing his thoughts. "First, the president's unpopularity. He is at a near historic low, and we are only a year out from the campaign. We lost the House, and the Senate is weakened. That cannot bode well for the immediate future. It is unsettling, to say the least. The resentment of this president is running high, very high."

Jerry looked over at Allison, then continued. "Second, the economy is free-falling. Real unemployment is in double digits—over twenty percent, if you factor in those who are no longer looking for jobs. People are having to take two part-time jobs. Inflation is at fifteen percent and climbing. We are not going to see serious relief before the election.

"The libertarians are suggesting that if he's not the Manchurian Candidate, he will fit the bill until the real one gets here."

Jerry stopped and looked around at each of his friends as though he were finished.

Finally, Allison jumped in. "That's two. What's your third thought?"

"Well, I don't quite know how to put this," Jerry continued. "But haven't we all wondered about just how he intends to pay for all he is spending? I mean, without a miracle or three, there will be no new *real* jobs. No new money, except for what he prints. … I'm seriously wondering where he is going with this. He isn't a stupid man. And his advisors are not stupid either. But I don't see how he intends to pull this off. I would like to think he has something fairly traditional up his sleeve, but for the life of me I can't imagine what it could be."

Allison recognized that Jerry had just dropped a bomb on the group. She looked down, as though waiting for Jerry to pick up and continue. Finally, realizing Jerry did not want to add anything, she looked up and said, "James, what's your take?"

James was ready but had not rehearsed. "We've got problems. And not just a few. All of what Jerry said is right on. I could not agree more. But it doesn't stop there. We've wrestled with gridlock for the past year. And it's only going to get worse. In November, we lose the Senate. The coalition probably wins the trifecta in the presidential election.

"The only bright side is that we might be able to shovel all these problems back onto them, and that might be good for the next midterm. But that's too far down the road. What if we have another war? We could easily get stuck out of power for eight years, maybe longer.

"Losing all those governors doesn't help. That will severely affect party leadership in those states for the next presidential election and for years to come. How many did we lose last November? Fourteen? I don't know, but it was a bunch. It's unprecedented. All of us could be old and senile by the time we see a friendly face in the White House.

"Now, consider that we could see two or more new Supremes retire. We have a serious problem. … Is that three? I could keep going."

"That'll do, James," Allison said. "Okay, Reg, what have you got for us?"

"I think Jerry and James have pretty accurately stated the obvious." Reginald had a unique way of relating what was on his mind. Everyone at the meeting knew him to be very blunt, often to the point of insult. He did not intend to demean. He simply said what he thought in as few words as was possible. "And I don't mean that to trivialize their comments. All of what they said had to be said. And they stated their points well. We have serious problems in all those areas. But one of the areas that they did not cover has to do with the way this guy has rendered impotent most, if not all, of the traditional solutions. Now I know we are not into solutions yet. And I am not going to go there—not yet. But the way the battlefield is being set here, the severity of the problems, and the overall ineffectiveness of this administration, all considered in front of a backdrop of the possibly rabid inflation, we will have a real problem implementing any of the standard attack mechanisms.

What I mean to say is this, it isn't going to matter to voters if we accuse the opposition candidates of raping children, beating wives, or pissing in public—none of that is going to matter. Anybody running against one of our guys, the levers are coming down for him. Traditional dirty tricks are not going to work. This guy has created a political, economic and social milieu that makes life very difficult for guys like me."

"I have no idea what you're talking about, Reg," Allison said in jest, but not smiling. "Steve, what do you think?"

Steve did not hesitate. "Reg might see a problem setting up the opposition. Well, I see an even bigger problem making our guys look good, much less electable. And I don't see any sunshine on the horizon."

Allison looked down and stayed silent, giving Steve a little time to jump back in. She knew him to weigh his words carefully.

After a moment, he continued. "We used to control the traditional mainstream media. I guess you could say we still do. But we don't control the social media, the bloggers, or the radio talk show hosts. The reality is that social media is the new 'mainstream media.' And we don't have a good way to counter it. People really don't trust the traditional outlets. And that's where we live, with the old mainstream. We have to find a new dynamic, something very new."

"We've all seen *Wag the Dog*. Is that what you're getting at?" Jerry asked.

"Not exactly, but you're not far off."

"That brings us to solutions," Allison interrupted. "Let's take them in reverse order, Steve going first. And each of you suggest and explain one possible solution at a time. During this round, any one of you should feel free to jump in and comment. Interrupt if you wish. Steve, you're up."

Steve stopped to think for another moment, and then he said, "When I was younger I used to take my nephews to this pizza place for their birthdays. The pizza was okay, but the games were the attraction. There was this one. You still see it around. There was this rubber mallet. And when you played the game, you had to hit this groundhog when he poked his head up out of a hole. There were about a dozen holes, and you didn't know which one he would use next. He would stick up his head, and you would try to hit it. But he was up and down so fast, it was hard to react quickly enough.

"The kids would wear themselves out trying to thump the groundhog on the head. Bang, bang, bang, bang. He just kept coming up. Then the game would be over. Their scores reflected points for every time they hit the groundhog.

"Well, that's what we're up against now. First the economy rears its ugly head, then this war, or that war, then jobs, or the lack of them, then the deficit, then inflation. Maybe double-dipping recession. Or deflation. We've just got too many problems, too many *big* problems, too many distractions.

"We need a single major issue to focus in on. Something the public can wrap its head around and something we can handle. Unless we are able to focus in, we are in big trouble. At least that's how I see it from a public relations perspective. I need one issue, not a ten-headed leviathan. That's what I think."

"Reg," Allison said, looking over at him.

"If we had a single enemy, a single target, I could create the weapon to destroy it, figuratively speaking, of course. Steve is right on with this one. He would like to be able to sell one major issue, I would like to limit the scope of my attack. Death by a thousand scratches is a good tactic, but it only works if those wounds are administrated to the same victim. Give me a single enemy, and I can be effective. Hell, I can be a lot more than effective, I can deliver a strategic blow, and they won't know what hit them.

"But there is just too much going on with this administration. It almost makes me wish I was on the other side. I could have a field day over there."

"Do you have anything else to add?" Allison asked.

Reginald scrunched up the corner of his mouth in a manner that bespoke virtual hopelessness. "Nope, not right now."

"James."

"I think Reg might have hit on something. Let's view this from the other guy's perspective. All of these things we see as problems, the other side sees as gifts. Day after day we keep giving the coalition gifts. Weapons. Ammunition to attack and destroy us. It's like we're playing dodge ball with them, except we chuck marshmallows at them, while they're lobbing an endless supply of manure at us—and most of them are hitting something important. When they run out, our guy loads up another dump truck, backs it up to their tent, smiles, bows politely, and asks them where they would like him to dump it.

"I don't think this guy knows how or when to stop. I don't think he ever will stop. I don't think he has a clue. It's as though he views this country like a college campus, and he's head of the debate team. He doesn't understand or appreciate consequences.

"I don't think he understands that the problems we have in this country are real ones. Not just here, but in Europe, the Middle East, Eastern Europe. You close your eyes and pick a spot on the map. And the next thing you know, it's a problem area.

"I hate to say it, but I see only one solution."

With that James suddenly stopped talking and just stared down at his hands, which were folded on the table in front of him. He then looked up at Allison, unfolded his hands, and slowly turned his palms upward.

"What are you suggesting, James?"

Jerry did not give his friend time to respond. "Did you feel that breeze?" Jerry asked.

"What breeze?" Allison asked. "I don't think James is finished."

"Oh, yes, James is finished. At least for now," Jerry continued. "The breeze we felt was that door opening. And you know who walked in? I'll tell you who came in. That damn proverbial eight-hundred-pound gorilla came in. And he sat his ass down right over there," he said, pointing to an empty leather recliner just a few feet from the table where the group was sitting.

"And we all well know what that gorilla is doing here. None of us wants to talk about it. We are all terrified to talk about it. But we all know. We are all headed in the same direction with this."

"Jerry," Allison said, "you need to be more specific."

"The hell I do—"

With that, James jumped back into the conversation, interrupting his friend. "What Jerry is stating is the obvious. He's right. We're all right. The only solution is to eliminate the source of our problem. That would open up a whole plethora of potential defenses and modes of attack. But with our guy where he is, we are faced with an impossible situation."

James took a deliberate moment to make eye contact with all the other members at the table and then continued. "Has this angle played into the strategies that any of the rest of you contemplated since the last meeting? That is, have any of you considered this approach?"

"And what do you mean by *this approach*?" Reginald asked.

"I guess I mean, have any of you pictured a scenario where the president was no longer the president?"

No one offered a comment. Finally, Jerry stood and said, "Al, we have to be very careful here. We have to exercise a lot of caution as to just where we go with this. Please consider this possibility. What if you adjourn this meeting, right now? It's not important what we've *thought* about, only what we are willing to state on record, at this table. Obviously, we are all a little reticent to verbalize what this might entail—as well we should be."

Allison said, "I think you're right, Jerry. I think we end this meeting right now. I want all of you to consider carefully all that we have discussed today, and all that we haven't discussed." She paused for a moment, and then joined Jerry standing. That, to all the others, signaled the end of the meeting. But Allison was not yet finished. "We could be venturing into some very tenuous territory here. Please be careful."

Everyone knew the meeting was over and that they should no longer be talking about anything related to the topics just discussed at the table.

"We'll meet again next Tuesday. I'll provide the details later. Have a safe drive home."

Allison stopped and stood motionless for a few seconds. "This can't wait that long. We'll meet on Thursday, the day after tomorrow."

Three of the men looked at Allison as she gave that last instruction, but they said nothing. Reginald, who had also stood to leave, simply stared at the table, not acknowledging what she had just said. He then turned toward the door. Allison did not say another word to any of them as she slipped silently out of the door behind Reginald.

Jerry spoke to his two remaining friends. "See you guys Thursday. I'll close up, after I let the gorilla out. Those stinky fellows can make a terrible mess. By the way, James, thanks for cleaning this barn up."

James looked in Jerry's direction and smiled. But still did not responded verbally.

Chapter 25—The drive home
7:11 p.m., Tuesday, December 20

As soon as Allison got in her car, she slipped on and adjusted Bernadette's wig and then put on her customary glasses. When she looked in the mirror, she surprised even herself with her sullen expression.

Allison was in a bad mood—and she remained in a bad mood for the whole trip home. Without a doubt, she had considered on many occasions just how much better the situation would be if she did not have to deal with President Butler. She truly hated the man. And she disrespected his leadership over the past two-plus years—to the point that she felt totally vindicated with her earlier assertions that she would have made a far better president.

Had he performed in even a mediocre way, she might have been jealous. Instead, she was locked into her anger and hate. Not only did she feel he was destroying his own chances at re-election, he was, in her opinion, helping the conservatives capture both houses of Congress—if not outright, they were likely at least to dramatically weaken her party's position.

Initially, her intention was to push for the second spot in his second term. From there she felt she had a pretty strong chance of winning at the end of it. And, should anything befall the president, she would step in and finish it out, then run for her own term—like Lyndon Johnson did when President Kennedy was assassinated.

Now, however, her prospects were beginning to look dim. She was becoming convinced that he would lose his second-term election and thereby take her down with him.

"That bitch Sophie. It is all her damn fault. If she had kept her nose out of the process, I would have won the nomination, and I would be president right now."

The "Sophie" to whom she referred was Sophie Monroe, a popular Philadelphia tabloid talk show host.

Not only did Allison believe that was true, when alone she would frequently verbalize it out loud. And that's what she was doing as she was driving back to the city. "What the hell did she mean by that anyway? She called him 'The Anointed One.' On national TV. Damn it all, that so sucks. All the time we felt that she was empowering women. Then she turns around and kisses this jerk's ass. God, I *hate* that woman."

Allison had no difficulty expressing her feelings about Sophie but only to herself, when she was by herself. She knew that if she ever verbalized her hatred of Sophie, even to her closest friends, eventually it would hit the media. And that could hurt her reputation with women. So, she saved that venom for when she was alone—totally alone.

Then, as was becoming her practice, she took a couple deep breaths and prepared herself to record her take on the meeting. She opened the center console and felt around until she found her miniature recording device. She then reached into her purse and retrieved a sealed envelope containing an empty thumb drive. Carefully she slid it into the recorder and hit the "Record" button.

"Tuesday, December 20. We met at Jerry's cottage. Present were James, Jerry, Reg, Steve, and myself. The meeting lasted ..." She paused to look at her watch. "The meeting lasted approximately fifty-five minutes. ... Jerry was kind enough to bring sandwiches."

She then hit the "Pause" button as she gathered her thoughts. Her intentions were never to redact the recordings. She never wanted any written account of the meetings. So it was important to her to be as concise and accurate as possible, as there was to be no editing done later.

She continued, "There were a few pleasantries extended to Jerry for allowing us to use his cottage and for his kind hospitality. Steve suggested he might have brought a hamburger for Reg. After those comments, I asked Jerry to open the discussion.

"I had asked that each member of the group provide two or three matters that he considered major problems facing us. Jerry brought up the three issues he considered to be the most pressing. First, he suggested the president's staggering unpopularity. He pointed out how badly we lost the House, and that he had real concerns about keeping the Senate the next time around. Then he suggested that the economy was in free fall and that nothing Butler was doing would or could help. Finally, he made a reference to the "Manchurian Candidate." He did not elaborate on that, but we all had a pretty good notion about what he was suggesting."

Allison paused the recording. After she had thought for a moment, she began again.

"James followed. He agreed with Jerry and added his own ideas. He said that there was not really a question about it—we would lose the presidency and the Senate in the next election. Not only that, the fact that we took such a huge hit on the state level during the midterm could greatly affect our ability to recover in the near future. We were in trouble. Our state organizations were severely weakened, and it would be hard to fix them. Not only would Butler almost certainly lose the election; if he happened *not* to be the candidate, the party's candidate would still likely lose."

Again Allison paused, but this time for only a couple of seconds.

"Reg suggested that even he could not be effective at smearing coalition candidates, he felt that nothing he could do would make anyone look worse than the guy in the White House.

"Steve pointed out that this time around the bloggers were going to exercise more power than the mainstream media. And that there was nothing he could do to paint an electable face on our party's candidates. He said we needed something fresh, a new dynamic. But he did not elaborate.

"After Steve, we discussed potential solutions. I started with Steve. Steve virtually continued with what he had been saying about the problems as he viewed them. He said that we needed to find a single issue, instead of the ten-headed leviathan of issues we seem to be dealing with. We needed one easy-to-understand point of attack, a huge, all-encompassing headline, one that voters could get their heads wrapped around. We needed to define that one issue, and own it.

"James then created an interesting metaphor. It had to do with our playing dodge ball with the opposition. And that every day Butler drove a truck full of horse manure into their camp, and dumped it. Then the opposition would scoop up the manure and heave it like snowballs at us. And a lot of it stuck. Then the next day, the president did the same thing.

"With that, James stopped talking. We all got the picture. James was suggesting that the president was not able to control himself ... that *he* was the problem.

"Jerry then jumped in, almost interrupting, and made the comment that an eight-hundred-pound gorilla had just walked into the room. No one wanted to state what was being suggested, but we all knew. We all knew that the situation would remain untenable as long as this president was in the White House. We stopped with that and agreed to meet again the following Thursday, which would be the twenty-second. At that time we would discuss options."

Allison flipped the recorder off and removed the thumb drive. She put the drive in an envelope in her purse and then dropped the recorder in her purse as well. She then took her cell out of her purse, reinstalled the battery, and called James.

Chapter 26—Allison contemplates
8:14 p.m., Tuesday, December 20

For a brief moment Allison thought she sensed a car following her on the trip back to the city. She kept an eye in the rearview mirror as she dialed James.

"James. Where are you right now? … Just leaving? … Same place. I suppose I should have cleared that with Jerry. I'm sure he won't mind. You can let the others know. … I'll give Jerry a call to confirm. Unless you hear otherwise, assume the same place." And she disconnected.

Allison stared intently into the New York night the rest of the way home. She had forgotten about the car in her mirror.

When she arrived at the parking garage she gave her keys to the parking attendant, along with her customary twenty dollars. But this time she could not even fake a smile. As far as she was concerned, the decision to eliminate the president had been made. All that remained were logistics. She had known, even before the first meeting, that there was only one viable solution to the problem, but she wanted her friends to verbalize it. It would be, after all, they who planned it out, made it happen, and engineered the proper outcomes.

As soon as Allison had successfully closed and locked the door to Bernadette's apartment behind her, she walked over to the bar and poured herself a double shot of Scotch. Then she slipped in an ice cube. Her plan was to nurse this drink, so she did not mind if it watered down a bit.

She took one sip from her glass and set it down beside her favorite chair. She then proceeded to stash the thumb drive from the last meeting in her safe.

Sitting down in the recliner, she immediately took her cell phone out of her purse and called James again.

"James, we need to talk. ... No, not the whole group, just you and me. I need to see you yet tonight. ... Where are you right now?"

James explained to her that he was on the Parkway, headed toward the city. He said that he could stop by the apartment and pick her up in half an hour. He would call her when he was ten minutes out. "That's perfect," she said. Allison then carefully put Bernadette's clothes in their proper places and officially became totally herself again. She then returned to Allison's apartment.

As promised, James called her about twenty minutes later. Allison told him to give her another call when he was outside the building. She really did not want to spend any unnecessary time making small talk with aides or agents. She did, however, notify her security detail that she would be leaving with James.

Just a short time later, James called again. And Allison went down to meet him. This time, as Allison, she greeted the doorman and gave him a twenty as he opened James's door. Everyone knew that James held a special place in the lives of Bob and Allison, so nothing suspicious was ever thought when James picked her up.

"I am sorry to inconvenience you like this. But these are very heavy times—very grave times," Allison said.

"I understand."

"Just drive until we find a good place to talk. I don't want to say anything right now. We need to do another security check."

"Sounds right."

Under normal conditions, James and Allison always had something to say to one another. But not this time—not until they had a chance to wand themselves and the vehicle one more time. They both knew that anything was possible. Someone could have slipped a magnetic transmitter under the car at a red light or in front of her apartment. Even the different clothes she had put on could contain a bug of some sort.

They drove around for several minutes, until Allison spotted an appropriate place to park. "Pull in here," she commanded.

James pulled his SUV into the parking lot and quickly wanded the car, himself and Allison. She had forgotten to take the battery out of her cell, so he had to check her out a second time.

"Okay, Al, we're good."

"Here's the deal. I know I told the group that there would be no meetings aside from meetings of the whole group. I'm changing that rule for tonight. I have to know from you, directly from your mouth, if what Jerry was suggesting is exactly what you were suggesting. Clarify it for me, please."

James sat in his seat for a moment, saying nothing. Finally, Allison asked him again, "James, I need you to clarify for me, right now, what you were suggesting at the meeting tonight. I need you to be honest, and I need you to verbalize it right now. I need to know where we are going with this. I need to know if what I think you are saying is actually what you are saying."

"Al, I see no way out of this as long as Butler remains president. He has to go."

"And what exactly does that mean? What are you suggesting be done?"

"Well, I don't think he will leave of his own free will. Do you?"

"So what do you propose?"

"I need some time to think about that—"

"The hell you do! Don't you sit there and mess with me. You can't convince me that you have not already spent time contemplating scenarios, various plans of action. Now you tell me where you are going with this."

"You want me come out and say it. And I am not comfortable verbalizing this. And neither should you be."

"Dammit! James, of course I'm not comfortable. I might not be able to sleep for a week. I am deeply troubled. I have to tell you that you are not alone in this. I have agonized for over a month. And that was the only answer I could come up with. I see no other way to get to where we need to be."

"I know what you mean. What we are discussing is the most indelicate of political solutions. But we must devise a very comprehensive plan to carry it out."

"Do you have any ideas?"

"Of course I do. You know me—my mind is working all the time."

"Where are you at with this right now?"

"Okay, this is how I see it. Impeachment won't work. Not even worth a minute's thought. He must be forcibly eliminated. Of course, there can be nothing delicate about that. An accident is possible. There are any number of ways that it could be carried out. But an accident would solve only half the problem."

"Explain."

"Well, accidental death would put John in the Oval Office. But it would not solve any of the problems. What we need to see happen is for the president to go away at the hands of the opposition. *That* would work."

"That might happen anyway. This guy has a lot of enemies who would love to see him dead."

"A lot of stupid and incompetent enemies. For us to satisfy ourselves with the 'possibility' of his demise is foolish. We cannot wait around for this. And if we're going to orchestrate it, we have to control all of the details. Nothing can be left to chance. In fact, the worst thing that could happen would be for some idiot opportunist to get successful without our being prepared to take the lead."

"Okay, I can see that I did not misinterpret what you were suggesting at the meeting. Quite obviously, Jerry got the same impression. In your eyes, how do we proceed?"

"Details, logistics. It will all come down to details and logistics and timing. It always does. The wildcard here is Reg. He has all the right contacts and the expertise. Plus, he is cold and calculating. He did not have much to say at the meeting. But he did not object. And he seemed as though he was headed in the same direction as Jerry and I were. We will need to feel him out at the next meeting."

"I don't think we can wait. The three of us—you, Reg, and I—must meet soon. We have to know where Reg is at. I agree that he would be instrumental. He's the only member of our group who could make it happen. But I don't know if he's ready to make that jump."

"He's loyal, Al. I think he would be in."

"Tomorrow. The three of us have to talk. Tomorrow. I'll set it up."

It had taken only seven minutes for the two friends to set in motion one of the most nefarious plans ever conceived in the history of the United States.

Allison immediately tried to dial Reginald's number but discovered the battery was not in her phone. Replacing it, she continued on her mission. "Reg. You, James, and I need to talk tomorrow." Encountering mild protest, Allison blurted out, "I don't give a rip about your plans. James will stop by tomorrow morning. Cancel whatever you think you have to do, and be ready for him at nine a.m. The regular place." Allison gave Reginald no time to protest—she pulled her cell away from her ear and disconnected.

No other words were spoken on the entire trip back to Allison's apartment. All that needed to be said had just been said. As she got out of the car, Allison said, "Pick me up before you stop for Reg. I'll look for you at eight-thirty."

Allison jumped out of the car before the doorman could open it for her. She shoved a twenty in his face as he scurried toward the car. She did not say a word to him, nor did she even make eye contact.

She spent a few minutes with her aides and with the Secret Service, and then she retired to her bedroom. Once there, she immediately entered the secret passageway up to Bernadette's apartment, sat down in Bernadette's favorite chair, and proceeded to summarize into the recorder her meeting with James. She then retired to her apartment, not expecting to get much sleep, but seeking at least some rest.

Surprisingly, she quickly fell asleep, not awaking until five a.m.

Chapter 27—Meeting with Reginald
8:30 a.m., Wednesday, December 21

As always, James called Allison to give her a heads-up ten minutes before he arrived. He was a little surprised that she had him pick her up before he gathered up Reginald. But he knew better than to question her about it.

James drove up at exactly eight-thirty a.m., just as Allison was walking out the door. Allison thanked the doorman graciously for opening the car door for her and handed him the customary tip.

"It's a ten-minute drive this morning to pick up Reg. Do you want to go someplace first?"

"No, he's always early. He'll be waiting."

Neither of them said a word as James sped through New York traffic. Finally, James asked, "Where do you want to go? After we pick up Reg?"

"Oh, I think we should just drive around. Reg is a man of few words. He's either in or out. If he's out, that could be a problem." She paused for a moment and then continued. "You seemed pretty confident he'll be with us, right?"

"Right."

James did not want to discuss anything of substance until he had again swept the car. So he just sat there silently the rest of the way, as did Allison.

The drive to pick up Reginald took a little over ten minutes, but they still arrived before the designated pickup time. And, just as Allison had predicted, Reginald was waiting for them. He spotted them coming and bolted out of the coffee shop. He tossed his newspaper and half-empty cup in a trashcan as James slid his SUV to the curb.

"Morning, Al, James."

"Good morning," Allison answered. "Say nothing for now."

Reginald immediately realized that this was going to be another private meeting, requiring the now all-too-familiar wanding. He then proceeded to remove the battery from his cell, as did Allison. James had already popped his battery out right after he had called to let Allison know he would be by her apartment soon.

James and Reginald were both keenly aware that the very existence of this meeting ran counter to Allison's rule against having meetings apart from the whole group, but both knew better than to question Allison about it.

"I know the regimen," she said as she removed the wand. She wanded James, then herself. Afterward, she turned and wanded Reginald, who was sitting in the backseat. Once finished with Reginald, she then returned the wand to its case.

After just a few contemplative moments, Allison turned around to face Reginald. "Okay, Reg. This is why we are meeting this morning. Our next meeting of the whole group is going to be a very significant one. And I'll tell you why. Just as Jerry and James suggested, there seems to be only one way to deal with this problem. I'm going to just lay it out for you. The three of us are convinced that the president must be eliminated. What do you say to that?"

Immediately Reginald's countenance changed. It was as though he had just been informed by his doctor that he had pancreatic cancer—stage four. All the blood drained from his face. He looked ten years older. Reginald stared into Allison's steel-cold eyes. Still, neither of them said a word after Allison had asked her question.

Reginald knew that his whole life was about to be changed—irreversibly. Were he to say the wrong thing or even assume an unacceptable posture, he knew he would not be allowed to get out of James's car alive. He knew after the previous meeting of the whole that it was coming to this, sooner or later. He also knew that Allison did not mess around. He had no doubt that he was either in all the way, or he, and perhaps his family, would suffer dramatically.

"I knew that this was coming," he finally answered. "We all knew yesterday. Except maybe Steve. No one knows what he's thinking half the time. But I knew."

"Well, are you in?" Allison repeated.

Reginald again hesitated as he gathered his thoughts. This was not a good time to say the wrong thing.

"Yes, I'm in. But this has to be done the right way. If this gets messed up, you not only can forget about your legacy—we'll all be dead. … It must be executed perfectly."

"Hell, if we continue in the direction we're going, I'll have no legacy anyway."

"That's exactly why the three of us are meeting right now, Reg," James said. He wanted Reginald to know that he was totally behind the plan. And just as James had intended, those words seemed to relieve Reginald a bit.

"And what do you mean by execute perfectly?" Allison asked.

"I will admit that I spent half the night thinking about this. Actually, I don't think I slept more than an hour, if that. When you called last night I knew exactly where this was going. I can't say that I was prepared for your bluntness, but I knew what to expect just the same.

"This is what I came up with as a preliminary workable plan. The only way to do this is soon. You have no idea just how much angst is out there, particularly in the other camp. And with the new radical right, anything could happen, and more sooner than later. If we are going to *manage* this thing for the greatest advantage, it all has to be on our terms, which means it must take place in our time frame. We cannot be caught playing catch-up."

"What are you suggesting as far as timing?" Allison asked.

"Weeks not months."

"Is that possible?"

"I've done projects in less. Certainly none this significant. But the magnitude of the job isn't really that different. Even a small job done wrong ruins lives. Look at Liddy and Watergate."

"You think a few weeks is enough?" James asked.

"Has to be. We really do not have any luxury here—it gets done soon, very soon, or it doesn't get done."

"Okay, Reg. I'm going to tell you something. Take it seriously. Not that I don't think that you will. But know I could not be more serious. Once we get out of this car today, we will have made a decision to assassinate the president of the United States. Are you up to that? Are you *really* up to it? You had better think about that before you say a word. Once you answer me, there can be no turning back."

Reginald knew that this bridge had already been crossed and had blown up behind him. He was well aware that Allison probably had a .38 pointed through the seat, at his gut, as they spoke.

"We all agreed, didn't we, that the alternative was just unacceptable? Is that not right? So, as far as I am concerned now, the outcome is inevitable, and in my eyes, this decision has already been made. ... This has become just another job to me. I am prepared to do what needs to be done."

"How about you, James?"

"You can count me in ... for the same reason."

That morning both men verbalized their commitment to this most dreadful of plots, even though Allison had warned them both that once they agreed to participate, they would not be able to turn back later. Both James and Reginald were nervous about the plot, but they both knew they already had too much information.

Allison trusted the resolve of her two friends, so she never revisited this issue with them. As far as she was concerned, they were committed. Glancing back at Reginald, she asked, "You said that you had worked up a tentative plan. Is that right? If so, we would like to hear about it."

Chapter 28—Reginald lays out plan

9:40 a.m., Wednesday, December 21

The SUV grew very quiet and remained so for an uncomfortable length of time.

"Kennedy will serve as our model," Reginald finally stated. "Even though that plan was severely flawed, both in design and implementation, it was exquisitely effective."

"How can you characterize it as exquisite?" James asked. "We do not even know who was ultimately responsible for it."

"Exactly. The public still does not know."

"And you do?" James asked.

"Of course. But that does not matter. The mere fact that initially Oswald appeared to be a lone gunman, and then he was taken out by Ruby, who just happened to be terminally ill and in need of money. The whole thing was a work of art. I got to know some of the operatives involved, and I have read every book written about it. I can assure you that the ultimate goal of those involved was realized. That's what makes it exquisite. We will use that assassination as our model, but with major modifications and, hopefully, improvements."

"How? How will you do it?" Allison asked.

"The only way to be sure anymore is with a bomb. Everything is bulletproof. And bullets get deflected—shooters miss their targets. There are just too many uncertainties with a rifle. Things can go wrong. This has to work perfectly, the first time. We will get only one shot at this."

"Where would you stage it?" James then asked.

"We would want it to be in the Midwest someplace. Somewhere conservatives, redneck conservatives, are thought to be in abundance."

"I assume the bomb would be placed outside, where he was speaking, perhaps?"

"No, we will blow up his car."

"How would you deal with the armor? Presidential motorcades are very well armored. I know that from personal experience," Allison said.

"Here's how we do this—at least as my plan stands right now. We will target the motorcade with rocket-propelled grenades. I'm even considering drones with rockets. We've tested this before, and it worked marvelously. We will not know for certain which car he will be riding in, so we take them all out. Every car in the motorcade, even if there are a dozen. It would not be a problem. We will hit the first and last cars with at least two grenades, or rockets, each."

Reginald paused for just a few seconds and looked first into James's eyes, then into Allison's. He clearly appeared to be enjoying himself. It was obvious that he had already given this matter a lot of thought, and he liked the way his audience reacted to him.

He then continued, "Now, we all know that it is a virtual certainty that POTUS will survive the initial attack. Those vehicles are battleships on wheels. But we are not actually seeking to destroy the target with this attack. All we are trying to do is to derail the motorcade, and get POTUS to break from it. It is a cinch that he will be immediately whisked off to a hospital. That's where the real hit actually occurs.

"Depending on how many hospitals there are in the city that we choose, we will have bombs buried at the emergency room entrances of each of them. Enough explosives to take out a whole wing of the building. The Secret Service will have checked everything along the route that the president will take, and all alternative routes. They will have welded all the manhole covers along those routes. But they will not have checked the hospital emergency room entrances—and there are always manholes outside the hospitals. All we have to do is select a trip that we know he won't back out of, and then set traps at the emergency room entrances."

"Now, we all know he's going to become more and more active, politically, supporting troubled candidates in key states. We should be able to nail one of those locations down to a high degree of certainty," James said.

"We won't take a chance on just one. We will be prepared for several targets. We can relocate the RPGs on a moment's notice, but the bombs will present a slightly different challenge. I will have to figure this part out. I'll need to contract the best people.

"But the beauty of it is, if for some reason he skips all the cities we have prepared for, no one will ever be the wiser. We will simply have to regroup a bit. I always have contingency plans."

Allison and James exchanged eye contact but said nothing. Then Reginald continued. "Now, back to the hospital emergency room entrances. We will also have placed smaller explosives inside the actual entrances of the hospitals, in the event that the president is delivered to the hospital in such a way that the original bomb placement might be ineffective. That could happen."

"How would you get the explosives into a hospital? Don't they have security?" James asked, a little like an advocate for the devil.

"All emergency room doors have electronic door openers. And they all are subject to inspections and scheduled maintenance. There is plenty of room inside the openers for a sizeable C-4 device. The metal of the enclosure would serve as shrapnel, making the explosion more lethal."

"Damn, Reg, you've certainly got all the details worked out," Allison said, obviously impressed.

"Not the case. Not at all the case," Reginald quickly countered. "I have a lot of details to work out. But I do have the overall structure planned. The tricky part is to make sure that the right people get blamed. Otherwise the whole plot will implode, our efforts will be wasted. If that happens, we are as good as dead."

"I might be of some help with that," James offered.

"How?" Reginald asked.

"I've got a friend, a spook, whose organization has a highly placed operative in one of the most radical of the opposition groups. I really think that we could do enough work with them to make them look responsible."

"That's not how it happens," Reginald said. "Too much can go wrong with that approach. You need to leave that part to me and to Steve. Once the event has occurred, we do not want to point the blame to any one person or organization. We will let the press and the pundits work at that. All we have to do is make it look like a right-wing conspiracy. We'll deal with generalities only—no specifics. And the rest will happen automatically. There will be a feeding frenzy. Steve and I will work out a series of press releases, plant the right rumors, and the rest will happen automatically.

"The critical thing here is timing. Because the conclusions drawn during the first twenty-four hours will rule the day."

"Day, month, and year," Allison immediately followed. "Steve will be instrumental here. If we have the stories ready, he can plant them."

"How much help are you going to need, Reg?" James asked.

"I'll let you know. But the less you guys know, the better, as far as I'm concerned. I've got some guys in the Secret Service that I can use in a limited way—a very limited way. And I have plenty of help available for work in the field. All I need is money, a lot of it."

"What do you need to get started?" Allison asked.

"All of it."

"Okay. And how much is that?"

"A hundred million."

"You can't be serious!" Allison exclaimed in shock, her chin dropping, exposing her lower teeth.

"What did you think? It isn't about lining my pockets. This job has to be done right. I will need to bring some very specialized talent on board—*expensive* people. I want to learn more about James's insiders. He and I will deal with that. We might find them helpful—at some point. But I am not going to do this on the cheap. I can promise you that I will not ever come back asking for more. And I will guarantee you that I will get the job done. But that is what it's going to cost. Can you come up with it?"

"I suppose I will have to."

Reginald countered, "Al, no one knows better than you that once you're president, you will have unlimited access to resources. Surely there are some foreign sources you can tap."

Allison did not have to consider the matter. As they all understood, the alternative was not acceptable. "When do you need it?"

"I need it in gold, by the end of next week."

"In gold?"

"I am not interested in dollars or any other currency. And neither are the people I am working with. You can do this, right?"

"You'll have it by next Friday—one week from tomorrow. But you need to get started now."

"I already have," Reginald replied. "Now, regarding payment. Let's say we base the amount on the close of the US markets today. I will expect payment by noon on Friday the thirtieth. Is that acceptable?"

Allison did not even acknowledge Reginald's last request. Her response was assumed.

Chapter 29—Allison arranges for Reginald's payment

10:18 a.m., Wednesday, December 21

Allison asked James to drop her off first. She had a lot of thinking and planning to do, not the least of which was putting together the hundred million dollars in gold, within one week.

As she got out of James's car, she did not say a word to either of the two men. She merely thanked the doorman, handed him a twenty, and went up to her apartment. As was becoming customary, she informed her aides that she would be retiring for the remainder of the day. Then, once inside, she quickly made her way up to Bernadette's apartment. It was almost as though she could think more clearly up there, where she was certain to be left alone.

Once seated in her favorite chair, she began recording all the events of the meeting with James and Reginald.

Strange, she thought, that Reg would come up with that figure without even having to take a moment to think about it. And, the fact that he wanted it in gold—that, too, was curious.

"Reg requested a hundred million dollars in gold. I suppose that given the way the dollar is falling, that's just good business. He said that the people he will be working with require payment in gold."

For a few moments she ceased recording. And then she started up again: "Sure, that's just good business. Given the way the dollar is falling. That's just prudent. Whoever Reg is going to be working with, they're not going to be interested in getting paid with anything but gold, especially if the economy really tanks in the aftermath. ... There is one good thing. At least I don't have to get my hands dirty. With Reg in charge, he will see to everything. This will be much neater and cleaner. The less I know, the better."

And, as she always did, once finished recording, she secured the thumb drive in her secret safe. She then poured herself a drink and returned to the chair.

With that, she put the battery back in her cell phone and made a call. The party she was calling did not pick up, and a very pedestrian recording of a female voice asked that she leave a message.

"My friend, I need to see you in the morning. Seven a.m., at the regular place." Allison then disconnected the call.

The person she had just called was Sid, her banker, so to speak. During her years in the White House she and Bob were able to amass a large fortune—nearly half a billion dollars. Two hundred million of it was in gold, the rest in various currencies, including dollars and Euros. The gold was to serve as a hedge against inflation, the currencies in the event of a worldwide depression.

She liked gold because it was practically untraceable. The sort of gold she and Bob held was a little more traceable, however, because much of it was in the form of antiquities. At the time they acquired it, gold was hovering around four hundred dollars an ounce. Now it had more than tripled. That meant the original two hundred million was now worth closer to seven or eight hundred million. So, a hundred million in gold, while putting a serious dent in her net worth, would not seriously deplete her fortune.

Interestingly, when she and Bob parted ways, she kept two-thirds of the gold and one-third of the cash. That was the deal she had worked out with her husband during his impeachment hearings. He was convinced that if she were to leave him at that time, he would be convicted and so be forced to resign. It seemed like a fair arrangement to him. But with gold increasing in value so precipitously, and the dollar falling in the same fashion, the deal turned out much to Allison's advantage.

Besides, that was not her only reserve. She and Bob had numerous Swiss bank accounts—mostly consisting of safe deposit boxes containing US dollars. Even though the value of those dollars had fallen off dramatically, their value was still significant.

At the time she and Bob came into the possession of the gold artifacts, they agreed that they should be preserved intact, rather than melted down. They thought this because as artifacts, there was additional intrinsic value attached to them. But now, with the price of gold at historic highs, the gold's additional value as artifacts was significantly diminished. Still, she could not yet bring herself to turn it into bullion.

She calculated that, not considering any additional value due to the gold's historical significance, her gold was now worth over six hundred million—perhaps more. She felt she could pay out a hundred million for a shot at the White House. Not only a shot, but if she played it smart, and if she lined up the right people to assist her, she believed she would win it.

Most important among the conditions she recognized were Reginald doing his thing perfectly and Steve spinning as only he was capable of spinning. "If those two do their jobs, this will work," she surmised.

First things first. Right now she was going to need Sid to fly to Switzerland and bring back enough gold to pay Reginald. And she needed him to get on it right away. She would meet with him in the morning and tell him what she needed him to do, and by next Wednesday, he would make the delivery to Reginald. She had no intention of seeing or touching any of the gold. Sid knew Reginald, and he would take care of it. In fact, Sid would make sure that the hundred million would be covered and then some—and he would have the gold in Reginald's hands earlier than required.

She knew Reginald would have the treasure weighed, and he would be pleased to find that he had received two to three percent more than he had bargained for. Allison had learned from her years with Bob that you never shortchanged a hit man. And, that's exactly what Reginald was, a very high-priced hit man.

Allison finished her drink and poured another. This second drink was celebratory. *It's hell when you have to celebrate something this huge by yourself*, she thought. *But this is only temporary. John will move up, and he will appoint me VP. The public will blame the serpent-headed conservatives, and I will unite the country. Then, in a little over a year, John will step aside, and I will run and win in the general. Everybody gets what he wants.*

With that she chuckled out loud, "And some bastards will get what they deserve."

She slowly sipped her drink. But still, stuck in the back of her mind, was the business about Reginald and just how quickly he came up with the price and his insistence that it be paid in gold. It made sense to her, but the way it all went down seemed more than a little curious.

She recognized the fact that she had too much to accomplish before the next meeting of the whole, and particularly with regard to Reginald's payment. So she begrudgingly moved on from her uneasiness— too much to get done, with no time to second-guess.

Chapter 30—Her "friend" Sid

5:14 a.m., Thursday, December 22

Allison was up and active by five a.m. That really was not unusually early for her.

She was thankful that Sid agreed to meet with her. Even though the two had not conversed, the mere fact that he did not call to cancel was a *de facto* acceptance.

Actually, Sid had never failed to meet with her or Bob when requested to do so. Initially, Sid was more strongly disposed to serve the fiduciary wants and needs of her husband. But when they went their separate ways, Bob found contacts other than Sid to handle his banking, while Allison leaned totally on Sid.

Aside from his financial wisdom, the thing about Sid that Bob missed most dearly was Sid's diplomatic clearance. Sid was part of the Israeli delegation, and as such had full diplomatic immunity. Therefore, thanks to Article 27 of the 1961 Vienna Convention on Diplomatic Relations, as long as he tagged his luggage as "Diplomatic Pouches," he could fly in and out of the Middle East, Europe, and the United States, without ever having a problem. His luggage, regardless of size, could never be subjected to inspections.

It was sort of funny, the way the whole thing turned out for Bob and Allison. When the First Couple learned just how much wealth could be acquired in the White House, Allison had her own people handling the couple's finances. Bob's principal role was coercing the wealth, while her job was to convert it to gold and currencies and stash it away abroad. That arrangement worked for a couple years. Then they found out that they were being ripped off in a major way.

Of course, they would not allow that to happen. People died, and they found Sid. Bob never really let her forget that it was her friends that were responsible for the problem. While the losses seemed substantial to them at the time (they lost over fifty million dollars), once Sid came on the scene, everything improved. Not only did they find more ingenious ways to extort, they also discovered that they had been selling themselves short. Instead of selling their influence for a million or two, now they would frequently close eight- and sometimes nine-digit deals.

The biggest challenge for them was to find better ways to hide their loot. That's where Sid came in. He was brilliant. It was his idea to acquire a percentage of their payments in gold artifacts, as opposed to currencies. It was also his plan to avoid investments of any type. Those were, in his estimation, much too traceable. He explained to them that there would be plenty of opportunity down the road to invest, just not while in office.

He told them that if they put away enough gold and currencies, they would leave the White House very wealthy people and virtually untouchable. Now, Bob no longer had Sid to help him.

But, Bob was outstandingly clever on his own even without Sid. Throughout his tenure as governor of Louisiana, Bob had built alliances—many of them international. It was while serving as the chief executive of that state (before he became the president) that he developed his very lucrative smuggling enterprises. Most of the monies he made on drugs remained in South and Central America, invested in real estate. He indirectly held the controlling interests in numerous resort properties and a major cruise line. Allison, while she knew that he had some investments south of the border, had no idea just how extensive they were. And she did not want to know. She knew Bob very well. She knew that people who pried too deeply into his personal affairs often met with a sudden death. She knew about his ruthless side, and she avoided crossing over into it.

On the other hand, she knew Bob could be a very good friend. For the most part, that was the relationship she opted for—that of friend and confidante.

As a husband, she trusted him. She knew that he would screw around on her whenever he wanted to. Faithfulness in that arena was never expected. When close friends would question her about it, she would frequently say, "Never expect people to deliver what they are incapable of delivering. If you do, you will be disappointed."

But, she could trust him to deal honestly with her regarding money. While they both loved money more than they loved each other, they were incredibly honest and loyal with regard to it. They never cheated there. If they owed money, they paid it. If they owed one another money, that debt too, was honored.

So, Allison was preparing to meet with Sid, a very loyal friend of the Fulbright's.

Unlike her meetings with James or Jerry, Allison did not have the same liberty when it came to dealing personally with Sid. She felt that it would be best if she donned her Bernadette persona when meeting with Sid. She reasoned that would be wise, because Sid was not a public figure, nor was he an acknowledged personal friend of the Fulbrights. His role, with regard to Allison, was strictly that of a financial confidante. She assumed that Sid probably had other clients for whom he provided similar services. While Allison should not be seen in public with such a figure, Bernadette certainly could.

Allison made a brief appearance outside her bedroom, contacted her aides, then feigned a headache and returned to her bedroom.

From there she quickly went up to Bernadette's apartment, emerging outside the building a half an hour later. "Need me to hail a cab, ma'am?" the doorman inquired. She handed him a twenty and flashed a small smile beneath her sunglasses. Within a minute, she had boarded a taxi and was on her way to meet Sid.

"Fiftieth and Broadway. And no need to hurry." Allison knew that she was running a little early. The driver shot over to Park Avenue, then headed south. The morning traffic was beginning to slow, but Park Avenue was clear down to 53rd. The driver started to turn west at 53rd, then opted to go further south. Even though Allison had told him that she was not in a rush, he was.

51st was pretty clear, so the driver laid on his horn and nosed his cab through the crosswalk, then accelerated for about one hundred feet. From that point, all he could do was inch along past the other taxis and morning delivery trucks.

When they approached Madison Avenue, Allison's patience was exhausted. "This will do just fine," she told the driver. "I'll walk from here. Just pull over. Thank you."

She paid and tipped the driver, then did a little window-shopping. Allison enjoyed doing that when she had a little extra time. That was a delicious little luxury indulged in only by her Bernadette persona. She knew that Sid would be waiting for her already, but that did not make her feel the need to hurry.

Bob had told her often that when dealing with people who work for you, you've got to make them wait for you. It should never work the other way. Friends are a different case. Never keep them waiting—never.

Sid worked for Allison. He was not a friend. So he should wait—at least for a few minutes. Allison checked her watch. It was seven-ten. "Perfect," she said aloud, as she entered the restaurant where they would meet whenever she wanted to talk to him. Sid had probably arrived for-ty-five minutes earlier, and got a booth.

"How are you?" Sid asked her.

"Fine, and you?"

"Well, thank you."

"I need you to make a trip," she said as the waiter walked up. "Just coffee and water, please."

"What do you need?"

"One hundred large. And it has to be hard."

Sid looked her in the eye and repeated what she had just said, "One hundred large and hard? Okay. When?"

"It has to be delivered by Wednesday, next week."

"Where?"

"I'll let you know. I do not want to see or touch it. Just pick it up and bring it back to the city. Someone else will receive it from you. I will let you know where and when."

Were this not Allison that Sid was dealing with, he might not have been willing to make the transfer of so large a sum to a stranger. But he knew that Allison would not put him in a vulnerable position. And, he knew better than to question her orders.

"Anything special about it? Do you want me to pick out the pieces? How do you want it?"

"You know, I hadn't considered that aspect." Allison sat there for a brief moment and then continued, "If there are pieces that seem to you to have greater historic value, leave them. And if there are others that you think are unusually traceable, leave them as well. I am not certain about the final outcome of the individual items, but I am pretty sure that most of them will be turned into cash, and quite quickly."

"I understand," Sid responded. "I do hope there will be discretion."

"Once the transfer is made, there will be no guarantees about that," Allison said.

Allison knew that Sid had a fine taste for artifacts. And she was not eager to run counter to his highly developed sensitivities. She wanted him to pick and choose. Even though there were a number of pieces that she loved dearly, she felt she needed to grant him this power. "Of course, you should take five percent for yourself, in the currency of your choice."

Typically his payment would be 3.5 percent.

"That's generous," Sid said. "Thank you."

"It's not generous. You are an invaluable personal friend. You mean a lot to me. And I know you will be professional about this."

Of course, Allison was lying to Sid with regard to his being a personal friend. And he knew it. But he still liked hearing the words come out of her mouth. It indicated to Sid that she viewed him as an indispensable *employee*. He had always known that his position in her eyes was not that of a personal friend. In fact, he was confident that she did not even consider him a close associate. He knew his place—that of a trusted employee. And that was fine with him.

With regard to his handling the transaction professionally—that was not hyperbole. They both knew Sid would conduct the deal discreetly, for not to do so would surely result in his death.

"What sort of arrangements do you think you can make at this short notice?"

"I can manage."

"I am sure you will. You have never let me down. I am giving you the liberty of one day. I would like to have you make the exchange on Wednesday, but we actually have until Thursday. Just keep that in mind in case things get tight."

"Thank you. I'm confident with Wednesday. ... perhaps a little sooner."

With that, Allison stood to leave. She had not received her coffee and water. "Call me when you get back."

"Will do."

Allison then left the restaurant. She thought for a few moments as to whether she should record a summary of her meeting with Sid, but she decided against it.

Chapter 31—Sid in Switzerland
11:05 a.m., Saturday, December 24

Sid was faithful, and he was smart. When he first received Allison's message, he correctly surmised what she had in mind for him. And he suspected that she would be in a hurry. So, immediately after he received the message requesting a meeting, he booked two seats on a Thursday evening flight to Zurich. Whenever he made trips such as this, he always took a diplomatic courier with him to render physical help. Sometimes he took two. Not knowing what would be the specifics of this trip, he opted for one helper. Had he to do it over, after learning about the magnitude of the operation, he would have taken two.

He and his courier left New York Thursday at eight p.m. from Kennedy and arrived in Zurich Friday morning just as the banks opened. They spent only a matter of hours there, and then caught a return flight Friday afternoon (Zurich time). Sid slept on the plane, arriving back in New York early Friday afternoon, New York time.

His plan was then to call Allison and receive her instructions for delivery. And that is exactly how it turned out, except he called Allison as he was boarding his plane in Switzerland and requested that she meet him at his New York apartment Monday afternoon. Sid was fully aware that Allison had specifically told him that she did not want to see or touch the gold. But the more he thought about this, the more apprehensive he became. There were a number of items that he knew Allison particularly liked, and some of those pieces were among those he was bringing back to the States.

"I said I did not want to be personally involved," she said. "Has something changed?"

They never used names when they were conversing—whether in person or on the phone. Sid had always insisted on having it that way.

"We've got time. And I would really feel more comfortable if you helped me pick out the drapery. It would please me greatly if you would be willing to help me with that."

"Of course, if you consider my input important enough to warrant it. What time should I be there?"

"How does one p.m. work for you?"

"That will be just fine. See you then."

It was actually not going to be a problem for her. In fact, she was looking forward to spending a little face time with Sid. He always had good advice to give her. And if he wanted to see her, if he thought that she needed to go through the pieces he had picked up, then she would be happy to accommodate.

Between the time she talked to Sid by phone on Wednesday and the next morning, Allison enjoyed a considerable level of satisfaction. She knew that Reginald was about to receive payment in full, and that of all the people she knew, Reginald was by the far the most single-minded and resourceful person she had ever worked with. Now that the payment was on its way back to New York, she was confident that she would not disappoint him. In Allison's eyes, all was going very well.

* * *

Before noon on the following Monday, Allison made a brief appearance outside her bedroom and met with her aides. Then she explained to them that she still was not feeling well, and that she was going to go back to bed. She then went up to Bernadette's apartment and exited the building.

Again, the doorman received his twenty, and she took a taxi down to Sid's West Village apartment.

Even though she arrived twenty minutes early, she proceeded directly to his building and rang the bell. Neither Allison nor Bernadette liked to shop in the West Village.

"Hello, my friend. How was your trip?"

"Exhausting, as usual." Neither of them had much to say, until they were in his apartment.

"I really appreciate your coming down to meet with me. I know I will feel much better once you have had a chance to see what I brought back."

Sid then opened up several large trunk-sized crates that were sitting in the middle of his living room. He had already broken the packing seals and loosened the covers. Inside the crates were dozens of the most exquisite pieces of antique gold a person could imagine.

"I brought these in for you to take a look at," he told her. "The more pedestrian pieces remain in storage. But some of these I have a question about. This is what I would suggest. If there are any of these pieces that you do not want to part with, then assign them to me as part of my payment. I will return them to the vault and exchange them on my next trip."

Allison knelt over the treasure and began to examine them, refraining, of course, from actually touching any of the pieces. "Here," Sid said to her, handing her a pair of latex gloves. "You must not touch any of them."

"Thanks," Allison said, slipping on the gloves. One by one, she picked up the pieces and examined them. She had seen them all before, but it had been years. "My God!" she exclaimed, as she picked up a gold mask. "I totally forgot about this one. This Egyptian death mask was always one of my favorites, for sure."

She stared at the mask for several moments. Finally, she picked it up, stood, and then walked over to a wall mirror. Holding the gold mask in front of her face, she looked at her image in the mirror. She was, however, careful not to allow the mask to touch her skin. She then turned to Sid, and said, "You know, there was a time that I imagined myself being buried in a mask like this. But that was a thousand years ago."

"Shall I put it aside and return it?"

"No, it's fine. I'm sure that I could find a hundred pieces that I like just as much as this one. But isn't it beautiful?"

"Exquisite, I like it as well."

"Then *you* should keep it."

"No, I would prefer to stick to the plan. But thank you."

"You're not afraid of the so-called curse are you?" she asked, smiling for the first time that day.

"Not at all. I don't believe in such things. ... Besides, once it's melted down, and all impurities removed, it'll just be gold—nothing special. Where'll the curse be then?"

Allison then stood, removed the gloves, and put them in her purse. Sid had taught her to do that as well, because inside the gloves would be not only her fingerprints, but possibly DNA as well. They exchanged a few more words, and Allison prepared to leave. "I'll call with the final word on where and when, okay?"

"I will be waiting to hear from you."

With those parting words, Allison headed back to Bernadette's apartment. And, as in the case of her last meeting with Sid, and for the same reasons, Allison did not record her recollections of this meeting.

Chapter 32—Reginald has a better idea
1:23 a.m., Monday, December 26

Reginald had followed closely behind Jack as he left Penn Station. Just as Jack reached the street, his friend walked up beside him. "Where do we go from here?" he asked Jack.

"Not sure yet," Jack said. "That arrogant bastard said to go back to the hotel and wait for another call. He has one more thing for me to do before he will release Kate."

"Then that wasn't Kate in the coffee shop?" Reginald asked. All he had seen was Jack rushing past him on his way out of Penn Station.

"No," Jack answered. "It was a lookalike. And the bastard used her to send me a message. He shot her right there as she sat across the table from him. Dead."

"Thank God it wasn't Kate," Reginald said, visibly relieved. ... "But do you believe him? ... That he has something else for you to do?"

"Oh, I believe he has more hoops for me to jump through," Jack said. "But I don't trust him. The problem is that I don't have a lot of options, I have to play along, at least for now." Jack waited just a moment, then continued. "Reg, we have to keep moving. There's a dead girl back there. We've got to get outta here."

"Right, but are you sure you want to go back to the hotel?" Reginald asked, glancing west in the direction of Jack's hotel. "That's got to be a crime scene by now."

Jack did not respond right away as he led the way east up 34th Street.

"We do need to get your stuff out of there—and soon," Reginald said. "I am pretty sure that fellow bled out inside, and that it will take a while to determine why, but by morning they will be poking around there in a major way. Good chance it's already been determined a murder. They might suspect a mugging, but that will change."

"Hang around here for twenty or thirty minutes," Jack said. "I'll gather up my stuff. Then we'll catch a cab and get out of here."

"I have a better idea," Reginald said. "Give me your card and the remote for the lock, and I will grab your stuff."

"… Yeah, that works," Jack said. After he thought for a moment, he continued. "What can you tell me about these guys? Do you think Kate is still alive? Or are they just jerking me around?"

"I think she is alive, Jack," Reginald said. "And we've got to act on that basis. But I think you need to get a proof of life before we proceed."

"That's what I think, too," Jack replied, a little relieved to hear those words come out of his friend's mouth.

"I really wonder what they're up to now," Reginald said. "I should think that they would be content. They got what they wanted. I can't see how Kate's value to them would exceed that. She had what they wanted, and we got it to them. I thought that they would be quite happy never to see either you or her again."

"Exactly how I saw it," Jack said. "Unfortunately, I now have some unfinished business with them—no matter how this turns out."

"Are you sure you don't just want to see this go away?" Reginald asked. "After all, once we get Kate back, what's to be gained by going after them?"

"Have to, Reg. It's the principle of the thing, now."

"Principle has nothing to do with this. Jack, these are agents of a foreign government. They're acting on orders. They don't know you, and they don't know your daughter. They were simply told to get their hands on the message and to get it deciphered. That's it."

"Yeah, well, that's apparently not all they're after," Jack responded. "Now they want something more. And I'm going to give them something more. But probably not what they'd hoped for."

The two men walked north up Seventh Avenue a couple blocks, until Jack spotted an available taxi. "I'm gonna catch this cab. Nothing's open around here. I'll have him pull up in front of Penn Station in forty minutes." Jack reached into his jacket pocket and took out the remote for the lock and his room card. Handing them to Reginald, he asked, "Will that give you enough time? The northwest corner, by the drugstore? What do you think?"

"That works," Reginald said. He then headed west on 36th Street, heading toward the hotel, as Jack disappeared in the taxi.

When Reginald reached Eighth Avenue, he crossed over to the west side to avoid the area where he had killed the agent earlier. And, just as he had suspected, the area was cordoned off by the police.

Reginald then continued on down Eighth. However, when he was still over a block north of the hotel, a man suddenly walked up behind him. "Reg," the man said, catching Reginald by surprise.

Chapter 33—Roger intercepts Reginald

2:13 a.m., Monday, December 26

The man grabbed Reginald's right arm above the elbow with his left hand.

"Roger!" Reginald exclaimed. "What's going on? What are you doing here?"

"Just keep walking," Roger said. "Don't look back. Just keep going." Roger continued to squeeze Reginald above the elbow and directed him toward a waiting van with deeply tinted windows. As the two men approached, a side door on the van opened, and Roger virtually pushed Reginald in. He then followed Reginald, and the van sped off.

Reginald knew Roger well. Roger was a veteran of the Secret Service and was currently heading up the detail assigned to Allison.

"I need to pick up some things from the hotel," Reginald said, looking around for familiar faces, but finding only one—that was Roger's.

"You can't go back there," Roger told him. "You wouldn't make it through the front door. ... You were planning to clean out Handler's room, right?"

"That's right," Reginald said. "How did you know that?"

"Doesn't matter," Roger replied. "We've got a man in the hotel, same floor. He'll take care of it for you."

"He'll need this," Reginald said, showing the remote to Roger.

"And what's this?" Roger asked.

"Jack has a special electronic lock he uses," Reginald explained. "This remote unlocks it."

Roger then immediately dialed his associate inside the hotel. "Alex.

Handler has an auxiliary lock on his hotel door. He uses a little remote to deactivate it. RF or IR? Reg, is this RF or IR?"

"It's like a car remote. I would assume that it operates on radio frequency. Check it. Are there any LEDs?"

Roger checked it out. "I don't see an LED," he said.

"Then it has to be RF," Reginald replied, still not comfortable with his virtual abduction.

"There's an electronic lock on the door. It's apparently an RF unit," Roger told his friend on the phone. "If you're ready, I'll activate it. ... Great. Give me forty ... fifty seconds."

Roger switched on a linear amplifier, and slid the remote into it. He then activated the remote for a few seconds. "That worked? ... Great," Roger said to the man in the hotel as he disconnected.

"That did it," he said. "We probably blew off every radio station in the city, but we unlocked Handler's door."

"Okay," Reginald said. "So what's the deal? Jack is not going to be happy about this."

"Would he prefer you to be dead?" Roger asked. "Because that's what would have happened to you had you walked into the hotel."

"What's going on?" Reginald persisted.

"We know all about the meetings," Roger said. "We know about Mossad too."

Roger's revelation regarding his knowledge of the meetings caught Reginald by surprise. For a moment, he was unable to say anything. He knew better than to press Roger for more information, at least at this time.

"Is that who's waiting for Jack in the hotel?" Reginald asked. "Mossad?"

"No," Roger said. "At least not exactly."

"What does that mean?" Reginald asked.

"The agent you stuck earlier tonight has friends in the CIA," Roger said.

"He was working both sides?" Reginald asked.

"It gets very complicated," Roger said. "Suffice it to say, these guys know it was you and Jack, and they're not very happy right now."

"I had no choice," Reginald said. "If I wouldn't have taken him out, he would have killed Jack."

Roger did not respond to Reginald's comment.

"What's your role in this?" Reginald then asked.

"My role?" Roger repeated. "Well, tonight, this morning, it's to save your life—and Jack's. Beyond that, it doesn't really matter. ... We're going to drop you back off to meet Jack."

"How about his stuff?" Reginald asked. "He's not going to be very happy if I turn up empty-handed."

"I was going to have it delivered later," Roger said. Taking his cell, he called Alex back. "Hey, you got it packed up yet? Okay, this is what you do. Get it together. Don't have to be fancy. Just get everything. Head over to Penn Station. We'll stop in front of the drugstore, in ... let's say fifteen minutes. Can you make it by then? ... Great."

Roger then disconnected and addressed the driver. "Head west toward the Hudson. Time it so that you can swing back to Penn Station in fourteen minutes."

No one spoke for a few moments. Finally, Reginald broke the silence. "Roger, I do not think you are working for Al tonight. Is that a safe assumption?"

"I'm not going to discuss this with you, Reg."

"I would know if you were working for her," Reginald replied. "That means you're moonlighting for Bob. Right? Just what is his involvement in this?"

"Drop it," Roger said, obviously angry with Reginald prying into his business. "I saved your life tonight. You would be dead right now if it weren't for me. So just drop it."

"This is important," Reginald persisted. "If Bob is involved, and I now suspect he might be, then that changes the whole dynamic."

"Reg. I respect you," Roger said. "I respect what you have done in the past for Bob and Al. I know very well what you are capable of. I know what Jack is capable of as well. If we wanted you out of the picture, you and I would not be here discussing this right now. So just be grateful you're still alive, and let it go. There is nothing else you need to know. We are not at odds. Our goals might be different, but they are not mutually exclusive. As far as you're concerned, my only official capacity is protecting Allison Fulbright. That's it.

"Unofficially, that's none of your concern. Just be happy to know that the people I sometimes help wanted you and Jack to live. ... Hell, Reg, someday you and I will probably work together again. Isn't that the way it always seems to turn out?"

Just then the van they were riding in approached the place they were planning to meet Alex, to retrieve Handler's belongings.

"There he is," Roger said, pointing to a man standing on the corner with two suitcases. "Pull up right here," he told the driver. Roger opened the door to let his associate in. Alex tossed the two suitcases into the open door, then fell face first on the van floor, and rolled back onto the sidewalk. Blood was oozing from his mouth, and his open eyes evidenced dilated pupils. Alex was nearly dead—apparently stabbed just before the van had driven up.

Chapter 34—Reginald delivers Jack's luggage

2:31 a.m., Monday, December 26

Roger reached over and grabbed the two bags and Alex. He pulled the dying man into the van. "Reg, shut the damn door!"

He then yelled at the driver, "Get us the hell outta here. ... Damn it, Reg, I don't know what the hell is going on around here. My guy has had nothing to do with this. We're dealing with rank amateurs. That's exactly what they are. Before this thing is done, we're gonna have bodies all over the whole damn city. This makes no sense at all."

Reginald put his fingers on the dying man's neck to see if there was a pulse.

"No need for that," Roger stated. "It's always the same, lately. A double poke from behind—lungs and heart. With a damn ice pick, no doubt. What is this business coming to? Whoever used ice picks before? It's insane."

"Why did they hit your man?" Reginald asked.

"Good question," Roger said. "He must have been spotted coming out of Jack's room. Or maybe they placed a transmitter in one of Jack's bags. Your guess is as good as mine. It's a damn shame. Alex's wife just had a baby—last week. ... Maybe the week before. I can't wake her up tonight—not with this news. Not tonight."

"Roger, I'm sorry. Truly. The guy I took out today was one step away from sticking Jack—it was his second attempt. If I had not taken him out, at the very least Jack would have lost his daughter, if not his own life. If I had it to do over again, I would have done the same thing. It might have made it worse for you, but I did what I *had* to."

Just at that moment Reginald spotted Jack's taxi. "There's Jack," he said. "I've got to get him to meet us somewhere else. How about 34th and Broadway?"

Grabbing his cell, he quickly called his friend.

"Jack," Reginald said. "I've got your bags. I'm with a friend—a *mutual* friend. …We can talk about it later. Just have your taxi shoot over to 34th and Broadway. I'm in a dark van. … Great."

Roger gave the revised instructions to his driver and then responded to Reginald's apology. "I'm not blaming you for this," he said. "I know you try to avoid problems. All of us old-school guys are discriminating, if given a chance. It's these younger guys. And the Russians in particular. They've lowered the bar. It's nothing for them to destroy a train to kill the cook. It's like they just don't worry about collateral. As long as they hit their target, they just don't care who else dies."

"I thought you said we were dealing with Mossad, not the Russians?" Reginald said.

"Mossad is who your group is dealing with," Roger said. "And they're not nearly done yet.

"But the Russians have an interest here as well. They apparently have a lot to gain, or so I've heard. And a lot to lose. We're pretty sure it's the Russians who are holding Jack's daughter."

"We all have a lot to lose, don't we?" Reginald asked, trying to squeeze some information out of his old friend.

"I suppose you could say that," Roger answered, careful not to be drawn too deeply into this conversation.

"Could you have the driver pull up there?" Reginald requested. "I see Jack's taxi right behind us." He then checked out Jack's suitcases to be sure there was no blood on them. Finding a small blood smear on the handle of the larger bag, he grabbed a paper napkin that was in a fast food bag on the floor and cleaned it off. Reginald looked up, as Roger had the driver pull as close to the curb as possible, three car lengths in front of Jack's taxi.

"Rog, thanks for the help tonight," Reginald said. "I truly appreciate it. I realize I owe my life to you. Feel free to call one in anytime. I owe you."

Roger did not respond to Reginald's offer. Instead, he handed Reginald a set of car keys. "Here, take these," he said. "It's the black Expedition parked in a loading zone just east of here on 34th—south side. Should have the four-ways flashing. ... Alex isn't going to need it any more. I think you and Jack can put it to good use."

Reginald received the keys and thanked Roger.

"See ya around, old friend," Roger said. "Take care of yourself. And say 'hi' to my old buddy."

"Will do," Reginald said, jumping out of the stopped van, then reaching back to snatch Jack's bags. As Reginald unloaded the luggage, one of the men in the van was already closing the door. Simultaneously, the driver raced the engine and shot out into traffic.

By the time Reginald had made it back to Jack's taxi, Jack had circled to the rear and was ordering the driver to open the trunk to stash his luggage.

"Did you get it all?" Jack asked. "Did you get my lock?"

"Can't say for sure," Reginald said. "We've gotta get outta here, and quickly. I'll explain after we get going," Reginald said. "And we're not going to need the cab. We've got a car—thanks to Roger Minsk."

"Roger gave us a car? What's going on here?" Jack asked as he handed the driver three twenties and told him he wouldn't be needing him anymore.

Reginald gave a cursory look around to see if he was being followed. He did not set the suitcases down, but he did wait for Jack to pay his driver. "Down 34th a bit," he said. "Look for a black Expedition, on the south side of the street. Four-ways flashing. ... I'll explain it all in a bit. Let's find that car."

"You don't know whether or not you packed my mag lock?" Jack asked.

"*I* didn't pack it," Reginald said. "One of Roger's men, a man named Alex, packed your belongings."

"I don't understand," Jack said. "You didn't go up to my room?"

"Nope," Reginald answered, now with Jack close behind him. "Alex took care of it."

"He got past my lock?" Jack asked.

"He did," Reginald said, "but not without help. Roger used a linear amplifier from down on the street."

"From the street?" Jack responded. "... It was *that* easy? He must have had my remote, right?"

"Right. His equipment learned the frequency and amplified it."

"I'm working on one that uses both RF and IR—redundant," Jack said, snatching one of the cases from Reginald's hand.

"Well, I'm glad that Roger was able to get his man in," Reginald said. "The tragic thing is, it cost him his life. Alex, his operative, was killed just as he was delivering your bags to us. Right on the street, with an ice pick."

"Lunacy," Jack said, as both men picked up their pace. "This is pure lunacy. I've seen more agents killed in one day than I've seen in the past ten years. It's unnatural. That's what happens when there are so many different interests represented. Everyone has his own agenda, and no one trusts the other guy. The only option that makes sense is to whack the other guy before he gets you. It's insane."

"There it is," Jack said, pointing in the direction of a dark SUV fifty feet away.

Reginald hit the unlock button on the remote that was attached to the key Roger had given him. They deposited Jack's bags in the rear seat.

"Here," Reginald said, tossing the keys to Jack. "You drive."

The two men got in, and Jack switched off the four-ways.

They had not gone more than a couple blocks when Reginald spoke up. "Jack, I think we've got a tail."

Jack glanced back through his mirror. "Which one?" he asked.

"Two back, same lane," Reginald said.

"How sure are you?" Jack asked.

"Good chance," Reginald answered. "It was pulled over behind the Expedition when we got in. Two occupants. I got a pretty good look—would bet Eastern European."

"Russian? Is that what you're thinking?"

"Could be. But at least Old Soviet," Reginald replied. "Shall we see if I'm right?"

Jack suddenly jerked the steering wheel to the right, turning east off 6th Avenue and onto 38th Street. He sped a few hundred feet down the street, then hit the brakes and pulled over to a tight double park.

The car directly behind them did not follow, but the second car back did. As soon as it rounded the corner, it too pulled into a double park and stopped. The driver obviously had spotted them.

"Stay put for a minute," Reginald told him as he opened his door and began rapidly walking back to the car that had been tailing them. He was swinging a Glock at the end of his right arm.

Immediately that car screeched its tires, pulling up to where Jack had stopped. The mystery car lowered the passenger side window and opened fire on Jack with what appeared to be a Glock 10mm. Instinctively, Jack dived face-first onto the passenger seat. Expecting to be showered with broken glass, he threw his left hand over the back of his head. Hearing the car speed away, he quickly sat back up, seeking to get a look at the license plate. "RFT 176," he said, reaching in and pulling out a pen and paper.

Reginald then got in and asked, "We gonna go after them?"

Jack took a long look in his rearview mirror, then turned his smiling face toward his friend. "Haven't we had enough fun for one day?"

"Suppose you could say we did," Reginald replied, chuckling just a bit.

Jack shoved the car in reverse and sped back to the intersection. Even though it was a one-way street, he thought it wiser to go back to Sixth Avenue than to continue east and perhaps run into the car that had fired on them.

"What the hell these windows made of?" Jack asked.

"Pretty cool, don't you think?" Reginald replied. "I suppose it's standard issue in Roger's world."

"That Glock didn't even nick the glass," Jack observed, pushing against the window.

"I've heard that a nine or ten won't faze it," Reginald said. "But an AK will. And so will a .357 or bigger, … or so I've heard."

"I think that was a ten," Jack said. "At least that's what the muzzle looked like to me. But, hell, even a BB gun looks pretty imposing from the business end. Still, I'm pretty sure it was a Glock 10mm."

"Still could be Russians," Reginald said. "They like that Glock, too."

"Can't tell by what they're using," Jack said. "All that I can say for sure is that the shooter didn't look much like a Boy Scout."

"What do you mean?" Reginald asked.

"Short cropped hair," Jack answered. "Steel blue eyes. Pale blue. Dead eyes. I think Russian too."

Jack reached Sixth Avenue, carefully backed into it, and continued northward.

"Where, exactly, are we headed?" he asked Reginald.

"I've got an apartment on the Island," Reginald said. "Let's crash there. We can figure stuff out in the morning."

"Sounds good to me," Jack replied. "You still haven't told me the whole story. What's going on here? There's got to be more to this?"

"Jack, your daughter is alive and well," Reginald said. "I think the danger for Kate is past, at least for right now. And we are both still alive. As of this minute, life isn't good, but it's okay. We'll get some sleep, and I will go over everything with you in the morning."

Jack was not happy with Reginald's evasive answer, but he accepted it.

When they arrived at the apartment, Reginald had Jack drive past it and circle around the block.

"Checking for a tail?" Jack asked.

"Yeah," Reginald answered. "Pull into that parking lot for a minute. Let's turn the engine off, and just wait to see what shakes."

Jack followed Reginald's instructions. After a good five minutes, they decided that there was no one following them, so Jack started the car and drove back toward the apartment.

"That's it," Reginald said, pointing over at a very average looking row house. "But don't park right in front. Drive down a couple numbers, and park in front of that van. I want to check it out."

Jack pulled past the van, and backed into the parking place in front of it. Then both men got out. As Jack retrieved his luggage, Reginald circled the van. He was relieved to see that the license plate was local, and that there was a window sticker on the back promoting a local high school. Both men were comfortable thinking that they had not been followed, and that the van was not a threat, so they continued on into Reginald's apartment. They were both totally exhausted.

What they failed to observe, as they disappeared behind the apartment door, was a rusty, blue sedan parked directly in front of Reginald's apartment, but on the opposite side of the street. In that car were two very tough-looking men. They had crouched down while Reginald and Jack scrutinized the van.

Chapter 35—Rest eludes Jack and Reginald

3:27 a.m., Monday, December 26

Reginald knew just how concerned his friend was about Kate. Still, he thought it best to get some rest and begin dealing with the problem in the morning.

"Are you okay with this for now?" Reginald asked. "Shall we drop this subject for the night? Then attack it fresh in the morning?" Reginald realized that the two of them were totally spent.

"I know I'd like to get some rest," Jack said. "Tomorrow will get here too soon, regardless."

"When are you expecting to hear about Kate?" Reginald asked.

"I don't really have a specific time," Jack answered. "He just said to go back to the hotel and wait to hear from him."

"In case you didn't notice, we're not at your hotel. Do you have a plan?"

"I do," Jack said, "but it's going to take a little time to implement. I need to hear from Kate—to hear her voice—proof of life. And to find out what exactly it is that they're looking for. Then I'll go after her. They're not going to give her up without a fight. I'm convinced of that now. But, I agree with you, as long as they think they still need me, they will keep her alive."

"And unharmed. As long as they still need you, they will not hurt her," Reginald added. "Do you want to tell me what you have in mind, as far as a plan?" Reginald asked.

"Not really—at least not right now," Jack said. "But I am gonna need your help, that's for sure—and Roger's. It's just that I would like to wind up this day without getting my juices going more than they already are. You know what I mean. I'll explain it all later ... and tell you what I'm going to need from you."

"You got it, Jack," Reginald said. "Just name it."

"I knew I could count on you."

"You take the bed, I'll grab the couch," Reginald offered.

Jack carried his two suitcases into the bedroom, found his toothbrush, and disappeared into the bathroom.

As is typical of New York row houses, single-bedroom second-floor apartments have only one view, and that can be from the front or the rear. In the case of Reginald's apartment, his view was the street. Casually Reginald walked over to the window to give the street one last look before going to bed. Just as he parted the curtains with an index finger, he spotted a dim light come on from inside the car parked below. He quickly closed the curtains and pulled back.

"Jack, we got company," he said.

Immediately the light in the bathroom went out, and Jack emerged. "Are you sure?" he asked.

"Most definitely," Reginald replied. "Two men got out of a car. Parked right in front, but across the street. Both packin'. I'm surprised we missed 'em."

"How will they attack?" Jack asked. ... "Damn it. I'm just too tired to deal with this tonight. We're gonna have to move on. Can't waste them here—not by your apartment. Right?"

"I say we kill 'em *in* the apartment, and in the morning stuff them in the trunk of their car," Reginald said. "That way we can still get some rest."

"That's good with me," Jack agreed. "What the hell is wrong with these bastards? What's the point? They got what they were after. Now they're after more."

"I think it's a bit more than that, now," Reginald said. "Now it's a bit of a vendetta. And who's to say it's the same organization. Roger suggested that we're dealing with the Russians *and* Mossad. With different agendas. … He even suggested some freelancing—working both sides."

"Damn it, this sucks!" Jack muttered. He was angry.

"Let's just get this over with," Reginald said. "… What do you say?"

"Yeah, let's get on with it," Jack said. "From the rear? Is that what you're thinking?"

"That would be my approach," Reginald said. "They can get to the back of the building about three doors down. There's an alley. They've undoubtedly scoped it out."

"Is the apartment in the rear occupied?" Jack asked.

"Nope."

"Great, let's go occupy it," Jack said.

"Let's go."

Reginald looked over the keys on his chain and selected one. "Pays to have a master."

"I've got one of those at the end of my right leg," Jack replied.

"Mine's quieter," Reginald said, reaching the rear apartment before his friend. He unlocked the door, and the two very tired men entered a dark hall.

"They will come in together," Jack said. "Right?"

"Absolutely."

"Which do you like, living room window or kitchen?" Jack asked.

"Fire escape is off the kitchen."

"You duck in the bathroom, I'll slide into the living room," Jack said, taking charge as usual. "Damn it, I hope these sonsofbitches are in a hurry. I know I am."

Within a few seconds, Jack heard the window being forced. "Thank God," he silently mouthed. The apartment was furnished. So he was able to take a position behind a couch. His intention was to allow both men to enter the empty apartment. Then, as they made their way down the hall toward the bathroom where Reginald was waiting, Jack would take an offensive position. Reginald would shoot the first one and possibly the second. As the two attackers retreated, Jack would make sure they did not make it back to the fire escape.

For a few moments it looked as though all was going to go as planned. Jack made out the form of the first man. But the second did not immediately appear. Reginald waited until the last moment. Just as the first man reached the bathroom where he was hiding, Reginald fired off a round that caught the attacker in the neck, severing his spinal column. As the man slumped to the floor, he squeezed off a second round that caught his attacker right in the middle of his forehead.

Reginald had expected Jack to cut down the second man. But that did not happen. Instead, Jack ran to the fire escape, just in time to spot the second man reaching the ground.

"Damn it!" Jack muttered. "Nothing is going to be easy tonight."

Jumping over the body of Reginald's kill, he ran past his friend and out the door toward the street.

"Back in a minute," Jack said as he ran down the steps.

He knew the second man would be heading back to the car. Jack did not know exactly which car, but he did recall what Reginald had told him about its being across the street.

Taking a position behind a tree across the street from the apartment, Jack waited for the man to emerge from the alley.

This idiot is not gonna wait for anything, Jack thought. *He's gonna run right out of the alley, and jump in one of these cars. I should have a couple seconds.*

Just then Jack saw a man running toward him.

That's better than I hoped for, he heard his mind saying. *The bastard's running right up to me.* Realizing that his target would be wearing body armor, Jack had to make a good first shot—head or neck.

Must be he's headed toward this car, Jack thought. *That poor stupid bastard.*

Just as Jack suspected, the attacker ran right up in front of him. The car was parked so that the driver's door was traffic side. Just as the fellow reached down to open the door, Jack lunged forward, and sliding his gun across the top of the car, he put a round right into his attacker's face. The man screamed once as he slumped to his knees on the pavement.

Jack ran around the front of the car, a 2001 dark blue Chevy, and fired again. The second round struck the man in the temple, destroying both lobes of the brain. Even though he was pretty sure his first shot was fatal, Jack never took chances.

The man had dropped to kneeling position, with the right side of his face resting against the car door. It was as though he had turned to watch Jack's approach, but his eyes looked dead, and he never moved when Jack put a second round in his head.

Jack then opened the driver's door and shoved the man in. He noticed that the blood flow had slowed, indicating the heart had stopped. The man was definitely dead.

"To hell with this stuff," Jack muttered. "This is much too messy. We're gonna have to get outta here—right now."

Chapter 36—Time to go

3:39 a.m., Monday, December 26

Jack squeezed the car door shut after he had deposited the body. He quickly glanced around to see if there was any movement or lights from any of the surrounding windows. Seeing none, he was hopeful that his killing had gone undetected. He always used a muzzle suppressor, so he felt reasonably confident that his action might not have aroused attention.

But it didn't matter at this point. There was blood on the street and on the car.

"This has just got way too messy. It's time to go. Time to go," Jack kept muttering as he briskly headed back to gather up his belongings and to check with Reginald where they might spend the night.

Before he had even reached the front door, he spotted his two suitcases ready for him. Reginald had set them outside and then returned to the apartment.

Jack grabbed his bags and headed toward the Expedition. Before he reached the car, he heard Reginald racing up behind him.

"Thirty seconds," Reginald said.

Jack glanced back at his friend. He knew exactly what Reginald had been up to.

Just as the two suitcases hit the floor behind the driver's seat, an orange flash from the apartment they had just vacated illuminated the night.

"Seems to me you could have given us just a bit longer," Jack quipped. "You damn near singed my ass. And I think I see a hole in that fancy jacket of yours."

"You're just getting old … and slow. Ten years ago you would have been half way to New Jersey."

By the time the two men reached the end of the block, the row home was totally engulfed.

"I think it will take a couple hours before they figure out that wasn't you up there on the floor," Jack said.

"What did you do with number two?"

"He's sleeping it off in his car," Jack answered. "They'll find him quickly enough. Too much blood. Probably about the same time his buddies show up—but they won't get close enough to figure anything out. Fire department will have it roped off. Our problems should be finished for the night. What do you think?"

"We should be good for now," Reginald agreed. "But I was pretty optimistic before all this went down."

"Reg, I'm getting a little sick of hearing how good you think we are," Jack said. "We're lucky just to be alive. That was damn near a disaster back there. Look, Reg. We've got to start pulling this together, if we're gonna get Kate back."

"We need some rest—we're not thinking straight. I've got a buddy we can crash with," Reginald said. "He's an old friend from my college days. Doesn't live far from here, either."

"Hell, Reg, I didn't know you went to college," Jack said. His mood had changed dramatically. He seemed genuinely more relaxed. Up until they killed their two attackers, he had sensed that a problem still lurked.

"Thanks, buddy."

"Hey," Jack said, "if your friend will let me sleep in a corner, out of the cold, I don't care how you got to know him. I do not recall ever being this tired. I nearly took a nap waiting for that last bastard to make it back to his car."

"Aren't you about ready for a nice vacation? Once we get Kate and complete this contract?" Reginald said, himself beginning to relax just a bit. "After all this is over, let's see if we can't find something in Hawaii. Actually, I think any place south of Newark would do for me right now."

"I agree with that," Jack replied, briefly allowing his mind to wander. "How far away is this friend of yours? Do you have to warn him?"

"Twenty minutes at the outside," Reginald said. "No need to call, I have a key."

"When are you gonna give me the details about this contract?" Jack asked. "And how does this relate to the fix Kate is in? Just give me the short version. Before someone else tries to kill us."

"Okay, Jack," Reginald said, after he had paused a moment, "Here goes. The fact is that I need your help in a very special way."

"Special? All of the people who hire me consider my services to be special," Jack replied. "So what makes this time different? And how do these guys holding Kate figure in?"

Chapter 37—Reginald discloses the entire story

3:47 a.m., Monday, December 26

Reginald weighed his words, and then replied. "In every other job we've worked together, there has always been a specific target," Reginald said. "Once we had eliminated that target, then the job was over. We collected our money and went our own ways. This time we have a target, but this time our goal is to prevent that target from being killed."

"Who the hell is going to pay us for that?" Jack asked.

"No one is going to knowingly pay us for not consummating the hit. We will be paid for the hit, the same as always—except substantially more.

"But, instead of killing the target, we must see to it he lives. And the people who originally contracted us, they must be convinced that their best choice will be to make the whole thing go away. Once we pull that off, there will be no one motivated to come after us. They might not ever realize that they paid us *not* to fulfill the contract."

"Well, that makes no sense to me," Jack said.

"It's very tricky," Reginald explained. "But this is the gist of it. First I have to convince the conspirators that *you* are the best man to pull this job off—to make the actual hit. I've already explained to them that I was bringing in some very specialized help. So, they're ready for someone exactly like you.

"Second, because this is a hugely high-profile job, with a lot of exposure, I insisted on cash up front. So, once I have the cash in hand, I start making the actual hit untenable."

"How do you make that happen?" Jack asked. "Once you've already been paid for it?"

"That's where you come in," Reginald said. "I need to take you to meet the group. You are a very imposing, and very believable figure. We will take advantage of that reputation, and use it as leverage."

"I think I follow you on that, but I don't see how we get to walk away with the money, without doing the job," Jack said.

"That's where it gets convoluted," Reginald said. "Perhaps 'complicated' is a better word."

"You know I always like to keep it simple," Jack said. "I don't like complicated, and I'm not sure I even know the meaning of convoluted."

"Your role in this is simple," Reginald said. "All you have to do is just be yourself."

"Well, 'myself' is beginning to think this whole mess is outta control," Jack complained. "How many people have we already killed just to get to where we are? What is it now? Three. Have we killed three men? And what's the point? I'm sure they needed killing, but I don't think we are any closer to resolution. And I still don't have Kate back. Then there was that beautiful girl—the one they killed in the coffee shop. She's someone's daughter, too.

"Reg, you are an old friend—an old trusted friend. But I'm not liking what you got me into this time. Right now I'm not feeling very good about all this."

"In a sense," Reginald replied, "it does all seem futile. Three dead guys on their end. Alex and the girl on ours. Not planned. Not organized. The guys we killed had it coming—they were trying to kill us. And there might be more. We can't know how many more will come after us. It is unlikely that those last two were working alone. Someone must have sent them. And that same someone knew where we were going. … Hopefully we have got ahead of this, at least for a while.

"We need to get some rest," Reginald continued. "We are tired. Right now nothing seems like it makes sense. I understand that. But we have worked together many times through the years.

"And I know you trust me just as much as I trust you. To this point, I have counted on that trust to be your incentive. But I am pretty sure that by now I have burned up all that capital."

"I would agree with you on that," Jack said. "It's time for you to make some sense out of all this."

"Try this on," Reginald said. "The person we are going to save is the president of the United States."

"I figured that," Jack said. "But how difficult is it to just say no?"

"Not difficult at all," Reginald agreed. "But if I would have refused this job, someone else would have taken it. I would have been eliminated. And this country would have an even bigger problem on its hands. We both know that we cannot afford the power vacuum an assassination would create. It could easily result in a revolution.

"The plan we developed was a logical one. Just as the group figured, the only way to move Al into the Oval Office is to assassinate the seated president. That would put the VP in, and he would appoint Al to replace him. If the whole thing could be blamed on the right, then Al would win in a landslide in the next presidential. And she would likely carry both houses with her."

"That's the *whole* plan?" Jack asked.

"That's it," Reginald said. "And, in theory it could work. You and I both would like to see Al and Bob back in the White House. But the big problem with it is that at best it could easily result in a revolution. Even worse—total anarchy."

"Assassinations are never manageable," Jack said. "This one would be no exception. But I would agree with you on one thing, I don't think there is any way that Al can get in using any traditional methods."

"That's exactly right," Reginald said. "I think if Bob could run for a third term, he might win. But that can't happen. And Allison would have little chance in a primary, and no chance in the general election, given the mess we're in."

"Some of us believe that there might not be another presidential election. We look for chaos—anarchy. We think that's what Butler and his backers want—to turn this country into a Venezuelan clone."

"That's why she concluded that Butler needed to disappear," Jack said. "Unless there is an assassination, it does not bode well for Al."

"Frankly," Reginald said, "I am quite certain that she would be happy to eliminate anyone who might get between herself and the Oval Office. Just as long as she becomes president, that's all that matters to her. And that's all that matters to the other members of our group. At least that's how it looks to me."

"It would be revolution, wouldn't it?" Jack said, after thinking about it for a moment. "If the president were to be assassinated, and the public thought it was some right-wing kook, half the country could be torched. Talk about nuclear holocaust—that could be just as devastating. It would rock the nation to its core. It might never recover."

"Now you've got the picture," Reginald said. "The ensuing chaos would be enormous. It could be a bloodbath. The military would have to be called in, regardless of *Posse Comitatus*. We could easily devolve into a military state. That's what we are trying to avert."

"What did your group determine the outcome would be if the president is neither challenged nor assassinated?" Jack asked.

"It would be hard to predict all the ramifications," Reginald said. "But a few things are likely. For one thing, it would officially end Al's hopes of being president. And that is totally unacceptable to her.

"Also, as I said before, if Butler is convinced that he would lose in a primary, or to the candidate of the other party in the general, then he would suspend the election. We think that this is where it's headed.

"But the real bottom line here is this—Al believes she was robbed during the last presidential. So, whatever she has to do to get in, she feels justified in doing it. ... To hell with the country—it's all about her."

"So," Jack asked, "if we are able to put the kibosh on this assassination, the worst thing that is likely to happen is for a resurgence of the opposition? Is that what you are suggesting? Because, even if Butler does postpone elections, he will eventually lose the hearts of the people, and they will somehow toss him out. Isn't that the most likely scenario?"

"That's how I see it," Reginald said. "If all works out like I hope, I guess we will find out."

"You are beginning to sound like a radical, my friend," Jack quipped.

"Far from it, Jack," Reginald said. "I just fear what this country might look like after the assassination of this president."

"I know that you are not alone in this. Besides Roger, who else are you working with?" Jack asked.

"Actually, until just a short time ago," Reginald said, "the only one I knew about for sure was you."

"You've got to be kidding me," Jack said. "I've never known you to be the Lone Ranger."

"I'm in this over my head," Reginald said. "The mere fact that Roger showed up tonight suggests there are some powerful people involved, with similar goals to ours. He would not talk to me much, but it is highly likely that there are some rogue CIA, or maybe not so rogue, working with him. I don't know. I just know that he has support from somewhere."

"Damn, this is complicated," Jack said. "Or what was that big word you used, convoluted?"

"You've got no idea," Reginald said. "Sometimes I get the feeling I'm in the middle of a stupid Mel Brooks movie.

"The thing is, Jack, this whole plot is so big, it has attracted all sorts of international attention. For one thing, somehow the Israelis have found out about it. And they are doing their best to stop it. They don't want a power vacuum either. They would rather have this guy as president than take a chance on seeing America implode. And that's what they fear. So, they have got their little thing going too.

"Then we've got the Russians. They don't mind seeing the US devolve, but they figure that right now they have more to gain by playing along with the current president. That's who we were dealing with tonight, at least I think so. Remember that message you deciphered. The Russians stand to gain Alaska. All they have to do is back up our currency, and we give the Russians Alaska … after fifty years.

"I have seen no specific evidence, but I would not be surprised if the Chinese were somehow involved as well. At least behind the scenes. They stand to gain Hawaii under similar terms. It is one big confused mess."

"And we are all actually working toward the same end?" Jack asked. "The Russians, the Chinese and the Israelis? Roger and his buddies? Is that about right?"

"Right," Reginald agreed. "In some weird sense, that's just about right. But the Russians and the Israelis do not know what our goal is. As far as they are concerned, they think we are intent on killing the president."

"Really!" Jack exclaimed. "I can't wait to see what happens next. Do we have a game plan?"

"We do," Reginald said. "If we don't get killed first."

"And what might that be?" Jack inquired. "And how do we still get paid? … We do get paid, right? You're more altruistic than anyone I know, but you don't work for free."

Chapter 38—Reginald wins Jack's support
4:31 a.m., Monday, December 26

Jack was not yet ready to put this situation to bed, even though that's where he would like to have put his weary head.

"Let's see if I've got this right," Jack said. "We've got a plan. The Israelis have a plan—and theirs is different from ours.

"The Russians have a plan, too—or at least an agenda. They want to see this guy remain in office for another few years because they want to see their deal for Alaska go through. If this guy gets killed, that deal is off. And then there are the Chinese. They have a vested interest in how this turns out because they own the whole country. But they're not satisfied—now they want the deed to it.

"And they all view us, you and me, as their *enemy*? Because they think we're spearheading the assassination? Is that about how you see it?"

"That's it," Reginald said. "And the only one we really have to fear is Al. She is the most ruthless of all. If she had any notion of our intentions, we would be dead in a second, and someone else would be in here running with it. She will let nothing stand in her way."

"So, that means that we're getting paid for not killing the principal target," Jack said. "We just have to kill off all those other guys who don't know what we're up to? And at the same time make Allison think we're doing her bidding?"

"That's just about right," Reginald said. "Our main objective is to give every appearance of intent and preparation. But in the end, we turn the plot back on the plotters."

"What are the chances of getting caught?" Jack asked. "I'm not liking the idea of having so many players. Who's to say they keep quiet once this is over?"

"You do," Reginald said.

"And how does that work?"

"You are the one person that I know who can pull this off. No one has the guts to buck you. They all know what you're capable of."

"And they're right," Jack agreed. "They had better be scared of me. I will certainly give them reason to be scared. … Hell, I'm not liking this much at all."

"That's why I want you to come to the next meeting," Reginald said. "I want you to put the fear of God in them. You know, make a statement. Also, you will be able to scrutinize the situation, and see just who cannot be trusted to keep silent afterward."

"When is this meeting?" Jack asked.

"Coming right up, Jack. Tuesday evening. I'll pick you up for it."

Jack did not have time to think much about the upcoming meeting, because his phone rang.

Chapter 39—Jack gets his marching orders
4:40 a.m., Monday, December 26

Jack looked at his phone, then back at Reginald.

"Handler here," Jack said. His voice was strong and direct. He could assume a posture of confidence because, just as he had explained to Reginald, he did have a plan to get Kate back. And that plan had nothing to do with his performing any of the deeds his adversary was about to outline.

"You didn't return to your hotel like we told you," the man said.

"Put my daughter on," Jack said. "I need to talk to her before we go any further."

"*I'm* giving the orders here—" the man started to say.

"Put her on, or we're done," Jack interrupted.

"You will do as I say—"

That was all Jack heard, as he disconnected the call.

"What was that all about?" Reginald asked.

"I just hung up on him," Jack said. "I'm going to talk to Kate before anything else happens."

Twenty long seconds passed. Then the kidnapper called back.

"Kate," Jack said.

"She's coming, hang on," the man said.

After about a minute, a weak voice came on the phone. "Dad?"

"Hi, babe," Jack said. "You okay?"

"Yeah, I'm doing okay," Kate answered.

Jack could tell by his daughter's voice that she was actually doing pretty well. She sounded weak and exhausted. But she did not strike him as being distraught. There followed immediately a rustling noise as the kidnapper snatched the cell out of Kate's hand.

"Put her back in the basement, and make sure she is secured," the kidnapper told his partner. "And use some rope, or tape. Those wire ties are cutting off circulation."

That was great information for Jack to have. For one thing, he now knew exactly where in the building they were holding his daughter. And, because the kidnapper made a reference to a basement, that meant there was a pretty good chance that they had her in a house.

Another thing Jack learned was that they were concerned about her welfare. That did not mean that they would not kill her in a second, if doing so would serve their purpose, or if she no longer had value to them. But it did suggest to Jack that she would most likely be strong enough to participate in the escape.

"This is what we need you to do," the kidnapper told Jack. "We need you to put an end to this assassination nonsense. We know that you and your friend have been contracted to assassinate the president of the United States. We *know* that. But you must see to it that this plot is stopped. And if you ever want to see your daughter again, you need to convince us that you have successfully put it to rest."

"I have no idea what you are talking about," Jack said.

"Of course you don't," the kidnapper said. "But I am going to call you back on Tuesday night at ten p.m. You need to give me some assurance, at that time, that you have been successful. Do you understand me?"

"Tuesday's no good," Jack said. "I can't get anything done by then. Hold on." Jack placed his hand over the mouthpiece and addressed Reginald. "Reg, I know I'm meeting the group with you on Tuesday, but when will the next meeting be? The one after that?"

"Thursday," Reginald said. "I can make sure we meet again on the following Thursday."

Jack then turned his attention back to the kidnapper. "Thursday at ten p.m.," he said. "Call me at ten on Thursday. I'll have something for you then."

"Why Thursday?" The kidnapper asked.

Jack did not respond to the question. Instead, he simply said, "But you need to know ahead of time, we are not going to talk about anything unless you put Kate on first. I will expect to hear from her before anything is discussed."

With that, Jack disconnected the kidnapper and again looked over at Reginald. He stared at his friend for what seemed an uncomfortable length of time.

Finally, he said, "We're on."

Chapter 40—Reginald notified

2:00 p.m., Monday, December 26

Once back at Bernadette's apartment, Allison sat down in her favorite chair to gather her thoughts. "I need to contact Reg today and set up delivery of his payment," she said aloud, at the same time writing "Reg" on a sheet of paper she had brought over to the chair with her.

She then thought to herself, *I wonder if I should set the time and place for delivery, or should I leave that up to Reg? Probably best if he determines that, because we are a little early, and he will have to establish the means to transport and store it. That will take time.*

Can that be correct? she thought to herself, as she scribbled some numbers down on her piece of paper. *Could one hundred million actually weigh three tons? And that's only if it is twenty-four karat—much of this gold is in the form of artifacts and so weighs substantially more than pure gold. There could easily be over four tons.*

Allison then took her cell phone and called Reginald. "Hi. We are ready to deliver. We could arrange for it later today, or tomorrow morning. I would like this to be done before our next meeting. What do you suggest?"

"I really cannot do anything about it today. But tomorrow morning would be fine. Let me know when the truck is on the way, and I will direct it to the drop. Shall we say seven a.m., west side of the city? South of 36th?"

"That works. Also, the meeting will be tomorrow evening—same place and time as the last one. I do not think it prudent to ever discuss this matter in front of the whole group. You should take your time checking it out. If you have questions or concerns, we will deal with them at a later time. We should not talk about it until Wednesday. I'll call you."

"Right. See you tomorrow evening."

As soon as she disconnected, she called Sid back. "The delivery is set for tomorrow morning at seven. You get the truck on the road, and I'll let you know exactly where to drop it off. I do know that it will be in the city, on the west side—Midtown Manhattan."

Sid wondered if he would need to get started earlier, but Allison assured him that a one-hour head start would be more than adequate. And she disconnected.

Allison realized it would take Reginald's people a fair amount of time to determine the actual value of the gold, given that much of it was not in the form of bullion. She was not concerned, however. For one thing, she knew the level of Sid's commitment to get his job done perfectly. In fact, she was positive that Sid could accurately calculate the value of any given item in her vault. In cases where the gold content might be in doubt, Sid would intentionally undervalue that piece.

In the end, when Reginald's people were finished evaluating the gold, she knew they would be pleased. The actual value would undoubtedly be closer to one hundred and five million dollars—five percent over expectations. Perhaps even more.

"You never try to cheat a hit man," she said to herself again, smiling broadly.

"I had better get back and be Allison for a while," she groaned, as she began changing back into Allison's clothes. "My aides are going to be calling for a doctor before long … or the coroner."

Chapter 41—The gold delivered

5:02 a.m., Tuesday, December 27

First thing on Tuesday morning, around five o'clock, Reginald called Allison and told her he was ready to take delivery. "Shall I talk to you about it, or should I talk directly to the driver?" he asked.

"I'm going to have you talk directly to my guy," she told him. "I'll have him give you a call within ten minutes."

"Sounds good."

Allison then called Sid, getting the same female voice on his recording. "Please call my friend. He is ready to take delivery," she said, giving him Reginald's phone number. She then disconnected. She knew Sid would be waiting for her call and that he would not delay in calling the number she had left him.

Just as planned, Sid immediately called Reginald. "I'm loaded and ready. Where and when would you like it?"

"I'm all set at my end. How long out are you from 29th and Tenth?"

"I can be there by seven, maybe a little earlier, depending on morning traffic."

"Let's shoot for that. If it's going to be later than seven, give me a call."

"Okay. What am I looking for?" Sid asked. Sid would be making the delivery himself, by himself. Something this important could not be assigned to others, nor did he feel this job should even be shared by others. Sid knew that at this stage of an operation of this magnitude, too many things can go wrong. He knew he needed specific instructions for unloading the crates, and he was going to need help. He assumed that this would all be understood, but he wanted to make sure. "I will be coming by myself in a fourteen-foot box. I'm going to need a dock and a forklift. And some muscle."

"I assumed that. What is it in?"

"Six wooden shipping crates, on three-foot pallets."

"Will standard docking do?"

"Yes. I assume you will want to weigh and examine the merchandise. If I'm there at seven, I would like to be out before nine. Does that sound right to you?"

"Perfect. This is what you will look for." Reginald gave Sid the address for a small warehouse on 29th Street, just west of Tenth Avenue.

"Remember that 29th runs west, so you will have to come in on 10th. Look for an Irish flag hanging over the door in the 500 block. That will be it."

"That will work just fine. If I have any questions or problems, I'll call you. I will give you a heads-up ten minutes out."

"I'll be waiting," Reginald responded. "And could you bring one extra pallet and empty crate?"

"I've got one of each on the truck," Sid replied. He assumed that whoever was receiving the gold would want to weigh an empty pallet and an empty crate to get a general idea of the weight of the gold contained in the shipment. Sid knew better than to short-ship. He knew beyond any doubt the weight and gold content of every item, and he made certain to provide greater than agreed upon value. He knew that the shipment would eventually be accurately scrutinized for value by a professional, so there was no point in creating any sense of mistrust on delivery. Sid was wise in these matters.

Reginald was a pragmatist. He knew that even a fourteen-foot box truck could have a problem maneuvering 29th Street on a weekday morning. But, he also knew that the best time to make such a delivery would be right when all the businesses were receiving deliveries.

So, to make it all easier, he had his friends from the city ribbon off a section of the north side of 29th Street, and he had his own semi-truck drop off a short trailer at that location. This was an unusual trailer, in that it had a roll-up door at both ends, so that when detached from the tractor it could be loaded or unloaded from either end.

Reginald's plan was to have the delivery driver pull past his trailer, then back up to the front roll-up. He would then drop a ramp between the delivery truck and his trailer.

This short trailer had one other special characteristic—an onboard overhead electric crane. This crane had an extendable track, which would allow Reginald to attach it to the roof of Sid's truck. Using the crane he could then transport each pallet across the ramp and onto a scale. He would then subtract the weight of the empty pallet and crate, thereby arriving at the approximate weight of each crate of gold.

While one of his people would roll the crane back to load another pallet, two of his men would transfer the gold into the empty crate, logging the individual pieces as they did.

Just as promised, Sid called Reginald to announce that he was on Tenth Avenue and should be arriving within eight to ten minutes.

"Describe your truck," Reginald said.

"It's a white fourteen-foot Mack. Older. Very dirty. I will turn on my four-ways when I hit 29th."

"That works," Reginald said. He then attached a small Irish flag to the east end of the trailer, and with the help of one of his men, removed the yellow ribbon that had cordoned off the area to the west. He did leave the cones in place, to prevent someone else from challenging.

As Sid's truck approached, Reginald's men removed the cones and directed the docking maneuver. It was a tight fit, and it took several attempts, but Sid eventually backed his truck up to within inches of Reginald's already-opened trailer. One of Reginald's men then opened Sid's roll-up door and directed Sid to back up tightly against the parked trailer.

Sid remained seated in his truck. None of the men ever used names. It was not a problem; they had all engaged in similar operations before.

Sid rolled down the window and handed Reginald a list of each crate's number and its contents. The men then positioned the ramp and engaged the crane, and the exchange began.

Sid recognized that Reginald and his men had no need of his help. If they needed something from him, they would know where to find him.

When Sid had originally acquired the pieces for the Fulbrights, he attached labels to each, listing weight and purity. So Reginald's people simply logged those labels, knowing that everything would be more carefully examined later. All they were guarding against was a careless error. Had they known Sid, they would have realized that he was not capable of such.

After about an hour, Reginald came around to the passenger door of Sid's truck and let himself in. "Looks good on the surface," he said to Sid. "But I am curious as to why so much of it is in pieces of art. I had anticipated more bullion."

"The actual artistic value of that load could very well be double its gold value. It's up to you how you choose to deal with it. None of the pieces appear on any lists. They can be bought and sold with impunity."

"That's interesting," Reginald replied. "Understand, I am not complaining. I just had my assumptions. And if your numbers are correct, and my people suspect that they look legitimate, you overpaid by nearly four percent."

"At least," Sid responded. "But that's the way it should be, don't you think?"

"That's a lot of money," Reginald said. "Are you looking for something?"

"Certainly not," Sid replied, just slightly offended. "My client always requires that we make good on deals such as this. You will be very pleased when you get the final tally. You're getting very good value."

"Is this a good number to call you back on? If I need to reach you?" Reginald asked.

"No, there will be no reason to call me. If you have issues, you can deal with my client," Sid told him. "I think we're done here. Right?"

"We are. It was nice doing business with you," Reginald said, as he let himself out of Sid's truck.

"It was a pleasure," Sid responded.

Neither man attempted to shake hands, as might have seemed customary—not when they first met, nor on parting. It never seems natural to offer a handshake while wearing latex gloves. As Reginald closed the passenger door behind him, he did offer a smile and a wave of his hand, and Sid responded in kind.

As he drove off, Sid called Allison and informed her that the delivery had successfully been accomplished. He then removed the SIM card from his phone and cut it into several pieces with a pair of wire cutters.

Before the end of the day, this fourteen-foot dirty Mack truck would be stripped and destroyed and left in pieces at a greasy little chop shop in South Newark.

Chapter 42—The third meeting

5:49 p.m., Tuesday December 27

Just as at the second meeting, James arrived first, opened up the cottage, and aired it out. And, of course, he swept the entire area for bugs and transmitters.

Again, Allison was the second to arrive. Initially, she started to remove the battery from her cell, then reconsidered and just left it in her vehicle. Just as at previous meetings, James thoroughly wanded Allison. And, she in turn passed the wand over James's entire torso, without a peep from the equipment in both cases.

"Jerry's not going to be coming tonight," he informed Allison.

"What!" she exclaimed, more angry than surprised. "What's the deal with him?"

"He had a medical emergency," James said. "His implant is acting up. Apparently he developed an infection and had to be hospitalized."

"When did he call you?" Allison asked, trying to determine whether she should be angry with James for not notifying her earlier.

"Thirty minutes ago. He was at the hospital," James replied. "It was weird. My phone rang, and it did not sound as though anyone was at the other end. Then, finally, Jerry answered. He said that he could not hear a thing, and that he was at the hospital having his equipment worked on. He apologized several times. He said something about an infection, and that he was running a high temperature. He asked me to go over business with him later, maybe tomorrow, if he gets out. Then he apologized one more time and disconnected. He sounded very distressed, as though it might be serious."

"Damn," Allison said. "We have some very important business to conduct tonight. Jerry should be here."

"Al," James tried to console her, "Jerry's on the same page with us. I know he is. And I promise I will stay on top of this. I will meet with him as soon as he is able, and feel him out. I will not provide him any information that I do not think he is ready for, just in case he balks. But I know Jerry, and I know he is good with it."

"You and I will meet with him, when he is able. I just wish he could be here tonight. He is the only one that Steve really likes." Allison paused for a moment, as she gathered her thoughts. "I agree with you that Jerry is into this thing with both feet. And that he is very loyal. But I'm going to miss him tonight, with Steve."

"I know what you mean. I will make every effort to be at the top of my game. Maybe I can take up the slack, when it comes to Steve. Reg just has a problem with gays. He's always been that way."

"Steve isn't gay. He's just not the sort of guy that Reg likes," Allison said. "Just pay some serious attention to whatever Steve contributes. And try to be a buffer between him and Reg."

"I will do my best," James responded. "I think you might be forgetting something here. Reg got paid earlier today. Right? He's going to be on his best behavior tonight. That is a hell of a lot of money he's going to have at his disposal. I'm sure a lot of it will work its way right into his pocket. He might surprise you a bit tonight."

"We'll soon know, won't we?"

Just then there was a knock on the door. "James, it's Reg. And I've brought a friend."

James looked over at the door, then back at Allison. "What is going on?" he said in Allison's direction. She did not utter a word. Dumbfounded would have been an understatement.

Chapter 43—*The surprise visitor*

6:02 p.m., Tuesday, December 27

James continued to stare at Allison, seeking to divine her reaction, "Al, wait here, and I'll check this out," he said.

"Do it," she said, reaching around under her jacket, momentarily resting the palm of her right hand on the grip of a five-shot hammerless Airlite Smith and Wesson .38 Special. "Don't let them in until you report to me."

"Right."

James walked over to the door and went out to see whom Reginald had brought to the meeting with him.

"Reg," James inquired, "what's this all about?"

"Sorry to spring this on you, especially on Al, but I had no choice."

"What does that mean?"

"James, this is Jack, Jack Handler. He has been a trusted associate of mine for over a quarter of a century. I have never engaged in a big job without him."

"I don't care who he is. … Reg, you knew the rules—Al did not even want us to *talk* to anyone outside the group, much less bring an outsider to a meeting." James paused for a moment and looked at Jack. "No offense, Mr. Handler, but we—Reg and I—had an agreement."

"Jack is not a stranger," Reg explained. "Al knows him. Bob and she introduced him to me. They knew him from the Louisiana days."

"Well, I will check this out with her. But even so, why is he here?"

"If there is going to be one instrumental figure in this, it is going to be Jack. What we are doing here cannot be done without his total participation. At least, it can't be done right. Jack has all the right contacts, and the right expertise—"

"Granted," James interrupted. "But that does not explain why he is here *tonight*. Of course, we expect you to use the right people. But why is he here, and why didn't we know in advance that you were considering this?"

"Fair question," Reginald answered. "He needs to know who he is working with in this. He needs to know that we understand the gravity of what we are doing. That we are not going to leave him hanging out there, blowing in the wind."

"And you couldn't convince him? ... Isn't he working for you?"

"Jack and I are working together, just like you and I are working together. He has never worked *for* me. And I will tell you something, if I were in his place, I would be doing the same thing. His life, his family, and his fortunes are on the line. He stands to lose everything if any one of us drops the ball. I can assure you that it is not yet even a given that he will agree to work with us. We still have some selling to do. But I can promise you that he's the best there is, and we need him."

"And what if he decides he does not like us? What then?"

"Then he's gone. When I tell you that he is the best there is, I mean it. He could have me put away for life in this country, and executed in half a dozen others. If I screwed with him, I'd be dead before dinner. So, when I tell you we need him, I mean just that. If we want this job to be done right, we need what he brings to the table. He can make things happen like no one else can."

"We thought *you* were that guy, Reg," James said. "Are you now telling me that we were wrong?"

"Not at all," Reginald said. "But we need Jack, and he needs to know all of us. It's that simple."

"Give me a minute, I need to consult with someone," James said as he turned to walk back into the cottage.

Allison was waiting for him. "Hell, yes, I know Jack Handler. I thought he was dead. He's supposed to be dead. And, yes, he was, perhaps is, the best. I'm not happy with Reg for bringing him here unannounced. But we are fortunate to have someone of his caliber involved on our side. That sonofabitch knows how to get stuff done." Allison's positive response surprised James.

"Shall I have them come in?" James asked, as he walked over to pick up the wand.

Allison did not immediately answer. Finally, she said, "Yes, tell them to come in. He's already here. Besides, that bastard has enough on both Bob and me to put us away too."

James was visibly shaken by this whole transaction. He was uneasy not only because Jack was forced on the group by surprise, but also because he had never been aware someone like Jack was lurking in the shadows. He always thought that he was privy to everything that occurred on the scurrilous side of the Fulbrights.

Walking back out of the door, he closed it behind him. "We're going to have to check you fellows out," he said.

"I've already given Jack a heads-up about this," Reginald said.

James continued toward them with the wand. "Reg, could you move over a few feet? I want to get a good reading on your friend first." James then passed the wand up and down both of Jack's legs and over his torso. "We're good here," James said, taking a few steps to the side and repeating the procedure with Reginald. "Okay, you're both good. Let's go in and see Allison."

James opened the cottage door and motioned for Reginald and Jack to go in ahead.

"Al, great to see you again," Jack said as his eyes met Allison's.

"Well, I can't say that I'm really surprised to see you again," she said, not smiling. "But I did not expect it to be at this meeting."

"That's my fault, Al," Reg said. He knew he was operating from a very strong position. First of all, he had the money—all the money. There was nothing Allison nor any of the others could do about that at this point. Second, Reginald knew that Allison was well aware of Jack's considerable credentials. Third, Reginald always did what he regarded as necessary. He never acted out of haste or fear. In this case, he knew that Jack would not work with him without a good look at the whole group. And fourth, as far as that group was concerned, Reginald was the action figure—the others were thinkers and talkers. But in the end, they were going to look to him to get the job done.

It was a fact—Reginald had every reason to feel good about his position in the group.

Plus, most important of all, Jack needed the opportunity to intimidate the other members—especially Steve and Jerry. They were the two Jack had doubts about.

Allison knew better than to go any further with her complaint. She had said what she did to drive home the point for James's benefit. She knew that as far as this meeting was concerned, she was no longer the boss. The eight-hundred-pound gorilla that Jerry had alluded to at the previous meeting had become anthropomorphized. And his name was Jack Handler.

Just then Steve opened the door. Before he had taken two steps into the cottage, he took a long look at Jack. "Jerry, you sure as hell have changed. Did you get a face implant this time?" He paused, and then said, "Well, I suppose this means no hamburgers tonight." He then waved a quick hand, turned, and walked out of the cottage and was headed back to his car.

"I was afraid of this," Allison said, walking after him. "Steve, hang on for just a moment."

Steve had already taken a dozen steps toward his car. At first, he did not want to stop. Then he had second thoughts. He realized that if he left this meeting, right now, he would be killed before he reached his car.

"Al, what is this all about?" Steve said, turning to face Allison as she walked briskly toward him.

Chapter 44—*The gravity of the plan*
6:10 p.m., Tuesday, December 27

Allison quickly caught up to Steve. "It caught me a little by surprise too. There is a lot going on here this evening. You need to turn around and come back in. It's all okay," Allison said, doing everything she could to mollify Steve.

Allison knew that she would not be able to let Steve leave. Even though Reginald did successfully challenge her authority by bringing Jack to the meeting without her knowledge or permission, she knew she must try to re-establish her leadership, at least in Steve's eyes. When she took that first step outside the cottage in pursuit of Steve, she was prepared to kill him on the spot had he not stopped.

Now, if he still persisted in his refusal to rejoin the group, she would do whatever was necessary.

Fortunately, Steve also appreciated the gravity of the situation. He was angry and more than a little baffled. "I thought we agreed that nothing like this would happen," he said to Allison in an obvious effort to see the matter resolved.

"That's right. You're correct. But this is okay. The gentleman with Reg is an old friend of mine, and of Bob's. I was not expecting Reg to bring him to the meeting, but for what we're planning to do, we are going to need this man. He is the best there is, and he also has to feel comfortable with us."

"What's up with Jerry? Isn't he coming?" Steve inquired, still not totally convinced he should remain. "Is he okay?"

"That depends on what you call okay. Jerry is in the hospital tonight with an infection. His implant is acting up, and this was an emergency. He called James and informed him."

"Can we still conduct business here without him? How will that work?"

"I will deal with Jerry later tonight, or tomorrow. Don't worry. Right now, we are going to lay some groundwork that primarily involves Reg and Jack Handler," Allison said.

"Jack Handler?" Steve repeated. "That name sounds familiar. How do I know him?"

"He was a close associate of Bob's back in Louisiana and also in the White House. Although he did not actually come to the White House, at least not as far as I am aware. He took care of special issues for Bob."

"That's how I remember him," Steve said. "I never met him before, but I remember hearing about him. He's a pretty dark figure, from what I've heard."

"He's a loyal asset," Allison said, correcting him. "People like him are indispensable in an operation such as this."

"And just what sort of operation is this?" Steve asked.

Allison, realizing that Steve had not been briefed on any of the recent matters she had discussed with James and Reginald, replied, placing her left hand on Steve's shoulder as she did. "That's what we have to discuss tonight. Shall we head back in and get this going?"

It was not until that point that Allison was fully confident that she was not going to be forced to terminate this long-time associate. But just as she mouthed those last words, Steve began nodding his head affirmatively. She was not sure whether he was buying into what she was saying or if he was contemplating what the alternative was going to be were he to continue walking toward his car. At any rate, Allison turned and began to walk back to the cottage, and Steve followed.

As they entered the cottage, James greeted Steve with the wand and proceeded to screen him. Afterward, he led him over to the group and suggested they all be seated. Allison sat down first, then the rest followed.

"Steve, this is Jack Handler," Allison said. "He's going to be working closely with Reg on some important matters." She then turned to Jack and introduced him to Steve. Neither Steve nor Jack verbally acknowledged one another, but their eyes briefly met.

Allison paused for a moment, then continued. "James, would you please inform the group about Jerry's predicament?"

"Jerry is in the hospital tonight," James said. "He is suffering complications, an infection, actually, resulting from his cochlear implant. He will be okay, but right now he is not able to hear anything, and we all know infections are nothing to toy with."

"Jack, you know Jerry, right?" Allison inquired.

"Not on a personal level," Jack answered, "but Reg informs me that we may have met."

"Steve," Allison said, looking directly at him. In fact, everyone's attention was on Steve. Every person in the room knew that Steve's reaction to what was about to be discussed was pivotal. Much had been discussed apart from him, and a great deal of money had already been paid, but nothing was going to happen if Steve did not get on board with the plan. And not just on board, but wholeheartedly behind it. Already he knew too much to walk out, and his end of the job could not now be handled by anyone else.

Again, Allison paused. Finally, after an uncomfortably long period of silence, she continued. "Guys, stop me if you think I am not explaining this very well, or if I am stating something with which you do not agree, but I am going to bring Steve up to speed."

"Reg, James and I met for a brief time after our last meeting. We discussed the matter that Jerry alluded to. When Jerry stated that an eight-hundred-pound gorilla had just entered the room. I think we all understood what he was saying. Is that correct, Steve?"

Steve sat there for just a moment, then responded. "Okay, let's see if I'm getting this right. The three of you met to discuss just how and when we were going to assassinate the president? Is that about right?"

Steve's candor caught them all by surprise. Jack looked at Reginald, then both looked down. James nodded his head affirmatively and said, "I think you've got the idea."

"Then let's cut the crap and get on with this."

"Can I assume that we are, at this point, all on the same page?" Allison asked. She then went around the table. "James?"

"Yes."

"Reg?"

"Yes."

"Jack?"

Jack looked down and did not respond verbally. He did nod his head affirmatively.

"And, Steve, you've already expressed yourself in this regard."

"I just wish Jerry was here," Steve said. "He's always the voice of reason."

"I will talk to Jerry myself," Allison said. "If there are any issues I will get back to you with them. Otherwise, assume all is okay. Is that agreeable?"

Three of the men responded affirmatively, only Jack remained silent to her request. "Jack," Allison said. "Do you have something to add here?"

"I know very little about Jerry, or his role. I would like to have a sit-down with him before I get too involved."

"Telephone good enough?"

"I'd be more comfortable if I had a chance to talk to him. There's a lot riding on each one of us. If you're going to meet with Jerry, I'd like to at least call you while you're there."

"Very well," Allison agreed. "I'll reach you through Reg with details."

Allison paused for a moment to get Jack's reaction. Jack looked over at Reginald, then turned his face toward Allison and nodded affirmatively. This indicated that he would be amenable to running the meeting with Jerry through Reginald.

"Okay," she said, "then I would like to have Reg go over what he is intending, and what he will be expecting from the rest of the group."

"This is where we are at," Reginald began. "In the very near future there will be a successful assassination of the president. It will be violent. When it happens, it will look like a group with radically conservative connections pulled it off. Are you with me so far?" There were no objections, so Reginald continued, "Okay, now when this happens, we will have a media window of twenty-four hours to make it stick to this conservative group. There will be strong enough evidence from the start to make it plausible. But, that's where you come in, Steve."

To this point, Steve had sat in his seat intently listening but not contributing. "What exactly do you expect from me?" he asked.

Reginald had surprised everyone by the deference he was showing Steve at this meeting. It was as though Reginald was wishing to put aside his animosity and begin to constructively work with him. "You've got two days to outline your blitz. Allison has not suggested it, but I would assume that we are going to meet again on Thursday. Is that correct, Al?"

"Originally I was leaning toward a Tuesday meeting. Next week. But Thursday, I think Jerry could make that. Does that sound okay?"

"It would be fine with me," Reginald said. "I think that Thursday would be perfect, at least from my standpoint. How about the rest of you? Does Thursday sound good?"

Once Allison had stated that she wanted to meet next on Thursday, compliance was a formality.

"Thursday sounds perfect," James said. "Jerry did say he could make it on Thursday."

"Thursday is fine for me," Steve agreed.

"Okay, then, Thursday it is—same place," Allison confirmed.

"So, Steve, this is what I need you to do," Reginald continued. "I need you to put your ducks in a row. You have to nail it down, immediately—your plan of action, that is. I cannot emphasize strongly enough just how critical the first hours are going to be, as far as media readiness."

"I get the point," Steve interrupted. "I will need all the details you can provide, in advance. I need to line up the appropriate interviews, with the right reporters. I would like the event to occur on a Wednesday evening. That would give me the full news cycle running through the weekend."

"Can't guarantee a Wednesday event, but I will work on it," Reginald said.

"If I have all day Thursday to roll it out, I can blitz the media. I can keep ahead of it through Friday, not allowing the radio talk shows to spin until the following week. The whole weekend would be delicious."

"Like I said, I cannot promise you that. Timing is largely contingent on the president's schedule. I will work hard to give it to you on a Wednesday, if I am able," Reginald said.

"But, you need to be prepared to take what you get. At least you will have some time to lay the groundwork, if you start now. You should work up a flexible contingency plan, if the event ends up taking place on a less desirable day of the week. As I perfect the details, I will let you know. I will need to be able to reach you twenty-four-seven. Is that a problem?"

"Not at all. The more you give me, the better job I will be able to do," Steve replied. "I do have a question for Mr. Handler." Steve then looked over at Reginald's associate and asked, "Is it okay to call you Jack?"

Jack did not answer. In fact, he did not even raise his eyes or look in Steve's direction.

"Jack," Steve continued, "exactly what is your role in this?"

Jack did not immediately respond to Steve's question, he just continued to stare down at his sizeable, weathered hands, which were folded on the table. Then, with a sudden burst of affected anger, he sprang to his feet, the back of his legs flinging his chair across the room and into the wall behind him. Everyone at the table snapped their attention to him. Leaning across the table, he grabbed Steve by the shirt and drew him out of his chair. And then, with his face only a few inches from Steve's, he said, "You listen to me, sonny, I'll tell you what I want you to know, when I want you to know it. I will never answer to you. Never! If you need something to make you feel better, you talk to Reg or James or your buddy Jerry. But don't you *ever* mouth my name again, not as long as you live. Do you totally understand me?"

Steve did not look directly at Jack. Instead, he just looked down and nodded his head.

"I'm talking to you, sonny. I asked you a question. Now you are going to look into my eyes and tell me you understand what I just said to you. I hate having to repeat myself. Now, you tell me, do you understand what I'm telling you?"

Steve looked up at Jack, focused his eyes on Jack's eyes, and said, "I understand completely what you are saying, and that will be fine with me."

"And that goes for the rest of you," Jack threatened, pointing his index finger at the noses of all those seated at the table, much like an angry man pointing a gun. "If any of you think you have something to say to me, talk to Reg. As far as anyone here is concerned, Jack Handler does not exist. ... Is there anyone in this room who does not understand what I just said?"

After a few nervous moments, Allison responded, "I think we all can get along with that."

"I will assume the lady has spoken for each one of you," Jack said as he retrieved his chair and slammed it up to the table. He did not sit down.

Then Reginald continued. "Now, to follow up a bit, I will be giving Steve all I can for his preparation. I have almost all the right people lined up. This is not going to be a slam dunk, but a job of this magnitude is not much more difficult than a small one—at least not in the preparation and execution. The big difference comes immediately afterward and down the road. I cannot emphasize enough just how important I view Steve's role in this. And, Steve, I realize that you and I have not always hit it off. But we are going to work together on this. I respect your position here, and I will help you in every way I can. I want you to feel free to contact me whenever you wish. And I assure you that I will be helpful. But, as my friend pointed out, you will be working through me, period. Does that work for you?"

"That's fine," Steve replied.

"On second thought," Jack said ... "about Jerry, I really do not want to be directly engaged with him. I would prefer to have Reg handle that as well." Then Jack looked over at Allison. "Does that work out?"

"That's fine with me, if it works for Reg," she said. "I will call him tomorrow to work out details."

At that point, Jack, who had remained standing, suddenly placed his right foot on the table. He then proceeded to very deliberately untie his shoe, tighten the strings, and retie it. He made sure that everyone in the room spotted the Walther semi-automatic pistol that was strapped to his calf.

"We're done here, right?" he said, as he turned and walked toward the door. And then, without looking back, he loudly announced, "Don't worry, I won't be coming back to your little coffee parties. ... At least, not unless for some reason I decide I need to."

With that, he opened the cottage door and exited through it, leaving it fully open behind him.

"Reg, I'll be waiting in the car."

Reginald watched his friend walk out the door and toward his car. The concern on his face was not feigned.

The members of the group knew that the meeting was over. It was obvious to all, including Allison, that Jack Handler had taken over this meeting. James and Steve were more than a little taken aback, but not Allison. She was very familiar with the way Jack worked. She had even seen him talk to her husband in the same fashion that he addressed this meeting. So, she figured if Bob was willing to tolerate Jack's heavy-handedness in order to get things done, so could she.

"Gentlemen," Allison said, "is there anything else any of you need from me, or from each other? We will meet back here on Thursday."

Steve never said a word to anyone as he left. It was obvious that he was not happy with the way Jack had treated him. But he knew he had no recourse. The way he viewed it, he was quite pleased that he was not going to have to be working directly with Jack—working with Reginald was bad enough.

Allison said goodbye to Reginald as he left, and she stuck around for just another moment to feel James out. "What do you think about the meeting?"

"Obviously, we knew going forward with this that we were going to be working with some shadowy characters. ... I was surprised that Reg brought Handler to the meeting. But, in reality it might be for the best. At least now we know Reg has got the best working for us; and I think Handler needed the chance to express himself. I think it was all good."

"That's pretty much my take on it as well. I've watched Bob and Jack work on jobs before, and often it didn't look any different than tonight," Allison concluded.

After just a few seconds, with a strained chuckle in her voice, she continued. "I recall Bob commenting after meeting with Jack that sometimes he was just happy that Handler didn't decide to kill him. ... Tonight was not all that unusual, when dealing with Handler."

"There is one thing that I think you should know, Al," James followed. "One of my friends in Mossad asked me an interesting question. He asked me if I had heard anything about a secret brains trust that was set up to alter the outcome of the presidential election. Now, that, all by itself, might not seem important. We all know that there are always brains trusts being set up—and many of them are secret. But, the fact that this fellow sought me out and asked me about this—that seems curious, don't you think?"

Allison stopped, turned, and looked directly at James. She waited until he turned to face her. It was obvious that she had taken his comment seriously. Finally, she responded, "How deep was your contact?"

"I wouldn't say he was deep. But he is significant."

"How close are you to him?"

"We talk about more than just football." James paused for a second, then continued. "We go back. ... Here's the thing. This fellow and I have known each other for years. I know a little about how he thinks, and he knows about as much about me. His comment could have been just casual conversation. He knows about my association with you. And he knows you have certain interests. He could have been just sticking his finger in the wind. But I think we need to be very careful about what we talk about outside the meetings, and to whom. Not that we haven't been. But I thought you should know what he asked me."

"Thanks, James. I'll keep my eyes and ears open as well."

Allison then walked toward her car. It was dark, and a little chilly. She pulled her collar up around her neck and got her keys out. She missed her remote starter, but she knew from experience that any radio remote would give James's wand a fit. She got in her car and started the engine. "Thirty-six degrees," she said, reading the digital thermometer. "It feels like zero to me tonight."

Before she even began her drive along the winding tree-lined dirt road that led away from Jerry's cottage, she slid a thumb drive into her recording device and began reliving the events of the meeting.

"Meeting of the Whole—Number Three: When I arrived at the cottage, James was already there. He told me that Jerry would not be coming due to an infection in his cochlear implant. We were both disappointed. He did feel that Jerry would be able to make a Thursday meeting. He said he would pick Jerry up and bring him to the meeting.

"We had a surprise visitor at the meeting. For some reason not clear to the group, Reg brought his associate, Jack Handler. We discussed the fact that Jerry was not able to come to the meeting but that he should be okay by Thursday. Handler was not happy about Jerry not being present. He insisted that Reg follow up with Jerry as soon as possible to make certain that Jerry was totally committed. Reg then laid out his preliminary plan of action. All present were in agreement—no one objected. Reg stressed his need for Steve to be actively engaged in the media coverage of the event after it occurred. He stated that it would point to a radical conservative group, but that it would be Steve's job to be sure that's where it went during the first twenty-four hours. Handler had a few choice words for Steve when Steve asked Handler what his role was in the meeting.

"Handler at first thought he needed to meet directly with Jerry, but later decided against his personal involvement.

"That is about all that was discussed, except that after the meeting, James told me that one of his associates asked him about some secret meetings designed to affect the outcome of the presidential election."

Allison was exhausted. She realized that her recollections were less detailed than usual. But she believed, even given her diminished energy level, she had summarized all the important details. *After all*, she thought, *nothing of much significance was actually discussed.*

She pulled the stick out of the recorder and dropped it in her purse. She then retrieved her cell from the glove box and dialed Jerry.

"Jerry, you can hear again."

"Yes, and I'm feeling much better. I'm back home. They've got me on about every kind of pill known to man—big red ones, smaller red ones, little white ones. I'm actually feeling almost back to normal. My temperature is coming down as well. But I still have to take these pills for ten days. Doctor's orders."

Jerry wanted to apologize for missing the meeting, before Allison could comment on it, so he just kept talking. "I'm really sorry to have missed the meeting, but up until an hour ago—"

With that, Allison interrupted. "Jerry, enough said. We're on for Thursday, the day after tomorrow. At your place again. Is that okay?"

"Certainly," Jerry replied.

"See you then," Allison said, disconnecting before Jerry could make additional small talk.

The remainder of the drive passed quickly for her, even though she was very tired. She could not get her mind off James's last comment, regarding what he had heard from his spook friend. *Does someone outside the group actually have information?* she wondered.

Chapter 45—Allison forced to vet Jerry

8:12 p.m., Tuesday, December 27

After she had checked in Bernadette's car and walked the six blocks back to her apartment, just as always, Bernadette nodded and smiled at the doorman but did not open her mouth. She then took the elevator up to Bernadette's apartment. Sitting down in her favorite chair to reflect, she slipped off her shoes and tucked her feet up under her. This was her relaxing posture—the position she loved most when she was a college student. She realized that it did not work well for "full-thighed" adult proper women—at least not in public. But there was no one around to observe her here. Perhaps, she reasoned, it was that sitting position that helped her think so clearly. She did not know that for a fact, but she thought it possible.

She had been seated for only a few moments when she realized that she might feel much better with a drink to sip on, so she sprang up, much like that college girl from years ago, walked over to the bar, and poured herself a Scotch. On the way back to her thinking chair, she started reflecting about how adamant Jack had been about making sure Jerry was on board. So, before she sat down, she grabbed her cell and dialed Jerry again.

"Sorry to be a pest, but I got to thinking about this a little more," she said.

"Not to worry. You may call me any time you wish," Jerry replied. "How can I be of service?"

"Reg's associate expressed more than a little concern about your level of commitment. Now, I do not question you, but I have promised Reg that I would talk to you about this.

"Besides, it would just be a good thing for you and me to get together before the next meeting. I'm thinking tomorrow morning, seven a.m. Does that work?"

"Certainly, whatever you suggest will be fine."

"Great. I'll pick you up at the regular spot?"

"That works."

"Are you sure you're up to it? Your infection is under control?"

"Sure, I might look a little pale. But I'm on the repair. I look forward to seeing you."

"Seven a.m. it is," Allison said, and she disconnected.

That will be for the best, she thought. *It is important to keep Jack Handler happy.*

Allison was not afraid of Jack. She knew that he had more to fear from her than she from him. And she had no doubt that Jack shared that belief.

That was one of the reasons Jack seemed to have no issue with her—at least with regard to her resolve or ruthlessness. His concern was with those with whom she had surrounded herself.

It was obvious that Jack trusted Reginald. They had worked together on numerous jobs. Allison knew that if it were not for Reginald, Jack would not be on board. And it was important to Allison that Reginald had enlisted someone with Jack's credentials to run point for him. Allison liked that.

Jack didn't really have a problem with James either. Everyone knew that James carried a big sword and that he was just waiting for the opportunity to fall on it. It wasn't that he was masochistic. It was just that James possessed the ultimate level of loyalty.

That left Steve and Jerry. That's why Jack had so aggressively confronted Steve at the meeting. He sought to instill fear in his heart.

As much as anything, Jack brokered in fear. He wanted Steve to see
his dark side, to know that there were at least two .380 rounds in his
Walther with Steve's name on them.

Truth be told, had Jack decided that Steve needed to disappear, he
would simply have dragged Steve over the table and crushed his throat
with his hands. And he knew that the operation was so important that,
had he opted to kill the young man on the spot, none of the others would
have objected, much less interfered.

Fortunately for all, Steve also appreciated the gravity of the encounter. He thoroughly understood just how close he had come to dying.
He also recognized that his life meant nothing to Jack or to the rest. He
knew that he was in, and that there was no way out.

That left Jerry. Jack was not yet comfortable with Jerry. Allison was
a little concerned that Jack had turned down the offer to meet with the
last member of the group. She knew enough about Jack to understand
the gravity of Jerry's situation—that Jack's refusal to meet with Jerry was
one step away from his putting a bullet in his brain.

Unfortunately, Jerry did not appreciate the danger. Allison now
needed to make Jack comfortable with this last member of her group.

She thought about this at length, then got up and poured herself
another drink. As she sat back down, she came to a conclusion. She decided to have Reginald join the two of them in the morning.

"Only Reg can make this palatable with Handler," she figured. And
she did not want to leave anything to chance. If Reginald were present
at the meeting with Jerry, he would be in a better position to help his
friend relax. Otherwise, she really feared that Jack might still feel con-
strained to kill Jerry.

So, she again grabbed her cell and dialed Reginald's number. "Reg," she said when he answered. "I need to have you meet with me and Jerry tomorrow morning. I'm picking him up at seven a.m. Where can I meet you?"

"Al, I've got a meeting at eight."

"Where's your meeting?"

"Near 59th and Broadway."

"That's fine. I'll pick you up at the usual place at six-thirty and drop you off on 59th before eight."

"That makes sense. You're a little concerned about Jack, right?"

"More than a little. You and I both know his volatility. We need to protect our assets, and both Jack and Jerry are assets." Allison was very concerned, but she understood that she needed to weigh her words carefully when describing her posture vis-à-vis Reginald's close associate. Allison simply did not want to lose either one of them.

Unlike Steve, Jerry was a personal friend, as well as an important member of her group. If Jack killed him, Allison would be expected to exact retribution. She wasn't sure whether Jack realized that. She was, however, quite certain that Reginald did.

"I'll be there. I think that is a wise move," Reginald said.

"Great," Allison said as she disconnected.

What Allison did not realize was that Jack was sitting beside Reginald during the whole conversation. "Well, you figured that one right," Reginald said to his friend. "You've got her attention. She wants me to be present at her meeting with Jerry—tomorrow morning, already."

"That's perfect," Jack said. "You can wear a wire. I would like to hear what the deaf guy has to say."

"It all depends. I doubt that she will bring a wand—that's usually James's job. What I will do is call you right before she picks me up, and carry my cell in my shirt pocket. Worst case, she might ask me to dump my battery.

"But I agree that it would be best for you to listen in on what he has to say. In the end, I think you'll find him totally committed."

"It's not so much his commitment I'm concerned about," Jack replied. "I've found that guys like Jerry are usually weak and ultimately untrustworthy. ... Do you think he's weak?"

Reginald did not like Jack's tone—already he was assuming the unacceptability of the last member of the group. Like Allison, Reginald liked and trusted Jerry. But even more important, Reginald did not think that it would be possible to keep Steve on board, much less energized, without Jerry.

"Jerry has a hearing problem," Reginald said, "but I don't think he is weak. I've worked with him before, and he has always been more than useful."

"We will see," Jack said, not buying anything Reginald said concerning Jerry. "I will be better able to make a decision after I hear his responses."

Reginald knew what that meant. Jerry's life was hanging by a thread, and Jack Handler held the scissors.

Chapter 46—Jerry's test

6:00 a.m., Wednesday, December 28

As far as Allison was concerned, this would not be a meeting that would require her to go as Bernadette. She was merely getting together with friends. Unfortunately, she was going to have to drive, and Allison did not drive her own car.

Therefore she got started early enough, as Bernadette, to walk over and retrieve Bernadette's vehicle. She contemplated as she walked along that familiar route, just how nice it would be when all this cloak and dagger business would no longer be necessary. Of course, that would not happen until she was in the White House. Until then, she would just have to buck up and do what had to be done.

She pulled her car out of the garage at six-fifteen a.m. and then headed over to pick up Reginald. She was a little early, but Reginald was already at the customary location watching for her.

As she drove up, he trotted out to meet her. She could not pull to the curb, so she stopped in traffic long enough for him to slide into the passenger seat.

"Good morning," he said. "Jerry's doing better?"

"I'm not sure about that," Allison responded, not acknowledging his initial greeting except with a small smile. "He says he's fine, but I suspect that could be his medication talking. … It really doesn't matter how he feels, at this point. We've got to get this issue resolved. … We'll know in a few minutes, one way or the other."

Suddenly Reginald's head jerked acutely. Without warning, Allison had shot across two lanes of traffic and made a right turn just as the light changed to red.

"What was that all about?" Reginald asked.

"I thought I noticed someone following me," she said, as she again darted into the right-turn lane, planning to circle back. After stopping briefly, she quickly made a right turn and then another at the end of the block. After the fourth right, she was back on course, confident that no one was tailing her. Reginald viewed her maneuver as possibly the result of a little paranoia, but he had no problem with it.

The two finally made it through the heavy New York morning traffic and arrived at the place where Jerry was waiting for them. Just as in the case with Reginald, Allison simply pulled as close to the curb as possible, and Jerry came running.

Allison hit the unlock button, granting access to her friend Jerry. "Good morning," he said as he got in. "Hello, Reg. I wasn't expecting to see you. To what do I owe this pleasure?"

"Allison just wanted me to tag along to be sure we got you up to speed," Reginald answered.

"This is how I want to handle this meeting, today," Allison said. "Reg is sort of in a hurry, so I am just going to drive around a bit."

Allison reached into the center console and removed a wand that looked nothing like the one James always used.

"What's that?" Reginald asked.

"It's a wand," Allison said. "Reg, please use it to scan yourself and Jerry for recording or transmission devices."

"That's not the one James uses, is it?" Jerry asked.

"No, it isn't," Allison replied. "It's left over from the White House. I suppose it might not be as up to date as the Mossad unit, but I think it's adequate."

"Well," Reginald said, as he adjusted the sensitivity downward, "it apparently doesn't like Jerry's implant any better than James's wand."

Jerry flashed Reginald an affected look of disgust, as Reginald proceeded to pass the device over their lower torsos. Reginald was careful not to bring the device even close to his shirt pocket. He then quickly turned the device off.

"You're still good for tomorrow's meeting?" Allison asked in Jerry's direction.

"Sure am. I am very sorry to have missed the last meeting, it's just that yesterday I was totally incapacitated—I could not hear, and I was heavily medicated," Jerry said, wanting to make sure his two friends understood his problem. "I will be there tomorrow. I promise."

"Jerry, what do you think about where we are going with this whole matter?" Allison asked, getting right to the point.

"Well, I think you knew that I had arrived at that conclusion even before most of the others did," Jerry said. "Look, I know that this was a tough decision to make. I fully understand all the implications and dangers inherent with it. But it has become clear to me that there was only one recourse possible. And that recourse is the elimination, the physical and violent elimination, of the current president of the United States.

"Now, I know that you needed to hear me say what I just did. I am not naïve about this matter. But I would appreciate it if you did not again make me utter those words. Suffice it to say, I am on board. I will do my part to carry this out—whatever is asked of me, I will do. I trust you guys fully. I am proud to be a part of this plan. We have to be successful, or we will lose our lives, and possibly our nation. I understand what is happening."

With that, Jerry paused for a moment and then looked first at Allison, then at Reg. "Not to be testy about this, but I must ask you both, did you get the answer you were seeking?"

Allison responded first, but not to Jerry. She asked Reginald, "I'm satisfied, how about you?"

"I heard what I needed to hear. I'm ready to proceed."

"Jerry," Allison said, "I want to thank you for your willingness to comply with my request for this meeting, I know you are not feeling well, but I also know you are totally aware of our concerns."

"I am," Jerry said, "and I have absolutely no problem with your caution. I would have expected the same thing had Reg missed a meeting. It was expected."

Allison, deciding that the meeting was over, had already headed back. "Drop you off where I picked you up?"

"That works," Reginald replied.

"I think you're going to be a bit early. Will that be a problem?" she asked, as she pulled to the curb to let him out.

"Not at all," Reginald said. "I suspect my party will be waiting for me. See you both tomorrow evening."

Both Allison and Jerry acknowledged Reginald's parting words.

Allison circled back toward Jerry's regular pickup and drop-off point. "Tomorrow evening at your cottage, Jerry."

"Definitely," Jerry responded.

Jerry understood that if there were to remain even a little insecurity regarding his commitment, it could cost him his life. He had, in fact, rehearsed his lines prior to this morning's meeting—he wanted to make sure he said everything that needed saying. Fortunately for him, he was adequately transparent, allowing his sincerity to register with both of his friends. As far as he was concerned, it had worked.

However, sitting in the coffee shop with an earbud on, waiting for Reginald to join him, was Jack Handler. He had listened intently to everything the three of them had said, and there was no smile on his face.

Chapter 47—Jack evaluates Jerry's performance

7:58 a.m., Wednesday, December 28

Reginald was in charge of Jack—at least as far as the rest of the group was concerned. But that was not actually the way the two of them regarded their relationship.

Theoretically, it was Reginald's responsibility to assign tasks for Jack and Jack's job to carry them out. But Reginald knew just how dangerous his associate was. In fact, throughout all his many exploits and intrigues, Reginald had never come across anyone he regarded more dangerous than Jack Handler. But that was okay with him. The two men had developed a comfort level that made it easy for them to get along and work effectively with each other.

It was as a result of that comfort level, that right now, as the two men sat at the table, Reginald knew better than to talk. Jack was deep in thought, and Reginald respected Jack's desire for silence. Finally, after an uncomfortable length of time, Jack broke the silence.

"Tell me again," Jack asked, "what exactly is this guy's role?"

"Jerry is a trusted friend of Allison's. ... Almost her superego. I think she relies on Jerry's levity as much as his common sense. Jerry runs deeper than you might think. He is a formidable ally. And totally loyal to Al. She bounces ideas off him all the time—always has. When she was in the White House, Jerry was always at her right hand. Bob also liked him. And you know Bob didn't actually like very many people."

"Is that it?" Jack followed.

"Not exactly," Reginald continued. "In a very real sense, he is the only one of us who likes Steve. I totally respect Steve's talents. For what he does, he is the best there is. But I really do not like him. They don't think I know what they're up to, but I'm sure they want Jerry around to serve as a buffer between Steve and me. And that's okay. I know we need Steve. I know what he is capable of. And I know he is loyal, too. But it totally irks me to have to deal with him. I just do not like the kid. Jerry does, at least he makes everyone think he likes Steve. Jerry's that kind of guy. He gets along with everyone."

"I've heard you refer to Steve as your 'little gay buddy.' Is that what you think of him?"

"Not at all," Reginald replied. "The president used to call him that when he was angry. I realize that there's no point antagonizing the kid. He already knows I don't like him. And I'm sure he feels the same about me. He just sometimes rubs me the wrong way."

"I don't think I would have a problem working with him, if it ever comes to that," Jack said.

"Yeah, but you and I both know what you would do if he got cocky with you. And, after last night, he has a pretty good idea as well. You made a lasting impression."

"Maybe that's what you need to do," Jack advised Reginald.

"It won't work for me," Reginald said. "I have to bounce ideas off of those around me. I cannot afford to intimidate any of them. You, on the other hand, can't do it any other way. They have to be scared of you. We're very different people. You're a hired gun. I'm the guy who hires guys like you. We make a pretty good team."

"I do intimidate most people, but I don't frighten Allison—never did. She's one tough lady."

"That she is," Reginald agreed. "But it was clear today, by the way she went after Jerry to bring him back into the fold, that she respects you."

"She respects me, all right," Jack said. "But I will guarantee you that she would kill me in a New York minute if she thought that would further her cause. I can live with that. She just has to believe she needs me. You've done a good job convincing these guys that no one can pull this off as well as you and I can. She has bought into that notion. I can see that."

"She does like the idea you and I are working together on her behalf," Reginald agreed. "That brings us back to Jerry. Are you going to be able to work with him?"

"For now," Jack said. "But I can't promise much once this job is done. It's fluffy guys like Jerry that make me nervous. But don't worry about it. For now, I'm okay with him."

Reginald subscribed to the concept that once you hear the words you want to hear, you end the meeting. He knew that this meeting was over. He also knew that for the time being, Jack was going to let Jerry live. That was all he really wanted to know.

So, excusing himself, Reginald left Jack in the coffee shop and went out to hail a taxi.

But Jack did not remain alone for long. No sooner had Reginald disappeared from the sidewalk out front, than a familiar figure approached Jack's table and sat down across from him, in the chair Reginald had just vacated.

Chapter 48—*The Yankees fan*

8:16 a.m., Wednesday, December 28

Jack did not immediately acknowledge his guest. Instead, he just continued reading his *New York Times*. It was obvious that he was not surprised. "Hey, bud," the man finally said to Jack.

The coffee shop was upscale, but Jack's guest looked anything but upscale. He was wearing a very soiled Yankees cap pulled down over a pair of dark sunglasses. His pants were worn and stained. When he sat down, they slid up his calves to expose a pair of once-white socks and well-travelled brown leather shoes. Threads dangled from each of the sleeves of his green waist-length jacket.

After at least a minute, Jack folded his newspaper and laid it on the table. He then glared into his guest's eyes. Still he said nothing.

After another long moment, his guest spoke, "Thanks for meeting me, bud. I know you're not excited about this, but I needed you to improve my comfort level." When the new arrival spoke, it was in a voice very well known to Jack. Roger Minsk, the head of Allison's Secret Service detail, had just joined him.

"I understand," Jack said. "At least you're up front about it. … And I'm going to need something from you."

Roger knew how to disguise himself without appearing unnatural. Reginald could have passed him on the sidewalk and not suspect he had just walked by his friend. In fact, he quite possibly just did.

"Are you going to be able to work with that group? At least nominally?" Roger asked, knowing that Jack would not tolerate small talk. He had picked up on Jack's comment that he needed his help, but he withheld comment on it until Jack was ready to bring it back up.

"That remains to be seen," Jack said. "Reg seems comfortable with Jerry. Jerry, for me, represents an unknown."

"Is he the only issue, as far as you're concerned?" Roger asked.

"He's my major dilemma. What's your take on this guy?"

"I know him through Allison. That's it. I haven't worked with him directly. From what I can tell, he is very loyal."

"Yeah, that's what Reg says," Jack said. "Reg thinks Allison wants him around to ease the strain between himself and Steve. Is that how you see it?"

"There's an element of truth to that. But I think Jerry also brings common sense to the table."

"Well, that makes him pretty useless, then. The time for common sense has long since passed. There is nothing common or sensible about what they are contemplating." Jack paused for a moment, then he pointed a very thick finger at Roger's chest. "What I wanna know is this: does this guy have the balls to do whatever needs doing? Can he keep his mouth shut? Could he squeeze the trigger on his own mother? Where does he draw the line?"

"I'm not sure I can answer that," Roger said. "Could you 'squeeze the trigger' on your mother?"

"I'm not the issue here," Jack said. "I can't work with anyone who senses any reservation."

"I'm not going to try to convince you of anything," Roger said.

"Hell, why should you have to do anything on his behalf? This guy has to stand on his own," Jack countered. "Look, what's the deal with his hearing problem? He wasn't born that way."

"He lost his hearing a year ago. As I understand it, he has Limbaugh's problem."

"You can't be serious!" Jack exclaimed. "Oxycodone?"

"That's the rumor," Roger answered. "And he doesn't deny it. It's not a real issue anymore, not with his cochlear implant."

"That's what I thought," Jack followed. "He's weak. People who abuse are weak. And if he's weak in one area, he's weak, period."

"He's not your typical drug abuser," Roger said. "Jerry had his back broken in a car crash a few years ago. The story is that he took a number of painkillers—oxy being one of them. Apparently it irritated his stomach, so he started breaking the pills up and mixing them in his food. That's how he got hooked. It didn't take long ..."

"So he says," Jack interrupted. "How long has he been clean?"

"He cleaned up as soon as he developed his hearing loss. I have no doubt that he's been straight ever since."

"Well, let's move ahead. But I do not want to work directly with this guy," Jack said. "Or any of the others, for that matter—except for Reg. He's going to be my only connection with that group. ... And you, of course."

"That makes sense," Roger agreed. "I don't think there is a better man for the job than Reg. And your reputation is stellar—"

"All that we are expecting of them is to keep their mouths shut, forever," Jack interrupted. "That's what worries me about Jerry. I don't think much of drug heads—regardless of how they acquired their habits. I fear he might be unreliable. If any part of this thing goes south, he could be a problem."

"Then we have to make sure it doesn't go south," Roger said, almost chiding Jack.

"That's right," Jack agreed.

"Now, what did you need me to do for you?" Roger asked, referring to what Jack had said earlier.

"You've got the equipment to trace and patch cells, right?"

"I can do that," Roger said. "What do you need?"

"They've got my daughter," Jack said. "Kidnaped. I need to get her back tomorrow night. It will be my one and only shot at it. I could use your help. I'll call you to set it up."

Jack observed that Roger was not surprised with the news of his daughter.

"Tomorrow?" Roger said.

"Right. Early evening"

"I'll be looking for the call," Roger said.

Thinking that the conversation was over, Roger stood and started to leave.

"Hold on a minute," Jack commanded. Roger, who had not totally risen to his feet, obligingly sat back down. "I've got something for you."

Jack reached down under the table and pulled a wrinkled brown paper bag out of his briefcase. "Here, take this," Jack said, as he handed Roger the bag.

"What is it," Roger asked.

"It's a gift for you," Jack said, pushing the bag across the table. "Take a look at it."

Roger received the surprisingly heavy bag and opened it enough to examine the contents. He looked back up at Jack and asked, "What is this about—and what's it for?"

"It's for you," Jack said. "It's worth a lot of money—ten, twenty thousand, I would guess. If you don't melt it down, probably a lot more. It's an antique. In fact, it's not just an antique, it's an antiquity."

"Why are you giving it to me?" Roger asked.

"When this job is over," Jack said, "you might have a use for it. They tell me it's a death mask—an ancient Egyptian burial mask. And they also tell me that you should not touch it. I don't know much about that. I'm really not superstitious. But I would take care not to show it around. There are certain parties who are familiar with it."

Jack then looked directly into Roger's sunglasses and stuck his very thick finger toward Roger's nose. Speaking in a frightening tone that was barely above a whisper, Jack said: "I might never see you again after Thursday night. Just know I'm expecting you to behave yourself too. I know you've always been a straight-up guy. There should not be anything to change that, right?"

"I'm good."

"Me too," Jack said, no longer looking at Roger.

Roger was Jack's friend. And it made Jack uncomfortable to talk to a friend as he had just done. But Jack knew of only one way to convey the gravity of the job ahead. And that's what he attempting to accomplish with this exchange.

After those chilling words, Roger turned and left. Neither of the men spoke as Roger walked away, carrying under his arm the gift Jack had given him. He was, however, careful not to touch the mask.

Chapter 49—Preparing for the next meeting

4:59 p.m., Thursday, December 29

Just as he had promised Allison, James arranged to pick up Jerry for the fourth meeting. James had planned to arrive at the cottage at least half an hour early, so that he could air it out. But Jerry kept him waiting for over fifteen minutes. So, it started to look to James like time might be a little tight. After the first five minutes, James texted Jerry to find out where he was. Jerry apologized and told him he would be fifteen or twenty minutes late. Rather than take the chance of arousing the interest of the police, James opted to drive around the block and return to the pickup spot about the time Jerry said he would be there.

As he pulled up, Jerry came trotting across the sidewalk toward him. James marveled at how relaxed and jovial Jerry appeared.

My God, James thought, *if he only knew all the trouble he was causing us, and just how close he was to attracting Jack's wrath. If he only knew the half of it.*

"Hi, Jerry," James said with a very friendly smile. Under some circumstances, he might have resented being made to wait—especially given the gravity of the meeting they were about to attend together. But he knew that any negativity expressed on his face would serve only to alienate his friend. And tonight, he wanted to draw out the best in all of them.

"Hey, James," Jerry said, "I am so sorry to keep you waiting. I do appreciate your picking me up and all."

"Not a problem," James responded. And he meant it—he did not consider it anything but the reasonable thing to do.

"I'm really doing much better," Jerry said. "For a while there I started thinking I might have to resort to reading lips. But I'm back to where I was before the infection. In fact, the way they have this thing set up this time, I can actually hear better now than I have since I lost my hearing." Jerry paused for a few seconds and then continued. "But don't bother to sing to me—I still can't appreciate music. It just sounds like noise. But I can't complain; at least I can hear and understand what people say."

"Not to worry, Jerry, I don't sing unless I'm in the shower or tipping a pint. And Allison's not going to let that happen tonight."

"That's the one thing that's been lacking," Jerry said. "When Bob was in charge, at least we could toss down a few beers. I suppose I can appreciate Al's position on that, but I think I would like it better with a drink in my hand. Might even lighten up Reg a bit. ... On second thought, I don't think anything would lighten him up. He is one intense dude."

"Too bad you missed the last meeting," James said, trying to prepare his friend a bit. "If you think Reg is a little heavy handed, you should have met his friend, Handler."

"No thanks," Jerry quickly replied. "I've heard enough about him to want to keep my distance. Steve gave me a call."

James was not pleased that calls were being made outside the meetings, but he did not let on.

"Oh yeah, what did he have to say about it?"

"He didn't say much—nothing about the meeting. He just said that this Handler guy made him very nervous."

"That's probably a good thing," James replied. "Handler is an imposing personality. A person would do well to stay on his good side."

"Or better yet," Jerry interrupted, "stay totally away. I really don't have a problem with him. I have a job to do, and I'm gonna do it. Come hell or high water—I'm just gonna do my job. I think that's all he's looking for. He's good for his end, and he expects the rest of us to carry our weight. That's fine with me."

"I hope you're right about that," James replied.

"Hey, let me tell you why I was late," Jerry said. "I ran into the most interesting old friend on my way to meet you—very strange. I hadn't seen him for years, and there he was, standing in the middle of Grand Central Terminal. I almost walked by him at first, then I recognized him. It was strange. ... You know the guy, too. He's a spook. Mossad. I think he must have been on an assignment. He seemed a little uncomfortable talking to me, but I could not miss him. You know how I am with faces."

"Who did you run into?" James asked, more than a little interested.

"Griffin. You remember him, don't you? I'm sure that was not his real name, but he was friendly with Bob back in the day."

"Yeah, sure," James responded. "... Doesn't that have a strange feel to it, Jerry? Running into Griffin like that?"

"Not at the time," Jerry said, "but when I stopped to think about it now, it does make me feel a little uneasy. ... What was his role, anyway? What do you remember about him?"

"I don't think he's that dangerous," James said. "I've not seen him since we left. I doubt that I would have picked him out. How did you spot him?"

"You're gonna get a kick outta this," Jerry said, a little embarrassed.

"Give me a try, I'm sure he wasn't wearing a name tag."

"When I walked by him, I accidently dropped part of my paper," Jerry explained. "It actually hit this guy's foot. How embarrassing. When I reached down to pick it up, I took a close look at the shoes he was wearing. I recognized them at once—two-thousand-dollar Italian Stefano Bemer shoes. In my whole life, I have seen only one person who wore those shoes, and that was Griffin.

"So, as I stood up, I took a close look at this guy. He was wearing shades and had a newspaper stuck in front of his face. But he answered when I said his name. And, like I said, he was definitely taken aback a bit. I suppose I might have blown his cover. I don't know. What do you think? ... Could *I* have been his target?"

"No, I don't think so," James answered. Even though he tried to placate Jerry's anxiety, James was troubled about that encounter.

What are the chances? James thought to himself. *That Griffin would be staking out the Terminal, at that particular time, and that he would just by chance run into Jerry?*

James was too savvy to even consider the possibility of coincidence. *Griffin was there because he knew Jerry would be passing through Grand Central at that time,* he was thinking. *There is ample reason to be concerned.*

Chapter 50—James and Jerry first to arrive

5:52 p.m., Thursday, December 29

Much as James suspected, he and Jerry reached the cottage later than he had hoped. They were, however, still the first ones to arrive.

"You're still parking way out here?" Jerry asked. "This is hard on my poor old legs."

"You'll survive. It just makes security so much easier."

Jerry reached into his pocket, pulled out his cell phone, and tossed it on the seat. "You're gonna lock this thing up?"

"I am," James replied, "but who do you think is going to steal your cell phone—Smokey the Bear?"

"You just can't be too careful," Jerry said, not totally joking. "Maybe some Mossad spook followed us, and he wants the numbers stored in my cell." Jerry paused for a moment. Then, looking back down the trail they had just motored up, continued, "You didn't see anyone following us, did you?"

"Actually I did, Jerry, but I think it was an exterminator. He must have heard about your critter-infested rat hole. ... Too bad I lost him."

Jerry appreciated James's good-natured humor and simply smiled at his friend.

James then followed Jerry's lead and tossed his cell phone into the middle console. He then walked to the rear of the car, opened the trunk, and removed the scanner.

"Still using that?" Jerry asked, rhetorically.

"You bet," James responded. "Have to find out what you're trying to sneak into the meeting."

"You can use me to test it," Jerry said, as the two men walked toward the cottage.

"Never mind the hidden key," Jerry said. "I've got one on my key chain."

"Just hold on, let me go ahead," James said. "I'll make sure no one planted anything while we were gone." James then removed a separate piece of equipment from the case, initiated it, and walked totally around the cottage. Jerry just smiled and shook his head.

When James emerged from the other side of the cottage, Jerry asked, "Okay if I unlock the door, now?"

"No," James said. "The cottage appears clean, now I have to wand you." Just as every time before, when James held the wand close to Jerry's head, the sounder emitted a distinctively positive signal.

"Looks like your penal implant is getting excited," James quipped.

"Here, let me see that thing," Jerry said, reaching over to remove it from James's hand. "I've gotta check you out, right? I have to be sure you're okay."

"Sure, check me out," James said, handing Jerry the wand.

"How does this thing work?"

"You just squeeze the trigger and hold it in," James informed him.

Jerry turned it on and started wanding James. "I don't think this thing is working," Jerry said. He then held it to his own head, to be sure he was doing it right. After the wand sounded, he said, "Looks like it's working okay now. Let me wand you again."

Jerry then proceeded to walk around James a second time. When he got behind James, he grabbed the wand with both hands, and rammed the end of it unceremoniously into James's backside. James figured he had it coming, so he simply removed the wand from Jerry's hand. "That's the last time you get to handle this piece of equipment," James said. "Al would not think much of that behavior."

Jerry then unlocked the cottage, and the two men began to enter. Just before James could close the door, he glanced back to the parking area and observed an unfamiliar car approaching.

Chapter 51—Meeting four

6:05 p.m., Thursday, December 29

James stopped and stood staring in the direction of the strange vehicle. Jerry noticed his hesitation, so he also turned to check it out.

"Recognize that car?" James asked.

"Can't say that I do," Jerry replied, squinting in an effort to get a more focused look. The two men just stood at the doorway, waiting to see who emerged. Finally, after nearly a minute, Steve jumped out, tossing his cell on the seat and closing the car door. He looked in their direction as he started walking toward the cottage, but he did not call out to them.

"Steve, nice ride," Jerry said to him as he approached. The car was obviously a rental or a loaner. There was nothing wrong with driving a three-year-old Chevy Malibu, but it was a major step down from his brand new Range Rover. Steve heard his friend's teasing, but he did not respond. James still had the wand in his hand, so he headed over to intercept Steve a dozen feet from the door. "What's with the car?" he asked.

"Some jerk stole my Range Rover," Steve said, as James ran the wand over his body. "It was parked in the ramp at my apartment and everything. The alarm was set. And some bastard got it anyway."

"What did the cops say?" James asked.

"They took a report. Is there something else that they do? … It just goes to show that there still is crime in New York—I guess Rudy didn't bust them all."

"Did they get anything else?" James inquired. "Did you have anything in the car that could be incriminating? … For any of us?"

"No, certainly not," Steve answered. "I did have a notebook in there, but there was nothing on it."

"Nothing on it? … Or nothing not erased on it?" Jerry asked.

"Nothing about these meetings, there or erased," Steve said. "I haven't logged anything regarding the meetings after we started them."

"What sort of stuff was on it?" James asked.

"No names, nothing like that," Steve said. "I did have a general outline of a time frame relating to the upcoming event, but no specifics. I never go online with that notebook, for that very reason. Anybody can get hacked."

"Tell me the sort of 'offline' stuff that you did have on it," James said as he completed clearing Steve. All three of the men then entered the cottage and closed the door.

"After Reg and his buddy, you know, Mr. Sunshine, threatened me last week, I decided that I would do well to get my game plan together. Few people do, but Handler scares the hell out of me. I wanted to have my stuff ready when I needed it."

"And you had some of that stuff on your notebook?" James asked.

"Yeah, but some stupid car thief will never figure out what it was, even if he got past my password," Steve said.

"That wasn't some stupid car thief, Steve, that was a targeted hit on your car," James informed him.

"There were no names, no specifics—only code words that only I would understand," Steve said. "Nothing could be proven."

"Not in a court of law," James said, "but the Russians, Mossad, or the CIA would decipher it in no time. … That is a problem."

"You're making too much out of this," Steve said, not willing to admit that there could be a security breach with his notebook at the center of it.

"No, I'm not," James said, "whoever stole your computer has a pretty good idea that something major is going down, and they know that it involves you, and they know who your friends are. …We have to bring Al up to speed on this. We will all be scrutinized from now on, if we haven't been already. Jerry ran into a Mossad spook one hour ago. Could be related. We're going to have to address this at the meeting. Guess we should be happy Handler isn't here tonight."

"Hell, he's probably the one who stole my car," Steve said. "I wouldn't put anything past him."

"That actually is a possibility," James agreed. "But I think he knows he's got your attention. The odds are that it was pulled off by an intelligence agency—ours or someone else's."

"How can we tell who is behind it?" Jerry asked.

"Oh, we'll find out eventually … when it suits their purpose," James said.

"I'm not so sure about that," Jerry said. "I've heard that it usually takes weeks or months to process any data like this. Those guys are so deep in bureaucracy—just like the rest of DC."

"You could be right about that," James agreed after thinking about it for a moment. "If it's the CIA. Except, whatever is viewed as a priority gets done immediately. We can't count on weeks or even days. Especially if it was Mossad."

"Well, I still think it was a garden-variety car thief," Steve said. "If my notebook was the main target, they would have smashed the window and grabbed it. But they stole the whole vehicle. I think it was a run-of-the-mill theft of a car. It's probably in some chop shop getting cut up for parts, and my computer is in a dumpster."

"Hope you're right," James said. "But I think we have to consider the possibility that we have had a significant breach and deal with it accordingly."

"How does that work?" Jerry asked.

"Well, for one thing, I think we are going to have to suspend our meetings," James said confidently. "We will see what Al thinks about it, but I see no other recourse. We were going to have only four of them anyway, according to Allison. Probably that's why—to avoid problems like this."

"Reg is going to have a few choice words about this," Steve said, obviously not excited about having to deal with his nemesis about a possible loss of information.

"Yeah, I know what you mean," James said matter-of-factly. "But we have to lay it all out, regardless of the consequences."

Just then, there was a loud knock at the door.

Chapter 52—The hard decision

6:21 p.m., Thursday, December 29

James walked over to the door and opened it. "Well, are you going to wand us in?" Allison asked, feigning impatience. She had arrived at the same time as Reginald, and they were now both standing outside the cottage door, waiting for James to screen them. It had been Allison who had delivered the exceptionally loud knock. Sometimes she over-did things such as that, wanting to exert her authority.

James had still not set the wand down, so he stepped outside the door and asked Reginald to take a couple steps backward while he veri-fied Allison had no transmitters on her person. None of the group both-ered anymore to remove the batteries from their cell phones—they sim-ply left them in their vehicles. Both Allison and Reginald were quickly cleared and invited in.

"Good to have you back," Reginald said to Jerry. "Feeling a little bet-ter? You look pretty healthy."

"I'm really A-Okay," Jerry said.

"Yes, it is good to see you again," Allison said.

"It's great to be back."

"Well, we're all here, shall we get started?" Allison said as she walked over to the chair she always used. With that, all four sat down at the table. Steve made sure he sat between Jerry and James.

"James, would you begin?" Allison said.

"Certainly," James responded, "before we discuss anything else, however, I need to make the group aware of some recent curious events.

First of all, Steve had his car stolen. He thinks it was a run-of-the mill case of vehicle theft. It is a simple fact that Steve lost his laptop as well as his car. He states that he had very little information relating to the current project on that computer—certainly there were no names, only generalizations of his anticipated media blitz.

"If he is correct, if the car was stolen for parts, then the laptop will end up in a dumpster, or simply sold as is to some student who will clean it up and use it for classroom notes. It is password protected. Usually, the hard drive is purged first, because the thief doesn't want to take a chance that there might be some sort of tracking device on it. If he doesn't consider it worthwhile to sell the laptop, he is most likely to just take a sledge hammer to it.

"It seems pretty obvious that whoever stole the car was fairly sophisticated. After all, he pulled it off in the middle of the day, in a parking garage at Steve's apartment. I assume that was very well surveilled. Steve's Range Rover would warrant theft for parts. But it is also possible, if not likely, that his laptop was the actual target."

"It could be both," Steve said. "If an agency wants the electronics from a vehicle, it can engage a competent chop shop to pull it off—the agency keeps the computer, the chop shop gets the car. That's been done before."

"At any rate," James went on, "we have to proceed under the assumption that some spook has Steve's computer. Even though there are no names on it, the information they glean will be significant.

"Now, there is another element that has to be considered. Jerry had an interesting encounter on his way to meet me earlier this evening. Jerry, why don't you tell the group what happened."

"Damn, this is starting to sound like an AA meeting," Jerry quipped. "Well, when I got off the train at Grand Central," Jerry said, "I ran smack dab into an old friend from our White House years—Griffin. Some of you probably remember him," Jerry said, as he looked over at Allison.

"Griffin?" Allison said, trying to remember how she should remember him.

"Right," Jerry continued, "he was actually a better friend of Bob's than any of the rest of us. Mossad—mid-level, maybe low-level at that time."

"I remember him," Allison said, looking as though a light bulb had been turned on. "He was the gay guy with the expensive shoes, right?"

"I don't think he was gay," Jerry said, not pleased with the obvious homophobia, but afraid to express his dismay. "Griffin just had an affinity for expensive Italian loafers—two grand a pair."

"Anyone who would wear shoes like that would have to be gay," Reginald stated in his usual denigrating tone when discussing matters of sexual orientation. "I've never seen a guy with tastes like that who wasn't ..."

"What the hell difference does that make," Steve interrupted, very irritated with Reginald's comment. "I don't care if the guy was gay, straight, or preferred farm animals—the critical thing is whether he was targeting Jerry *specifically*, or if it was a chance encounter. That's the salient factor here."

"He's right," Jerry stated. "By the way, this fellow tried to hide his face from me. When I approached him he ducked behind a newspaper, and he was wearing sunglasses. I strongly suspect he was on some sort of assignment. At first I didn't think I could be the target. But James got me thinking about it. I now think that I definitely could have been the object of his attention. He sure got nervous when I started talking to him."

"What made you recognize him, anyway?" Allison asked.

"Actually, I spotted his shoes first," Jerry explained. "As I walked past him, part of my newspaper fell to the floor, right on his two-thousand-dollar Italian shoes. I recognized them right away. The only pair I'd ever seen like them was on Griffin's feet, over a decade ago. They are easy to identify. As soon as I saw them, I knew I needed to get a look at the guy's face who was wearing them—to see if this really was my old buddy. So when I stood up, I actually pulled the fellow's newspaper down. And there he was, Griffin. He looked a little older, but even behind those dark shades, I had no problem making him."

"And he recognized you right away as well?" Reginald asked him.

"You know, that was a little strange," Jerry explained. "He acted as though he did not remember me at first. Then, finally, he greeted me like his long-lost friend. He took off his sunglasses, and we shook hands. … But we didn't hug."

"He took off his sunglasses?" James asked.

"Yeah, doesn't that sound a little strange?" Jerry asked.

"Very," Reginald said, "that means that he no longer needed his disguise. That would strongly suggest that you were his target."

"I agree," James said.

"Okay," Allison said, jumping in to gain control. "It looks to me that we have aroused the attention of someone, perhaps Mossad."

"Not necessarily," James said. "Sometimes the agencies share notes. It actually could be a CIA operation. Griffin worked with them before. He worked with your husband too."

"Whoever is working this," Allison continued, "it just means that we have to be more careful. We knew we could not continue to get together forever without attracting some unwanted attention. The fact remains that they, whoever they might be, are on a fishing expedition. They do not know what we're up to. We simply need to stop having these meetings, at least as a group. We each know what we have to do. We do not need to have any more meetings. Do we agree on that?"

"I have all the information I need for now," Reginald said. "Steve, Jerry, and James, I am sure, feel the same. We each have our own jobs to do. I see nothing productive coming out of additional meetings. Jack is comfortable enough to get on with it. And, Steve, a lot of this is going to fall on you, now. Are you ready?"

"I'm good. I just need you to keep me in the loop."

"That will happen," Reginald told him, sincerely meaning what he said.

"I see no reason to go on with these meetings, then," Allison announced, virtually dismissing the current one, as well as the process itself. "From now on, we will move on independently, at least until after the actual event. Each of us will perform our assigned tasks, and we will communicate only when necessary. Is that how you each see it?"

All four men nodded in agreement.

"Jerry," Allison said, "thank you very much for making your cottage available to us."

"Not a problem."

The meeting was now over. Steve offered to take Jerry back to the city, and Jerry accepted the invitation, poking fun at Steve's rental car.

"I'll close it up this time," Jerry told James. "Now you know where I hide my key; I'm going to have to find a new spot."

"Great," James said, "then you can clean it up too."

"Yeah, right, it doesn't much look like you did any dusting."

The five friendly conspirators all left together, cracking jokes and making small talk all the way back to their cars. Based on their jovial mood, it hardly seemed possible that so deadly a process was underway.

Driving back to the city, James and Allison were basically doing the same thing, though driving separate vehicles—both were playing back in their minds the events of the evening. The main difference being, Alison was recording her thoughts.

James was less than twenty minutes on the drive back when his cell phone rang. "Hello," James said.

"James?" An unfamiliar voice asked. "I need to get your input on a story I've written."

"Who is this?" James asked, "And how did you get this number?"

"That's not important—"

"The hell it isn't!" James exclaimed. "You're calling on my private number. You should not *have* this number."

"Forget about that," the voice said, "I've got a story that you need to read."

"Get off my phone!" James demanded.

"Wait," the caller said, as James disconnected.

Only a few seconds passed when James's phone rang again.

"Get off my phone," James commanded the caller.

But before he could disconnect the call, the caller said one word: "Assassination."

Chapter 53—Plan to rescue Kate

6:52 p.m., Thursday, December 29

Reginald left the meeting and drove directly to meet Jack at a predetermined location—an all-night diner less than fifteen minutes from Jerry's cottage.

As he drove up, Reginald quickly spotted Jack sitting in his vehicle waiting for him. Reginald parked three cars away and walked over to the black SUV. He got in the passenger side and closed the door. Jack pulled out of the parking lot and headed toward Brooklyn. The two rode together for a couple miles before a word was spoken.

"Want to fill me in on your plan?" Reginald finally asked.

"This is what I have in mind," Jack replied. "Roger is positioned outside the hotel. By Penn Station. And you and I are headed to Brooklyn. That's where we think they are holding Kate." Jack paused for a moment, then asked, "You are armed?"

"I'm good," Reginald said. "Let's roll."

Roger had determined on the basis of triangulation of cell phone signals that Kate was being held in that borough.

"Roger has some specialized electronics with him," Jack said. "He also has my cell right now. So, when the kidnapper calls, the call will first hit my cell that Roger has in Midtown Manhattan, and his equipment will patch the call to this one," Jack said, holding up a new cell phone for Reginald to see. "If the kidnappers have equipment sophisticated enough to trace cell activity, and we have to assume they do, then it will appear to them that my response is coming from Midtown Manhattan, because that's where my cell actually will be. My response will be routed through my cell downtown. This will give us a small window of opportunity to rescue Kate. We miss this chance, they will most certainly kill her."

"I understand," Reginald said. "How will we determine the location?"

"With this little device that Roger loaned me," Jack said, pointing at a metal carrying case lying on the console between them. It was about the size of a thin briefcase.

"Actually," Jack continued, "Roger will pinpoint the source of the kidnapper's call while I try to keep them talking for as long as I can. Once Roger has determined the coordinates, he will feed that info through to this device."

Jack then flipped open the latches on the metal case, exposing a brightly illuminated screen. "Roger's feed will come up on this GPS map. All we have to do is follow it, and it will take us to the house where they are holding Kate. ... I tested it, and it is simple to operate."

"Can we do a dry run?" Reginald asked.

"No time," Jack replied. "But trust me, if we can get a fix on the location, it will lock in, and we can't miss it. It's accurate to within inches. Roger is controlling the whole thing from his end. He will be monitoring it and feeding our GPS the coordinates. ... It's all going to come down to our reacting quickly and decisively. We're up to it. I won't fail Kate."

"We *can't* fail Kate," Reginald quickly interjected. "I got her into this, and I am with you all the way. We will get her out, my friend."

Chapter 54—*The unexpected phone call*
7:18 p.m., Thursday, December 29

That one word more than got James's attention. "What did you say?" he asked the caller.

"I said you are plotting the assassination of the president of the United States," the caller said. "You and four of your associates have been meeting for at least two weeks, and you have decided to kill the president. Now, would you like to get a look at my story before you hear about it on cable news?"

"You're crazy," James said. "Where did you ever get an insane notion like that?"

"I'm crazy, am I?" the caller asked. "Well let me tell you just a little about what I know. Right now you are driving back from your fourth planning meeting. … Would you like me to name names right now? Because I am prepared to do it."

"What are you looking for?" James interrupted, not wanting to discuss the subject over his caller's cell. At that point James began to suspect a possible extortion plot.

"I want you to read my story."

"I'll read it, but I still think you're crazy," James said.

"Good," the caller said. "And we'll see just how crazy you think I am after you've read it."

"How are you going to get it to me?" James asked.

"It will be inside the mailbox at your apartment."

"You mailed it?" James asked.

"No, I just slipped it into your box."

"That's pretty damn stupid," James said. "What if someone else gets hold of it?"

"Well, I suppose you should probably get there first, don't you think?" With that, James heard his mystery caller disconnect.

For the next several moments James just stared numbly out of his windshield but continued driving. He could feel his heart race and beads of perspiration forming on his forehead. Finally, he called Allison.

"Al," he said, "we've got a situation."

"What's up?" Allison asked. "You're still on the road, right?"

"I am, but I just got a very disturbing phone call."

Allison paused before responding and then asked, "Okay, what exactly does that mean?"

"We can't discuss it now, or over our cell phones—but just imagine the worst. And just assume that everything's been compromised. We have got to get together tonight. There's no time to waste."

"Okay, I suppose I could meet you somewhere," she said. "What do you recommend?"

"I have to stop by my apartment, then we should meet at your place."

"My place?"

"It will have to be your place."

"In an hour?" she asked. "Is that about right?"

"Hour and a half—maybe even two. Can't be sure what the traffic will be like."

"That's fine, call me about ten minutes out," Allison said.

They disconnected, and James continued to drive and to stare straight ahead with unfocused eyes.

When James arrived at his apartment, he stopped outside at the curb and engaged his four-ways. He asked the doorman to keep an eye on his car as he ran into his building. When he opened his mailbox, he found a thick manila envelope. It was taped shut at the top. *Won't find any DNA on this one,* he thought, as he ripped it open.

Inside he found a neatly printed document of about forty pages, with a short table of contents on the first page: "Meeting One, Meeting Two, Meeting Three, Meeting Four." Immediately he turned to the last segment—Meeting Four. There he found a transcript of the entire meeting he had just attended. Quickly he slid the material back into the envelope and raced back to his car, thanking the doorman with a ten-dollar bill on the way.

James realized just how disconcerted this had made him, and he started to check himself on everything he was doing. He took a look at his gas gauge. He made sure to turn his flashers off. He was careful to observe traffic signals and obey the speed limit. The last thing he needed to have happen would be to get stopped for a violation.

The whole drive over to Allison's apartment seemed to take only a moment. "I'm here already?" he muttered, as he speed dialed her number. "I'm nearly there," he said, when she answered.

"James, this is how we have to do this," Allison said. She was having second thoughts about having James join her in her personal apartment. "Park in the rear ramp. Combination is 61113. That gets you in the ramp. Then ring Bernadette from the rear entry, and I will buzz you in. Get on elevator three. The code for that is 11613. Get off on the fourth floor—Bernadette's apartment is the only apartment on the fourth floor."

Allison was loath to surrender the privacy she enjoyed as Bernadette. But this was a special circumstance—an emergency. She needed to avoid Secret Service scrutiny. James would have to get past the Service at the rear door. That would be no problem. But she could not allow him into Allison's apartment. Once he was inside the building, she reasoned, he would have no problem getting to Bernadette's apartment, provided she give him the proper codes.

James did as she directed. He parked in the rear private parking garage, and she buzzed him in the building. He then rode the elevator to the fourth floor and knocked on her door.

As she opened the door, she went on the attack. "What's this you're telling me?" she spit out, looking more agitated than inquisitive.

Under ordinary circumstances James would have made a comment about the secret apartment. But he was altogether too troubled at this time. "I don't know yet," he replied. "This fellow called me on my private cell. He shouldn't have had that number. At first I hung up. But he called back immediately, and said this one word—assassination. That got my attention. He then told me that he had deposited a document in my mailbox."

Holding up the envelope for Allison to see, James said, "This is what he left for me. He said it is an article he is set to publish.

"I have no idea yet what it involves, but I soon should. I've only just begun to scrutinize it. I will say, at least on the surface, it looks to be very detailed, and very damaging."

Allison had already poured herself and James large drinking glasses of Scotch. Each drink had a single rapidly dissolving ice cube floating on top. She knew this was going to be a very long night. And she knew James would be studying this document, line by line and word by word. She was used to his style. She knew he would not be asking her opinion about anything, at least not for a long time.

At some point, she had no idea when it might be, James would determine the document's origin and, more importantly, the motive behind it. He might, along the way, need to ask her about certain specifics—details that only she would know about. But he would not be looking to her for any help drawing a conclusion. There might be opportunities down the road for her input, but for right now, the best service Allison could offer would be to remain at his side and keep quiet until called upon. She had found that Scotch, and plenty of it, helped her relax enough not to interrupt.

Allison quickly found her glass to be half empty. She realized that she had already dramatically mellowed out. But James had not yet shouted his customary "I've got it!" So Allison slid her glass over to him and took his. Within twenty minutes, she took both glasses, announcing that she was going to "freshen them up." She topped both off (this time skipping the ice altogether), and returned to where he was working.

Finally, after over two hours of poring over the transcript, it was obvious even to a substantially inebriated Allison that James was on to something. Rapidly he started flipping pages, checking notations, then skipping from the middle of the document to the end. Then back. He repeated this nervous exercise in a near feverish frenzy.

Then it all stopped. He slid his chair back and just stared at the ceiling. "Al, I've got something here. I'm not exactly sure what it is, but I see a definite pattern. Take a look at this. Let me show you what I am talking about. It is just plain shocking."

Chapter 55—James reveals the transcript to Allison

11:47 p.m., Thursday, December 29

James had been intently studying the document for some time. Finally, he reached over to take his first sip of the drink Allison had poured for him. "Where's that Scotch?" he asked, as he made room for Allison to slide up close enough to read some passages he wanted to show her. "Here, take a look at this. These are the notes from the first meeting. Notice how specific everything is. … For instance, it quotes verbatim what everyone says."

"Let me see that," Allison demanded, sliding the paper close enough so she could read it easily. "Oh my God, James, somehow they recorded it. How the hell did they do that? You put that damn wand on each one of us. How did they *do* that?"

"That threw me off at first," James said. "But then I took a long hard look at the notes from the third meeting. There is a major difference."

"What do you mean?" she asked.

"Look," James said, "the rendering of the first two meetings is virtually word for word. The only way that could have been accomplished is if the meeting was recorded. But meeting three is different. Look at this. It's not word for word—it's summarized. Meeting three was either not recorded, or it was transcribed by a different person. But I don't think it was a different person. I'm certain the same person is responsible for the whole transcript. Look at the words I have underlined. They represent misspellings. The transcriber misspelled the same words throughout— and they are simple words. That's not uncommon for a person, even an intelligent, well-educated person, if that person has learned English as a second language. Frequently foreign operatives make slip-ups like that.

"Now, if we take that one step further and look at the *specific* words that are misspelled, then, if we get lucky we might be able to ascertain the nationality of the transcriber."

James then slid the transcript closer to Allison, so he could better demonstrate to her what he was suggesting. "This word, 'still,' is misspelled 'stil' throughout. And it is misspelled in the same way. That is a key. Israelis who have learned English as a second language frequently make that mistake. Now, it might seem strange that an Israeli would make such a mistake, given so many have been educated in the States, but this transcriber must have been educated primarily in Israel. Whatever the reason, I am quite sure we are dealing with Israeli Intelligence—Mossad. Maybe we did just get lucky."

"Mossad?" Allison said. "That's what you had suspected from the start, right?"

"It is," James responded.

"But how did Mossad record us?" Allison asked.

"This is what I think happened," James said. "All the meetings, except for the third, were recorded and transcribed virtually verbatim. The third meeting, however, was not recorded. Instead, someone who was at that meeting, who then took notes about the meeting, produced it. Here, let me show you," James said, turning back to the first meeting, and reading from the transcription:

Allison: "As I said, the meetings will be no longer than one hour in length. And there will be no more than four of them. If we find we can't get done what we need to get done under those constraints, that would indicate a lack of consensus, then we'll simply dissolve the group. Unless we are on the same page, unless we all view the problem in a similar fashion, it wouldn't matter how many meetings we held, or how long they were.

"All of you probably already know why we are having these meetings. But just in case you're not sure about it, I'll tell you.

"Virtually every contested seat in the House went south—we lost them all. Same is likely to happen in the Senate next election. It seems likely that whatever we did not lose in the midterm will be lost in the presidential. Unless things change—and I mean radically change. This guy is about to run the country into the ground, and the people know it. They don't believe a word he says, and he can't sell anything. ... That is, even if he had something to sell."

Steve: "Do you size him up as a one-termer?"

Allison: "Definitely. And even if I were the nominee instead, if the libertarian coalition puts up a strong candidate, I might not win. The direction we're going, and the speed we're traveling, who knows what will be left in two years. If they take control of both houses *and* the White House, they will consider it a mandate, and overturn all the gains we have made over the past twenty-five years."

Jerry: "What are you looking for from us?"

"The transcript for the first meeting is the product of a recording, Al," James said, "there is no doubt about it."

"But that is impossible," Allison said. "You checked carefully for any type of recording devices."

"I did, but I am now virtually positive I know how they did it," James said. "Here, check this out," he said, turning to the transcript of the third meeting. "See the difference between the two?" He then began reading from the transcript's rendering of the third meeting.

James: "Jerry's not going to be coming tonight. He has an infection."

Allison: "I am disappointed, we have some important business to discuss, and Jerry should be here."

James: "Jerry apologized. But he simply cannot hear right now, and he is running a temperature. I am sure Jerry is in agreement with the direction we are going."

Allison: "We need Jerry here to help Reg and Steve to get along."

James: "I will step in and help in that regard. ..."

"That, Al, is a redaction—a summary," James said confidently. "The transcriber did not have a recording of that meeting to work from—only a summarization. He then turned it back into a dialog. Whoever wrote the summary left out a lot of the details, such as the comments about Steve being gay. I don't see anything about that in the transcription of the third meeting. Yet I recall that comment. And I promise you that if the transcriber would have heard that, he would have made mention of it. The fact that it is lacking is significant."

"My God, you're right!" Allison exclaimed.

"And this begs two questions," James continued. "Why did the transcriber *not* have a recording of meeting three? And where did he get the summary? One of us had to have written notes, from memory, after the meeting. I know it was not I who wrote them. That leaves Jerry, Reg, or Steve—"

"James, I think I know where the notes of meeting three might have come from," Allison said. "*I* made a recording after every meeting. I could have been the source."

"That definitely could explain it," James said. "I sort of suspected that might be the case, as the comments from the third meeting seemed to be more from your perspective, just a bit." James paused for a moment, then continued. "We need to take a look at how they got those notes, but it is more critical to find out how the other meetings were recorded. I am also pretty certain I know how that was done, as well."

Allison did not respond, she simply looked deeply into James's eyes. She was eager to learn what he had concluded.

"The only possibility, as I see it, was that Jerry was the source," James said.

Allison, still looking squarely at James, asked, "What are you saying? I have known Jerry for two decades. I always have trusted him."

"Well, he is responsible for this breach," James stated confidently. "But he might not have even been aware of what he was doing. He could have been an unwitting accomplice."

"Unwilling or unwitting?" Allison asked.

"At least unwitting," James answered. "Actually, I doubt that he was even aware it was happening. His cochlear implant was the instrument used. It must have been fitted with a recorder and a transmitter of some sort. Most likely the same mic that it used to help Jerry hear, also fed a digital recorder. Then, after the meetings, Mossad sent a signal to it that caused the transmitter to come alive and transmit what had been recorded at our meetings. Perhaps it transmitted on a set schedule. Jerry missed only that third meeting. And that was the one that the transcriber had the problems with. He had to work from a summary."

"Jerry was the source?" Allison asked. "Are you sure about that?"

"As sure as I can be," James said. "But, as I said, I'm quite sure that he did not knowingly cooperate.

"There is one more interesting aspect here," James said, fingering his way through the document. "It is quite obvious that while the source for meeting number three was different from the others, it is equally clear that the transcriber was the same for all."

"How can you possibly be sure of that?" Allison asked, struggling to understand what her friend was suggesting.

"Here, take a look at this," James said, turning to the page that contained the notes from the first meeting held at Jerry's cottage—which was actually the second meeting overall. He had folded the right top corner of that page so he could find it easily. "Here Steve requests hamburgers instead of sandwiches for Reg," James read. "Check out how the transcriber misspells hamburger." James then pointed out that part of the text, and read it slowly. "h-u-m-b-o-r-g-e-r."

"Now," James continued, "if we turn to Steve's comment before meeting three, when he first realized that Jerry would not be there. Again he made a reference to hamburgers, and again it is misspelled in exactly the same way—"h-u-m-b-o-r-g-e-r."

"You're right," Allison agreed, "but what does that prove?"

"It doesn't actually *prove* anything," James said, "but it does strongly suggest two things. First, that the same transcriber was employed to deal with the recording of the second meeting and with the redaction of the third meeting. But that is not all. By the very nature of the misspelling, we can also surmise that the transcriber is Israeli. Again, most likely a Mossad agent."

"That sounds like a leap," Allison said.

"Not really," James said. "The Israelis are an independent bunch. It is common for restaurants in Tel Aviv to have handwritten English menus. And it is a common occurrence for them to misspell hamburger the same way our transcriber misspelled it."

"Oh my God," Allison said. "James, you are a genius!"

"It's no different from solving any puzzle," James said.

Neither of them said anything for a moment. Finally, Allison leaned back onto the pillows, reached down, and took another long drink from her much-used glass of Scotch. "What do we do now?" she asked. "What do we do about Jerry?"

"It's not so much what we do about Jerry," James said. "The real problem is what we do about this transcript."

"What *can* we do?" she asked.

"First, we have to consider what the real purpose of it is. I am convinced that it was made by Mossad, and that Mossad has all the original recordings. And that is the best of all possibilities."

"Why is that?" Allison asked.

"Because Mossad is both thoughtful and predictable," James answered.

Just then there was a loud banging at the door.

Chapter 56—*The not-so-safe safe room*
3:20 a.m., Friday, December 30

Their attention immediately turned to figuring out a way to get out of the building. "Has to be a fire escape—code demands it."

"There's a fire escape off the back. But you can bet your sweet ass they're watching it."

"FBI. Open the door or we'll smash it down. We have a search warrant."

"Don't worry about that door," Allison consoled James, "it's very sturdy. This whole apartment is a safe room. Even the fire escape window is designed to resist entry from the outside."

"Al. If that actually is the FBI, they will get in. They'll cut through the wall."

"Two layers of tempered steel, concrete filled, it is one-hour cutting-bar rated." Allison thought for a short moment, then stood. "Grab all your stuff, James. This will buy us a little time." She grabbed James's hand and led him into the bedroom, and then into the walk-in closet. There she opened the top left drawer of a built-in cabinet. She pulled it out until it stopped, then firmly yanked it. It was that last inch that released the latch securing the wall panel behind it. She then pushed the drawer back in, leaving it open just enough for her to slide her fingers into the cavity. She gripped the ridge above the drawer and pulled firmly. The whole cabinet was part of the door mechanism leading from the Bernadette apartment into the spiral staircase. Allison then pulled the heavy door open. As she did, a motion sensor turned on a small battery-powered light that illuminated the staircase.

"What is this?" James asked, not believing his eyes.

"This is how we get outta here."

"I can't believe this. I always wondered how you did this. You're some kind of a James Bond."

"This is how we do it. Take a piss right now, because you might spend a while in here."

James just stared at Allison for a few seconds. "Go ahead—do it."

James recognized Allison's tone of command. *She's back on her game,* he thought, as he started unzipping his trousers on the way to the toilet.

Allison then briskly went into the kitchen, opened a drawer, and removed two one-gallon Ziploc bags, three bottles of water, and a roll of paper towels. She then headed back toward the secret staircase. But, instead of entering the closet to wait for James, she detoured into the bedroom, closing the door behind her. Quickly she changed from the robe into a pants suit and found a pair of Allison's shoes.

She then walked over to the bed and removed a Walther semi-automatic pistol from beneath a pillow. She lifted her top, exposing a small roll of fat that hung just a bit over the top of her slacks. At first she slid the pistol under her pants. Realizing that it was not secure there, she removed it and tossed it onto her bed. She then grabbed a thin belt out of a drawer. Again lifting her top, she placed the belt around her midsection and tightened it until it was snug but not uncomfortable. She then tucked the Walther under the belt and pulled her top over it. *This is going to be a crazy day. Never know what might come in handy,* she thought as she made her way to the staircase, where James was waiting.

"Here, take this," she said, handing James the bags and paper towels.

"What is this for?"

"Use your imagination," Allison barked, glaring into his eyes over her glasses. "Take it!" Allison had given James the roll of paper towel and Ziploc bags in the event that he were to be stuck in the stairwell for an extended period of time. She did not want to reveal the storage cabinet to him, at least not now, because she did not want to have to restock it later.

James smiled and took the bags and towels from her and stepped into the staircase shaft. Allison still remained in the closet. She was nearly, if not totally, sober by now. Adrenalin was kicking in, counteracting the alcohol.

She carefully slid the magic drawer back into the cabinet until she heard a familiar click. That indicated the latching mechanism on the door could be engaged. She then entered the stairwell with James and began to pull the door closed behind them.

"Hold on. Stop." James squeezed past her and trotted to the office where they had been talking. He snatched up the laptop, yanking the power cord out of it, and hurriedly made his way back to the stairway. Allison had followed him to see what he was doing.

"Can't believe I almost forgot this. I must be getting old, Al."

James then walked down the first three steps and waited. Allison re-entered the stairwell and pulled the heavy door closed behind her. She gave a final tug on the door handle until she heard the lock engage. Then, she engaged a second lock, this one on the inside of the stairwell.

With the door closed and double-locked, the stairwell became a secret inner sanctum within Allison's safe room complex.

"Okay, James, let me squeeze through," she said, as she gripped his elbow and pushed past him. "This is not going to be very comfortable, but I'll get you outta here as quickly as I can. If the light goes out, just move around a bit, and it will come back on."

"Wonderful," James muttered.

Just as Allison reached the door leading into her lower apartment bedroom, there was a large explosion, followed by the building's fire alarm sirens. It was obviously coming from the door to Bernadette's upper apartment.

Chapter 57—Bernadette's apartment under attack

3:31 a.m., Friday, December 30

The whole building shook as the result of the explosion.

"Holy crap," James exclaimed in a very loud whisper. "Shock and awe. So much for your 'safe door,' Al. Nothing's safe when you get the FBI involved."

"Damn it all," Allison muttered as she continued on down the steps and opened the door at the bottom. "I'll let you know what's going on as soon as possible. There's an intercom. I'll hit you on it."

Allison then entered her bedroom closet and secured the door behind her.

Even though there was steel in the walls, James could hear several people tearing through the apartment he and Allison had just vacated. Placing the roll of paper towel on the floor of the upper landing, he carefully sat down on it, using it to cushion the hard surface of the stairs. *This could be a while*, he thought. Then, realizing that his phone was still on, he carefully took it out of its holster and removed the battery. He checked to be sure that the Wi-Fi feature on the laptop was not engaged.

James then sensed the smell of DMDNB, a common C-4 odorizing taggant, wafting through the ventilation system. "C-4? Whoever pulled this off was *highly* motivated," he mouthed, as he settled in for the wait.

After a few minutes, the timer on the light cycled, and the light turned off. For a few moments James just sat there motionless, his eyes adjusting to the total darkness. That is when he noticed the glow of a small red LED squinting from under a partially closed steel cover on the wall beside the upper staircase door. He lifted himself to his feet to inspect it. The motion of his rising triggered the stairwell light.

He quietly walked over to the box and opened it. Inside he found a seventeen-inch LCD flat panel monitor. Directly below the monitor was what looked like a CCTV multiplexer. He pushed the "View" button, and it came to life.

"Holy cow!" he whispered. "What has Allison got here?" He quickly realized that he was watching the ransacking of the upper-level apartment. It was then that he noticed that something did not look right. He drew his face closer to the monitor.

"Hold on. That is not the FBI. But who could they be? Must be some spooks, or rogue spooks. Could be the Russians. ... or Mossad."

He continued watching as the band of seven or eight intruders tossed the apartment. Then, apparently not finding what they were looking for, they left.

"Just what I thought—definitely not the FBI. If it were the FBI, they would have secured the scene. These guys, whoever they were, just took off. Who could they be?"

James pondered what had just transpired before his eyes. "I would bet on Mossad. But I thought they already had everything they needed."

James stood there scrutinizing the monitor. He found a little joystick and zoomed in on the entry door, at least what was left of it. Even after ten minutes, there remained a detectable haze throughout the entry area from the explosion.

"Looks like six distinct charges were used—all relatively small," he whispered to himself. "C-4. That smacks of spooks. Somebody's spooks. Almost surgical but definitely effective. They took half the wall down on each side. So much for the cutting-bar-rated safe-room door," he chuckled audibly.

James zoomed in farther and noticed that several plastic crime-scene tapes had been secured across the gaping hole where the door used to be. "They're not coming back. If they were going to come back, they would have secured and occupied. They were looking for something and didn't find it. Maybe they were looking for Al and me."

James then saw a button on the monitor that read "Area Two" and pushed it. With that, a new set of images appeared on the screen. He immediately recognized what he was looking at. "That's Al's bedroom. And there's Al."

Feeling just a bit like a peeping Tom, he zoomed in on Allison anyway.

"And what is this?" he whispered. "Al's packing iron? My God, what is this world comin' to?"

Allison had just removed her top, exposing the tightly secured belt around her midsection with a small Walther semi-auto tucked under it. "I wonder if she has a permit for that?"

Just then Allison stopped in her tracks. Even though totally preoccupied with what was about to confront her outside her bedroom, she suddenly realized that James would most certainly have found the camera system and figured out how to operate it. She pulled the Walther out from under the belt and pointed it in the direction of the camera. She then emulated the recoil of discharging a round. Smirking as only Allison could smirk, she lowered the pistol and delivered a very deliberate middle finger at the camera.

Of all the faults James might have had, voyeurism was not one of them. He then switched to a group of cameras called "Area Three."

"Okay, here we go. That looks like the rest of Al's lower apartment. And all hell has broken out."

James's observation was correct. The apartment was full of FBI and

Secret Service agents. "One, two, three, four, five, six, seven. There must be a dozen. That's way more than usual. I wonder how that rogue unit got past them?"

James then switched on "Area Four." Suddenly the images on the screen became very tiny. "Holy crap. That's a lot of cameras." He squinted to see if he could determine exactly what he was looking at and touched the top left image. Immediately a full-screen video opened, showing the lobby. "That's more like it," James exclaimed out loud.

In the lobby were a dozen uniformed and heavily armed men. "That's our guys," he said, going back to his whisper voice. He then found the street cameras and began moving them around with the joystick. "The street is totally cordoned off.

"How did those fellows who broke in here get into the building in the first place?" James whispered. "There must be some sort of recording device on these cameras."

Now James was on a mission. He had taken his contacts out earlier, so he reached into his pocket and pulled out a pair of reading glasses. "Okay, James, you should be able to figure this out," he muttered to himself.

James continued to fiddle with some of the buttons but still to no avail. He then stopped and leaned back a little. *I'm at least average intelligence,* he reasoned. *Surely this box has to be simple enough for me to figure out.*

He then touched an on-screen button that read: "View History." Immediately the images disappeared from the screen, and a list came up. "Let's see, Area Three."

He touched "Area Three," and another list appeared. He then looked down at his watch. It was five a.m. He then touched "3 AM" on the screen, and the screen filled with all the images in Area Three, but from two hours ago.

"Okay, let's start with this one," James whispered as he touched the lobby camera. He then hit "Fast Forward" to expedite the process. Initially, there was only a single Secret Service agent in the lobby. As the video replay approached the time of the explosion, James slowed it down. At 3:34 the camera shook.

That's when they blew the door in, James reasoned. *But I did not see those fellows come into the building.*

James then repeated the process viewing the rear courtyard entrance. Still he saw no one entering.

James removed his glasses and sat down on the steps to think. "Think, James. Use your brain."

He then smiled broadly, as though he had just developed the unified theory. "Could they *live* here? Do our friends live right here in Allison's building?"

James's eyes just glared at the wall and beyond. He sat there for a few more moments, trying to assimilate all the data and to determine his course of action.

As he always seemed to do, James continued whispering aloud what he was doing. He liked to hear his own words as his thoughts produced them—he felt that was useful in putting everything in order. "Okay, so they're either tenants of the building, or rogue Secret Service." He paused another few seconds. "Can't be rogue agents, 'cuz there were just too many of them. They *must* live here!"

James needed a plan, and he needed it immediately. He knew that the men who broke into the upper apartment had to have been aware of the private entrance to that apartment. And, therefore, would probably have known that he had entered Allison's secret apartment. He then grabbed his cell phone and put the battery back in. He hated doing this, because he knew that it could be traced and monitored, but he had to contact Allison immediately.

As soon as it came alive, he dialed Allison's cell. By this time, Bernadette had transformed back to Allison, and she was preparing to leave her bedroom. When the phone vibrated, Allison stopped and answered it. "Yes."

"Hey, hold on. I'm coming down."

"What?"

"Al, those guys that blew up this apartment live in this building. They knew about the secret apartment, and they knew about your secret identity. They have to know about me as well."

"So?"

"Look, our cover is blown. If they know about this, soon everyone will. Our DNA is all over this place."

"If you come up here now, we can make it look like we're having an affair."

"Right! How the hell is that gonna go over? A former first lady screwing around with her husband's former top aide? I want to be president. Not on the cover of grocery store tabloids. You're not gonna make a fool of me. I've worked too—"

"Al, half the people in the country think you're a lesbian. Most of them still love you, and all of them respect you. This sort of steamy, sordid thing can do nothing but help. And it will deflect—"

"James, you can't talk to me like that."

"I'm right. You know I'm right."

Allison paused for a moment. "I've got to go out there. The Secret Service has to be going nuts."

"Hang on for a few minutes, and I'm coming down." James then again checked the camera monitor, Area One. He went from camera to camera, making sure that no one was in the upper apartment. He then found the latch on the door and re-entered the Bernadette apartment. He ran over to the bed and yanked all the covers off. He then took a handful of saliva and smeared it on a pillow.

"That's my DNA; but what about Al's. I doubt that she ever slept in this bed." James thought for a moment, then walked quickly over to the bowl that Allison had used when she was vomiting. He dumped the smelly remains in the toilet and flushed. He rinsed the larger residue out and dumped it into the toilet as well, and flushed again. Taking the bowl over to the bed, he wiped it dry using the pillow on the other side of the bed.

"And that's Al's DNA. We're now officially lovers. Who would ever have thought that?"

James then returned to the secret passage way, securely closed the door behind him, and went down the spiral staircase to join his "lover." An involuntary smile, almost sardonic, locked his face.

"We are going to pull this off—it's gonna work!" he said aloud as he prepared to confront Allison.

By the time he reached the bottom of the stairs, Allison had opened the door and was waiting for him.

It was immediately obvious to James that Allison was not sold on his idea. She looked very angry, but she did not open her mouth. Instead, she just stood in front of him, blocking his departure from the stairs, arms crossed, and with her Walther tightly gripped in her right hand.

"Al, it has to be this way. We need a distraction. We have to get the press looking in a different direction."

"Continue," Allison said, still not allowing James past her.

"It's the old story, 'sex sells.' Given two stories, a harmless explosion in your building, or a steamy sex scandal, they will run with the sex. In fact, I doubt that the explosion will even get out there at all. The Secret Service won't be talking about it."

"You bastard. How could you let this happen? I should just shoot you now and leave your body in the stairwell until you rot. *Damn* you."

"You wouldn't do that. I don't smell so good now, imagine how it would be after a couple warm days in *that* coffin? Just trust me on this one, you know I have never let you down."

"Tell me how this is gonna work." Allison backed up and let James out and then secured the stairwell door behind him.

"This is what we do."

"Make it fast, I've got to go out there and face the music."

"Right. I put our DNA on the bed upstairs. It will look like that apartment was our private love nest."

"How'd you do that?"

"Not important. Now we simply have to put on our 'guilty' faces and walk out of your bedroom door. Everyone will assume the obvious, and they will do everything they can to cover it up. That's what the Service does best."

"That's how Bob survived those eight years," Allison said, agreeing with him.

"That's all we have to do—at least for right now. Our friends who blew up the apartment know better, but they're not going to be talking. They have other interests. I have to get to the bottom of that, but not right this second.

"Ready? Let's do it."

"Wait!" Allison commanded, grabbing James's arm just before they left the bedroom. "What do you mean, they *blew up the apartment*?"

"The door, right after you left. Seven or eight guys with jackets, not uniforms. They used C-4 and blew in the door. They just rushed in, tossed it, didn't find what they were looking for—or at least I assume they didn't find it—and then they left."

"Were they in the bedroom?"

"Yes, but only for a minute. I reviewed the video. I didn't see them entering the building, so I think they must have been here earlier. I think they might even live in your building."

"I've gotta check something," Allison said, briskly moving to the secret stairway. She quickly opened the cabinet drawer and pulled the stairway door open. With James right behind her, she started up the spiral staircase at a rapid clip. This time she did not bother to remove her shoes. As she reached the top of the stairs, she stopped to view the status of the alarm panel and the cameras in the apartment. She wanted to be sure that no one was waiting for them in the apartment. Satisfied that the Secret Service had not yet secured the area, she opened the door to the upper apartment and entered.

With James right behind her, she quickly moved from the closet staircase to the bathroom. There she saw that the toilet paper dispenser had been removed from the wall and was lying on the floor.

"Those bastards took them!" she exclaimed.

"Took what?"

"The memory sticks—thumb drives, among other things, possibly."

"Thumb drives?"

"Yes. The sticks I recorded the meetings on. That's where I stored them. And now they have them all."

"Why would they still want them?" James asked. "They have the other recordings, and they copied most of those sticks already." He paused for a moment and just stared without focusing, which he commonly did when deep in thought. "They want to have the originals. For down the road. They will use them for leverage when you're president.

It makes sense. Those original sticks will even have your prints on them. That's what they wanted—real, hard evidence. ... Nothing's changed, Al. We know who we're dealing with, and we know what they're up to."

"I want to know how they knew where to look." Allison paused for just a moment, then continued. "Those nosey bastards must have cameras in here. Right here in my bathroom. Right in my damn *bathroom!*"

"Could be. But don't bother to look for them, they'd be gone now," James said. "They would have been wireless cameras, and the guys who broke in would have grabbed them before they left. ... They must have been in earlier and copied the drives. That's how they had the notes from the third meeting. They probably had covert mics in here as well. Didn't you ever have this place swept?"

"No one was supposed to know this apartment even existed," Allison said defensively. "I used the equipment Bob got us when we were in the White House. It never turned up anything."

"That old stuff is useless against what the agencies are using now. What else did they get?"

"Nothing critical, just some jewelry."

"Jewelry?"

"Right, when I was going out as Bernadette, I would slip my rings in a Ziploc bag and hide them in here. Then when I came back, I would remove Bernadette's rings and put mine back on. This time I didn't bother. I still have Bernadette's jewelry on."

"You mean these rings?" James asked, picking a small plastic bag up from the floor.

"Yes. Those are my rings. There's over fifty thousand dollars in that bag, and they just tossed it on the floor."

"That just proves that it couldn't have been FBI, CIA, or the Russians," James said, chuckling. "Any one of them would have taken the jewelry."

"Tell me again why they wanted my recordings?" Allison asked.

"Evidence, hard evidence. Fingerprints … DNA. Once you're president, they will expect favors. Then, when you retire, you'll receive a package with them in. They really do not want to hurt, or even embarrass, you." James thought for just a moment, then smiled and continued. "You could probably display them in your presidential library someday. Do you plan to have your own, or just an annex on Bob's?"

Allison heard James's comments, but did not respond.

"Okay, let's summarize," James said. "Your recordings were not the primary source of the leak. They did not have the last thumb drive until just a few minutes ago, but they really did not need it, because they had the recording through Jerry's implant. So, now they have *all* your recordings—your redactions. They don't really have anything they didn't have before, except that they now have your originals. Unless there was something else on those sticks besides your recollections of the meetings. Was there anything else?"

"No, the only thing on those drives were the recordings of notes from the meetings."

"And there is nothing else missing?"

"Correct. The jewelry is all here; only the thumb drives are missing."

Allison snatched up the bag of rings as they turned to leave, but James intercepted her. "You need to put that back. This whole place just might become a crime scene before long. Here, let me have it."

Allison reluctantly handed the bag to James. He wiped his fingerprints off with a damp tissue and dropped it back into the compartment in the wall. Then, using another tissue, placed the toilet paper holder back into its place.

As they headed back to the staircase, James said, "Nothing has changed, Al. We're dealing with the same people. We can't be totally certain as to why they wanted those recordings. But nothing fundamental has changed."

After they both entered the stairwell and closed the door behind them, James took Allison's arm and said, "Here's the plan. We go out and face the Secret Service, and anyone else waiting on the other side of your bedroom door. It doesn't matter who's there. We go out together. We say nothing about it, but our actions amount to confessing an affair. That's no problem."

Allison was not pleased about this aspect of James's plan, but she knew that if James considered it their only recourse, most likely it was.

"The only thing we say is that you will be holding a press conference later today."

"And what, exactly, am I going to say at that press conference?"

"We'll work out those details. Just the announcement that there will be a press conference buys us the time we need. We have to determine just what is known, and what is only suspected. Then we will know how to handle the press. One thing for sure, we want the questions to be about our affair. You can plead ignorance about everything else. But you will have to be convincing and contrite about the affair. No pointing of fingers. No denying. You confess that you and I are having an affair. Don't call it an affair. Use words like 'indiscretion,' and 'became intimate.' Avoid calling it an affair. And that is all they're going to be interested in. That announcement will run the weekend news cycle and beyond, and that will buy us the time we need to get the rest of this stuff in order."

James and Allison continued down the stairs and entered the lower-level apartment, securing the door behind them.

As they walked over to the bedroom door, James took Allison's hand. At first she started to pull away. James looked down into her eyes and took her hand again. He then reached down and unlocked the door, and the two of them walked out, hand in hand.

Positioned throughout the room were over a dozen heavily armed and fully uniformed men, all pointing automatic weapons in their direction.

"Get on the floor, face down," the leader loudly commanded.

Chapter 58—Let's see what flies

4:10 a.m., Friday, December 30

Roger Minsk was the Secret Service agent in charge of Allison's detail. Without hesitation he jumped between the former first lady and the FBI agent. "Hold everything!" he commanded, "I'm in charge here, and the first lady will not be intimidated by you. Call your superior if you have a problem with this. But you keep your hands off her. And the same goes for her advisor, James. When he's with her, I'm in charge of him as well. You have *no* authority here."

The FBI agent backed down, lowered his rifle, and ordered his men to stand down.

"You may be investigating a crime, but that crime did not occur here. So take your men out of this apartment."

"I need to question these two," the FBI agent protested.

"No you don't. You need to leave here immediately. These two are my responsibility. You have no business here. Get your men out of here. Now!"

Roger was very familiar with Allison's erratic antics during her years in the White House. The two had bonded. Allison was not the easiest person in the world to get along with, but Roger had mastered the art. He genuinely liked her. That's why she requested him to protect her. Not only did she trust him, but she was very fond of Roger. Most of the time, if not all of it, Allison felt closer to Roger than she did her own husband. She knew that Roger always had her best interests at heart—and as far as she was concerned, the same could not be said of her husband. She admired and respected the former president, but she could not trust him, and there certainly were many times during their marriage when she questioned his love for her. Allison knew that Bob would always look out for his own interests over hers.

When, however, their interests overlapped, Bob could be counted on as a solid ally.

That was not the case with Roger. Her friend was ready, on this and every day, to do physical battle for her, even if it meant he had to tangle with a heavily armed FBI agent. Had Bob, her husband, been there instead of Roger, he would have acquiesced to the wishes of the FBI, as long as it did not directly involve him.

That is not to say that Bob was a coward. Bob actually liked to fight. Many times, even during his presidency, Bob would grab a man whom he judged to be out of line and throw him to the floor. He sometimes slapped senseless those he perceived to be his enemies. But he would not defend Allison in that way. It was as though Bob had detached himself from her to the degree that he was willing to let her fight her own battles. Fortunately for Allison, Roger was in charge on this occasion.

The FBI agent in charge was not happy about Roger's intervention, but he did recognize the fact that the Secret Service actually was the agency of authority in this situation. "I'll be back," he said, pointing his finger in James's face. "And I'll have the proper warrant." He turned and started to walk away, but then he twisted his body around enough to make eye contact with James and blurted out, "at the very least you two are material witnesses. You will have to answer my questions sooner or later."

James knew better than to open his mouth. It was not his nature to get pushed around, but he did not want to say anything that could somehow be used against him later.

Once the FBI had cleared the apartment, Roger requested that everyone else leave the room except for Allison, James, and himself. No one ever questioned Roger's orders, so the room immediately emptied. Then, after he was certain no one except for the three of them remained within earshot, he addressed Allison. "We've got a situation in the building. There was some sort of explosion upstairs. Did you know about that?"

"I felt the building shake a little. What was it all about?" Allison asked.

"Don't know much about it. It might have been a gas leak. There was no fire. The FBI has taken over the investigation. I don't know what they want with you. I know you were in your bedroom the whole time. They, and Homeland Security, they get a little overzealous sometimes."

"We've been busy preparing for Allison's press conference this afternoon," James jumped in.

Roger looked over at James, shaking his head slowly in surprise. "There's no press conference on the schedule for today. What press conference are you talking about?" Roger asked.

Roger did not like surprises. He ran her security detail like a finely tuned machine. It was, in fact, his almost inordinate attention to minutia that made him so effective. Roger would even monitor the amount of liquid Allison drank and the type of food she ate, so that he could predict the frequency of her restroom breaks. When he suspected that she was going to need a break, he would send a female agent in ahead to inspect the facilities.

Allison knew that the news about the unplanned press conference would frustrate Roger, so she tried to calm him down.

"I'm sorry to do this to you, Roger, but this is an emergency. James received a very disturbing call a few hours ago. Apparently a local news outlet is about to release a story that could be very embarrassing, particularly for me."

"What sort of story?" Roger asked.

"I can't really discuss it right now," Allison explained. "But that's what this press conference is going to be about."

"Where are you going to hold it?" Roger asked. He knew that if he were going to secure the area, he would have to know precisely where and when it was going to be held.

"Downstairs in the lobby," James interrupted. "No point making your job tougher than it already is."

James had not selected the lobby for Roger's benefit. James wanted to get the press tightly packed into the lobby of Allison's building. That would make the conference seem more intimate and impromptu on TV. Plus, holding it near Allison's apartment would add weight to the sexual nature of his relationship with her, which was actually the concept that he was going to sell.

"Roger, would you please bring Janet and Lesley back in? I need to talk to them," Allison said, more in a tone of request than command.

Janet and Lesley served as Allison's principal aides. When she was in her apartment, or traveling, those two young ladies were always close by.

Both Allison and Roger knew that a Secret Service agent, even the agent in charge, did not have the authority to "clear the room," particularly when two of the people in the room were members of her personal staff. But she understood what Roger was trying to accomplish. So, for that reason, she had acquiesced to his request that her staff leave. Allison was not in any sense threatened by Roger. But now she needed to get some business done, and she needed Janet and Lesley to help her do it.

"Yes, ma'am," Roger responded. "But, before I get them, may I have your permission to do a quick inspection of your bedroom? I just want to be sure there is no obvious presence of gas or other explosives."

"Please. Check it out," Allison replied. "Then lock the door and send my aides in. James and I will be in the study."

"Yes, ma'am." Roger then opened a case he always seemed to have nearby and removed and activated a curious-looking little sniffing device. Then, briskly making his way through Allison's bedroom, he poked and prodded with the little instrument along the door, on the floor, and generally throughout the apartment bedroom, constantly checking readouts on the tool's small digital screen.

About two minutes later, he came out and locked the door behind him. He then entered the hall outside the apartment, where Janet and Lesley were waiting, and asked them to join Allison in the study. He also thanked the rest of the staff for their patience, and said it was okay for them to return.

As this group of trusted employees, along with the two Secret Service agents who were on duty that day, headed back to their positions in Allison's apartment, Roger closed and secured the door behind them. He then turned around and headed toward the stairs. Even though Roger was not a young man, he was in great shape. He ran down the steel edged concrete stairs like a man half his age. Emerging at the main level, he virtually trotted over to where the doorman was stationed. "I'm gonna need one of these," he said as he grabbed an envelope from a small box the doorman kept there for messages. "Thanks."

Roger scribbled "Deliver to Buck," on the envelope. Reaching in his pants pocket, he pulled out four small black thumb drives and inserted them into the envelope. After licking the envelope's flap, he ran his fingers along it several times to be sure it sealed. He then folded it and put it back into his pocket.

Just then a heavy hand gripped his shoulder. "I will want to talk to you as well," said the same FBI agent he had confronted in Allison's apartment.

"Not right now you don't," Roger replied firmly. "And I'm gonna need you to pull back from the lobby as well. The first lady is going to have a press conference here."

"You can't do that. This is a crime scene."

Roger then started pulling down the plastic tape the FBI had strung up. "Your crime scene, if there was a crime, is upstairs. We're going to hold a press conference right here. And I don't want you guys to be on camera."

"You sonofabitch. I'm calling my superiors. You can't interfere with an FBI investigation."

"Call whoever you want. I am in charge here. Your so-called crime scene is upstairs. You can use the rear entrance. Get all your men out of the lobby and off the front sidewalk. You can park back there as well. I don't want to even see you around here."

As the FBI began pulling back, a tall dark-haired man got off the elevator and walked through the lobby toward the front entrance. As he walked past, Roger removed the envelope from his pocket and slid it into the man's hand. Their eyes never met, nor did they speak.

Chapter 59—Preparing for the press conference

6:10 a.m., Friday, December 30

Janet was used to taking orders from James, because it was understood that he spoke for Allison. So when he told her to close the door behind her, she simply complied with his command. Neither she nor Lesley took issue with that arrangement. Actually, the two aides both greatly admired James. They viewed him as possessing genius intellect. He was always able to see the larger picture and always seemed able to solve a problem.

"Allison has some important news for you. But first, when this short meeting is over, we want you to get hold of Cal. Tell him that James and Allison need him to get over here ASAP. Tell him to cancel all his meetings for today. We'll be keeping him busy here."

Cal was a special lawyer. Allison and James both trusted him as much as anyone can trust a lawyer. You could probably say that Cal was one step up the ladder from being a mob lawyer. Or maybe below—it depends on how you look at it. But just like a mob lawyer, Cal knew where all the bodies were buried, and he knew he would end up in the same place if he ever broke a confidence. So, when James told the aide to have Cal cancel all his appointments, there were no questions to be asked about it. If Cal was burying his mother, it was understood that he would have to miss the funeral. Cal had to come when beckoned by James or Allison.

"Okay, we're going to make this quick," James continued. "We've got a lot to get done. A lot. Al, would you tell them about the call?"

"Earlier this evening James got a call. It was from a reporter neither of us had ever heard of. He said he was from *The New York Times*. We can't verify it, but he did have James's phone number. He wanted to get a comment on an article he intends to run. The article is based on some bogus information. We don't have any idea yet who's behind it. Probably some right-wing group. Who knows. There are so many kooks out there. Anyway, we denied it. We called the *Times*, and they had no idea who this so-called reporter was, and they knew nothing about the story."

"Why is that a problem?" Janet asked. "If the *Times* won't back it up, why is that a problem?"

"Normally that would be right," James jumped in. "But this could create a very dangerous situation for Al. There is one element of truth about what the reporter was saying. That has to do with the fact that Allison and I have been intimate. We have no idea where this reporter is getting his information. But he is right about Allison and me.

"Therefore, we are holding a press conference—so we can announce it to the press before this reporter can. We're going to pre-empt him."

Allison then added, "It's a cinch that the *Times* won't touch it, but once it hits the Internet and the idiot bloggers start running with it, all hell could break loose."

Neither Janet nor Lesley opened their mouths. They both just stood there trying to imagine all the ramifications. James then continued. "Used to be all we had to worry about was the *Times*—east and west, and the Post. Not so anymore. Once a rumor hits the Web, there's no controlling it."

The news about the sexual intimacy was hard for both Janet and Lesley to believe. In all the years they had known Allison and James, they not once ever suspected there was anything going on between them, other than the business of politics. In fact, they had never once suspected that James ever screwed around. He certainly had plenty of opportunities—late nights on the campaign trail, hotels, bars, and endless airports and smelly airplanes. But not once had either of them ever witnessed James making a pass at anyone, not even after a few beers. They viewed him as the consummately boring faithful husband. They were shocked to hear about the affair.

"Unfortunately, we are being forced to admit it," Allison said. "There is no point denying it. There is just too much evidence."

Janet and Lesley both wondered about that. They had served on Allison's staff when she was in the White House, and they knew that almost anything, even the most obvious, could and would be denied, if it suited their purposes. Neither of them commented, but if a thought bubble were to have appeared above their heads it would have contained the image of Bob continually denying his indiscretions.

But wisdom dictated they remain silent, and they did.

James looked at his watch. "We are having a press conference, downstairs in the lobby, at ten a.m. today. That way it will hit the network news fresh, as well as cable. Janet, you can take care of that announcement. Are we competing with any breaking news?"

"Not that I know about," said Lesley. "But if the president's press secretary gets wind of this, she might generate something. It is Thursday, after all."

James was not worried about that. He knew from his vast experience that sex drives the news. And a salacious scandal drives it even harder. It would not be a good time for anyone to try to step on this. In fact, this would be a great opportunity for some senator or representative to fess up to a DUI. This sex scandal would drive a DUI right off the front page. James knew that this story would steal the above-the-fold headline slot in all the major papers, as well as own cable and network coverage, at least through the weekend news cycle. He realized that no one can predict what the bloggers might do, but they could not be controlled anyway. James had decided the best way to deal with the potential disclosure of the assassination plot was to provide the piranha with a better story. That, he calculated, would give him time to do some damage control. At least, that's how he viewed it and how he had explained it to Allison.

James looked down at his watch for the fifth time. "Fifteen minutes till show time. Are you good to go?"

"I'm ready," Allison said. It was, however, obvious that she was not totally sold on James's concept.

Allison then turned and addressed her two aides. "Both of you might be useful in getting this set up. Go down and offer any assistance you can."

Once Janet and Lesley had gone, Allison turned back to James. "During my eight years in the White House, press conferences like this were set up to *deny* extramarital sex, not to admit it. Why are you so sure we're handling this in the right way? Once we make this announcement, there'll be no putting the feathers back in this pillow."

"By admitting to this one- or two-night stand with your chief advisor, we will deflect every other news story out there. That's all anyone will be interested in. I swear, Russia could attack Alaska and China could invade Hawaii, and no one would care. All they're gonna be caring about is, 'What's Bob gonna think about this?' And they're gonna be checking into our backgrounds trying to find out how long this has been going on. They will be so busy they'll have no time for anything else. ... And, of course, they will not be able to dig up anything more than what we give them."

"Speaking of Bob, how sure are you he'll get on board with this?

Have you talked to him?"

"No time. But he's a smart guy. He'll know exactly what we're up to. Anyway, it's best that he be caught off guard. That way his face will get red, and he will blow a gasket. But once he talks to us, he'll play along."

James took one more look at his watch, then asked, "Well, Al, ready to rock and roll?"

"You sonofabitch, you better know what you're doing here, or your head will roll. Bob will kick it around like a soccer ball."

Chapter 60—Meeting the press
10:00 a.m., Friday, December 30

James faced the assembled journalists.

"Ladies and gentlemen, I want to thank you for coming out on such short notice. I realize that this is what you do for a living, but I am sure each one of you has a schedule to keep as well." James knew that each reporter was very happy to be there, short notice or not, but he also knew that you could never be too polite to the press.

He continued, "Allison will make a short statement. After that she will answer a few questions. She has a very tight schedule today, so she won't be able to take follow-ups." James then turned to Allison and said, "Allison."

Allison had conducted hundreds of press conferences, but the unusual circumstances behind this one made her uneasy. However, her ability to act and her immense self-confidence, allowed her to completely mask her reservations. "Ladies and gentlemen of the press, thank you for coming out today, particularly on such short notice." She paused for a few seconds, and then continued. "I have something very personal to share with you. I hope you will appreciate the sincerity with which I come to you and afterward afford me and my family some time to heal."

Allison again paused for a moment, to give the impression that she was speaking impromptu.

"As you know very well, James has for decades served both myself and my husband as a very close advisor, and as a trusted personal friend. He remains so to this day."

Again she paused, feigning an attempt to gather her thoughts. "Recently, however, our relationship changed. Neither of us ever imagined it would happen, but we became intimate."

Looking down, she paused for a moment, allowing the assembled to digest what she had just told them. She then raised her head and made eye contact with a number of the reporters.

"Both James and I regret this indiscretion very much. We apologize to the people of our great land, and to our families, for any hurt this may have caused."

With those words, a collective gasp swept over the reporters and advisors alike. No one had ever seen a press conference quite like this one.

"Both James and I are happily married, and we assure you and our families, that the intimate aspect of our relationship has ended. We both acknowledge that we acted foolishly and ask your understanding, and our families' forgiveness. I will now take a few questions." She barely got those words out of her mouth before the deluge began. "Mrs. Fulbright," flew from the mouths of every person wearing press credentials. James acknowledged his favorite, Janice Hume, of CNN. "Miss Hume."

"Mrs. Fulbright, we are floored—"

James interrupted, "Do you have a question?"

"Yes. How long has this affair been going on?"

"I don't regard it as an affair. But James and I were intimate on three occasions, starting two weeks ago and ending last night."

Again a chorus of "Mrs. Fulbrights" rang out.

This time James acknowledged another of his favorite reporters.

"Roger."

"Mrs. Fulbright, did you just say that it ended last night?"

"That's correct."

James then pointed at a network news reporter.

"Bob."

"Mrs. Fulbright, have either, or both of you, discussed this with your respective families?"

"We will do that later. We wanted to make this announcement at this time, before it was dragged through the mud on the blogs."

Another frenzied shouting match ensued. This time the reporters were jumping up and down trying to get James's attention. But, as is the case with most press conferences he conducted, James had his list of favorites, and once he had exhausted those, he would end the press conference.

"Yes. Karen."

"Mrs. Fulbright, you stated that this intimate relationship with James started two weeks ago. Were you ever intimate prior to that date? And, if so, how are we …"

Again, James interrupted, "No follow-up questions, please." He then looked at Allison.

"James and I were intimate for the first time exactly two weeks ago today."

James then acknowledged a reporter from a conservative New York newspaper. He really didn't like the guy, but he thought he could predict the sort of question he might ask.

"Mr. Laskey."

"Mrs. Fulbright, you know that every reporter in the country will start digging into your past. Are they going to find out that you and James had an ongoing affair, perhaps dating back to your days in the White House?"

Allison had a genuine dislike for this reporter. Without even looking in his direction, she said, "Already asked and answered."

James could barely conceal his amusement at the way Allison dismissed this hated reporter. He then pointed toward the back of the room and acknowledged another reporter of whom he was fond.

"Larry."

"Mrs. Fulbright, I'm sure I am speaking for nearly everyone in this room when I ask you this question. Why are you making this announcement, at this time? We are not used to public figures making such confessions. Don't you think this is political suicide?"

"Perhaps so, but we wanted to do the right thing. I think the American people are smart enough, and good enough, to understand what this is all about. We are very sorry it happened. But it did. And we are apologizing for the indiscretion. It most certainly was a mistake, and we want to put it behind us so we can get on with doing the work of the people. I don't view it a political suicide. I view it as being honest."

James liked Allison's response to the reporter's question. He had hoped for shorter answers, but so far he was very pleased with Allison's feigned candor. Up to that point Allison and James had anticipated all the questions and therefore had scripted the answers. However, Allison's answer to the last question went a little beyond what they had prepared for, and it caused James to think it might be time to start wrapping up the press conference.

James then spotted the reporter for Fox News. He always had reservations when it came to Fox, but he determined that if he wanted this story to carry the weekend, he had better deal with Fox.

"Gerald."

"Mrs. Fulbright, my question is on a little different matter. Last night I got a very disturbing phone call from a freelance reporter. He asked me if I was aware of some secret meetings you have had recently. He did not get into detail regarding the purpose of those meetings. I think he was trying to feel me out and see what I knew. Would you please comment on those meetings or at least tell us if there were any such meetings?"

That was exactly the question Allison did not want to hear, but she knew that she had to respond in some fashion. "The only meetings I know about are the ones with James. They started two weeks ago, and they have now ended. Thank you, ladies and gentlemen. I have to go now. Thank you."

While the last question caught Allison off guard, she didn't show it. As Allison turned and walked away, James gathered up his belongings and followed. Usually, after press conferences, James would stick around and cozy up to the reporters. This time, however, he was too much a part of the story and thought it best to look for some taller grass.

Janet and Lesley, Allison's advisors, were still visibly shaken by the whole matter, and they too did not want to be subjected to additional feeding frenzy questions; so they followed closely behind Allison and James.

Once in Allison's apartment, the discussion and planning continued; but only after Allison had tossed a large book in James's direction, narrowly missing him. Allison was furious. She kicked Janet and Lesley out of her apartment and told her Secret Service agent to "take a hike."

"You sonofabitch. James, I would never let you touch me. I have too much self-respect. How in hell did you ever talk me into this?"

"Al, didn't you hear that last question? That is exactly what we are guarding against. *That's* what we have to fear. That reporter, the one who called me last night, he's out there trying to start a fire. Well, what we did will deflect it. At least for the short term. Until we can get our heads wrapped around it better. We don't know what they're gonna say. We don't know exactly how they intend to use what they've got. I think I've got a pretty good handle on it, but I'm still doing a lot of guessing.

"It's a little like shooting a horsefly with a shotgun. You kill the horsefly, but you might kill the horse as well. It's just the chance we had to take."

James could see that Allison had at least started to listen to him. "We bought some time today, Al. We bought a little time. That's the best we could hope for."

"Get the hell outta my sight. Go call your rich wife. Go make peace with her bastard father. Do whatever the hell you have to do." Allison paused for a second, and then she stuck her finger under his nose. "This better turn out just like you said, or I'll cut your balls off myself. ... And I'll stick them right down your damn throat."

James had seen Allison angry before. Usually, however, that anger and those words had been reserved for and directed at her husband. James had observed that Allison often took several hours to calm down when she was this hot, so he took her advice and left the apartment.

Chapter 61—The aftermath

10:46 a.m., Friday, December 30

Roger had observed the whole press conference. And, as is the manner of a good Secret Service agent, he did not allow his facial expression to reflect what was going on inside his head or his heart. At its conclusion he had followed Allison up to the apartment but had remained outside the door, assuming the posture of a sentry guarding a gate.

Even though the apartment door was extraordinarily thick, and even though he did not attempt to eavesdrop, he could not help but hear the shouting going on inside. He did observe that the only voice piercing the door was the high-pitched screams of Allison.

He would have been concerned had other voices risen to that level. He knew that Allison's screams were her way of venting anger and did not represent distress. He had experienced similar shouting episodes on numerous occasions in the White House. He thought for a moment, then realized that this was the first time he had heard Allison this worked up when Bob was not the target.

"Rog, Al is having a difficult time," James said on his way out of the apartment. "I'm sure you're already aware of that. I'm headed home. You know how to get hold of me if you need to. Don't hesitate to call me."

Roger nodded, making eye contact with James, but he did not say anything.

As James walked away, Roger pulled up a chair outside the apartment door and sat down.

Inside the apartment Allison's private telephone rang. All of her phone circuits were supposed to be secure. Allison immediately recognized this as the line Bob used when he wanted to talk to her. She intentionally allowed the phone to ring three times, then picked it up.

"Hello."

"Al, what the hell is going on? You're on every TV. Even the business channels. What's this talk about you and James? And why did you have that stupid press conference?"

"It's complicated. We can't talk about it over the phone."

Allison knew that her phone lines were as secure as the government could make them, but she did not trust them anyway. She knew that for every security measure taken, there were very smart people staying up nights figuring out ways to defeat it. But even beyond her skepticism about phone security, she really wanted to air this whole thing out with her husband face to face.

"Can we get together? Right away?"

"Sure," he said. "Where shall we meet?"

"How about here?"

"I'll be deluged. No good."

"What works, then?" The tone of Allison's voice was not harsh or loud. Not only was she no longer angry, but she truly did wish to seek Bob's advice. Even more than the wisdom of James, she always respected what Bob had to say. She knew that once she explained why they had opted for this strategy, and why James thought it necessary, Bob could be useful. Besides, she understood that her husband had a vested interest in a successful conclusion to the whole matter. They were, after all, still husband and wife, even though that relationship was frequently strained, particularly by Bob's numerous affairs.

"I'll swing by and pick you up. Who's working? Is Rog around?"

"Yes, he's sitting outside my door right now."

"Really! Call him in and put him on."

Allison detested whenever anyone ordered her around. Anyone, except for Bob. He was her first love, and her only love. And the same could be said for Bob. They had both had more than their share of extramarital flings, resulting in some of the most vicious fights ever known to have occurred off a battlefield; but neither of them ever doubted their mutual love for each other. So, when Bob told her to go get Roger, she immediately complied.

She set the phone down, walked over, and opened the door. "Roger, Bob wants to talk to you."

"Yes, ma'am."

Roger entered the apartment as Allison secured the door behind him. He felt a little uneasy, allowing her to escort him. Typically it would have been him holding the door for her.

"Over here," Allison said, directing Roger to the phone.

"Hello."

"Rog, how are you?"

"Well, sir."

"Wonderful. Wonderful. It's great to talk to you again."

"Thank you, sir. It's good to talk to you as well."

"Rog, Al and I have to get together, and right away. I need your help with it."

"Yes, sir."

"This is what I want you to do." Bob paused to gather his thoughts. "I'm going to swing by there in one hour. I'm not coming up. I'll let you know when I'm ten minutes out. Allison is going to ride with me. You follow with my agent. Drive separately if you wish. But the fewer cars the better."

"Yes, sir. Do I need to know where we're going?"

"Soon as I do."

"Yes, sir."

"Would you put Allison back on?"

"Yes, sir," Roger answered, as he handed the phone back to Allison.

"Bob," she said.

"Here's how we're going to do this. I'm going to stop by in an hour. Roger will escort you down to my car, and he will ride with my agent." Bob paused, but only for a couple seconds. "Put Rog back on."

Allison called to Roger, who had walked over toward the door. "Roger, Bob wants you back."

Roger briskly returned, and Allison handed him the phone.

"Yes, Mr. President."

"Rog, I want you to ride with my security detail. Okay?"

"That's fine, sir. Who is on for you today? If I might ask."

"I have two today. I think you know them both—Smith and Harmon, male and female. You know them, right?"

"Yes, sir, I do."

"Okay. I'll call this number when I'm ten out. You accompany Allison to my car. Then you ride with my detail. Right?"

"Yes, sir. I'll wait for your call."

"Let me have Allison again. It was great talking to you again. I look forward to seeing you."

"Thank you, sir," Roger said, again handing the phone to Allison.

"Bob, things are not as they might seem."

"Don't say anything else. I'll be there in an hour. We'll talk then."

"Where are we going?"

"Someplace really nice. And private. I'll fill you in when I get there."

"Great. I have always loved your surprises." As was always the case, her husband had a way of making even the worst of circumstances seem bearable. For the first time that day, Allison was starting to feel confident that James's plan might work. Even though Bob did not come up with this strategy, she believed that once Bob was fully engaged, it had a chance. She was not smiling, but something close to a smile had emerged on her face. Roger even noticed it.

"I'll wait outside," Roger said, after Allison had hung up the phone.

"I'll let you know when Bob calls back."

"Thank you, ma'am."

Roger then walked through the door and assumed his position outside.

Chapter 62—Allison to confront Bob

11:09 a.m., Friday, December 30

Once Allison had closed the door to her apartment, Roger Minsk arose from his chair outside her door and began walking around in the narrow confines of the corridor. He removed a throwaway cell phone from his jacket pocket. He double-checked to be sure he was using the right phone, and then he dialed a number.

"It's me," he said, after a male voice answered.

"She's gonna be fine. She just talked with her husband. They're meeting."

"In about an hour. ... But you know how he is—always late."

"He's gonna pull up. Allison will ride in his car, and I will trail with his people. Total, two cars."

"I have no idea where we're going, neither does Allison. Hell, I'll bet her husband hasn't decided that yet. We'll know when we get there."

"I wasn't there. She called me in at the end. I just heard one side of the end of it."

"I don't think anyone has her phone. It's the best we've got. But I really don't think they discussed anything. That's what the meeting's about."

"I'm sure I won't be there. When we were in the White House, we would do it like this. The president would pick up whoever it was he wanted to meet with, and they would go someplace different every time, and they would talk in his car. He always was most comfortable in his car. I'm sure that's how this will be. Just like Meatloaf, I guess. You know,

Bat Outta Hell."

Roger paused for a moment, listening intently to the party at the other end. Then he said, "I thought it went pretty much as expected."

"They ate it up, don't you think? That's all we'll see on the news this weekend. That's what you wanted, right?"

"Then you would consider it a success?"

"Even that *last* question. Perfect ending. Her face was shining. I've never seen her sweat before."

"We'll talk later."

With that, Roger hung up the phone and waited for Allison to call him in.

Inside the apartment, Allison was preparing to meet with her husband. Even though they no longer shared the same bed, she still loved him. She wanted to look her best today. It had been weeks since they had last talked, and over a month since they had met face to face.

She walked into her bathroom and looked in the mirror. "I look horrible," she muttered. She began washing off the makeup she was wearing for the cameras. While it gave her color under the lights, she hated how it made her look in natural light. "I'm going to need some help here," she said, picking up a cell phone. "Lesley, can you get in here now, I'm meeting Bob and I need your help. Right now! I need you right now!"

When Allison had kicked everyone out of her apartment, Lesley had walked across the street with Janet and was sipping a latte with her. They knew that when Allison got like that, it might last a few minutes or she might stay mad all day. In any case, they knew that they should stay close enough to be available, yet far enough removed to be safe.

Officially, Lesley's duties did not include hairdressing and makeup. But she had a gift with those sorts of things. At Bryn Mawr half the ladies sought out Lesley for her opinion before a party or even a date. At the time, Lesley thought it a bit tedious, but as it turned out, it was that talent that endeared her to Allison. Lesley could always make her boss look her best. And that's the look Allison was after today.

"Sorry," Lesley said to her friend, as she got up from the table. "The boss needs me. Must be she's meeting with somebody special."

"Her husband, you think?" Janet asked.

"That's probably correct. She doesn't usually get over these things so fast. Could be she's playing dress up for him."

"She'll be calling me, in a minute. I'm gonna hide out till she does."

"Good idea."

"See ya later."

"See ya." Lesley smiled and gave a girly wave to the girls behind the counter. They all knew who she was and whom she worked for. In that little coffee shop, Lesley and Janet were rock stars.

* * *

"Roger, would you come in and talk to Bob?"

"Yes, ma'am," Roger replied as he arose from where he was sitting and entered the apartment.

Even though she couched it as a question, it was anything but. Had Roger responded any differently or arose from his chair more slowly or been engaged on his cell and ignored her "request," her choice of words would have been much different.

"He's waiting to talk to you."

As he walked over to pick up the phone, Roger observed just how beautiful Allison looked, but he knew better than to comment. *Lesley worked her magic again*, he was thinking. *Al must still love that guy.*

As he placed the phone to his ear, he could hear the former president talking to someone else, even though Bob apparently was trying muffle his words with his hand. "Don't argue with me. Rog is going to ride with you, period. Got that?"

Roger, not wanting to embarrass his former boss, rattled the phone slightly on the table, then raised it again to his ear. "Mr. President."

"Hey, Rog. Thanks for picking up. ... Rog, traffic is light today, must be the price of gas. Anyway, I'm only about ten minutes away. I would like you to escort Al downstairs and be there with her as I drive up."

"I think we're all set at our end. Have you discussed that detail with Allison?"

"She's good with it. Neither of us wants to engage anyone until we've had a chance to talk. I think she's all set."

"Very well, is there anything else?"

"That should do it. You're good to ride with my guys? *They're* not happy about it. But I'll be damned if I'm gonna make this a parade. ... You're by yourself on this, right?"

"Yes, Mr. President."

"Great, I know you can handle them. You always could. Right, Rog?"

"That's not a problem for me."

"Great. See you, ah, in about seven minutes."

Even though the former president said he was running early, Roger did not buy it. He knew that his old boss absolutely detested waiting for anyone and, so, always misstated his schedule to accommodate that penchant.

"Yes, sir, Mr. President. I'll give you back to Allison."

"Thanks, Rog."

Roger then looked over at Allison. She had not taken her eyes off the phone since laying it on the table for him. There was a small but detectable smile on her face as she received the phone from Roger.

"Roger, go do whatever you have to do. I'm all set." Allison knew better than to place her hand over the mouthpiece while addressing

Roger. She knew that her husband loathed it when people did that to him. He was adamant about that. "If you are on the phone with me, then you're on the phone with me. Our conversation is over when I hang up." He had told her (and others) that before, and everyone complied.

"Bob."

"Rog knows what to do. I'm about seven to ten minutes out."

"I'll be ready when you get here."

"Great. See you in a few."

As Allison hung up the phone, she looked at her watch, then called over to Lesley, who had removed herself somewhat from the vicinity, so as not to appear to be eavesdropping.

"Les, get me my diamond watch," she commanded as she unhooked the large-faced Tiffany that she generally wore. She was, after all, meeting with her husband to discuss an alleged affair with a staff member. She frequently had received compliments on her diamond-studded watch. It had been a gift from a Middle Eastern head of state, and Allison loved the way it looked. It had been one of the items that she took with her after leaving the White House. It meant a lot to her, partly because she had to declare its value and pay for it when she left. Lesley helped her slip it on.

"Les, check me over one more time. … What do you think?"

Allison never sought any other person's opinion of her appearance—only Lesley's.

Lesley took a step back, then walked around behind Allison and said, "Ma'am, you look wonderful. Everything is perfect."

"Thank you, Lesley."

The dismissive tone of Allison's voice was Lesley's cue to step back, which she did.

Allison looked down at her watch again. "Damn, I can't read this thing. Lesley, what time have you got?"

Lesley checked the time and said, "eleven-fifty."

"Call Roger and see where he's at."

"Yes, ma'am," Lesley said, using her cell to page Roger.

"He's right outside the door, ma'am." Allison knew that it would take three minutes to get to the street. She also knew that her husband, under any normal circumstances, would be at least ten minutes late, perhaps more. Something would come up—traffic, a phone call, something. But it didn't really matter. She knew she had better be downstairs awaiting his arrival. If not, her husband would be furious—not angry, but furious.

"Call Roger in, and we will get started."

"Yes, ma'am." Lesley walked over to the door and opened it. "Rog, Mrs. Fulbright would like you to step in for a moment?"

Allison had logged on to the front camera and had zoomed in on approaching traffic. Spotting a white Mercedes limo, with a single trailing-SUV, she said, "There he is, on time. ... Damn, what is this world coming to?"

Roger's replacement had arrived, so she and Roger exchanged a few words as he, Allison, and Lesley headed toward the elevator.

Chapter 63—Allison and Bob

12:02 p.m., Friday, December 30

The group emerged from the building just as Bob's limo pulled up. Bob did not get out of the car to greet his wife. Instead, Roger opened the door across from where her husband was sitting and offered his arm to Allison as she slid in. Bob then leaned over and said, "Rog, how are you?"

"Fine, Mr. President. … Anything I need to know before I join your boy and girl?"

"No, they're expecting you."

"Thanks, Mr. President," Roger said, as he closed the limo door and walked back to join the agents in the trailing SUV.

There was no real animosity between Roger and the former president's detail. Actually, they all knew each other and were friendly when not on duty. But when on the job, all good agents become highly territorial, with that "territory" being the geography under the feet of the one they have been assigned to protect. So, as Roger opened the rear door of the trailing SUV, the agents seated in the front did not turn around to acknowledge him. Instead, Sammy, the driver, started humming an old RL Burnside blues song. Sammy and Roger had a history. They both worked on the White House detail when Bob was president. They got along fine then. They were okay now—it was just that Sammy was not pleased to have Roger tagging along. The reason for the Burnside song was that Roger had come to be called RL during his years in the White House. Roger's middle name was Lawrence, and he liked the blues. Roger got in and sat down.

"Got your seat belt on, RL?"

"All set here."

"Wouldn't want to see you get hurt. The president's driver thinks he's a cabby."

"Hell," the female agent added, "he thinks he's Jimmy Johnson."

Roger did not respond to either comment.

The limo sat at the curb for only a few seconds when the driver lowered the passenger side window and summoned the doorman over to talk to him. Sammy and Roger both chuckled, as they could see that the doorman was feverishly nodding his head in agreement. It was obvious that he was getting his ass chewed out by Bob's driver.

The doorman then turned toward oncoming traffic and started blowing his whistle. The idea was to signal traffic to stop, clearing a path for the two vehicles. But Bob's driver did not wait for the doorman's signal. He just hit the accelerator and shot out into traffic, as though he were aiming at the doorman's left kneecap. The terrified doorman jumped out of the way at the last split second.

"Look at that bastard!" Sammy exclaimed, laughing loudly. "He thinks he is pulling out of the pits at Talladega. He damn near ran his crew chief down."

The rear of the limo dropped as it accelerated. Heavy dark smoke shot out from dual chrome exhaust pipes. Sammy floored the accelerator, causing Roger's head to jerk back and forth like a bobble-head doll.

"That's novel," Roger observed. "No lead car."

"Oh, there's a lead car, all right. We're following it. Sometimes we lead, but only when we know where we're goin'. Like some formal function."

"Not one of those times, I suppose."

"No, not one of those times. Only the president knows where we're headed, and he might not have made up his mind yet. … He might just drive around and talk. Depends on how heavy the traffic is. Wouldn't surprise me if he hit the Lincoln and headed down the turnpike. That's probably what he will do."

Both cars flashed alternating four-ways as they repeatedly sped up and stopped, doing the best job possible to get through traffic. Sammy kept his left foot on the brake all the time, with his right on the accelerator.

"If we hang a left in the vicinity of 59th, we're goin' to Brooklyn," Sammy said. "My money is still on the Lincoln. Turnpike traffic is usually not so bad this time of day.

"Hell, I've seen him cut through Central Park when he thought it'd be quicker. And I mean cut through. I've followed him over the curb and through the park. Cops don't bother with him. As long as he doesn't hit one of their mounted."

"Where'd the president get this guy?" Roger asked.

"You remember his father. Everyone called him by his last name— Jones. He was the president's driver back in the White House days."

"From Louisiana, right?" Roger asked.

"Exactly. He was a Louisiana State Trooper. Well, so was his son. The president brought him up to drive for him earlier this year, when the old man had a heart attack. The president calls him Jones Junior."

"Holy hell, did I see that right?" Roger asked in amazement.

Sammy had no time to respond as he flew over the curb and down a sidewalk, doing his best to stick to the rear bumper of the limo. The two vehicles passed a horse-drawn carriage and pulled back into traffic.

"The kid wears a baseball cap with a number '8' on it. That should tell you all you need to know about Jones Junior," Sammy said, after he imitated the curb maneuver.

"There, I was right. We're headed to Jersey," Sammy concluded, as the mini-motorcade crossed 59th Street, continuing to head south down Fifth Avenue.

Inside the limo there was far more silence than usual. After some perfunctory greetings, the former president and his wife did not talk. Instead, Bob busied himself directing Jones Junior through New York traffic.

"Where to, Mr. President?" Jones Junior asked. Bob pushed the "talk" button and said to his driver, "Stay on Fifth. Then find the best route west when you can and head to the Lincoln."

"Yes, sir."

As the limo crossed 60th Street, Bob looked over at Allison and said, "This guy, the driver, is the son of Jones, our old driver. Isn't he some-thin' special?"

"Something special all right. He scares the hell out of me."

"He was a trooper down in Louisiana, just like his daddy."

"That figures," Allison said in a sarcastic tone. She had not liked Jones the senior. She felt that Jones was loyal only to Bob. She suspected that it was he who set up "dates" for her husband and that it was he who would secretly squirrel him out of the White House in the middle of the night to meet women. She could never prove it, nor did she ever really wish to, but she resented the rumors just the same.

After several minutes of silence, Allison finally asked, "where are we going?"

"Oh, if traffic permits, we're takin' the Lincoln to the Jersey Turnpike. Then we'll see. Maybe I'll take you to a motel. You'd like *that*, wouldn't you?"

Allison did not respond audibly, but she couldn't block a small smile.

Bob continued, "Maybe we'll go to the motel where you and James meet up. Shall we do that?"

Bob then hit the "silence" button on car's intercom, ensuring privacy—then he loosened his collar. His face was visibly growing red, as it always did when he was beginning to lose his temper. Sometimes he just unbuttoned his collar to intimidate—like a male lion exposing his mane.

Chapter 64—Allison explains, Bob listens

12:22 p.m., Friday, December 30

Allison's face flushed with anger. "You asshole. You know what that was all about," she said. "That business between James and me. Don't even pretend you don't know the story behind it."

"I'm not sure what the *real* story is. Why don't you tell me?" Bob said.

"The phony affair, the press conference, it was all part of James's insane idea to draw attention away from what could be a much larger problem."

"Really?" Bob chuckled. He always got a kick out of Allison's foul mouth. "Just what is it that this asshole husband of yours is supposed to know about?"

"I've got a problem—actually we've got a problem."

"What sort of problem do we have?" Bob asked.

"There have been a series of meetings—four meetings, perhaps five, if you count the one with Jerry. They were supposed to be secret meetings. But somehow they were recorded. If this comes out, it could be very embarrassing."

"Meetings? You didn't ever mention any secret meetings. What was the purpose of these secret meetings, and who took part?"

"A month ago Jerry came to me with an idea—"

"Jerry! That sissy sonofabitch. I didn't think he ever had any real ideas."

"Well, as it turns out, he's the source of the problem. No way to know for absolute certain, but according to James, it looks like Jerry might be the one who leaked most of the recordings."

"That doesn't sound like something he'd do. He's not the smartest person in the world, but he knows better than to cross us."

"We don't think he meant to. We think that someone, James thinks Mossad, planted an eavesdropping device on him without his knowledge."

"What the hell does that mean?" Bob asked. "How does something like that happen?"

"He's developed a hearing problem, and he had an implant. We think that a bug was implanted in his head along with the cochlear implant."

Bob started laughing, "Jerry—a damn bionic man? I don't believe this. What the hell did you get us into? And I mean *us*. You go down, I go down. ... What were these secret meetings all about?"

"Well, when Jerry originally came to me with his idea—"

"Hold on just a second," Bob interrupted. "Explain what you just said a minute ago. That Jerry might have been the source of some of the recordings. Was there another source?"

Chapter 65—Allison dances
around the recordings

12:30 p.m., Friday, December 30

Allison reluctantly confessed: "Apparently someone got hold of my summaries. After every meeting I recorded a summary on a thumb drive. It looks like they used my recorded notes for the third meeting—the one Jerry missed."

"What a bunch of jackasses. Reminds me of the gang that couldn't shoot straight—"

Allison interrupted Bob's diatribe before she totally lost her temper. "Shall I go on?" she asked rhetorically. "Anyway, I thought Jerry's suggestion was a stretch, but it got me thinking. He suggested that there was a powerful undercurrent in this country, and that it might end up in a shortened term for the current president, and that I needed a game plan should that occur."

"Fat damn chance of an impeachment. Look what fools I made of them when they tried to screw me over. Won't happen. Especially with our guys in the Senate—the ones that are still there. Won't happen."

Allison paused and then said, "He wasn't talking about impeachment."

There was dead silence in the car for an uncomfortable length of time. "Al, exactly what the hell are you suggesting?"

"What Jerry was alluding to was what he considers to be a very real possibility—that the radical right, the fringe, might try to pull something off."

"Are you talking about an assassination of the president of the United States? That's serious business—too damn serious. And someone recorded these meetings?" Bob said, sounding very agitated.

"Appears to be so," Allison answered, "but we do not know for sure exactly who it was or what their intentions were. But it does appear … actually, it's virtually certain, someone has tapes. And, as I said, James is confident that it is Mossad."

"Do you know for certain that there are tapes?" Bob asked.

"We received a phone call—actually James received a phone call— from a reporter we had never heard of, and he read segments of what he said was a transcription of some private conversations. Then this reporter dropped off a transcript in James's mailbox. James and I read it, and it appears to be very accurate."

"Was James a party at those meetings?" Bob asked.

"Yes, he was one of four, plus myself."

"What did you discuss at those meetings?"

"At first, it was all speculative—such as what sort of things we could do to improve our chances with Congress. Then it quickly turned to where Jerry suspected it would go—what might we expect to happen should the president die, or be killed? How should we react to it? How can we position ourselves to be ready to step in? After all, there is a VP."

"Oh my God," Bob said. "God help us if that old lying bastard ever becomes president. If anyone ever earned an early demise, he would get my vote. This new guy is a panty waist, but he's not as stupid as his VP."

Bob paused a moment and then continued, "Well, what did you come up with? How did you determine you should posture yourself in that event?"

"That's when it started to get a little troublesome. Vice President Roberts is an old man—some think he is getting senile. Jerry thought that we should strike a deal with him. In the event of an assassination,

Roberts would nominate me for VP. We would meet immediately after the event, and he would choose me. That would help provide stability. And it would be quite logical, my having served with you in the White House. I should have no problem with confirmation. Roberts could finish out the term, and he would be too old to run in the next general."

"Yeah, that way he could get his picture on a postage stamp," Bob quipped. "That ought to make him happy." Bob thought for a moment. "Well, those tapes are a problem all right. But they demonstrate bad judgment, not a crime. At least not yet. Hell, the president has contingency plans to bomb every city in the world—but that does not mean anything. Just that he is being prudent. There's nothing wrong for the VP to have a contingency plan in the event that he should suddenly become president."

"Unfortunately, it didn't stop there," Allison said.

"What does that mean?"

"At the second meeting, Jerry made a comment that got us all thinking. He said something like this: look, we could spend a long time getting ready for something that might or might not happen. And if it does happen, who knows the when or the how? And if it doesn't, we would have wasted a lot of time and resources. Too bad we could not nail it down, so that we could work our way up to it in an orderly fashion."

Allison stopped talking for a moment. She wanted Bob to have a chance to digest what she had just laid out for him. For a few moments—that seemed like an eternity—both were silent.

She then continued, "We all just stared at each other for a minute. Then Jerry suggested that if we infiltrated the radical right and found out just what they were planning, it would help us plan."

Bob, who was growing more angry by the second, interrupted: "Jerry has always been full of it. What the hell was he thinking? You can't infiltrate those buffoons. Nobody on our side is that stupid, or that ugly. Besides, if an assassination were to happen, it would not be organized. Two skinheads would get to talking about it. Then they would get drunk—or high on something. That would lead to bragging, and then they would try to pull it off. If they're any good, or lucky—and if they have half a brain between them—they might actually be successful.

"But that, my dear Allison, is a whole bunch of 'ifs.' The only person who could do any contingency planning is the guy who is actually plotting the assassination."

"And that's what we concluded," Allison said.

"That's what you *concluded*? Exactly what does that mean?"

"That's what meetings three and four were about: possible facilitation."

"Facilitation? Facilitation of exactly what?" Bob asked.

"We discussed, hypothetically, the pros and cons of facilitating the event, just in case the right never could successfully pull it off. We thought it would be good to set up a time frame. We could not control when the earliest possibility might be, so we thought it wise to start gearing up immediately. Initially, our guess was that it could not happen before the middle of his fourth year. But Reginald changed our thinking. He said the sooner the better. He was talking weeks.

"The plan was to make it look like the assassination was the work of the other guys. You know how that works—our guy gets killed by the other side, so our guys get the sympathy vote."

"I cannot believe it. You were plotting the assassination of a sitting president." Bob glared over his glasses at a nervous Allison as he slowly mouthed these words.

"It was all hypothetical at first. Our reasoning was this: if I did not become VP until the middle of the fourth year of the president's term, I would have too little time to establish my positions, vis-à-vis the current president. And Roberts would need some time to prove just what a fool he is. Later than that, he might somehow get himself nominated and elected. We could not allow that."

"Let me see if I've got this right. You and your buddies were meeting privately, secretly, and the topic of your conversations centered around the assassination of the president. Is that about right?"

"You make it sound so callous. As I said, we feared that it was going to happen whether or not we facilitated it. We calculated that the best thing for the country was simply to use it to our advantage."

"Callous? Just how delicate would you like it? When you start talking about 'facilitating' an assassination, it is anything but hypothetical—and it is never genteel. That's called 'conspiring to assassinate a president.' You and your buddies were hatching a plot. That's exactly what that was. Get caught and convicted—you hang. Now you've got me involved. Al, I thought you were smarter than this."

"Are you here to help, or drive in another dagger?"

"Al, I want to help, but you've dug a very deep hole."

"I know it's bad—that's why we're talking. We have to find a solution. That's what that business with James is all about, something to buy us some time."

It had been several minutes since Bob had actually looked at Allison. "How does that work?" he asked. "That business about your affair with James?"

"James thought that if we cooked up this story about an affair between him and me, it would steal the news cycle, for this weekend at least. We don't know what this reporter has in mind with the story—if he's going to run with it or not. And if so, where? We don't even know if he is a real reporter. These are all unknowns. Altogether too many unknowns. We needed some time to sort it out, and James thought this bogus affair would provide it."

"You mean you're not sleeping with James?"

"Of course not."

Bob chuckled slightly and said, "So, you have just confessed to an affair that did not happen? Oh my God, am I hearing what I think I'm hearing?"

"I don't believe for a second that you are surprised to hear that," Allison said with a note of sarcasm.

"Actually," Bob said, turning to look at Allison, "I'm not at all shocked that the two of you hatched this scheme. It sounds a lot like something James would come up with."

The two of them sat there for a few moments, without either of them speaking a word. Finally, Bob broke the silence. "If you don't know who this guy is, or what outlet he represents, what makes you so sure he is a reporter? Maybe this is some sort of blackmail scheme."

"We considered that. But nothing was ever mentioned about money, quid pro quo, or anything that resembled what one might expect if it were extortion. It had the sense of a story. It just felt typical, like this guy got hold of these transcripts and wanted to publish them. It had the smell of a Watergate."

"Watergate?" Bob said. "Hell, this is nothing like Watergate. Watergate was chewing gum compared to what you guys got on your shoes." He paused a moment then said, "Transcripts, you say? Not tapes? Not recordings?" Bob appeared to be deep in thought.

"No recordings, but from what we read it seemed as though it had been transcribed verbatim. They had to have been transcribed from a recording."

"Then what is this?" Bob asked Allison, removing a small thumb drive from his pocket and holding it up. He did it almost as though he were sticking it in her face.

Allison got a quick glimpse of it and turned away. "I don't know, what is it?" she replied.

"It sounds like you dictating something. What's this all about?"

Allison snatched the stick from his hand and briefly examined it. She immediately recognized the writing on it as her own.

"How did you get this?" she asked, exhibiting extreme signs of frustration. It appeared as though her husband had her summarizations of the meetings. She could not be sure without putting it in a computer, but it certainly did look like her drive, the one that had, just hours earlier, been stolen from her by who she thought to be Mossad agents.

"If that's what I think it is, then I want to know how you got it," Allison said, now in full attack mode.

"Well, I'm pretty sure it is what you think it is," Bob replied. "It's okay, you can keep it. I just want to know how you could be so careless. The encryption on the original was child's play. Any fifteen-year-old could have cracked it. What's that old cliché? Loose lips sink ships."

"So, did you listen to it?" Allison asked, her voice signaling her anger. She was furious that Bob had the thumb drive, that he had made fun of her attempts to secure it, that he had let her go on when he already knew about the plot, and that he was lecturing her about the whole matter.

She was deeply embarrassed that she had allowed this potential disaster to occur. The only bright side, in her mind, was that Bob was now totally engaged. And when Bob accepted a challenge, things happened. And problems, even big ones, always seemed to have a way of going away—when Bob was fully engaged.

Allison thought it best to just sit there until she had calmed down.

Bob knew she was angry, and he was willing to back off the sarcasm and shift into solution mode.

"Okay, let's see if I've got this straight," Bob said as he began to summarize the situation. "Stop me if I'm wrong, or if I'm leaving something important out. You and four others began meeting a short time ago, discussing a strategy in the event that the president were to leave office before the end of his term."

Bob paused, to give Allison a chance to add something should she wish to. "That's where it went, but initially we were discussing election strategies," she said.

"Whatever," Bob continued. "Then, Jerry, acting like that damn idiot I've always known him to be, suggested that it might be a good idea to become a bit more proactive. In other words, he thought you guys should prepare to take matters into your own hands, should the other idiots, those Nazis in that other party, not be able to pull it off in a timely fashion. Is that about right, so far?"

Bob then stopped to again give Allison a chance to speak. He had not wanted to lose his temper, but he was very furious about this whole incident. Allison did not even acknowledge the pause. She did not acknowledge her husband or anything he was saying. Had he been wrong, she would have spoken up, but her silence could rightly be interpreted as agreement.

Bob then continued. "Now, it turns out, someone tapped into Bionic Jerry's cochlear implant." Bob stopped, fuming again. "Why does this remind me of the Four Stooges? Damn it. All those years we worked together. All the tough times we've been through, and you pull this—"

"Shut your damn mouth, you sonofabitch."

Chapter 66—Telling Bob off

12:39 p.m., Friday, December 30

Allison's face was on fire. "I stuck with you through all those affairs, all those blowjobs, and a whole damn truckload of your filthy cheating deeds. Do we need to talk about the drugs? Then there were the murders of your so-called friends? I had nothing to do with them—not with any of that. But I stuck it out with you. Now, damn you, you're going come down off your high horse and help save our careers."

Allison paused as Bob contemplated. She then continued. "I completely realize the mess I've created. I know I'm in over my head. But we've been there before. Many times before. And we always got out. Are you suggesting we give up this time? What makes it so damn different, except for the fact that it was me screwing up and not you?"

Bob knew she was right. He knew before he had picked her up that they were going to work this out—that they would come up with a game plan, pick up the pieces, and move on. He was not about to give up on her or, more importantly, on his own career.

"This is what we're left with," Bob continued, visibly settled down. "Someone has tapes of four of the five meetings. The reason he doesn't have the one meeting is because good old Jerry's bionic ear wasn't there to record it. Is that right?"

"That's what we have surmised. Seems to be totally logical, and James is convinced that's the way it was."

"Okay, now we know that the tapes exist and that they have been transcribed. And that some reporter, or some possibly non-reporter, has the transcriptions. And he is intimating that he will publish them. Is that correct?"

"He did actually threaten to publish them," Allison replied. "But it was kind of strange. It seemed as though he was more interested in our being aware that he had them than in meeting a deadline."

"Blackmail?" Bob again suggested.

"Hard to say, but it didn't feel like blackmail. It was very strange." Allison paused again and then continued, "The one thing that stood out was that the caller was missing the transcription for meeting three. That's what turned us on to Jerry and his implant."

"How sure are you about his being the source?"

"Totally," Allison said. "James determined that it had to have been Jerry's implant. Jerry missed one meeting, and the nature of the transcript changed dramatically. James determined that my recording was the source used by the transcriber for that meeting. Besides, before every meeting, James would wand the members of the group, and every time Jerry's implant would trigger the device. Jerry was the principal source."

"The implant triggered the wand, and you still let him into the meeting? Why did you do that?"

"James assumed that it was just the nature of the device to activate the wand. I suppose because it had a microphone. But there was no evidence of a transmitter. James thought it was acceptable—the fact that there was no evidence of a transmitter."

"Hell, that sounds pretty stupid to me. If a transmitter was turned off, it would not be detected. All that was required would be to record the audio and then have the transmitter activate later. I thought James was more careful than that."

"Well, we screwed up," Allison admitted. "It was as much my fault as James's."

"Tell me again, who does James think is responsible?" Bob asked.

"James suspects Mossad."

"Sounds like James, he blames them for everything. ... You can buy most of that stuff over the Internet now. Could have been anyone. Could have been the Russians."

"James is pretty sure that the transcriber was Israeli. He concluded that from some spelling mistakes in the transcript," Allison said. She could see that Bob had settled down a bit, so after a few seconds she asked him, "So, how did you come up with my thumb drive?"

"Rumor had it that you had summarized all the meetings and stored the audio on thumb drives hidden in your second apartment. I had some of my people retrieve 'em."

"Rumor! Screw your rumor! You've been spying on me. Damn you, don't you *ever* quit?"

"You should be damn happy I secured the originals of those recordings for you. That is exactly the sort of thing that brings presidencies down. I thought you were a student of history, Al, don't you remember Nixon?"

Allison again grew silent. She knew Bob was pontificating. Regardless of what James said, she knew that the thumb drives could have brought her down, were she to have become president.

"Don't worry, Al, the rest of the thumb drives—I've destroyed them. And I mean destroyed them, with my own two hands. And then I fed the pieces to the SOB that had them. Just wanted to send a message."

There were distinct tones of pride and anger in Bob's words. He liked taking matters into his own hands, at every opportunity.

"There are no other copies out there? Aside from the one I have in my hand?" Allison asked.

"Not unless you made some others, but I don't think you did.

Right?" Bob asked, in a quasi-rhetorical manner. "… Of course, the reporter would have made a copy—or copies. But if James is right, and if it is Mossad, it won't be a major problem. Besides, copies are not the same as originals."

Allison did not respond because of his condescending tone.

Again the two of them rode along together without saying a word. It was an uneasy silence. The best that Allison could hope to come out of this meeting was for the two of them to form a united front. So very many times before they had attacked problems in just this way—a lot of friction, a lot of sarcasm and name calling, but in the end, unity. Something akin to unity was what Allison was seeking now.

But, in this case, while she felt unity was getting closer, she sensed it had not yet materialized. Finally, Bob broke the silence.

"Al, do you know how embarrassing it is for me that the whole world thinks you are screwing around with one of my closest friends?"

Chapter 67—Bob frightens Allison

12:30 p.m., Saturday, December 31

Allison recognized those words. She had thrown them in Bob's face on numerous occasions in the past. She knew that Bob was not the least bit embarrassed about the planted rumor. He simply wanted to get a dig in. So she did not respond to his question.

Then Bob turned his attention back to the recordings and the transcriptions. "Let's assume, for the sake of this discussion, that James was right, that Mossad is behind this. I would agree with James that this is actually quite likely, given the way it is being handled. Besides, I have a lot of confidence in James's intellect. If he is convinced it is Mossad, it probably is."

Bob paused to catch his breath and then went on. "Mossad would like to use their knowledge of these meetings for two things. First, I do think they would like to see an end put to this assassination thing. They abhor the unknown and political turmoil. Even though they do not like this guy, the current president, they would rather see him voted out than killed. I think these tapes effectively have put an end to this notion. Right?"

Allison, by her silence, signaled her acquiescence on this matter.

"Then, if the plan is dead, they will back off, and that could be the end of it. But, in the future, you can expect to see them use the intel to leverage something out of you, or me—especially should you become president. We can count on their doing that."

"That's exactly what James said," Allison added.

"Now," Bob continued, "can I safely assume that there are no other recordings in your voice regarding those meetings? Would that be correct?"

"Not in my voice. One of the others might have made some after-the-fact recordings, or transcriptions, but they would not stand up in hearings."

"You're damn right about that. And if this thing ever saw the light of day, quite a few things wouldn't be standing up," Bob said, again venting some anger. After a few moments, Bob continued, "So, what we're left with are these transcriptions ... and these very mysterious recordings. And, of course, this ridiculous rumor about your affair with James," Bob said, making an attempt at conclusion.

"And the four other members of our group," Allison added.

"Loose ends," Bob said. "I hate loose ends."

"They're my friends, Bob."

"Friends? They're not friends. They're all a bunch of jackasses. That's exactly what they are, a bunch of damn jackasses."

Allison recognized that tone of voice. She feared heads were going to roll.

Chapter 68— *The plan to free Kate unfolds*
8:33 p.m., Thursday, December 29

Jack drove directly to a Long Island residential neighborhood and parked.

"Do you have a specific reason to think Kate is being held nearby?" Reginald asked.

"We can't be sure," Jack replied. "But Roger and I talked about this earlier and concluded that it just made sense that the kidnappers would have rented a house quite close to where Kate lived. So they could keep an eye on her prior to the kidnapping."

"Kate lived near here?" Reginald asked.

"She did," Jack said. "Her apartment was only a few blocks west of here. We concluded that it would be likely that the kidnappers would have rented a house, not an apartment. So that their activities would attract less attention. It really would not be difficult to find a house to rent in this area, given the number that are on the market. It's just a guess. But it feels like a pretty safe bet."

"Tell me again how this is going to go down," Reginald said.

"I told the kidnappers to call right at ten," Jack said. "I'm thinking that they're going to want to get the upper hand—catch me off guard. So I am expecting them to call early. When they call, Roger will immediately patch the call through to this phone."

Jack held up his throwaway phone for Reginald to see.

"As far as they are concerned," Jack said, "If they put a track on my phone, it will give them a location around Penn Station. That will make them comfortable.

"They already know that I'm not going to talk to them until they put Kate on. That will take some time. I will do all I can to keep them on the phone until Roger can pinpoint their location. His equipment is the best there is. He thinks that he can locate them within the first twenty seconds or so—even if they engage in some sneaky routing. He said he might even locate them more quickly."

"So, when we get the location, I direct you to it?" Reginald asked.

"I think it would be better if I concentrated on the conversation and you drove," Jack said. "I've got to take a piss. When I get out, let's switch seats."

"We've got over an hour," Reginald said. "At least we should have."

"I'm not so sure about that hour," Jack replied, getting out of the SUV. "I spotted a very friendly group of evergreens on the way here. I'm gonna go back and visit them. It was only a block or so back. Damn prostate. Your day will come, my friend."

"Don't get yourself arrested, Jack. You'll end up on some sexual offender list."

"Is that how you did it?" Jack chuckled as he closed the door and headed back down the street.

He located the clump of evergreens right where he had remembered them, and disappeared into it.

Just as he was zipping up his pants, his phone rang.

Chapter 69— *The early call*

8:51 p.m., Thursday, December 29

Jack quickly parted the trees and headed for the sidewalk, answering his phone as he walked.

"Yeah," he said.

"Handler, is that you?"

"You're early," Jack scolded. "I'm taking a piss. Call me back in ten minutes."

Jack did not give the caller time to argue, disconnecting the call without listening for a response. He started jogging back to the car where Reginald was waiting. Just as he was reaching for the door handle, his phone rang again. This time it was Roger.

"Didn't get it," Roger said. "You should keep them on the phone a little longer next time."

"Got it," Jack replied, hanging up on Roger.

"I was right," he told Reginald when he got in. "They called me while I was taking a leak. Start the car."

Reginald started the engine. He had shut it off only moments earlier so as not to attract attention with the exhaust.

"At least I know Roger's on his toes," Jack said. "I told them to call back in ten. If they managed a trace on my cell phone, they should be satisfied to see it pop up in Midtown. But they probably didn't have time—Roger didn't."

"Are you sure they will call back?" Reginald asked.

"Absolutely," Jack said. "They want something from me. They must have some information that makes them think I can exert influence over something of interest to them. Maybe someone at the meeting talked. Who knows? But they will call tonight. And when they do, we have to act quickly. They will keep Kate alive only as long as they need her. And they won't need her after tonight."

"I'm as ready as I can be," Reginald assured his friend. "Maybe they will wait until ten—the time they were supposed to call."

"They will be calling any second," Jack countered. "They're not concerned now that I'll be tracing their call. If I were, I would have kept them on the first call. They're ready to move."

Jack took a deep breath, laid his head on the back of the seat, and stared at the ceiling of the SUV. "This is the worst part of it—the waiting."

Just as those words tumbled from his mouth, his phone rang. Jack looked at his cell, then over at Reginald and said, "This is it."

Chapter 70—Time to roll

9:02 p.m., Thursday, December 29

Reginald slid the shifter into drive and waited with his right foot on the gas and his left on the brake.

"Yeah," Jack said.

"Handler?" the kidnapper asked.

"Right," Jack said.

"I know what you and your friends are planning," the kidnapper began.

"Hold everything! I need to talk to my daughter before we discuss anything. So if you will kindly go get her, and let me be sure she is okay, then we can talk. But there will be no conversation until that happens. Do you understand me?"

Normally Jack was a man of few words. Tonight, however, he was trying to drag it out. Not only did he want to give Roger time to run his trace, but he needed to keep the men who were holding Kate on the phone long enough for Reginald to locate the house once Roger had done his job. Jack knew that as soon as he was finished talking to his daughter, she was expendable.

"We were anticipating that," the kidnapper said. "We've got Kate right here for you to talk to."

"Then put her the hell on," Jack demanded.

Jack had barely got those words out of his mouth when the GPS lit up. Roger had located the kidnappers. Reginald studied it for only a couple seconds before he determined the best route to take to free Kate.

Just as Roger and Jack had surmised—the kidnappers had chosen a house six blocks from where Kate lived. Unfortunately, Jack and Reginald had stationed themselves slightly in the opposite direction. It would take Reginald nearly five minutes to reach the location. But traffic was light, which would expedite their effort.

"Daddy?" Kate said.

Jack recognized his daughter's voice, but he could tell that she was under duress. She never called him Daddy.

"Kitty," he said. "What's wrong? Have they hurt you?"

She did not respond immediately.

"No, Daddy, they've not hurt me," she said. "I'm just so tired. I haven't slept much. But they haven't hurt me."

With that, one of the kidnappers wrenched the phone from Kate, and addressed Jack.

"Okay, Jack? Satisfied?" he asked.

"No," Jack replied, again trying to stretch out the phone call. "My daughter sounds terrible. What have you done to her? Have you drugged her? I need some assurance that—"

Reginald looked at his watch, "Four minutes to go," he silently mouthed in Jack's direction.

"You got what you wanted, Handler," the kidnapper said. "Now let's talk business."

"I want you to put Kate back on," Jack said. He knew that would not happen, but he was again trying to buy a little time.

"Forget it, Handler," he said. "Your daughter is fine. She wants you to do the right thing so she can go home. You talked to her—you can tell she is doing fine. That's all you're gonna get until you help me."

"Just give her the cell phone and send her out the door," Jack said. "As soon as she is safe, I will do whatever you want."

"Two minutes," Reginald mouthed, checking the GPS another time to be sure he was on track, while he held up two fingers.

"You'll do what I want now, Jack," the kidnapper snapped. "I've got all the power here. All I have to do is say the word and Kate loses some of her beautiful teeth. Is that what you want, Jack?"

"Back off," Jack said. "I said I would help you if I could."

"Oh, you can help us all right," the kidnapper said.

"One minute," Reginald mouthed, turning down the street listed on the GPS. He started checking house numbers and looking for a place to park. Then, spotting the house, he pointed it out to Jack, making sure to keep his gesture below the bottom of the windshield as he drove past. The window in the door of the SUV was heavily tinted, but the windshield was quite clear. There was a man posted on the porch of the home.

Reginald did not want to park directly in front of the house, so he drove past it and found the first parking place on the opposite side of the street.

"Let's just do this," Jack said. "Tell me what you want."

Reginald knew how this had to be done. There was no opportunity to talk to Jack right now, so he got out of the SUV, crossed the street and headed toward the house where Kate was being held.

Reginald never smoked. But he always carried a pack of cigarettes and a broken lighter. Nothing works better to start a conversation than to ask someone for a light. It used to be a more effective ploy, before all the anti-smoking laws were passed. But it still worked outside.

Reginald continued down the sidewalk, fumbling in his pocket for his lighter. While he did not look at the sentry posted on the porch, Reginald knew that the man's radar had picked him up.

When Reginald reached a point about fifteen feet before the steps leading up to the house, he stopped and triggered his lighter several times. Of course, it did not work. He then pulled it away from his cigarette, and flicked it several more times.

"Damn it," he said, as he started up walking again.

He then glanced up at the man on the porch. He turned and took a couple steps toward the house, and said, "Hey, buddy, could you help me out with a light?"

All Reginald was looking for was a clean shot. He had one, and he popped the man in the face and in the neck. The silencer muffled almost all the noise. He knew the fellow would be wearing body armor, so he made sure his two rounds hit their mark.

"We know you have been contracted to assassinate the president of the United States," the kidnapper said to Jack. "Don't deny it. We know all about it."

Now Jack wanted to get this phone call over with. He watched Reginald get past the guard and into the house.

"I don't know where you're getting your information. But that's a bunch of bull."

Jack got out of the SUV and headed to the rear of the house. "I don't have a clue what you're talking about."

Jack knew that he did not have any more time, so he just tossed the phone to the ground and drew his gun.

As he arrived at the rear door, he saw a number of flashes illuminate the curtains on the windows of the second floor. He then heard several rounds from an unsuppressed semi-automatic. He surmised a 10mm.

When Jack reached the door he kicked it in. He could smell smoke. At first he suspected tear gas but then realized that the kidnappers had triggered an incendiary device. Jack continued on into the building, searching for Kate.

What he did not know was that Reginald had already found his daughter and had spirited her out the front door.

Jack made it as far as the stairs leading to the second floor, when he was suddenly hammered from behind by what he thought could have been a baseball bat. Apparently Reginald had shot and wounded one of the kidnappers. Thinking he was dead, Reginald removed the man's gun and continued on in his search for Kate.

So, when Jack ran into the wounded kidnapper, the man found the first blunt object, a ceramic-based lamp, and clubbed Jack over the head with it.

However, even though he was knocked to the floor and stunned, Jack was able to turn and discharge his semi-auto six times, hitting his attacker with three rounds. Jack's first shot struck the man squarely in the chest. Body armor prevented the shot from killing the attacker, but it was sufficient to knock him backward. Jack's second shot missed its mark altogether, but the third caught him squarely in the left forehead.

Reginald managed to help Kate to a tree about seventy-five feet from the house. He carefully leaned her against the trunk. "Kate, are you hit?" he asked her.

"I'm okay," she replied. "Where's my dad?"

"I think he's still in the house," Reginald said. "That sounded like his 10mm. I'm gonna go get him. You should be fine here."

Reginald turned and trotted back toward the house. He was limping noticeably.

"Jack! Jack!" Reginald shouted. "You in here?"

"Reg, over here," Jack answered.

The blow to Jack's head had disoriented him. Adding to that, at the stairwell the fire on the second floor was beginning to lick down and along on the ceiling of the first. The heat was intense, and the smoke thick and black.

Reginald could see his friend crumpled on the floor at the bottom of the stairs. He knew that he had to get Jack out of the house as quickly as possible, so he grabbed him by the wrists and began to drag him to the front door.

"No!" Jack shouted, "I've got to get Kate."

"She's good, Jack," Reginald assured his friend as he continued toward the door. "She's outside."

"Is she hurt?"

"She says she's fine. I'm sure she's in shock. But she looks fine to me."

Once outside, Reginald helped Jack to his feet and pointed over to the tree where Kate was sitting.

"See for yourself, Jack. I think Kate looks pretty good for what she's been through. But go check her out. ... She was asking about you."

The mention of his daughter's name, along with the fresh air, began to bring Jack around. Looking in the direction Reginald had indicated, he spotted his daughter and began stumbling over to her. "Kate!" Jack implored, "Kate, it's your dad. Can you hear me?"

Kate opened her eyes, and forced a smile as he approached. "What happened?" she asked.

"Are you okay?" Jack asked, kneeling beside his daughter. "Are you *okay*?"

"I think so," Kate said. "I don't remember much. What happened? ... How did you find me? There was *so* much smoke."

"Reginald found you," Jack said. "He saved you. He saved me too. Are you sure you're okay? Were you shot?"

"My lungs are on fire," she said. "I breathed some smoke, but I think I'm gonna be fine. I wasn't shot. Where's Reg?"

Jack suddenly realized that Reginald was not with them, and he attempted to stand up to search for him. As soon as he stood, he fell. He, too, had breathed a lot of smoke, and he was still groggy from the blow to the head. But during that brief moment when he tried to stand up he did spot Reginald lying fifty feet from where he had found Kate.

Jack struggled again to stand and this time was successful. Staggering like a drunk, Jack finally made it back to his friend.

"Reg!" Jack cried. "Talk to me. Reg!"

Chapter 71— Jack comforts fallen friend

9:36 p.m., Thursday, December 29

It appeared to Jack that Reginald had tried to make it over to where Kate was sitting but had fallen flat on his face only a few yards from where Jack had left him. Jack placed his fingers on Reginald's neck, searching for a pulse. He adjusted his probing fingers several times but detected nothing.

Jack then gently rolled his friend over. It was clear from his blank stare and lack of color that Reginald was either dead or dying.

Jack immediately began CPR, delivering repeated cycles of thirty chest compressions followed by two rescue breaths. He continued this process without slowing. He was totally oblivious to what was transpiring around him. He didn't hear the sirens growing ever closer. He didn't even notice the two black SUVs with darkly tinted glass, that had bolted over the curb and had pulled up within a few feet from where he knelt with Reginald on the cold, damp concrete.

All he could see was the emptiness that now owned his friend's eyes.

"Roger sent us to clean up," a man said, as he jumped out of the first vehicle. Jack had seen this fellow before. He never knew his real name, always referring to him as "Scarface," for obvious reasons.

Before Jack had time to react, another man had run around from the other side of the SUV, and the two of them were lifting Jack up. They dragged him to the rear of the SUV and virtually tossed him into the grasp of a third man inside the vehicle.

As soon as they had pulled Jack in, the two men then snatched up

Reginald and rolled him into the rear hatch of a second SUV. The men both jumped inside with Reginald and closed the hatch behind them.

The man attending Jack slammed the doors of their vehicle. And then the two SUVs took off in different directions.

Jack struggled to look back in the direction of his daughter. "You can't leave Kate behind! We have to go back for her!"

"There's nothing you can do for your daughter," the driver shouted. "An ambulance has already arrived, and it will take her to the hospital. Roger's orders. ... Staying with her, or taking her with us—it would raise too many questions. ... Roger has this under control. Kate appears to be okay, but we're getting her to the hospital for observation. ... Mark, he's the man with your daughter right now. Mark will brief her on her story."

"You're *sure* she's okay?" Jack asked.

"Mark is one of our best," the driver reassured Jack. "He will check her out thoroughly and let us know. For sure she is in good hands. ... And she's headed to the hospital."

The driver paused for a moment and then continued. "You've got to understand what's at stake here, Jack. It's *imperative* that you be left out of this. And the same goes for Reg and Roger. ... Kate's bright; she will appreciate the ramifications in this for her, and her department, if any of you three are tied to this."

"Kate knows nothing about what I do or who I know," Jack responded.

"And we're gonna keep it that way," the driver said. "Anything that gets you involved in this business with Kate would ultimately drag Roger into it too. Who knows where that could go. And it certainly would not help her career. It has to be handled this way."

"What hospital are you taking my daughter?" Jack asked.

"Not determined yet—we'll have to let you know later," the driver said. "First we have to get you cleaned up. We've got a room for you at a hotel by LaGuardia. According to their records, you've been there since the twenty-fifth. We've moved your stuff in and have a car parked in the garage under your name. It is also dated from the twenty-fifth. We've got to create separation between you and all that went down over by Penn Station. And now this as well."

"You got yourself pretty messed up," the man attending Jack observed. "How bad you hurt? I see you got some blood in your hair and a *very* nasty lump on your head. Any bullet holes we don't know about?"

"I'm not hurt," Jack said. "I just inhaled too much smoke."

"We've got to get you out of those clothes before you get to the hotel," Scarface said. "You can't walk in looking and smelling like this."

"He's about your size," the driver said. "Switch with him. And help him get washed up too."

The man sitting beside Jack immediately started removing his clothes, and so did Jack. When Jack handed the man his bloody shirt and jacket, the man just wadded them up and tossed them in the back. "Thanks, but I don't think I'll be needing these," he said with a laugh.

Using a bottle of water, and his undershirt, Jack washed the blood off his face and hands, and put on the fresh shirt and jacket.

"You've still got blood on the back of your left hand," Scarface told Jack. "Once you get that off, I think you'll be fine until you get to the hotel.

"Here's the card for your room," Scarface said, handing Jack the mag-striped plastic card. "And here's the keys for your rental. It's parked on level three, section two. Just hit the remote, and you will find it. It's a black Chevy Tahoe. I also wrote your room number on the key card in case you forget it. I suspect you are still in shock. ... *I* would be."

Jack took the key card and the car keys from Scarface and examined them. "You guys think of everything," he said.

"We have to," Scarface said, "if we want to keep working for Roger. I'm also giving you a new cell phone. Roger's orders. He does not want you using your old cell anymore. Same number, just some additional security built in. Your old one might have been compromised. Once you get settled, Roger will call you, and we'll go from there."

"And you're gonna fill me in on Kate?" Jack asked.

"Sure will," Scarface said. "Most likely Roger will give you that info. Probably you will be able to see her yet tonight."

"Maybe," Jack said. "Sure bet the cops are going to be debriefing her as soon as possible. I might not be able to talk to her until after they're done."

"Probably so," Scarface said. "Just remember, you were not on the scene when Kate was rescued. Just let Kate fill you in on all the details. She will be the source of *all* your information. Go along with what she says."

Just then the driver's cell phone rang. "It's Roger," he said, checking the caller ID. "Yes, Rog," he said.

There followed a period of silence lasting for nearly a full minute. Finally, the driver asked, "And just how badly is she injured?"

Chapter 72—Jack learns that Kate was shot

10:16 p.m., Thursday, December 29

There was another pause. "I will let Jack know what you told me."

The driver then turned so he could momentarily look Jack in the eye, and he spoke clearly and deliberately to him. "Mark discovered that Kate had been shot. She did not even know it herself. He found the wound when he checked her out. He found quite a lot of blood on her. At first he suspected that the blood was from Reg—that it got transferred to her when he carried her out of the building. But when Mark examined her he found an entry wound in her lower back."

"Lower back?" Jack asked. "Where in her lower back? And was there an exit wound?"

"No exit wound," the driver said. "It's still in there. The entry wound is fairly large. So it appears that the round may have passed through or ricocheted off of something else, then hit Kate. It also appears to have been from a handgun. Probably 9 or 10mm. Nothing bigger. Not high velocity."

"Where on her lower back?" Jack asked again.

"Just above her left hip," the driver answered. "It's impossible to get an accurate reading as to the angle of penetration, because the bullet appears to have been substantially degraded by the time it hit Kate. Both the origin and angle of entry are unclear. They will determine that when they get her into the emergency room."

"I need to get to the hospital," Jack said, in a commanding tone. "I need you to turn this around and get me to my daughter."

Almost immediately the driver jerked the big SUV into a gas station and pulled up to a pump.

"You can run in here and wash up a little better," the driver told Jack, as he peeled off a twenty and handed it to Scarface to top off the tank. "The hospital's gonna be crawling with cops."

Jack was happy to be running into the restroom, because his bladder was already topped off.

Lower back, above the left hip, Jack thought to himself as he trotted toward the restroom. *Degraded with no exit. That could be bad. Could be a kidney. Or worse yet, it could have ripped open her colon.*

Jack stopped himself with that last thought. He always tried to be positive about everything, because he did not like the effect negative energy had on his performance.

It could be resting harmlessly on her hipbone, he concluded. *Good she's getting to the hospital.*

Out of the corner of Jack's eye, he spotted a full-sized sedan that had just pulled in behind them and had backed into a dimly lit parking space. Two men were sitting in the car, and they appeared to be watching him as he entered the service station.

Jack knew the driver was right about his need to wash up. The hospital would be crawling with New York City cops, FBI agents, and who knows what. The mere fact that Kate's father was there checking on the condition of his daughter was not a problem. But if he came in with blood on his clothes or his hands—that would raise questions. So Jack took his time and made sure he looked presentable. All the time, however, the thought of the two men in the sedan played on his mind.

As he left the restroom, Jack took a detour. Rather than coming out of the front door where he had entered, he exited from the rear—toward the big-rig diesel pumps. Once outside, he turned right until he reached the corner of the building. From the darkness he carefully peered over until he spotted the sedan.

The two men in the car had their eyes fixed on the front door of the gas station, obviously waiting for Jack to emerge. But that was not going to happen. Sneaking up from behind were Scarface and another of Roger's men.

Time to create a distraction, Jack thought. Careful not to glance again in the direction of the sedan, Jack proceeded to walk around the side of the building in plain sight of the men in the car. As soon as they spotted Jack, their eyes followed him intently as he rounded the front corner and approached the waiting SUV.

Just before he got in, he heard the familiar sound of several rounds of suppressed 10mm smashing through the tempered glass of car windows. He then heard the engine of that car race.

He also knew what was causing that, but he still did not turn around to observe. Jack had seen that happen several times before. When a man is shot through the temple, his natural involuntary reaction is to stiffen. Obviously, the driver of the car had his foot on the accelerator and was now pushing down on it.

"About now," Jack reasoned, "the driver's side shooter will be reaching in and shutting off the engine."

And, just as Jack anticipated, the engine stopped.

When Jack got into the SUV, he observed that the driver and the fourth man were not there. Jack also knew what that meant. "One carefully placed round through the DVR," he reasoned.

In fact, just as Jack surmised, the driver and the fourth man had entered the station at the same time Scarface and his friend sneaked back to take out the men who had been tailing them. While the man with the driver took a soda and a bag of chips to the counter, the driver stepped quickly into the little office and fired off three suppressed .38 Special rounds into the video recording equipment.

The driver was a professional. He had chosen a revolver over the more popular semi-automatic pistol because he did not like the sound of spent cartridges bouncing on the floor. His Smith and Wesson .38 Special could also fire .357 magnum rounds, but he never used those more powerful rounds under normal conditions, because he wanted to avoid collateral damage. A .357 magnum can explode through a wall and injure or kill someone on the other side.

Almost at the very second that the driver was destroying the DVR, his cohort at the counter squeezed the bag of chips, causing the bag to explode, spewing chips all over the counter.

"Damn," the man said, "I never had that happen before. Must be a cheap bag."

"No problem," the cashier said. "I'll clean it up."

"Sorry, buddy," the man said, as he took a chip from the bag and stuck it in his mouth. "I guess I won't open a bag like that again." For a few moments the odor of the airborne chips covered up the pungent smell of the spent gunpowder.

Immediately the driver and his friend paid for the chips and walked out of the gas station together. As they did they observed Scarface getting in the SUV. The interior light illuminated when the car door opened, and the driver could make out that there were three men in the vehicle—his two men and Jack.

Just as the driver reached the SUV, his cell rang.

"Is she conscious?" he asked. "I see. What's the hospital looking like?" There was a pause, then the driver continued. "We'll be there in fifteen. Twenty at worst. I think I'll just drop Jack off. You're not gonna need us there, are you? … I'll stay close."

After he disconnected, but before he pulled away from the pump, the driver turned to face Jack. "Not as good as we might hope, Jack," he said. "Roger says that they've got Kate in the ER. But that now she's in some pain. They're going to stabilize her and get her scanned as soon as possible. They suspect some internal bleeding, but they're not quite sure where that bullet is. I'm sorry, buddy, but you know how these things go. That is a great hospital, and they will fix her up, I'm sure of that."

For the remainder of the drive to the hospital, Jack sat virtually silent. In fact, no one in the vehicle said very much.

Then, just as they approached the hospital, the driver exclaimed, "What the hell—this looks like a scene from a Bruce Willis movie!"

Chapter 73—Jack arrives at hospital

10:30 p.m., Thursday, December 29

The driver turned around once more, facing Jack. "I'm gonna drop you off here, Jack. If I try to drive through we might get trapped in there and *never* get out."

"That's fine," Jack replied. "I'll just jump out here. … Hey, you said my stuff was already at the hotel? When's my checkout?"

"Don't worry," the driver said. "We'll take care of that. You can stay with Kate as long as necessary. The address of the hotel is on the card."

"Thanks for all the help," Jack said. "What about Reg? Did he make it?"

"Roger says that Reg passed," the driver answered. "The official cause of death is an auto accident. We'll clean him up and get the body to an appropriate funeral home."

"Send his clothes to me, okay?" Jack requested. "Buy him some new ones to send to his family. But I want his clothes."

"Certainly," the driver replied. "You take care, and we'll be in touch." With that, Jack looked over at Scarface and nodded his gratitude, then closed the door. *He was right about the Bruce Willis movie,* Jack thought, as he took in the sea of red and blue surrounding the ER entrance.

Best way to do this is through reception, Jack concluded. So he walked around to the main entrance and stood in line at the desk.

"New patient. Kate Handler—H-a-n-d-l-e-r," he said. "I'm her father."

The woman at the desk started checking on her screen to see if she had an admission by that name.

"She was just brought in," Jack said. "Might not be in your database yet. I believe she suffered a gunshot wound."

With that information, the attendant ceased looking at her computer and made a call. "Have you got a Kate Handler—H-a-n-d-l-e-r? … I have her father here. I'll let him know."

The woman then hung up the phone and addressed Jack. "Your daughter is in surgery right now. I have no more information for you than that. She was admitted into the ER about a half hour ago. There is a waiting room right outside surgery. I will give you a map."

The woman then presented Jack with a sheet of paper outlining the route he should take to get to the proper waiting room. "You are here," she said. "You need to follow the blue line over to the elevator. Take the elevator down one level. That will be level one. When you get off the elevator, there will be another blue line. Follow that blue line to the ER waiting room. There will be nurses there that can give you more information."

"Thanks," Jack said as he turned to follow the woman's instructions.

Wonder what I'll find there? he asked himself. *That waiting room will no doubt be full of cops—cops asking questions.*

Jack scrutinized every person he encountered along the way, looking for familiar faces but finding none. As he approached a bank of three elevators at the end of the helpful blue line, Jack pushed the button, and there was the familiar "ding." Jack looked up to see that the elevator on the left was arriving at his floor.

After several passengers got off, Jack entered and pushed the button marked "ER." When he turned around to face the closing doors, he observed a man walking up to that same bank of elevators. As the door closed in front of Jack, for a split second their eyes met. It was Kate's "friend" Kurt, from the Penn Station coffee shop.

What the hell is he doing here? Jack wondered, as the elevator door closed between them.

Chapter 74—*The bullet's path*

10:42 p.m., Thursday, December 29

When the elevator reached the ER floor, Jack got out and waited for the next elevator. He wanted to confront Kurt and see just what Kate's old associate was really up to. But the next elevator arrived, and Kurt was not on it. After the second elevator emptied, Jack figured out that Kurt was not going to be getting out.

I must have spooked him, Jack surmised.

Before approaching the nurse station, Jack surveyed the entire area. He figured that if one questionable guy showed up in Kate's hospital, there might be others. Not seeing anyone he recognized, he proceeded to check on Kate's status.

"I would like to check on a patient. I think she is in surgery," Jack said. "Kate Handler. Can you give me an update?"

"We do have a patient by that name," the nurse at the desk told him. "Are you related?"

"Yes, my name is Jack Handler. Kate's my daughter."

"We don't have any recent updates," the nurse said. "All I can tell you right now is that your daughter is still in surgery. Dr. Phillips is the emergency room surgeon tonight. He is our chief surgeon on this shift. If you will wait in the waiting room, as soon as he comes out I will have him talk to you."

"That would be great," Jack replied. "Do you have any idea how long that might be?"

"I really have no more information than I just gave you," she said.

"I'm sorry. You do know that she suffered a gunshot wound in the left hip. And that there has been some internal bleeding. As soon as the doctor is confident that she will be stable, he will come out and talk to you."

"I'll have a seat right over there," Jack said, pointing to a chair just outside the waiting room.

"Thank you, Mr. Handler," the nurse said. "I'll be sure and send Dr. Phillips over to talk to you. I just want you to know that Dr. Phillips is the best we've got. In fact, he is greatly respected by his peers. Your daughter is in good hands."

Jack did not audibly respond, but he did smile, and he nodded in a manner suggesting he was pleased to hear that.

It's not just the doctor that I worry about, Jack thought as he walked over to the seat he had just pointed out. *It's the guy administering the anesthetic or the nurse with the flu or the intern on pills. Any one of them could kill my Kate.*

Just as Jack sat down, a man in a black suit walked over to him until their knees touched and said, "Jack Handler? You are Jack Handler? Right?"

Jack sized him up quickly: *cheap suit. Big man. All muscle. Distinctive bulge right where you'd expect to find a Glock. Very big, heavy hands.*

"Who's asking?" Jack demanded, not at all comfortable about having his space violated and wondering where this guy had come from.

Chapter 75—Big Hands quizzes Jack

10:55 p.m., Thursday, December 29

For a long moment the two men just stared at each other.

"I think we have a mutual friend," Big Hands said. "You do know Reginald Black, don't you?"

Jack did not like getting bullied, and it was obvious to him that was exactly what was going down. His adrenaline-induced inclination was to sucker punch Big Hands in the groin. But he thought better of it for a couple of reasons. First of all, even though he was thoroughly convinced that Big Hands was a bad character, he was equally certain that the man did not pose a serious threat on this stage. Besides, no one who really knew what he was doing would leave himself so open to attack. "Might be a cop," Jack reasoned. "Or a private dick. Whatever the case, this guy is not who he purports to be, and he is likely a minor player."

But there was a stronger reason Jack wished to avoid an altercation—he needed to behave himself if he wished to stick around for his daughter. Besides, for some reason he could not immediately figure out, there seemed to be something vaguely familiar about Big Hands—perhaps in the way he looked, his mannerisms, or in the way he talked.

I don't have time for this now, Jack thought. So, he glanced over to the nurses' station as though being summoned and started to get up. "Excuse me," he said to Big Hands, uncrossing his legs and driving his heel heavily into Big Hands's instep. "Sorry about that," Jack said, as he rose to his feet and walked toward the desk.

After taking a half dozen steps, he turned back to address Big Hands. However, the big fellow had already disappeared.

Now that was very strange, Jack thought, taking another moment to fully survey the entire area. But the big fellow was nowhere to be seen. *Damn strange. First I almost ran into that Kurt fellow. Now this guy asking about Reg.*

Jack continued over to the nurses' station and asked, "Is there a coffee machine around here?"

"Sure is, Mr. Handler," the nurse in charge said. "Right over there by the telephones and the elevators," she said, pointing toward a couple coin-operated machines.

Jack had noticed them when he initially got off the elevator as he stood waiting for Kurt to emerge. He really did not want any stale machine coffee, but he needed an excuse to quickly extricate himself from Big Hands.

Jack did proceed over to the concession area, inserted a dollar bill into a machine, and pulled the lever on a Diet Coke. The can clunked down loudly. He retrieved it and popped the top open. *Better figure out where the toilets are now. … It's only a matter of time.*

Just then he caught sight of a man approaching quickly to his right. Jack's head snapped around, just as the chief surgeon finished slipping on a fresh surgical jacket. "Mr. Handler?" the doctor asked.

"Yes, I'm Jack Handler."

"I'm Dr. Phillips," the doctor said. "I believe you are Kate Handler's father. Is that right?"

"I am," Jack said. "How's my daughter?"

"We've located the bullet," the doctor said. "And we've stopped the bleeding."

"Well," Jack said. "That would have to be good news. Right?"

"That is good news," the doctor said. "But there are complications."

Chapter 76—Kate's boss

11:10 p.m., Thursday, December 29

Just then a man in a tailored gray suit walked up to Jack's right, joining Jack and the doctor. It was obvious that this third man viewed himself as important and that he intended to take part in the conversation.

"You're Kate Handler's surgeon?" he asked.

"Yes I am," the doctor replied. "And who might you be?"

"I'm Captain Lawrence Spencer. Your patient, Kate Handler, works for me," the man in the gray suit answered, opening his wallet to display his badge. "Kate is one of my detectives. I just learned that she was wounded. Can you update me?"

The doctor glanced down at the detective's badge. "I was just explaining to Kate's father here that we did locate the bullet. Unfortunately it had fragmented. We removed several pieces of it, and we did manage to control the bleeding. But there is a problem, and we have not gained the upper hand on that yet."

"A problem?" Jack asked. "What sort of problem?" Jack was a little irritated that his daughter's boss had interrupted.

"Well," the doctor replied, showing the men a basic diagram of the human anatomy. "It will be easier to show you than to tell you."

"Here's where the bullet entered Ms. Handler," he said, pointing to a spot just above the left hipbone. "As you might already know, the entry wound was substantially larger than it should have been. This would suggest strongly that the bullet had bounced around a bit before it hit your daughter. Because it had flattened out considerably, and lost velocity, it did not penetrate as deeply as it might have. That's good and bad.

It's good in the sense that it did not do damage to her intestines or vital organs. But because it was quite large, it did do some tearing. And, unfortunately, one of the things that it tore into was a large blood vein—a renal vein.

"Again, your daughter was fortunate. The bullet did not strike her kidney. In fact, the damage to the vein was minimal, but it did cause significant internal bleeding. Most of bullet's energy had been spent by that time. All the bleeding we were seeing, it was from that hole in the vein."

"But you were able to patch that up, right?" Jack asked.

"Yes we were," the doctor said. "But there might be more to it than that. You see, when the bullet reached that point in Kate's body, it had begun to disintegrate. I already alluded to that. As we followed its path, we found and removed several very tiny fragments. They had separated from the bullet, and had become lodged in the surrounding muscle tissue.

"The problem is, it is possible that we missed one or more of the fragments, because they were so tiny."

Jack interrupted at that point. "If they are so small, and lodged in the muscle, that wouldn't hurt anything, would it?"

"If the fragments remain in muscle tissue, that would be correct. They would not significantly impact her recovery, if at all."

"The problem, rather, the potential problem, that we encountered involves the point at which the bullet struck the vein. While we were able to remove the major part of bullet itself and repair the hole, we did find a much smaller hole directly above where the bullet came to rest. That hole was tiny by comparison—not much larger than a pin might make if pushed head and all through a sheet of paper. It was very small."

"You know I'm gonna need that bullet," Kate's boss interjected.

"I understand the procedure," the doctor said. "But we're not done with it. Even though it was tiny, it was a hole just the same. The curious thing about it was its location. It was only a couple millimeters above the larger hole. Now, there are only two ways that hole could have been created. First, we could have inadvertently caused it during the process of removing the bullet and making the repair. While that is a possibility, it seems unlikely. The more feasible explanation would be that the hole was caused by a fragment of the bullet."

"When will I be able to get that bullet?" Captain Spencer interrupted.

Dr. Phillips glanced in the detective's direction but did not address his question.

"Now, if that is the case, if a fragment became separated from the bullet itself and caused that puncture, then we would have liked to have found that piece. But we did not."

"Are you saying that there could be a piece of the bullet still in Kate's body? Floating around in her blood stream?" Jack asked.

The doctor nodded affirmatively. "And if that is the case, it still would not necessarily present a problem. At least not in and of itself. If that little piece of shrapnel, which would likely be about the size of a grain of sand or smaller, if that tiny piece of metal simply ripped a hole through the tough wall of the vein, then bounced off and lodged itself in surrounding tissue, then that will never be a problem. It would never cause Kate any discomfort.

"But, it could be a different matter altogether if that piece, small as it is, passed through the wall of the vein and got into her blood stream. If that happened, and we're not at all sure that it did, then it could float around until it got lodged somewhere else. But if it made its way to her brain, it could plug a vessel, cause a clot, and that could be serious."

"Can't you stick a magnet in there, or something like that, and get it out?" Kate's boss said.

"It's possible we could find it with a scan," the doctor said, trying not to patronize the detective. "If we knew where to look. But it is virtually impossible to locate something so tiny. At this point, about all we can do is wait. Chances are great that it will end up someplace where it will do her no harm. The human anatomy has a way of dealing with things like that. Most likely there will never be any repercussions from this. But I wanted to give you as accurate a picture as possible. There can always be complications. In this case, I think the chances are excellent that nothing will ever come of it. But we will be keeping her for a few days, and we will be looking for signs of additional bleeding as well."

"Then, given this piece of the bullet never presents a problem, what would you say is the prognosis for full recovery?" Jack asked.

"Excellent," the doctor said with an air of confidence. "In addition to the gunshot wound, your daughter was unusually dehydrated when brought in. We found that curious. But we're getting that under control. I would say that we'll have her on her feet tomorrow, then watch her for a couple days. She should be totally mobile by that time. A little sore, perhaps, because of all the digging around we had to do. But other than that, she should be back to normal within a week or so. That is, as long as there are no further complications."

Just as Jack reached out to shake hands with Dr. Phillips, Big Hands walked up. At first Jack did not notice him. But when he saw Detective Spencer slide over to make room, he realized they had company.

And, it was also at that time that Jack remembered just what it was about Big Hands that had seemed familiar to him earlier.

Chapter 77—Who
Big Hands really is

11:19 p.m., Thursday, December 29

Jack caught the scent of the Big Hand's cologne. But it was not the cologne that got Jack's attention. Jack realized that the cologne was intended only to cover the telltale odor of smoke—incendiary smoke. *This man with the big hands must have been at the house where Kate was held. He must be one of her kidnappers,* Jack thought.

Jack did not initially acknowledge Big Hands. Instead, he played back in his mind all that he could recall about the kidnappers: *The voice was wrong. Big Hands was definitely not the spokesman. I always talked to the same man. No way to know exactly how many of them there were. They could have operated in shifts—two on, two off. And a lookout. Possibly three at any given time. I believe we left three bodies at the scene. Then there's this guy—smelling like smoke.*

But what was this guy's role? Why is he here now? Certainly can't be revenge. Must be he is concerned Kate will be able to identify him. That would make sense only if the guys who took Kate were not foreign agents. They must be our guys! And this fellow is on the inside. Captain Spencer probably knows him. That's why he slid over to let him in."

Jack's mind continued to race as he stood there, still not acknowledging Big Hands. "I have to make sure I don't let him know that I might be on to him."

"So Kate's gonna make it," Big Hands interrupted.

"I'm sorry," the doctor said. "I don't believe we've been introduced."

"My name is William Smith," Big Hands said. "Dr. William Smith. I am a consultant for the NYPD. Captain Spencer here will vouch for me."

I'll be damned, Jack thought. *He is the inside man. And of course Kate would recognize him. Certainly she never saw him before her abduction. But now, if he consulted in her department, she eventually would have contact with him. He's here to kill her.*

"As I explained in detail to Mr. Handler," the doctor said, "Ms. Handler was seriously wounded by a bullet, but we expect her to make a full and speedy recovery."

"Wonderful!" Big Hands Smith said. "What great news."

Then, directing his comments to Jack, Big Hands Smith continued. "I'm sure you're relieved. I am so happy for you."

"Now," the doctor said, as he took half a step backward. "If you will excuse me, I will get back to work. Nice to have met all you gentlemen. If you have further questions, the nurses at the desk will be happy to help you."

All three men smiled, acknowledging the doctor's effort to move on. But only Jack spoke. "Thanks, Doctor," he said. "I appreciate your candor."

With that, Dr. Phillips reached out to Jack to shake his hand. "I'm glad I had good news for you. All too often it doesn't work out that way." He then smiled in the direction of the other two and proceeded over to the nurses' station. He picked up a folder, glanced at it for a few seconds, and then headed back through the swinging doors into the treatment area.

"Gentlemen," Jack said, as he started to walk back to his seat.

"Jack," Big Hands Smith said, reaching out to shake Jack's hand. "We've not formally met. I just want you to know how pleased I am that your daughter is going to be okay."

"I believe you had said that you were an associate of Reginald's." Jack inquired. "How do you know Reginald?"

"He and I go back forever," Big Hands Smith said. "I consulted with him on different matters through the years. Not recently, though. I did not know that he was involved with anything in the city until I heard from a third party that he was seen with Kate earlier tonight."

"Is that right?" Jack asked. "I haven't seen Reginald around here, have you?"

"No, I haven't," Big Hands Smith said. "But I've only been here a short time. How about you, Jack, have you been here long?"

Jack believed that whenever a person used your common name in conversation, it suggested he was not comfortable with you. Jack was not comfortable with Big Hands either.

"Not long," Jack said. "I need a cigarette. How about you?"

"Sounds good," Big Hands Smith replied. "But I doubt that they have a smoking room in this hospital."

"Yeah they do. And I know exactly where it is," Jack said. "I've been here before."

Jack had no idea where to go to have a cigarette. He did not even smoke. But Jack did know where to take a man he was about to kill. Jack headed down the stairs and all the way to the basement maintenance area. He could have taken an elevator but did not want to be stuck in one having to make conversation with the man who intended to kill his daughter.

"Right through here," Jack said, sliding in behind Big Hands Smith as they walked toward the dumpsters. "We can talk while we smoke."

But there would be no cigarettes lit. Not even a celebratory cigar. Instead, just as they reached the largest of three dumpsters, Jack flipped open the knife he always carried. Locking both hands together around the knife in order to drive it deeply into Big Hands's back, he thrust if forward with all his strength. The blade pierced the big man's suit coat and ripped through his left kidney. The force of the blow knocked Big Hands off his feet, slamming him face-first into the front of the dumpster. Big Hands instinctively grabbed the front of the open dumpster to break his fall.

Pulling the knife from Big Hands's back, Jack reached over the top of Big Hands's head. Grabbing his forehead in his left hand, he pulled Big Hands's head back toward him. Then, with the knife in his right hand, Jack slit the big fellow's throat from ear to ear.

Jack was careful to avoid the blood that was spurting out of Big Hands' neck. Dropping the knife on the concrete in front of the dumpster, Jack gripped the big man's legs just below the knees, lifted him up and slid his dying body into the dumpster. As Jack bent down to pick up his knife, he could hear Big Hands thrashing around. But by the time Jack had wiped the excess blood off the front of the dumpster with some trash paper he had found nearby, the noise had stopped.

Jack knew that if there were a surveillance camera, it would be directly above the door. So he chose to walk around to the front of the building, rather than turn to face the camera. Most middle-aged men look about the same from behind. There would be no way to make a positive identification without an image of his face.

Kate should be safe for the night, Jack reasoned, as he approached an intersection a block from the hospital.

"I need a cab. I need some sleep," Jack then complained out loud.

Jack started to hail a cab that was headed his way. But as he did, a black sedan cut in front of the cab and pulled up right in front of him.

"Get in, Jack," the driver said, as he rolled down the passenger side window. Jack recognized the man in the car. It was the guy that he had seen earlier in the hospital just as he was getting on the elevator.

"Kurt?" Jack responded, placing his hands on the car as he leaned in to get a closer look at the driver.

"Jack, get in the car," Kurt said. "You are in danger."

Chapter 78—Kurt comes back
11:41 p.m., Thursday, December 29

Jack just stared at Kurt for a moment and then said, "What else is new? Hell, I'm always in danger—at least lately."

Jack did not really have to think much about it. He wasn't particularly concerned about a threat on his life. But he did want to find out just what this guy was all about. When he initially encountered the man in the coffee shop, Kate was with him, so he was hesitant to feel him out. Now, however, it was different. Now Kate lay helpless in a hospital bed with a bullet hole in her back, and Reginald—Jack's best friend—was dead.

What do I have to lose? Jack reasoned as he got in the black sedan with Kate's strange friend Kurt.

"How 'bout I drop you off at your hotel?" Kurt asked.

"What hotel?" Jack asked.

"By the airport," Kurt replied. "Roger set you up there, but I don't think you've been there yet. Isn't that right?"

"How do you know Roger?" Jack asked.

"I know a lot about this whole mess," Kurt replied. "I'm the fellow who picked up Reg."

That surprised Jack. He had not suspected that this fellow from the coffee shop was in any way involved with Roger. But, it did not surprise him. Roger always seemed to be on top of every situation.

"Where did you take Reg?" Jack asked.

"Roger will be in touch with you later," Kurt said. "Right now we need to get you to your hotel room. Have you seen yourself? You've got blood all over your right sleeve. That's not from Reginald is it? Looks like you've been busy again."

"You said someone is after me? That I'm in danger?" Jack inquired. "What do you mean? Who's after me?"

"One of the fellows who was holding your daughter," Kurt said. "A big guy. Well, he consults with the NYPD. He was actually at the house where they were holding Kate. He somehow escaped tonight. We have every reason to think that he is coming after you. He was spotted in the hospital tonight."

"Actually, I think Kate was his target," Jack said. "But I don't think he will present any problem for me or my daughter. I had a little talk with him, and he decided that he would rather take a little ride to New Jersey in the morning."

"I see," Kurt said.

Jack had wanted to see just how quickly Kurt would catch on. If he truly was a trusted associate of Roger's, he would know that a morning trip to New Jersey would mean that Big Hands Smith was about to become landfill. Jack observed that Kurt understood exactly what he had just said.

"Anything else I should know?" Jack asked.

"The detective in charge," Kurt replied, "Spencer, Captain Spencer. He's a pompous ass—and a not-terribly-bright one at that. But, generally speaking, he's cool. He's been responsible for moving your daughter up the ladder. Don't get me wrong. She deserved every promotion. But it never hurts to have someone like Spencer promoting you."

"Are you suggesting that his intentions are not righteous?" Jack asked.

"I've never heard of him trying to pull anything with a female subordinate," Kurt replied. "He's working his way up the ladder too, and he knows that Kate is one of the department's darlings. She is a very competent detective, and it doesn't hurt that she is a female detective. Spencer is looking out for himself. But you can't fault him for that. He's one of the good guys. Kate is lucky to be working under him. And he is just as fortunate to have your daughter watching his back. They are a good team."

"That's good to know," Jack said. "There might be some waves when Big Hands doesn't show up for the morning briefing."

"Spencer won't be aware of anything right away," Kurt said. "He had no idea that this Smith guy was working for the other side."

"Then they weren't using Kate as bait to draw him out?" Jack asked, exhibiting a little agitation.

"No," Kurt said. "It was not at all like that. Kate is in a secure area. And a female detective is actually sleeping in the room listed as Kate's. Had Smith, or anyone else, made an attempt, Spencer would have busted him."

"So," Jack said, "I wasted a man who might have been a valuable witness?"

"You could say that," Kurt replied, with just a hint of a smile on his youthful face. "But don't worry about it. This whole mess has presented us with more detours than a summer drive through downtown Chicago. You know a little about that, don't you?"

Jack did not respond. The mere fact that Kurt had all the right answers gave Jack all the confidence he needed for this night. *This guy is legit,* Jack thought. *I will certainly welcome a shower and a change of clothes. And a warm bed would be okay, too.*

Jack reached into his pocket and pulled out a chocolate bar. "No offense if I don't offer you some, Kurt. I don't remember the last time I ate anything," Jack said.

"You go right ahead," Kurt replied with a chuckle.

Jack looked down at his right hand. It was thoroughly stained with Big Hands's blood. So he took care to grip the candy bar by the wrapper. Even though he did not touch the candy with his bloodied hand, he could still smell the dead man's blood. But it did not stop him from enjoying the sweet chocolate.

However, his pleasure was suddenly interrupted. Just as he slid the last piece of the candy bar into his mouth, he heard the thud of a bullet piercing safety glass, accompanied by a shower of warm, sticky blood. Kurt had been shot.

Chapter 79—Jack escapes death car

12:06, a.m., Friday, December 30

Jack grabbed the steering wheel with his right hand and used his left to prop up Kurt's limp body as a shield to block a barrage of rounds being fired in rapid succession from a vehicle that had pulled alongside at a traffic light. He could feel the shockwave of each bullet as it struck Kurt's torso. In most cases the 9mm slugs bounced off of the man's vest. But some missed the protection and continued on into flesh.

It was those rounds that posed the greatest threat to Jack. A bullet striking a shoulder bone could easily bounce off and lodge in his own body. Almost immediately Jack jammed the accelerator to the floor with his left foot, jetting through the intersection. Fortunately, the attack occurred just as the cross-traffic light turned green. So when Jack bolted ahead, all the other vehicles were able to stop before striking his car.

As soon as the shooting stopped, Jack sat up and checked out where he was going. It was a good thing he did, because he found his car right on the rear bumper of traffic stopped at the next traffic signal.

Jack would not have been able to hit the brake, even had he wished to, because Kurt's right foot was in the way. Instead, he steered to the left and drove into the oncoming traffic until he reached the light. He then turned left, going the wrong way down a one-way street. Finding no room on the street, he steered his car onto the sidewalk and bounced it off a brick building.

"I'm outta here," he yelled, with only himself to hear. He turned the wheel into the parked vehicles to stop.

Reaching into Kurt's holster, he removed a Glock 10mm. He had remembered that gun from when he brushed up against Kurt in the Penn Station coffee shop. *Didn't know this was going to come in so handy,* Jack thought as he checked the semi-auto to make sure it had a full clip. He yanked back on the action, ejecting a round. He had to make sure there was a live round in the magazine. Sometimes private detectives, and most private citizens, do not keep a live round in the magazine for safety reasons.

"Bet this guy is FBI," Jack muttered.

He felt Kurt's neck for a pulse. Realizing the man was still alive, he removed Kurt's phone and dialed 911.

"Man shot! Need help!" Jack shouted at the dispatcher.

As always, Jack remained calm. He set the phone on the seat and then removed his jacket and wiped off all the blood he could with the lining. He then looked in the rear seat and found a half-empty plastic bottle of water. He poured some of it in his hands, and washed his face and hands, again wiping it off using the jacket lining, and then he slowly opened the door of the vehicle.

Looking around, Jack caught a glimpse of a subway entrance. A crowd was beginning to gather. "We need an ambulance here," Jack announced. "I think my friend had a stroke. Somebody call 911."

Seeing his way was clear, Jack hurried down into the subway tunnel. However, before he reached the bottom of the steps, he turned around and headed back up. He knew that there would be cameras in the tunnel.

When he got to the surface, he did not look in the direction of the smoking car. Instead, he hurried back across the street and headed to the point from where the shots were originally fired. He knew that the gun used to shoot Kurt was a 9mm semi-auto. He also knew that spent rounds would be all over the street.

When he reached that intersection, he walked out into the stopped traffic and found three casings. One had been run over, but two appeared to be intact. If this fellow, Kurt, was actually working with or for Roger, Jack knew that Roger would appreciate the evidence. Poking a pen into the hollow end, he picked up the two undamaged casings and wrapped them in a handkerchief. He picked up the third casing with his bare hand and slipped it into his pants pocket.

He then stood up and continued on across the street.

Roger would be able to tell a great deal about the shooter from the two casings. For one thing, if the shooter did not wear gloves when loading the clip, he would leave his fingerprints on the round. It is possible that the prints were in the system, so Roger would be able to determine who shot Kurt.

Even if there were no prints, every firearm, especially semi-automatics, leaves distinct markings on the round as it ejects it from the magazine. Eventually Roger might still be able to make a positive identification of the shooter.

This type of information was especially valuable in light of the fact that Roger might never recover any of the bullets that were fired. The one that hit Kurt in the head probably ended up in the gutter, because after striking Kurt in the side of the head, it bounced off and whizzed past Jack's candy bar, and then out of the open window.

The other bullets, the ones lodged in Kurt's protective vest, or in his body, would be held by the NYPD and might never be accessible to Roger.

That's why Jack made sure that his friend would have a good opportunity to identify the shooter.

Just as Jack reached the sidewalk on the other side of the street, a large, dark Ford Expedition pulled up beside him as he walked.

A passenger in the rear seat of the SUV opened the back door and said, "Jack, get in."

Hell, Jack thought, *where have I heard that before?*

Initially, Jack was hesitant about getting in. But when he got a look at the driver through the open door, he smiled. "Good to see you again," Jack said as he sat down. "You might want to start ducking right now, 'cuz all my friends are getting shot tonight."

Chapter 80—Roger to the rescue

12:21, a.m., Friday, December 30

Jack welcomed getting in off the street. For one thing, as soon as he spotted Roger behind the wheel, he knew that this Ford Expedition was virtually a personnel carrier. Jack had heard Roger say on numerous occasions that he had too many enemies and too many friends with targets on their backs.

Roger always insisted on tinted windows capable of stopping an AK-47, with doors and an undercarriage strong enough to withstand almost any IED. The roof and engine compartment of Roger's vehicles were fortified as well. The tires were constructed of solid, explosion-resistant material.

Jack got in, sat down, and took a deep breath.

"Kurt was shot—might be dead," Jack told Roger.

"I know," Roger said. "He is a good man. He's only been on my team for a few months, but he had already proved his worth. That's why I sent him to gather you up. … Did you get a look at the shooter?"

"I didn't," Jack replied. "But I did scoop up some of the spent rounds." Jack then pulled the handkerchief containing the cartridges out of his pocket and handed them over the seat to Roger.

"Did you say that Kurt *is* a good man?" Jack asked. "Does that mean he's going to make it?"

"Right. The first on the scene are reporting that the round to the head will not be fatal. Now we just have to worry about the ones that missed his vest. Never know about that stuff. But it looks pretty good right now."

"That's great news," Jack said. "I took him to be FBI. He didn't fit the profile of the Secret Service. At least that's not how he struck me."

"He *is* FBI," Roger said. "He's on loan. The director himself signed off on him. He's a great asset."

"Didn't know that happened," Jack responded.

"Doesn't often. … Kate is looking good," Roger said. "I'm sure that's on your mind too. She's been through the ringer, but from what I hear she's going to be fine."

"You've taken care of Reg?" Jack asked.

"Kurt did," Roger said. "His wife will eventually get the body. We scrubbed him up and got some new clothes. No telling whose blood he had on him. For sure he carried some of Kate's DNA—and yours."

"I would like his clothes," Jack said. "They weren't in Kurt's car, were they?"

"I've got them, and I'll see they get to you," Roger said. "Any particular reason? They are pretty messed up."

"I'm not sure," Jack replied. "But if it weren't for Reg, neither Kate nor I would be alive right now. Reg was a true friend."

The real reason behind Jack wanting to get his hands on Reg's clothes was based less on sentiment than his belief that there might be some useful information hidden in them.

"That he was," Roger said. "I also regarded him as a friend. There are some people in this world you can simply count on—no matter what. Reg was one of them."

"You're dropping me off at my new hotel?" Jack asked.

"That's the plan," Roger said, "unless you have someplace else you'd rather be."

"The hotel would be perfect," Jack said. "… Actually, I'd accept anyplace with a bed."

Strangely, or perhaps by design, Roger drove by the gas station where earlier they had stopped so that Jack could wash up. There were at least a dozen emergency vehicles parked there, most with their red and blue lights flashing.

"That place appears to be cordoned off," Roger said. "I hope you don't need to wash up again."

"Not there, for sure," Jack said.

The remainder of the ride was uneventful. Jack sat in his seat, staring out the window next to him. However, he was not looking at anything in particular. First he thought about Kate and that perhaps he ought to go back to the hospital and sit with her.

But then he thought better. His presence would do nothing except raise more questions. When Kate came out of the anesthetic, she would tell her side of the story to Captain Spencer. Jack needed to remain out of reach through the preliminary debriefing. She knew she must leave Reginald out of it.

Once that had taken place, he would visit her and find out what she had told her superiors. That way they could keep their stories straight. Better to have his absence questioned than his presence result in conflicting versions of the story.

"Are they all dead?" Jack asked Roger.

"The fellows responsible for Kate's abduction?" Roger asked.

"Right. Are there any loose ends?"

"One fewer since that big fellow went dumpster diving behind the hospital," Roger replied. "You barely beat us to that one. But better you than us, I suppose."

"You knew about him?" Jack asked, a little surprised.

"We did, but we didn't have a clean shot at him until he was outside the hospital. But you took care of him first—and in a pretty efficient manner. … You might be happy to learn that we cleaned it up. Our guys emptied the dumpster and erased the hard drive of the camera that caught you slicing him up. All they had was your back, but we took care of it anyway."

"Thanks."

"No big deal," Roger said. "This is New York City after all. You know what they say here: 'no body, no murder.' Especially when it comes to dirt bags like that."

For a dozen seconds neither Roger nor Jack spoke. Then Roger broke the silence. "But I don't think I truly answered your question. We're not sure if we got them all. We have no reason to think we haven't, but it seems to us unlikely that they're all dead. That was a fairly large operation—with a lot of people involved. Certainly we have not got very high up the ladder. But we just can't be sure that some remain that Kate could identify. She is still in danger. … I think that is what you were getting at."

For the rest of the drive to Jack's hotel, no one in the Expedition said a single word. They all knew that Jack was whipped. And so they left him alone.

Even though Jack sat silently, his mind was anything but quiet. While he did sense a degree of relief that Kate was recovering from her wound, he knew Roger was right—that there could be others who felt the need to do his daughter harm.

Also, he could not reconcile himself with the fact that his good friend was dead. Had it been almost anyone other than Reginald, Jack would have felt only the highest level of satisfaction that Kate was rescued. But the grief that befell him at the loss of this good friend was not going to be easy for Jack to shake.

"Well, this is it," Roger said, as he brought the SUV to a stop at the main entrance to the hotel. "You should be all set. You know how to reach me."

"Thanks for all your help," Jack said. "Kate and I are both most grateful."

"See ya, buddy."

Jack got out of the Expedition and entered the lobby of the hotel. Initially, he thought about checking at the front desk for messages, then thought better. "I guess what I don't know can't kill me," he muttered to himself, as he headed to the elevator.

Just then his cell vibrated. Jack looked at his phone, and read the display, "Kate?" Jack hesitated before answering.

"Hello?" he finally said, but with a question mark.

There was a long moment of dead silence on the other end. Finally, a male voice answered, "Handler?"

"Who is this?" Jack asked.

Chapter 81—His worst nightmare?

12:59, a.m., Friday, December 30

After several more seconds of silence, the caller replied, "Who am I? Jack, I'm your worst nightmare, you sonofabitch. That's who I am." With that ominous declaration, the call went dead.

Jack had reached the elevator but had not yet pushed the button. He just stood there, dumbfounded. He thought for a moment, then dialed Kate's phone. The call went immediately to voicemail.

Enough of this, Jack was thinking as he took the battery out of the phone. *This puts a whole new wrinkle in things. ... And I'm altogether too tired.*

"Going up, mister?" a young man asked as he held the elevator door open.

"Up," Jack replied, stepping on with the young man. "Yes, I want to go up."

"What floor? I'll hit it for you?"

"Ah, good question," Jack said. "I'll have to check. Just go to your floor, I'll check my key."

"It's cool, I'll hold it for you," the young man said. "Just arriving?"

"Yeah," Jack said. Ah, let me see. ... 1150. Eleventh floor. ... Thanks."

"No problem," the young man said, taking his finger off the "Door Open" button and hitting the one for the eleventh floor.

"Have you stayed here before?" the young man asked, just trying to make conversation.

"No," Jack replied, beginning to grow annoyed with the questions.

"Restaurant sucks," the young man informed him, "but the coffee shop is okay. And it's open all night."

"Good to know," Jack replied, not making eye contact with the young man.

"Here it is," the young man said. "This is your floor."

"So it is," Jack responded as he passed through the elevator door as it opened. "Have a good evening … night … day, whatever it is."

"You as well," the young man said, grabbing the elevator door as it closed. "Hey, care to join me for a late night cup of coffee … later?"

Jack turned around and, for the first time, looked at the fellow. "Thanks, but I'm pretty tired. Maybe I'll see you around."

"Yeah," the young man said. "That would be great. I'm here by myself, and I don't know anyone. So, if you change your mind, I'm in 1440. My name is Brian."

"I'll keep that in mind, Brian," Jack replied, "Good night now."

"Good night," the young man replied, releasing the door.

That was an overly friendly young fellow, Jack thought as he started checking for his room number.

"Eleven fifty. There we go," Jack said aloud as he reached his room.

He presented his card to the heavy-duty brass-plated steel lock. Happily, he saw the green LED illuminate, and he could hear the lock disengage.

Jack opened the door slowly and held it wide as he reached in to switch on the light. *Not bad. At least it looks clean. Smells okay. I should be able to get a good night's rest here.*

Jack quickly located his two suitcases, tossed them onto one of the two double beds and began searching for his special lock. He was surprised to see that everything was neatly packed. It was obvious to him that someone had probably inspected all the contents. He was certain that when Roger's man originally "packed" them up at the Penn Station hotel, that he most certainly would have just jammed everything in the suitcases as quickly as he could.

But everything was now neatly packed. That did not trouble him, because he really did not have anything with him that could possibly compromise him or his job. He always assumed that someone would gain access to his personal belongings. So he made it a practice to commit to memory critical matters, such as names and places. Phone numbers and addresses were encoded and electronically stored so that he could access them via his cell when needed.

"Doesn't look like anything is missing," he determined as he removed his electronic lock and secured the door. Not intending to leave for the evening, he plugged it in. That way the battery would charge as well.

While the stranger that called him on Kate's cell phone troubled him, he was most interested right now in getting a little rest.

However, the more he thought about it, the more concerned he grew. *So, he's my worst nightmare, is he? I wonder what he meant by that.*

Even though Jack was overtired, he could not forget what the caller had said. While the threat was not leveled against Kate, Jack realized that the best way for a person to get at him would be through his daughter. So Jack dialed Roger.

"Hey. I just got an interesting phone call. It initiated from Kate's cell. What do you make of that?"

"What did he want—your caller?" Roger asked.

"At first he seemed a little surprised when I answered. But he called me by name. Not a friendly call. Who could have ended up with Kate's cell phone? Any ideas on that?"

"Well, we never did retrieve it," Roger said. "You know, at that house. We thought that it might have burned up in the fire. But I guess that was not the case. Must be there is one more, at least one, that we have not yet accounted for."

"It did not sound like the fellow I had talked to earlier," Jack said. "I would have recognized that voice."

"I had hoped that we were done with these front line guys, after you saw Smith off," Roger said. There was a short period of silence as both men thought. "You know, this fellow might not be one of the fellows who held Kate. You know what I mean? His involvement might be on a different level."

"I'm not sure what you're getting at," Jack said.

"Look," Roger said. "We suspected that there were a lot of players, and that not all of them were directly connected. … Who would have had access to that phone?"

"Well, we know that it was last located at the house where Kate was held," Jack said. "But she certainly never had control over it once the whole thing got started."

"Right," Roger said. "Now you said that the caller sounded a little surprised when you answered the call. Right?"

"Right," Jack said. "That is curious. If he were one of the group I was dealing with, he would *not* have been surprised to hear my voice."

"Exactly," Roger said.

"One of the cops," Jack said. "That's what you are thinking. Right?"

"Possibility," Roger said.

"Who else could it be?" Jack asked.

"At this point," Roger said, "it becomes less important just who is still out there than it is what his immediate intentions are."

"There's nothing to be gained now by killing me," Jack said. "Kate's the target, isn't she?"

"I'm afraid so," Roger said.

"And motive?" Jack asked, after pondering Roger's words. "What would be the reason for going after Kate at this point?"

"The most obvious motive would be," Roger replied, "because someone thinks that Kate has additional information that they're afraid of."

"You know they never intended to let her live," Jack said. "Once they had used her up, they had to kill her. I think that they planned to terminate her right after my last call."

"I agree," Roger replied.

"You're thinking this could happen soon," Jack said. "How soon?"

"I have no doubt that your daughter was Smith's target," Roger said. "It's unlikely that two contractors would have been sent at the same time. When you eliminated Smith, you probably bought yourself a day or two. What do you think?"

"Normally true," Jack said. "But if we're right, if there are some cops involved in this, on any level, then we might be looking at a different paradigm. I think they've got two men on her right now. And a hospital full of doctors and nurses. All potential witnesses. I think that by tomorrow she will be a bit more isolated. Think tomorrow."

"I'll tell you what," Roger said. "You get some rest. I'll poke around down there tonight. Spencer and I have a history—he's okay. He'll be in and out. He will likely head up the debriefing. I'll stay down there until I see you."

"How well do you know Kate?" Jack asked.

"I don't," Roger replied. "But I'll tell her that you sent me. Do you think she'll buy that?"

"Hopefully not," Jack said. "But if you tell her that her dad said Nanny Val sent you, she will believe that."

"Nanny Val?"

"Right," Jack replied. "She will know immediately that I sent you."

"Keep your cell close," Roger said. "I might need to have her talk to you—to validate my creds."

"I'll be here," Jack said. "Not going anywhere."

"If anything comes up, I'll let you know," Roger said. "Otherwise, I'll remain as close to Kate as possible until I see you tomorrow."

"Sounds great, my friend," Jack said. "See you then."

"Hasta la vista," Roger replied as he disconnected.

Jack knew that he needed to get some rest. He was as confident as he could be that Roger would protect his daughter. He walked into the bathroom to brush his teeth. As he stood there in front of the mirror, he could not help but observe the deep wrinkles and darkened eyes. "Damn, Jack, you're getting old," he said out loud. "Too old for this nonsense. This killing business is a young man's game."

After he brushed his teeth, he splashed water on his face and blotted it off. Looking at himself in the mirror again, he said: "I think I'm going to find my bed now, Mr. Handler. See you in the morning."

Jack then walked over to his bed and turned it down. But before he climbed in, there was a muted knock on his door. "Jack," the man outside said. "You here? I need to talk to you. It's important."

"Shit!" Jack muttered as he headed over to the door. "What could he want?"

Even though Jack knew that the man at the door was his newfound young friend, he still did not simply open the door for him.

"Yeah," Jack said. "What can I do for you?"

"I have some information about your daughter," the young man said. "Kate. That's her name, right?"

"Just a minute," Jack said. "I have to find my glasses."

This was totally unexpected. Not only did it catch Jack by surprise, but he was highly apprehensive about this young man, now.

So, instead of opening the door, Jack found the Glock that he had removed from Kurt's body. As quietly as he could, he disengaged the safety. He slipped his shoes off to ensure silence.

Thank God this is a double room, he reasoned.

He knew that standard procedure dictated that whenever registering a room with a door connecting it to the adjoining room, operatives would always take both, then make sure both were accessible from the occupied side. That allowed for a quick escape in an emergency. Plus it prevented someone renting the adjoining room, then using it for an attack.

Carefully Jack unlocked and opened the door on his side. And, just as he anticipated, the door on the other side was propped open.

Jack slid a waste basket between the two doors to hold them open, and to prevent the noise that would be generated should the latches engage.

He then made his way over to the door in the other room that opened into the corridor. He disengaged the secondary latch. Grabbing a towel from the bathroom, he put it over the primary lock, and slowly unlocked the door.

He assumed that the young man at the door, and whoever might be with him, would hear the door being opened. But that could not be avoided. At least, he reasoned that he would be standing four to six feet away from his visitor.

Pulling the door open quickly, Jack stuck his head out to see who was there. Just as he had suspected, the young man was not alone. Jack had positioned the gun slightly behind his right buttocks, which was partly behind the door. He held the door open with his right foot.

Fortunately, his visitors did not have time to reposition.

Jack did not recognize the man who was standing behind the young man. But he knew what this was all about just the same. The stranger was a contractor.

This young fool is dead, Jack was thinking. *Nothing can change that at this point.*

Ideally, Jack would have liked to see both of the stranger's hands, but he could see only the right. Jack assumed that the left hand held a gun.

As usual, Jack was correct.

The 10mm Glock was not Jack's gun of choice—at least not for this application. But it was rigged with a suppressor. To Jack, a semi-auto with a silencer did not make a lot of sense. Sure, the silencer cut the noise down substantially. Jack liked that. But it also spit out the brass jackets with every shot. Sounding like tinkling bells, the spent rounds would bounce off walls and ceiling, leaving all the evidence necessary to trace the gun that birthed them.

Jack was not surprised to see the older man use the young man as a shield. In fact, he expected it. Only seconds after Jack stepped into the corridor, he saw the gunman poke his weapon under the young man's left arm.

Thirty-eight revolver with a silencer, Jack observed.

As soon as Jack was certain his attacker had committed himself to that mode of attack, he took a rapid step to his left, which provided him with a clear shot to the man's right side.

Jack rapidly lit off six rounds. As he fired, he tried to miss the human shield but knew that there was going to be collateral damage. Jack wanted to get a couple rounds into his attacker's arm—the one holding the gun. Without immobilizing the bone and muscle in the shooting arm, he knew that he could be killed.

The only other approach would have been to get off a perfect head shot. But that would have been very risky, because the target was moving.

His first two rounds did graze his attacker's right arm, passing through to the right side of his upper torso. But just as Jack suspected, the man had on body armor. While the impact of the bullets did get the man's attention, it did not stop him.

The gunman pushed his gun forward, under his hostage's arm, and attempted to point it at Jack. Taking an additional step and a half step to his left to avoid the muzzle, Jack fired off four more rounds, all in the direction of his attacker's gun hand.

Three of the rounds tore through the soft tissue of the young man's left side, while one round struck a rib and bounced off. Two, however, found and disabled the attacker's wrist and lower arm after passing through the young man, causing the attacker to lose his motor functions in his gun hand. At that point, the battle was over.

The young man slumped forward in shock and fell face-down on the floor. When he did, he peeled the attacker's gun out of his hand and pulled it to the floor with him.

Jack smiled at his attacker for a split second, then popped him once in the head and a second time in the neck. The man was dead before he hit the floor.

"Damn," Jack muttered, "will I ever get a night's sleep?"

Without hesitation, Jack grabbed the young man by the collar and dragged him into the still-open door of the adjoining room.

As soon as he was certain the young man's feet were going to clear the open door, he returned and grabbed his attacker and dragged him into the room as well.

Jack was pleased that no one had responded to the ruckus, so he took a few moments and picked up all the spent cartridges.

He removed the empty ice bucket from its tray, filled it with water, then grabbed two large bath towels.

Opening the door a bit, he checked to see if there was any activity in the hall. Finding no one out there, he walked over to the two relatively small bloodstains and poured the water on them. He then began blotting up the blood and water. As he did this, Jack looked around to see if there were any cameras, and was relieved to find none.

The water had dispersed the blood enough so that by the time he was finished with the two towels, all that appeared on the carpet were a couple of innocuous-looking water stains. Jack was sure that once the water completely dried up, a significant bloodstain would emerge. But for now, the water stains would not attract attention.

"Time to pack it up," Jack reasoned. It would be impossible for him to dispose of two bodies by himself. He would need some help cleaning it up.

"Roger," Jack said, after he had dialed his friend. "Hey, buddy, can you get some help cleaning up my room?"

"You've been naughty, again?" Roger asked.

"I suppose you could say that," Jack said.

"I'll take care of it," Roger said. "You'd better move on."

"Right, I'm on my way."

Jack knew that the attacker was already dead. But, aware of the nature of gut wounds, he suspected the same could not be said for the young man. So, without further hesitation, Jack lowered the muzzle of his Glock to a point sure to sever the brain stem, and he fired.

The bullet passed through the young man's lower skull, struck the concrete floor beneath the carpet, and ricocheted up into the side of the man's face, lodging in his brain. The unconscious young man was now dead.

Jack searched until he found that last brass casing and put it in his pocket with the rest.

He knew that Roger's people would totally sanitize the room, so he did not concern himself with fingerprints.

Good thing that I had not totally unpacked yet, Jack thought, as he tossed his toothbrush, razor, and other items back into his suitcase. He took one slow look around, to be sure he had all of his belongings, then left the room and headed toward the bank of elevators.

"Jack, I need you to come with me," a man said from behind him as he got off the elevator on the ground floor. "Roger sent me."

Chapter 82—William

1:22 a.m., Friday, December 30

The man caught Jack by surprise. "I think you misunderstand what I need," Jack said, turning to look the man in the eye. "I need someone to tidy up my room."

"That's taken care of," the man said. "My name is William, and Roger sent me to bring you to the hospital. He will take care of you from there. ... Don't worry about your room. Roger's men are going to take care of it."

"I can't come back here again," Jack said.

"Exactly. We've got a new place for you," William told him, as he handed an envelope to him. "This is your new hotel and your new room key. Hope you like it better."

"That last place was okay, but it did seem to be a little noisy at times," Jack quipped, checking to see where Roger had set him up. "The Penn Station Central," Jack read on the envelope. "Back to Penn Station."

"Will that suit your needs?" William asked.

"Recently renovated," Jack said. "It was quite the hotel back in the day. Popular for visiting NBA teams."

"Seventeen hundred rooms, you know," William said. "You should be able to melt right in."

"As long as it has a bed," Jack said.

"It's a club room."

"What does that mean?" Jack asked.

"Refrigerator and a flat screen."

"The refrigerator sounds good," Jack said. "I would like to hibernate in there until I leave town. It seems as though every time I move around I draw attention."

"What's up with your daughter?"

"Not sure yet," Jack said. "Roger might have some additional info on that. I should find out more when I get to the hospital. ... You sure that's where Roger wants you to take me?"

"That's my orders," William replied. "He believes that there is one more important issue out there that he needs to discuss with you. Not sure where it's coming from, but if anyone can get to the bottom of it, Roger will. And quickly."

"That's what I'm hoping for," Jack said. "I wonder why he didn't mention it when I talked to him."

"I'll drop you off at the hospital," William said. "Then I'll make sure your belongings end up in your new room. Roger has a ride for you to the hotel."

"You gonna turn down my bed and leave a piece of chocolate on my pillow?" Jack responded.

"Doubtful," William said, cracking a slight smile. "But I will sweep it for bugs."

William removed the car keys from his jacket and hit the remote to find his car. "That's the thing about rentals. I can never remember what I'm driving. Sometimes I'm happy to remember the level where I left it."

Jack thought it curious that Roger's man should be driving a rental, but he let it pass.

At first there was no sound. So the two men just kept walking. Finally, after the third attempt, they could hear the horn blow about a hundred feet away. William hit the remote a couple more times to confirm he had found the right car.

"How long is this gonna take?" Jack asked. "To get to the hospital?"

"Under decent conditions it takes about half an hour. I would guess that would be about it tonight."

"Then, if you don't mind," Jack said. "I'm gonna get some sleep."

"Sounds good," William said. "I'll wake you up when we get there."

Jack fastened his seatbelt and tilted his seat back. Within seconds, he was sound asleep.

It seemed only a matter of seconds to Jack when he heard William giving him instructions. "Jack, better wake up. We've got a little company. And they've got guns."

Chapter 83—Lots of cops

1:44 a.m., Friday, December 30

William's words startled Jack out of his nap. "What's this all about?" he asked, forcing his eyes wide open.

"Cops. And lots of them," William said. "They seem fixated on you. Don't make any quick move."

Jack had an uncanny ability to go from zero to sixty in record time. He had been sleeping deeply. But when William warned him about the cops, Jack woke up immediately. Strangely, there was something in William's voice when he sounded the alarm that seemed vaguely familiar to Jack. *Damn*, Jack thought. *I've got it. I recall that voice.* But there was no time to ponder this, with half a dozen pistols pointing at the car.

"What the hell is this all about?" Jack asked aloud, beginning to roll down his window.

"Get your hands up," said the officer closest to the driver's side of William's rental. "I want to see both hands—in the air. Get 'em up, I said. And get the hell out of the car."

Jack had lowered the window about four inches when an officer on his side of the car began yelling at him. The officer shouting orders at Jack was a uniformed officer. In fact, he was one of about ten or eleven uniforms that Jack spotted.

Jack sized up the situation and determined that the man pointing the gun at him meant what he was saying. Jack rested both hands on the dash, as the cop who had yelled at him opened the car door and dragged him to the ground. But that's when it all got strange.

Just as Jack hit the ground, there was suddenly a barrage of gunfire,

all directed at William. Jack did not know what was going down, because there were two officers lying on top of him.

He tried to count the rounds being fired, but it was impossible. As
near as Jack could tell all the fire was from relatively close range. Glass
and warm human tissue struck him on the face as he lay beside the car.

"Get the door open and drag him outta the car," one man shouted
from the other side of where William was sitting. "He's still got a gun.
He's armed. Grab it and cuff him." That was followed by some mumbling
and the sound of a car door being opened.

"I don't give a flying fart if you think he's dead," the same man said.
"Secure his weapon and cuff him."

At first Jack was half expecting a bullet to the back of his head. But
the way the officers were holding him to the concrete seemed strange to
him. No one had attempted to cuff him or even to pat him down. It was
more like they were trying to protect him.

It was then that Jack heard a familiar voice. "It's all secure, you can
let him up now."

Jack welcomed that sentiment, because the second officer who was
pinning him down must have weighed two hundred and fifty pounds.

Slowly the two officers stood, and the officer who had initially
dragged Jack out of the car reached down to help him to his feet.

"Hey, Buddy," he said to Jack. "Hope you understand why we did
that to you."

"I sure as hell don't," Jack retorted, looking up to see Roger. "But I'll
bet this fellow can explain it to me. He probably even ordered you to
toss me down."

Chapter 84—The ubiquitous Roger

1:49 a.m., Friday, December 30

Roger chuckled when he saw Jack stretched on the concrete. "What the hell are you doing on the ground?" Roger asked.

"I don't know, Rog, why don't you ask my good buddies here about that?"

"We only did what the captain told us to do," said the cop who had helped Jack to his feet. "Hope we didn't hurt you."

"I'm fine," Jack said. "I suppose I ought to thank you for pinning me down."

"Take a look at this," Roger said, leaning into the car and, using a pen, picking up a Glock with a suppressor. "William here was about to do you in."

"I take it he was not working for you?" Jack asked rhetorically.

"Hardly. William, I'm convinced, was the head of the group that kidnaped your daughter. ... Or at least the spokesman."

"I just figured that out," Jack said. "When we drove up, it came to me where I remembered that voice. He was the mouth on the phone. He had been able to disguise it right up until he ran into your posse."

"You two should get the hell outta here," Captain Spencer said. He then looked around and spotted a nearby patrol car. "Jack, you and Roger accompany this officer to that patrol car." Then, firmly gripping the shoulder of the cop in charge, Captain Spencer turned him in the direction of the car and commanded, "Sergeant, take my friends over to that patrol car, seat them in the back until I can debrief them. And leave the door open so they can get some fresh air. Got it?"

"Yes, sir," the officer said. "Gentlemen, please follow me."

Neither Jack nor Roger hesitated. They followed the sergeant to the car and seated themselves in the back seat.

"Please wait here," the officer said, "The captain will be right with you."

"Thanks, Sergeant," Jack said as he slid in the back seat beside Roger.

The two men sat there silently until the officer was safely out of range.

"Okay," Roger said. "This is how I see it. This guy, William, the fellow who drove you here, was the last of the kidnappers directly involved with the kidnapping—the one logistically in charge of that operation. He intended to use you tonight to get to Kate."

"How did you make him?" Jack asked.

"The cleaners I sent to sanitize the mess you left in your hotel spotted him."

"And they recognized him?" Jack asked.

"Not exactly. But they snapped a picture and emailed it to me. I identified him from an HLS warning. He had been spotted at JFK. He's got quite a sheet."

"Freelance?" Jack asked.

"He is," Roger confirmed. "A bit of a mercenary—always works for the Eastern Europeans. The fellows with him accompanied him on all his operations. It's a team."

"Big bucks, would you say?" Jack asked.

"Very," Roger replied. "I'm guessing high six figures."

"Significant," Jack said. "Do you know who footed the bill?"

While Jack was trying to find out as much as he could about the men who had held his daughter against her will, he could not resist the urge to find out as much as he could about his competition and potential new clients.

"Not for certain," Roger said. "But I still like someone associated with law enforcement. Could be high up. Hell, has to be high up. But I do not like the Feds for this—*much* too messy. And I think we can rule out all foreign entities. For the same reason. The operation was probably financed by some foreign entity, but that would have been the extent of their involvement. ... Nothing direct."

"You suspect a city official?" Jack asked, looking his friend in the eye.

"You know, Jack. It's impossible to point a finger. But, at this point, it is quite likely that we will never know for certain."

"That's what I was thinking," Jack said. "But I do think that Kate should be safe at this point."

"I would agree. ... But, from everything I know, this William character was almost certainly the last one directly involved with Kate's abduction. And the only reason he was still coming after Kate was because he believed she could identify him. And their job was to get the information from Kate—and they did that. So they fulfilled the contract. Whoever hired them got what he wanted. There should be no point in pursuing this any further."

"That's how I see it," Roger said. "Do you intend to go after whoever hired them?"

"Counterproductive at this point," Jack said. "Kate is safe now, that's really all I ever cared about."

"We agree on that," Roger said.

"I would really like to check in with my daughter," Jack said. "I'm tired, but as long as I'm here, I'd like to see her."

"You do that," Roger said, and I'll move your stuff into a new hotel."

"I thought Captain Spencer would have my suitcases sealed for evidence by now."

"Take a look in the front seat of this cruiser," Roger said.

Jack leaned forward and looked on the floor and passenger seat and spotted his two suitcases.

"How the hell did you manage that so quickly?" Jack asked, chuckling.

"I'm not gonna tell you all my secrets," Roger said laughingly. "Then you'd know as much as I know."

"My head would explode," Jack said. "… Where you gonna place me this time?"

"I'll call you later with that," Roger said. "I think it's time for us to boogie on outta here. What say you?"

"Yeah, sounds good."

Both men then slid out of the open rear door of the patrol car. As they did, Roger nodded to one of his men to retrieve Jack's belongings.

"Hey, Jack," Roger said as the two men were about to split up. "Are you going to behave yourself? Or am I going to have to fly some help in from LA? I think I'm running out of mops."

"I'm gonna check in on my Kitty," Jack said. "As soon as I hear from you, I'm hailing a taxi. And if you don't call, you'll find me curled up under one of these trees."

Both men chuckled and parted ways.

But before Jack was able to enter the hospital, he felt a powerful hand fall on his shoulder.

"Jack, we need to talk," the man said.

Chapter 85—Jack talks to Kate

2:21 a.m., Friday, December 30

Instinctively, Jack's hand reached for his knife, but he no longer had it with him.

"Captain Spencer," Jack said, turning to face his daughter's boss. "Kate's in her same room?"

"She is, and she will be very happy to see you."

"No complications?" Jack asked, as the two men continued on into the hospital.

"She's great," Captain Spencer said. "I talked to the doc before he went home, and he was very optimistic that they got all of the round. Forensics took the bullet. When they pieced it together, they determined that the doctor gave them everything that had entered your daughter. So our hopes are high. We should all be encouraged."

"How about the bleeding?" Jack asked. "Did he have any further thoughts on that? Did he think they got that all squared away?"

"No further word on that. But they were confident about that from the beginning. The bullet did not penetrate deeply. It did some significant tearing, but once they made the repairs, it cleaned up well. At least from what I gathered. Anyway, no one expressed any additional concern about that. I would say that her prognosis is excellent. Especially after she gets to see her old man. She has been asking about you."

"All good news—I can use some of that," Jack said. "I'm happy it turned out as well as it did. I didn't have a very good feeling about it about ninety percent of the time. ... The only downer ... and it's a big one ... is the loss of Reg."

"And Reginald Black wasn't our only casualty, you know," Captain Spencer said. "That big fellow we were talking to just outside of surgery, with the doctor. Well, he was one of us. He was consulting with the department. And it appears he came up missing. You wouldn't know anything about that, would you?"

"What do you mean by *consulting*? Was he actively involved in what Kate was working on?"

"You might say that," Captain Spencer responded. "But they did not work directly together. In fact, I'm pretty sure that Kate never even met Smith. The chief sent him over to me when it became clear that we were in over our heads with that State Department fellow."

"State Department fellow?" Jack asked, attempting to determine just how much Kate's boss knew about his involvement.

"I know you were working with Kate on those puzzles," the captain said. "She told me that you were pretty good at figuring that stuff out. It's okay. She cleared that with me before she called you in. The big fellow, Smith, he was supposed to be some kind of an expert with that stuff too. Anyway, he worked on it for a few days and got nowhere."

"What was he—this Smith?" Jack asked. "Some kind of computer nerd? He was pretty old for that."

"No, not at all," the captain said. "He had friends. I have no idea who they were. But he had people with some special expertise. Spooks, maybe. I don't know. The chief said that I should give him everything he needed. But we did not have anything besides the puzzles, so we gave him copies of them. We did not have any additional info. Anyway, he took the puzzles and had his guys work on them. But they did not have any success."

"Kate never met the man?" Jack asked.

"Like I said," the captain said, "not as far as I know. In fact, I'm damn near positive that I was the only one in the precinct that Smith ever talked to. That's how he wanted it."

"Do you have any video of this Smith guy?" Jack asked. "I'd like for Kate to have a look."

"No, not that we produced," Captain Spencer said. "We'd hoped that his recent visit to the hospital would be on some of the hospital's surveillance. That might have helped us figure out where he disappeared to. Except, for some strange reason, it has all been deleted."

"Deleted?" Jack asked. "That's weird."

"Right. When he came up missing, I tried to access what they had, and it had all been erased. Must have been a malfunction. At least that's what hospital security said."

"That's too bad," Jack replied. "I would like to get an image of the fellow in there for Kate to take a look at. When she's feeling a little better."

"You're gonna be surprised, my friend. Your daughter is one tough woman. Wouldn't shock me a bit to see her checking outta here in the morning and on the job by noon."

"Dad," Kate said, as the two men walked into her room. "I heard you were coming up."

"Kitty," Jack said, tears filling his eyes. Generally speaking, Jack was not one to get emotional about anything. But he and his daughter had been through so much over the past few days, and he was so dramatically overtired, that he could not control his feelings.

"Come here and give your daughter a hug."

"I'm sure you two will excuse me," Captain Spencer said. "I think I'm done here for the night. I will keep an officer outside until she leaves the hospital. And then we will have an officer assigned to her until we get this all sorted out."

"Thanks, boss," Kate said, flashing a big smile in Captain Spencer's direction.

"Yeah," Jack said, turning to shake hands with the captain. "I look forward to talking to you again, when all this settles down a bit."

"We are going to want to debrief you both, but that will wait for tomorrow."

"See ya, boss. Thanks for sticking in with me."

With Kate's last comment, Captain Spencer waved and winked at Kate, then nodded at Jack and left the room.

"How are you, Kitty?" Jack asked. "I mean, really, how are you holding up?"

"Dad, is this over?" Kate asked. "Am I safe now?"

"You are, darling," Jack said reassuringly. "We are convinced that all of your kidnappers are now dead. The last one, the ringleader we think, bought it right outside the hospital—just a short time ago. We think he was on his way up to pay you a visit."

"Oh my God!" Kate said. "Are you sure he was the last one?"

"Can't be sure. But it has that feel," Jack said. "At least he is probably the last one you could pick out of a lineup. We're pretty certain about that. However, not all news is good. We are convinced that there is a main man, or an agency of some sort, that financed this whole thing. But we strongly believe that all of the men who would be intent on killing you are now gone."

"That sounds good to me," Kate replied.

"Now, we've got to get our story straight," Jack said. "There won't be any time tomorrow. So let's go over some things right now."

Just then Captain Spencer reappeared at the door. "One more thing I forgot to tell you."

Chapter 86—Confrontation with Captain Spencer

2:34 a.m., Friday, December 30

Both Kate and Jack turned their heads to face the captain.

"Captain," Kate responded.

"Kate," the captain said, taking several steps in her direction. "When we found you, leaning against the tree, you were alone."

"That's right, and was I happy to see those uniforms," Kate said, smiling.

"We were all pretty happy," Captain Spencer replied. He paused for just a moment and then glanced in Jack's direction. "We were not sure this story was going to have a good ending, if you know what I mean. But, the thing is, witnesses are coming forward who put a couple men on the scene along with you. One of the men allegedly carried you out of the burning building. And then he went back in and came out helping a fellow that seems to fit your general description, Jack. Can you tell me anything about that?"

"Really," Jack said, looking first at Captain Spencer, then at his daughter. "I would sure like to shake that man's hand. Do you have any idea who he is?"

"No, Dad," Kate replied. "I don't remember much before waking up in recovery. How about you, boss, do you know who it might have been?"

"Not yet, but we're investigating. ... Then can I assume that the man this mythical superhero saved was *not* you, Jack?"

"I don't know anything about that," Jack said. "But when you do ID him, I would like to thank him personally for saving my daughter."

"I'll keep in touch, you can count on that," the captain said. "And, Jack, I expect you'll be sticking around town for a while, right? I'm definitely going to want to talk to you some more about this."

"Yeah," Jack said. "I'm going to keep my daughter company till she gets back on her feet."

"You can take this as an official request," the captain said, this time in a very ominous tone. "I will want to talk to you again about this, and other things. So do not leave town."

"No problem, Captain," Jack said. "Like I said, my daughter will know how to reach me. I do hope you'll let me sleep in tomorrow. I don't remember the last time I closed my eyes."

"Just make sure we can get hold of you when we need to."

Jack had already responded affirmatively to the captain's initial request. He did not appreciate the repeat. He was exhausted. His patience was gone. Jack turned toward Captain Spencer and took a couple short steps in his direction. When his nose got to within about ten inches from the captain's chest, he said. "I realize you are my daughter's boss. So I'll be polite. But you listen to me, because I don't like repeating myself. I told you that I would be available. Now, unless you are going to cuff me and haul me in, turn your ass around and get the hell out of this room. I'm going to spend a little time with my daughter right now, and I've had my fill of you for this night. Do you understand me?"

"Sounds good, Jack. I appreciate your candor."

With that, Captain Spencer stepped to the side and backward. Looking over at Kate and smiling, he said, "Glad you're doing well, Kate. You get some rest. Can't wait till you're back on the job." He then looked back at Jack. "And I do look forward to continuing this conversation." He then flashed an officious smile at Jack and left the room.

"You're a bit testy, aren't you?" Kate observed after Captain Spencer had left her room. "He is my boss, Dad."

"Yes, he is. But he's not mine. I wasn't rude. I'm sure he gets a lot worse on the streets."

"He hasn't seen the streets in years," Kate said.

"Maybe he should," Jack retorted, smiling at his daughter. "Okay, this is how I say we handle this."

Chapter 87—Getting the story straight

2:52 a.m., Friday, December 30

Jack walked over to the hospital room door, glanced at the officer stationed outside, and smiled. "I'm gonna spend a little private time with my daughter. ... So, if anyone one else comes through this door, I will kick his ass and dump him on your lap."

The officer nodded in agreement and smiled back at Jack. The officer had overheard Jack dressing down the captain, and he wanted no part of Jack's anger.

Jack then smiled at the officer and closed the door.

He pulled up a chair around the back of the bed and drew it in close to his daughter. He wanted to be able to speak in private and to keep his eye on the door as he did.

"How much do you remember, Kitty?" Jack asked. "You know, about the whole thing—kidnapping and all?"

"How much do you think I should remember?" she asked, signaling her father that he was making the calls. "After all, I was traumatized. And shot."

"This is how I see it," Jack said. "We need to leave Roger and Reg out of this whole thing. Roger would want it this way. The less known about his involvement, the better. And there is nothing to be gained by bringing Reg into it, either."

"You saved me by yourself?" Kate asked.

"Not exactly," Jack said. "Beyond the business with my working on the puzzles for you, you should leave me out of this as well. That's the safest approach. ... Reg is dead, nothing will bring him back. Roger will take care of the cover story as far as Reg is concerned. You know, with his family and so forth."

"Nothing else about Reg?" Kate asked.

"Nothing," Jack said. "No need to. No one can say for sure that he was there, except for you, me, and Roger. There's some talk that there was a third party, and that he died on the scene. But no one knows anything about that for sure. Roger's men sanitized the scene pretty well. What they could not clean up, they contaminated. You can state that you do not recall *anything* about your escape. There was an explosion, and you ran out. There were no cameras. All the kidnappers are dead. That part worked out well. Two of them came after you, and they are both dead. So there is really no one left to refute your story ... or lack of a story. Besides, just tell them you've been drugged. You can easily claim loss of memory."

"Will they want to get me on the machine?"

"They *can't* do that," Jack said. "They can't force you to do it. And you should not volunteer. Besides, if it becomes an issue, get your union rep in. He will back up your refusal. Makes no sense to put a wounded warrior on the machine."

"Can they *force* you to do it?" Kate asked.

"They could request it, but I cannot be forced to take one either."

"Could they be recording us now?" Kate asked.

"Sure," Jack said. "Anything is possible. But if they did that would be eavesdropping. They would be in deeper water than us. We're on pretty solid ground here, Kitty."

"Who do you think is behind this?" Kate asked.

"Beats me," Jack said. "Roger and I think it is someone in the department—pretty high up the food chain. Whoever it is, it is clear that they pushed that big guy, Smith, on your boss. He was in on it." Jack paused for a moment, then continued. "I don't think you met that fellow, did you?"

"Not any new guy named Smith," Kate answered. Can you describe him?"

"Tall, with enormous hands," Jack said. "Must have gone six two, two-seventy. No fat."

"That sounds like one of the men who I saw in that house," Kate said. "Big man. *Really* big. Not one of the kidnappers, but he showed up a couple times. Could that be him?"

"Most certainly," Jack said. "I suspected that he was one of them from the beginning. He seemed much too interested in your condition. He had come back to kill you. He knew you could recognize him. ... Damn, kiddo, they never intended to free you."

Jack reached over and took his daughter's hand. "My God, Kitty. We have so much to be thankful for. If it weren't for Reg, and Roger, we'd both be dead now."

"Well," Kate said. "Reg did what he did because he was your friend. You would have done the same thing for him."

"I'd like to think so," Jack said, turning his eyes to the side. "We've been through a lot together—that's for sure. And we always had each other's back."

"Dad, if Reg had not wanted it this way, he would not have gone in there after me. ... He did what he did because he was your friend. You don't need to feel guilty about anything."

"It's not guilt," Jack said. "I don't sense guilt. It's my loss. I will always wonder what I could have done differently. How I could have protected him better. I will never have another friend like him. Every time I look at you, I will think about what Reg did ... for both of us."

Kate looked up at her father's rugged face. Not only was the fatigue evident, but his eyes were red as though he'd been crying. She reached over and touched his cheek with her hand. "Dad, I don't remember ever seeing you cry before."

Jack smiled at his daughter, swiped two napkins from her tray, and wiped his face off.

"You are safe, and that is all—absolutely all—that I need to think about right now."

Jack then stroked his daughter's hair as he stood to leave. "I'll call you in the morning," he said. "Or you call me. If you need something in the meantime, call me anytime."

He then took another napkin and wrote his cell phone number on it. "Put this away—don't leave it laying around for your boss. I know you probably have it committed to memory, but you've been through so much."

"Dad, could he—Captain Spencer—could he be involved?"

"Definitely not," Jack assured her. "He's not talking about it, but he knows he got snookered by that Smith fellow. And I suspect he has a pretty good idea who in his department set it up. At least he probably can narrow it down to a few—all of them his superiors. That's got to be hell for him."

"Does that affect us?" Kate asked.

"Not really," Jack said. "But Spencer, that's a different story. He might opt for early retirement. Especially if more people start dying around him. Who knows? But it won't be our problem."

Jack bent over his daughter and tenderly kissed her on the head. "You get some rest now, kitten," he said. They exchanged smiles, and Jack turned and began walking toward the door.

But before he reached it, his phone rang.

Chapter 88—New digs

3:27 a.m., Friday, December 30

Jack looked down at his phone just as he was walking through the door. He did not recognize who was calling. "Hello," he said.

"Jack, Roger here."

"I didn't recognize your number," Jack said.

"Right. Well, you ready to head up to your apartment?"

"Apartment?" Jack asked, a little surprised.

"We're thinking that you're going to be in town a while," Roger said. "At least until Kate repairs a bit."

"As long as there's a bed," Jack said. "I think it's been a lifetime since I've touched a pillow."

"Running on nervous energy," Roger said.

"Way past that," Jack said. "I'm ready to shoot somebody just to buy a bed in lockup. You got an address and a key for me?"

"Better than that," Roger said. "If you can make it downstairs without help, I'll be waiting. Black Expedition."

"If I'm not there in five," Jack chuckled, "check in the elevators. I'll be curled up on the floor of the express."

"I'll take care not to startle you. I've seen what you can do."

"See you in a bit," Jack replied, disconnecting the call just as he entered the elevator.

There was no one else on the elevator when Jack got in. He just stood there staring at the buttons. For the longest time he tried to think. Had someone stuck a pistol in his face, his reflexes would have taken over. But he was so exhausted that he could not figure out which button he needed to push to go to the lobby.

Just then another man got in the car with him. "Excuse me," the man said, reaching in front of Jack to push the "Lobby" button.

Jack forced a slight smile and took a step backward. He had been this tired before. Factoring in the stress element, right at this moment he did not care whether he lived or died.

When the elevator door opened, he took a look around, surveying his surroundings as he exited. He always exercised caution, even in exhaustion.

Immediately he spotted Captain Spencer standing over a well-dressed man who was seated in a chair. It occurred to Jack that Spencer appeared to be agitated. For one thing, he was standing very close to the seated man. *That would be uncomfortable,* Jack thought. *Spencer does not look happy.*

At first Jack was unable to get a good look at the other fellow because Spencer was blocking his view. But as he doglegged toward the hospital exit, he caught a good look at the seated man's face. *I've seen him before,* Jack thought. *That is the police commissioner. What would he be doing at the hospital? And why would Spencer be so animated? Could he be the one who set the captain up? Anything's possible, I suppose.*

Jack was not eager to be spotted leaving. But, as should be expected, he was unable to escape the attention of the two over-the-hill detectives.

"Jack," Spencer shouted across the lobby. "I'll be in touch tomorrow."

Jack did not respond. In fact he did not even glance in the captain's direction. But he did wave his left hand in a perfunctory manner as he walked past. "If I have to talk to that bastard one more time today, I'm gonna shoot him," he muttered as he reached the revolving door.

The cool early morning air felt refreshing on his face. It revived him just enough that he was able to locate Roger's Expedition.

As he approached to get in, the heavily tinted window on the front passenger side opened, and he heard a familiar voice. "Get in the front," Roger said. "I've got a black coffee waiting for you."

Jack opened the door and slid in.

"Great," Jack said, popping the lid off the hot black coffee. "That's just what I need. Maybe you won't have to carry me up to my bed."

"Let's hope not," Roger chuckled. "I'm not getting any younger, and you're not getting any lighter."

Jack took a quick sip of the hot coffee. Just enough to determine that it was not too hot to drink and that it did not have any sugar. "Perfect," he said, taking a full-mouth gulp. He held the coffee in his mouth, savoring the flavor. And then he swallowed.

"What's the status on Reg?" Jack asked.

"Hey, buddy," Roger said. "He's still dead."

"Have you contacted his wife?" Jack asked.

"I have," Roger answered. "And the ME has signed off on his accident."

"His wife's okay with that?" Jack questioned. "She knows better, right?"

"Probably," Roger said. "But she also knows better than to question me. She's good with it."

"And his belongings?" Jack asked. "Where are they?"

"You requested his clothes, shoes, etc. Right, Jack?"

"That's right," Jack responded. "Is that now a problem?"

"No, not at all," Roger said. "Officially Reg was killed in a car accident. There'll be no autopsy. I believe his wife has been talking cremation, but I think we'll push for standard burial. End of story. Of course, his personal effects—wallet, jewelry, wristwatch, cash, stuff like that— his wife gets that bag. And you get the clothes. That's what you want, right?"

"That would be great," Jack said. "Any idea when I'll get it?"

"I'm dropping you off at the apartment right now. Maybe it'll beat you there."

"Really?"

"Do you think we should hold off until morning with that?" Roger said. "Don't you think that would be best? Get some sleep now without distractions?"

"I'd like it as soon as possible," Jack replied. "I'll sleep regardless."

There was a moment when neither man spoke, during which Jack nearly fell asleep.

"You gonna tell me what you want with it?" Roger asked.

Jack paused for a moment. He did not want to sound overly sentimental. And he wanted to avoid the macabre; after all, Reginald's death clothes could have been riddled with bullet holes, soaked in blood, and saturated with the smell of incendiary smoke. "You know, Rog," Jack finally said. "I do not have so much as a Polaroid of Reg. Not a single picture. After all we have been through together. And the way he died. Saving my daughter ... and me. Yet I have nothing to remember him by. I know his wife doesn't need this kind of reminder lying around in her attic—especially with the blood and all. Better she go with the story of the accident. So those clothes are of no value to anyone else in the world."

"What will you do with them?" Roger asked. It was quite possible that Roger was more interested in keeping Jack awake until they arrived at Jack's apartment, than he was in listening to any of Jack's actual answers.

"You would have just burned them," Jack said.

There was no conversation in the SUV for a few moments. Roger suspected that his friend had fallen asleep. Finally, Jack broke the silence. "Reg was a bit of an odd duck. He was a hard one to understand. I can't imagine him gone. In our line of work, there just aren't very many people who really get to know you. Reg knew me."

"Yeah," Roger responded. "He was the consummate professional. But you would have done the same thing for him. Isn't that true?"

"I always thought I would. We've been through a lot together—some really tight places. But it never got to this point before. Had it been his daughter or him trapped in a burning building, I would like to think that I would have reacted the same way. But you never really know about such things."

There was another lengthy pause before Jack started back up.

"But, it was always easier for me. I died the day my wife was killed. Nothing was ever the same after that. Then, when Kitty got her job in New York, I felt as though she did not need me so much. At least not the way she did growing up. Back then I felt like I had something to live for—something to get me going every morning. ... I'm sure glad I was around during this mess. I'm not so sure how that would have turned out if all Kate had to count on was old Captain Spencer. Without Reg, and *you*, Kate would not be around right now. Something like this makes a guy re-evaluate his existence. I don't want to let go of Reg, of his memory. Aside from Beth, my wife, there has never been another person in my life that I could count on in an emergency. And they're both dead now, because of me. In a sense, I killed them both. It doesn't seem right. ... It's not right."

"You are not responsible for Reg's death."

"No, not directly. But it should have been me. I should have found Kate and pulled her out. I should have taken that bullet. Reg should be home with his wife right now bitchin' about *my* getting killed. If someone had to die, it should have been me."

"We don't get to make those choices," Roger consoled his friend. "As long as we do the best we can, that's all that matters. It just happened that Reg reached Kate first. And, thank God, he got her out safely. That's just the way it went down. I'm sure Reg would not change a thing. Were he to have known that he would die saving his friends, he would have done it exactly as he did."

"Sure, but that doesn't lighten my load tonight," Jack said. "I lost a very dear friend—my only friend. ...You know, Rog, I don't even have a picture of him—not in all the decades that I've known him ..."

Roger chuckled as he interrupted. "You already said that, Jack. You just keep repeating yourself. ... God, I'll be glad to deliver your sorry ass. ... Besides, my friend, just how professional would that be—to keep a hit-man photo album? Would you have captions under the pictures? Like, 'This is Reg and me after we killed the senator.' I can't imagine Reg allowing that. I'll bet his wife doesn't even have *any* pictures of him after their wedding."

"Hit man? What the hell are you talking about? And what do you know about that senator?" Jack asked, feigning a scowl.

"I'm just kidding, you sonofabitch," Roger snapped. "You know what I mean."

"... I need some sleep," Jack confessed one more time.

"Just hang in for a couple more minutes," Roger said. "I don't want to carry you into your apartment. ... This is it. The one with the bag by the door."

"What the hell is that?" Jack asked.

"My guess is that bag contains Reg's personal belongings."

"Already?" Jack asked.

"Yeah," Roger said. "You said you wanted it yet tonight—this morning. And my man just texted me that he was dropping it off in a taped black plastic bag. That would be it."

"And he just leaves it at the door?"

"That's him sitting in the running car. When you take possession, he will pull away. He's a bit bashful around men like you."

Jack thanked Roger again.

"You've got your key, right?" Roger asked as he bid farewell.

"Sure do," Jacked answered as he started to exit the SUV.

"Hang on a second," Roger said. "Here, take this." Roger then handed Jack a small Smith and Wesson .38 Special. "I share your aversion to semis. Just promise me you won't shoot yourself in the foot before you get some rest."

Jack smiled as he slid the hammerless revolver into his pocket.

He looked around to see Roger's deliveryman pulling away. Picking up the plastic bag containing Reginald's clothes, Jack turned and waved to Roger.

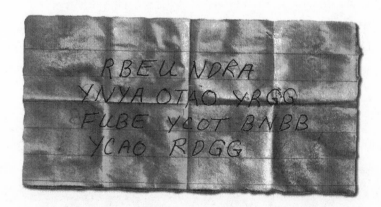

Chapter 89—Reginald's belongings

3:34 a.m., Friday, December 30

Jack placed the bag in the center of his kitchen table. For a few long moments he just stood there, staring at it, as though not wishing to open it. Perhaps he was too tired. Perhaps he simply did not want to go there. But for some reason unknown to him, Jack just could not bring himself to open the bag—at least not immediately.

Finally, he turned and walked over to the refrigerator and opened it. He was amazed to find it totally stocked. Obviously, Roger had something to do with that. "Someone knows what I can eat and drink," Jack quipped, actually wishing that he would find a cold beer. Ever since his heart attack, his doctor had insisted he not drink.

"Of course," Doc Rivers told him, "you must never drink again."

That was not a major problem for Jack, because he never really liked to drink. But to be told that he must never drink again was not an easy thing for him to accept. The doctor also told him that he must not smoke or drink more than one caffeinated drink a day. And, of course, he had to give up salt also.

There were two things that irked Jack about this new regimen—one was the issue of the salt. Okay, so he did have a heart attack. It was a minor one. So what. A lot of people have heart attacks. Jack reasoned that if he gave up beer and cigarettes, then it should be okay to have a little salt on his food, followed by a coffee chaser. It just made sense to him—something about the quality of life trumping longevity.

So, as Jack inventoried the contents of his refrigerator, he immediately realized that there were no processed foods, no beer, no soft drinks, no red meat, and no milk.

Jack continued to look around until he found four bottles of water. He took one out and unscrewed the cap.

He opened the cupboard just to the left of the refrigerator and took out a clean drinking glass. As he poured the water into it, he looked into the cupboard just to the left of where he had found his glass and found a bag of sodium-free pretzels. "I guess this will have to do for now," he muttered, tearing the bag open. "I sure as hell am not going to go shopping tonight."

He then returned to the bag of Reginald's belongings, still lying in the middle of his table, held closed with gray duct tape. Jack placed his right hand on the package, as though he were placing it on his friend's shoulder. For a time, that seemed to satisfy him.

After a moment or two, he walked over to the cupboard drawers and opened them until he found a sharp knife. He used it to cut the tape.

He then opened the mouth of the bag and carefully dumped its contents onto the table.

The first thing to tumble out was Reginald's jacket. Jack immediately chuckled when he looked at it. He recalled all the times he teased Reginald about that jacket. "Who bought that for you, Reg?" Jack had said to Reginald on a recent encounter. "I'll bet it's from that boyfriend you never talk about."

The next article of clothing that dumped out when Jack turned the bag up and shook it was a rolled up pair of slacks. Jack noted the large quantity of still-damp blood that soaked the pants. "Amazing," Jack noted, "the amount of blood that pours out of a dying human being. ... Over a gallon, on average. And, in Reg's case, most of it was left on the street."

Jack carefully unfolded the blood-soaked pants. His act was not in any sense dictated by morbidity. No, Jack had experienced death blood many times in his life. And a few of those times the blood was that of someone close to him. That was the case this time.

Of course, the blood was sticky and cold.

Jack then slid the pants and jacket to the side and dumped out Reginald's shirt, underwear, socks, and shoes. They all seemed to come out as a single unit.

Reginald always wore white socks. Jack had teased him about that as well.

Tonight, however, there was only one white sock. The second sock was mostly brown, so stained by the large amount of blood that had flowed down Reginald's right leg. "He must have bled out from his right side," Jack surmised. "Must have caught a round through his right femoral artery."

For just a moment Jack considered examining Reginald's pants to find the bullet hole but then thought better of it.

Instead, he pulled the jacket from the bottom of the stack and examined all the pockets. Upon finding nothing, Jack concluded that Roger's men had removed all contents in order to return it to his wife.

Jack then looked through Reginald's pants pockets. The first one he examined was the right front. Initially, it appeared empty. But upon a more careful inspection, he detected a small, tightly folded and blood-soaked piece of paper stuck to the bottom of the pocket.

Fearful that he might destroy it in an attempt to remove it, he instead looked for a pair of scissors to cut the pocket open.

Not finding any, Jack instead took the sharp knife he had used to cut the tape and cut the stitching on the bottom of the pocket. He then opened it up to get a better look. Sliding the knife between the damp paper and the inside of the pocket, he carefully pried it loose and re-moved it.

It appeared to have been folded three times.

He took the folded note and laid it on a clear spot on the table.

"I should open this up now, before the blood gets totally dry," he reasoned.

So, carefully he unfolded the paper until it lay flat on the table—face up.

"You sonofabitch," Jack quipped, realizing that the words on this little piece of paper were undoubtedly the last words his friend had written. And, fittingly, they could not be read as written. Reginald's last words were encoded.

"Another cryptogram," Jack said. "Reg, even from the other side, you still find a way to devil me. Don't you?"

Chapter 90—Reginald's final surprise

3:40 a.m., Friday, December 30

Smiling, Jack leaned back in his chair and fixed an unfocused stare at the ceiling.

"Who was supposed to read this, ol' buddy?" Jack mumbled. "Was this intended for me?"

Jack looked around until he found a piece of paper and pencil, and then he began copying the puzzle.

RBEU NDRA YNYA OTAO

YRGG FUBE YCOT BNBB

YCAO RDGG

This thing is altogether too short to solve without a key, Jack observed. *So, Reg, here we go again.*

Jack slid his knife under the piece of paper, and carefully flipped it over to see if the key might be on the back. He remembered what Reginald had told him about the puzzles he exchanged with his operatives.

"Conrad Courtyard Hotel," he read.

Could it be that simple? he wondered. *Probably not. This thing looks damn near inscrutable!*

Jack copied the words from the back of Reginald's bloody note onto his handwritten copy of the puzzle.

"Not gonna happen tonight," he said, as he left the brown stained piece of paper on the kitchen table to dry. "I am going to get some rest."

Jack put his transcription of the puzzle in his wallet, shoved Reginald's clothes back in the plastic bag, and headed off to bed.

Normally Jack would have performed his regular nighttime routine. But he was much too exhausted. After he had washed his hands, he removed his clothes down to his undershirt and boxers, and crawled under the covers. He never even bothered to see if his electronic lock was packed. He didn't even brush his teeth. He just didn't want to remain awake another moment.

Almost before his head hit his pillow, Jack was sound asleep.

The next thing he knew his phone was ringing.

"Kitty," he said. "What're you doing calling me so early. Everything okay?"

"Dad, it's almost noon. I was just checking up on you to see if you were okay. I hope you got some good sleep. You're gonna need your wits about you today. My boss is eager to talk to you."

"Noon, you say. I can't believe I slept that long. I was whipped."

Jack jumped out of bed and headed to the kitchen to get a glass of water. As he approached the kitchen sink, he noticed that the apartment door was slightly ajar.

"Kitty, I'll call you back," Jack said as he disconnected.

Chapter 91—Jack slept deeply (perhaps too deeply)

11:27 a.m., Friday, December 30

Instinctively, Jack quickly reached into his jacket pocket and removed the small .38 Special revolver Roger had given him earlier. He walked over to the door and examined the lock. There were no signs of forced entry. "Whoever got in here either picked it or had a key," he muttered.

Jack then locked the door and glanced around to see what might be missing. *The bag with Reg's belongings,* he observed. *It's gone.*

Jack had slept so soundly that he never heard the burglar slip in and take the bag.

They obviously didn't want to kill me, Jack reasoned. *And apparently they didn't want anything except for that bag of Reg's clothes.*

He then looked down and saw the rectangular stain on the table where he had spread out the note from Reginald. "They took the puzzle," Jack said aloud. "Could it be that's really what they were after?"

With the .38 still in his hand, Jack walked back into the bedroom. He found all of his belongings right where he had left them.

Must be they were only after Reg's stuff, he thought. *The puzzle probably escaped Roger's attention, because it was stuck by the blood to the inside of the pocket. But these guys knew that there was something else. And they knew that Roger had returned Reg's belongings to me. The intrigue here just doesn't stop.*

Jack reasoned that there must be some serious significance to the puzzle that Reg had created. *The only two things that I can think of that would prompt Reg to create such a puzzle would be money or his work. At this point, it seems unlikely that it had to do with the job. The note must have related to money.*

The more Jack thought about it, the more certain he grew that Reginald would be writing about money. *And that would make a lot of sense,* he reasoned. *Reg had all that gold to deal with. Perhaps that note explains where he hid it.*

Just then Jack's cell phone rang again.

Chapter 92—Moving on

11:58 a.m., Friday, December 30

Booming from his phone even before he had lifted it to his ear was the all too familiar resonating voice of Captain Spencer. "Handler?"

"Yeah," Jack said.

"I need to talk to you," Spencer said, in a tone Jack did not appreciate.

Jack took a deep breath. *This is Kate's boss,* he thought. *I'm either going to humor him or kill him.*

Jack knew that he was not actually going to kill the man, even though he might like to—at least not right now, and certainly not with witnesses.

"I'm headed down to see Kate," Jack said. "I would like to spend an hour with her, then I could meet with you. Say in the hospital coffee shop, around three."

"Make it two," Spencer said.

"I'll be in the coffee shop at three."

"Three it is, Jack. See you there."

The meeting was set. And on Jack's terms—that made him feel a little better. Forcing Spencer into an option made the prospects of talking to a man that he was beginning to regard as a nuisance only a bit more palatable. Jack knew that it was imperative that he accommodate, but not patronize, Kate's boss. It was important to his daughter. There was, after all, only one way that Spencer got his cell phone number, and that was from Kate.

On the brighter side, Jack was amazed at just how fit he felt after his sound night's sleep. He was not happy that he allowed someone to get so close to him, but he actually was not all that upset about it.

Keeping Reginald's clothes was never the object. He wanted to search the clothes, because he suspected that Reg would leave a message for him. And it turned out he was right.

All is well, Jack reasoned. *I have a transcription of the note, and someone else has what could be all the incriminating evidence. That's not a bad tradeoff.*

Jack then jumped in the shower, looked through his luggage for a clean change of clothes, and shaved.

Looking at himself in the mirror for the first time since he woke up and shaved, he thought, *not bad for an old man who's been through hell and back. Now I get a chance to see my daughter's beautiful smile.*

Jack briskly left the apartment, this time affixing his magnetic lock on the door before he left.

When he reached the street, he had a surprise waiting for him.

Chapter 93—The last thing he expected

12:30 p.m., Friday, December 30

The last thing Jack expected was to be intercepted outside his new apartment.

"Jack. Over here."

Jack did not recognize the voice.

Jack placed his fingers around the pistol he was carrying. "Yeah, what can I do for you?"

The driver had leaned over and opened the door of a black Expedition with highly tinted windows and said, "Roger sent me."

"Hang on for a second," Jack said, taking his cell out of his pocket but still keeping an eye on the driver.

"Rog," Jack said, "Did you send someone to pick me up? ... Thanks. I just wanted to check out his story. Jackson, you say? Well, thanks again."

"What the hell, Jackson, did you sleep out here?" Jack said, as he got into the front passenger seat.

"Actually I just got here, Mr. Handler," Jackson replied. "But Roger did have a man posted outside all night."

"He did? Did he see anything unusual?" Jack asked.

"Not really. Unless you're referring to the two idiots who broke into your apartment."

"That's exactly what I mean. Who were they? Do you know?"

"We snapped a couple of images," Jackson said, reaching into the center console and pulling out half a dozen plain-paper prints. "Take a look and tell me if you recognize either of them."

Jack took the pictures and scrutinized each of them. "The light is pretty poor, but even so, I would have to say that I've never seen these fellows before."

"We were surprised when they walked back out," Jackson chuckled. "We figured you would have them gutted and hanging in the shower."

"I never heard a thing," Jack said. "Rog must have drugged me."

"You're kidding me. Right?" Jackson quipped.

"They could have killed me, if they'd wanted to. I was dead to the world. I did not hear a thing. The first thing I knew about it was when Kate, my daughter, woke me up with her call. That's when I discovered the burglary."

"Well, I promise we'll never tell a soul," Jackson said, pulling onto the highway. "I take it you're headed to the hospital?"

"Right," Jack replied. "I've got a date with Capt'n Spencer, right after I check up on my daughter. That guy is becoming a royal pain in the ass."

"Tell me about it," Jackson replied. "But, I'll confess that I've worked with Rog for ten years and have known Spencer for that long, and I can tell you that both Roger and I believe him to be harmless. He's a bit of a Columbo. ... What does Kate think of him?"

"You know," Jack said. "I've never actually asked her. And she's never offered her opinion."

"Roger said that she's a total pro."

"I think so."

"Actually," Jackson added. "I've heard others comment that Spencer might be a little thick, but he is a straight shooter—"

"Well," Jack interrupted, "he might be a straight shooter, but he better not be pushing my buttons anymore, or he might not be collecting his pension."

"Do you want to know who those fellows were? The ones who broke into your apartment?" Jackson asked, wanting to change the subject.

"Or, even better, who sent them?"

"Yeah, I would like to know who burglarized me," Jack said.

"Promise no retribution?"

"Depends on who they were, and what they were working for," Jack said. "What do you know about them? Do you have that info?"

"We ran facial recognition," Jackson said. "And we came up with these names. They don't mean much to us and probably won't to you. But I think you might find interesting just who they work for."

Almost as soon as Jackson handed him the printout, Jack's mouth dropped. His eyes lifted from the pictures and turned into a blank stare out of the windshield.

"What the hell would she want with Reg's things?" Jack asked.

His question was sincere. He really did wonder why anyone would have an interest in Reginald's bloody clothes. But he had a pretty good notion why Allison would want to get her hands on the puzzle.

Neither Roger nor his people knew anything about the puzzle. Jack decided to keep it that way.

Chapter 94—The Presidents talk

9:32 p.m., Thursday, January 12

Former President Bob Fulbright had just stopped at a red light when he looked down at his cell phone and dialed a number.

After a few rings, the party he called answered.

"Mr. President."

"Mr. President."

"Where are you right now?"

"I'm just entering Fort Marcy. I'm supposed to be in bed sleeping. Instead, I'm goin' out whoring with you. … By the way, I don't see you."

"So that's what you call it," Bob said. "Ain't it hell, what we have to do for a little privacy?"

"It is. How do you suppose FDR handled it? I guess all he had to worry about was a gimpy set of wheels."

"And Eleanor. Rumor has it she had more secrets than he did," Bob said. "Pull in and park here. I'm right behind you."

President Butler did as Bob asked and turned off the engine.

Just then Bob knocked on the passenger side window of President Butler's car. He opened the door as it unlocked and said, "Times have changed."

"I'm not so certain about that." President Butler said. He paused for a moment and then continued. "This must be pretty important, Bob, to want to meet me like this. What's on your mind?"

As President Butler put his car in reverse, Bob answered his question: "Just wanted to iron out a couple details, you know. Just wanted to be sure we were on the same page."

"Well, you did your part. And, obviously you did it well, or I would not be here right now."

"Yeah, but consider just how revered you would have been had we let this thing play out. You'd need a library twice as big as mine just to house what would have been written this year alone."

"Oh, there will be plenty written anyway."

"I'm sure that's true," Bob said. He then took a look at President Butler and started to chuckle. "You look like you just walked out of the gym, Barry. You're not gonna pick up girls in warm-ups."

"What were you expecting—a pimp hat and bling?"

"Well, maybe."

The two presidents continued on for a few moments without speaking. Finally, Butler said, "I spoke to Alexander, and he's ready to move on it—on your appointment."

"Really? Were you surprised?"

"Not at all. We knew going in what the deal was. When you first came to me with your plan to weaken Allison. It was all part of our agreement."

"So how do you see it transitioning? And how soon?"

"It's common knowledge that the UN is broke, and deeply in debt. It will be relocated in Europe. Alexander is leaning toward Eastern Europe—perhaps Hungary."

"Hungary? Damn it, Barry—why Hungary? Why not Paris?"

"Alexander favors an Eastern European site. He's more comfortable with that. Besides, he doesn't want to deal with the French."

"But Hungary? My God, Barry, that might as well be a third-world country."

"Just because the headquarters is located in Eastern Europe, that doesn't mean that's where you have to live. You can live anywhere you want. You could move back in with Allison, if you wanted to. Or, Depp has a nice place in Southern France, I've heard. You like him, right?"

"That's a low blow, Barry. ... The Allison comment—not the Depp part." Bob paused for a moment, and then continued, "I didn't know you had a sense of humor." President Butler did not respond to Bob's comment, except for a small smile.

"Well, one thing for sure, we're gonna find out if all those ignorant rednecks were truly serious about getting the UN out of New York. Now that they're not gonna have a choice about it, I'll bet they'll be pissin' and moanin' more than ever. Those bastards didn't know when they had it good. I swear, they don't know what the hell they want. "

"I know what you mean. And they're not even gonna know what the hell hit 'em, either. Damn, they're gonna be mad. This is like a double shot of poison for them—me as president and you as God. And there's not a damn thing they can do about it."

Both men chuckled audibly as they contemplated that scenario.

Finally, Bob queried, "Did Alexander have a problem with creating the new position? *UN president?*"

"No, but he was not excited about weakening the role of the general secretary."

"Weakening the role of the general secretary? You've got to be kidding me. Barry, the only weaker person in the world is the French secretary of defense. He was just messin' with your head. ... But, seriously, Barry, he was okay with the new position, and the fact that it would be permanent?"

"He had no problem with that. You and I both know that if he ever wanted you out, you'd be out. But as long as he likes you, and you play ball, you're good."

"What's gonna happen to the current UN Headquarters? That property can never be privately developed."

"Right. It will always be under the direction of the United Nations, at least until the charter gets changed. I think he intends to use if for archiving. Eventually I see him moving his institute there. It would just make sense.

"Allison ever figure out what happened? Do you think she has any idea that you were the one who foiled her plans?"

"She never trusts me—at least not entirely. Never did. When my appointment comes through, and the UN moves out of New York, with me in it, she might start to see what hit her. But, more than likely, she will think I'm just being opportunistic—taking advantage of the situation for personal reasons. Hell, ain't that exactly what I *am* doing?"

"I'd say it was a win-win all the way around. You get what you want, I stay alive. Alexander gets what he wants, even. And, who's to say, if Allison plays her cards right, she might still get to be president."

"Hell, that'll never happen, Barry. My man, you're a definite two-termer."

"You think?"

"Absolutely. And after that, who knows? But it won't be Allison. She knows that. A man can be elected if he looks old. Just means he's 'distinguished looking.' Gravitas. But a woman. When a woman gets old, that's what she is—old. That's why she was so desperate."

The president liked what he heard. More than anything, he liked hearing those words come out of the mouth of someone he admired more than any other person in the world. A small smile crept across his face as he contemplated what his friend Bob had just told him.

"You've got to dump that old bastard, you know. He can't stay on the ticket. But whatever you do, don't put Allison on it. Not unless you have a death wish."

"We've been through that once. I'm not going there."

"Pick a more conservative running mate. You know, one with some downhome appeal. Just not that old fart."

Again both men chuckled.

"Ever consider suspending the election?" President Fulbright asked. "You could do that, you know—Homeland Security, executive orders. Hell, I'm sure you've thought about it. Right?"

President Butler did not respond to the question.

"And think about running a redneck conservative on a third-party ticket—split their vote. Remember good old Jacque? He was Alexander's man, you know. And with regard to your VP selection. I'd say a Christian from the South." Bob paused for a moment then continued. "Hell, Barry, find out what Elvis has been up to lately."

"I thought Elvis was going to be heading up the new UN."

"That's me, all right. ... Damn, Barry, I *never* imagined you could be funny."

As the two presidents headed back to their original meeting place, for a few moments no words were shared. But there was no lack of mental activity. The current president was already mentally composing his second inaugural address, while the past president contemplated how he might expedite his UN placement. *This sonofabitch is politically dead in the water,* he thought. *And so is Allison. How good could it get? Hell, if I wanted to be president again, I'll bet I could pull it off. ... But, I'd rather be God for life.*

Just then Bob remembered that he had brought a present for his friend. "Hey, Barry, I almost forgot," he said, pulling a heavy velvet bag out of his briefcase. "I brought you a present, something to help you remember this meeting." Bob then carefully removed a brilliant gold object from the bag and pretended he was polishing it with the soft cloth of the bag. "Just a little token of our enduring friendship," he said, as he presented the current president with a beautiful gold Egyptian burial mask.

As he had always been, Bob was careful not to touch the death mask with his bare hand.

"What have we here?" President Butler asked, reaching out to receive the gift. "This is beautiful. It must be worth a fortune for the gold alone. What is it?"

"Oh, it's just something that has been in our family for a while. Actually, it was a gift to Allison and me when we were in the White House."

"And you're *giving* it to me?"

"I sure am, Barry. You're not superstitious, are you?"

"What do you mean?"

"There's a story, a legend, attached to this mask. At least that's what the Egyptian government official told me. I don't know if he was serious or not. You know how people like that make things up."

"Not sure what you mean?"

"He told me that it was removed from an old Egyptian tomb—a pharaoh's tomb. Couldn't tell me which one. But the story goes that the raiders who found it all died immediately after touching it."

"You're shitting me. Right?"

"That's what he told me," Bob said with a smile. "But he said that only *after* he had handed it to me. You know, like it was a joke. He presented it to me in this same velvet bag. ... It's kinda funny. I'm not a superstitious person. But I still have never touched that damn mask with my bare hand. And neither has Allison. I guess it's just one of those stupid things, like walking under a ladder."

"So, that's what you just did to me. You handed it to me and then told me it was unlucky."

"Not unlucky—*deadly*," Bob said, again laughing. "… But you, my friend, *you* touched it."

"Well, I don't believe in stuff like that," President Butler said.

"I don't either," Bob agreed. "But those stories are out there. And there are people who believe them. I suppose a less worldly person than yourself might think themselves into an early grave. You know, psycho-somatically. … Hell, you touched it, and you're fine. I'm sure others have as well. It's just one of those Indiana Jones stories. That's all it is.

"You should try it on your wife. … Maybe looking at this would help you get it up."

Both men chuckled.

And then Bob continued, "I'll have to admit that it would have taken a lot more than an Egyptian gold death mask on Al. … Although I *am* rather fond of gold."

"That's what that little blue pill is for," President Butler said.

"I don't think that would have helped either."

Again both men laughed. With that, the two went their separate ways.

Epilogue—The fate of the notables

President Barry Butler: Shortly after their meeting, Bob did get his appointment. Contrary to what Jerry had suggested, there was no right-wing attempt on the life of the president. He successfully (if it could be called that) completed his full term.

The following November the opposition candidate overwhelmed President Butler's party in the midterm election, resulting in that party controlling both the House and the Senate.

And, just as Bob had thought (but didn't say), Barry lost in a landslide in the presidential race.

Just before he went to bed on the night of the election Bob Fulbright was overheard saying, "He should have suspended the election—some guys just don't know good advice when they hear it."

No one, however, was very much surprised at President Butler's fate—especially once he had "sold" Alaska to Russia, and Hawaii to China, ostensibly to get them to pick up some of the US debt.

Strangely, even after losing those two states, many thought he still had a chance to win a second term, given the enormous secret war chest he had accumulated, and with the opposition vote split caused by the emergence of a third-party candidate (whom many thought was funded by Alexander). But, when President Butler voiced his support for allowing Texas to secede from the union, his hopes were totally dashed. In fact, with the Texas fiasco, even Alexander, the president's largest benefactor, pulled his support.

Tragically for President Butler, all he was left with was the legacy of bringing down the American Empire.

And, of course, a very valuable gold death mask.

Kate Handler: Because she was young and healthy, Kate healed nicely from her injuries and was back on the job after the minimum leave of absence permitted by her union. Happily for her, there were no repercussions resulting from her father's involvement in the puzzle case.

While there were some men in her life, there were none with whom she considered marriage. Jack thought his reputation might have frightened some off, but Kate was actually more interested in building her career at this point.

Captain Lawrence Spencer: Kate's boss grew frustrated when he was unable to get to the bottom of the Big Hands Smith question. During the first six months following Kate's abduction and release, he worked diligently trying to figure out who above him was involved, but his every effort was discouraged.

Within the year Captain Spencer requested early retirement, but the police commissioner coaxed him to stay on with the department for an unspecified period of time.

He relished the idea of eventually being off the hook, but he was never completely satisfied with the way he was leaving.

Kate was aware of his frustration.

Allison Fulbright: As far as the former first lady was concerned, Jack already knew where all her bodies were buried—he had placed many of them in the ground himself. He felt he had nothing to fear from her. He even entertained the notion that he might be working for her or her husband in the future. Therefore, Allison got a pass from Jack.

As far as her career was concerned, thanks (at least in part) to the efforts of her husband, she never again was thought of as a viable candidate for president. She weakly challenged Barry Butler for the nomination, but nothing came of her efforts.

When it was clear that she would lose the nomination, Allison pulled out of the race and threw her support behind Barry Butler. She considered seeking the nod as his running mate, but he had no interest—for obvious reasons. President Butler instead selected a young, more conservative up-and-coming Elvis from the South. Most think that the only thing he had going for him was his VP's popularity.

Soon after the election, the UN was pulled out of New York and moved to Hungary. And, of course, Bob relocated there, with a lifetime appointment.

Allison maintained her New York apartment. James had been the only one who knew all of her secrets, and (as was expected) he never broke a confidence.

Allison was never satisfied with the fact that she had poured one hundred million dollars into the plot to assassinate the president. While that loss did not break her bank, it did amount to a sizeable dent.

Jack knew that it was Allison who had orchestrated the burglary of his apartment. But that did not trouble him.

He also knew that she held Reginald's original puzzle. It was his guess that this puzzle somehow pointed to the location of the gold Allison had given to Reginald. In the back of his mind, he imagined a scenario whereby Allison would someday hire him to locate the treasure. But that did not happen right away.

Allison also believed that the puzzle would lead to the gold. And, she did entertain the thought of hiring Jack to find it for her. But, she wanted to wait for the right time. She sometimes suspected that Mossad remained interested in her political pursuits—that they suspected she might still have designs on the White House. She was also convinced that her activities were under scrutiny by her own government.

After her failed presidential run, Allison packed up and moved to Paris to live with her daughter.

Strange as it might seem, at this point in her life she was as much interested in maintaining some level of contact with her husband than she was in becoming president or finding the gold. And that she was able to do by residing in Paris. While Bob did run the United Nations out of Hungary, he lived only a few blocks from the Sorbonne. She did not, however, give up her desire to be president.

The residence Allison shared with her daughter was across the rue from the Sénat, which was within walking distance of the university.

Frequently the three of them would share a meal at one of the Bohemian restaurants in the Latin Quarter. And when they did, Bob never failed to pose some veiled inquiry about the disposition of the gold. He knew that would be a sore point for her, and he relished irritating the wound.

But, even without her husband's prodding, there was certainly no lack of interest on Allison's part regarding the gold. Seldom did a day pass that Allison did not consider her options concerning reacquiring her treasure. It was the "how and when" that most seemed to elude her— at least at this time.

Tragically, just as Allison appeared to be getting her life back in order, she received startling news after a routine physical. She hated the long flight from Paris to New York, but she had scheduled the appointment months earlier to check out some discomfort she was sensing. So she flew in for the exam and resulting tests. Her total stay in New York was less than a week.

By the time she got back to Paris, there was a message waiting for her to call her physician.

"Allison, we got the results back, and we found an abnormality near your pancreas," the doctor told her. "We would like to do further MRIs to get a better look at it. Possibly some X-rays as well. When can we schedule these tests?"

"I'm back in Paris already," she told him. "Can't they wait?"

The other conspirators: After the plot to assassinate the president was abandoned, many of those close to it wondered who would suffer most for its failure.

Everyone correctly assumed that Reginald's legacy would get a free pass—his untimely death secured it. Not even those close to the operation were aware that both he and Jack Handler were actually doing the bidding of the former president. In fact, not even Jack suspected. So, as far as most of the other conspirators were concerned, Reginald's memory remained dear.

Allison, however, while always kind to Reg's memory, was not pleased to have lost so much of her personal treasure. She held Reg responsible for that.

Steve: It had been clear from the third meeting that Jack Handler disliked this young man. At one point Jack even considered eliminating Steve.

However, on the basis of Jack's lengthy discussions about Steve with Reginald early on, Jack determined that Steve would not pose a problem to him. Not only was Steve altogether too frightened ever to discuss the plot, Jack knew that he could always return to the matter and kill him. Besides, as Reginald had pointed out, Steve's talents and connections might come in handy down the road. Jack decided to let Steve live.

James: Initially, Jack did give some heavy thought as to how best to deal with James. However, his concern about James was short-lived. Shortly after the scandal broke (surrounding the affair between James and Allison), James was killed in a mysterious plane crash in Eastern

Europe.

While investigators determined the accident was due to pilot error, many suspected the plane was brought down intentionally through misinformation provided to the pilot from the ground.

Those closest to the incident did not buy into the official report, but no one could successfully point a finger.

Some of the theories involved Allison having him killed to put an end to the gossip about their alleged affair. That rumor seemed to have merit, because with his "accidental" death, all the talk about the infidelity ended, as it was deemed disrespectful to his family and his memory.

Others suspected Bob had him killed. That prospect did not seem out of character to many who speculate about such things, particularly the daytime radio talk shows.

Then there was the story floated by the hardcore conspiracy buffs. They suspected that James was killed by spooks—either the CIA, the Russians, or Mossad.

As far as Jack was concerned, he didn't think that any of the above did James in. Jack had heard that James's wife might have had him killed. She was from a very wealthy southern family, and the embarrassment of the affair had seriously affected her social status.

Ironically, while James's concocted story might have spared Allison's having to deal with the fallout of the assassination plot, it very well may have led to his own death. Of course, it is totally possible that the accident really was just that, an accident.

Sometimes things like that actually do happen, without any help, particularly in Eastern Europe.

Jerry: Of all the conspirators, Jack Handler singled out only one for termination—Bionic Jerry.

It was not that Jack bore ill will toward Jerry. And it was not that he considered Jerry to be an inherently evil man or that he might somehow threaten Jack.

It was just that Jack believed Jerry to be weak, and so he could not be trusted.

If asked why, Jack would not have had to think about it. He would have stoically said, "Everybody dies sometime. It's just that in some cases the process gets expedited."

In Jack's eyes, Jerry needed nudging in this regard. So he developed and implemented a plan to do just that.

* * *

7:00 a.m., Friday, January 13

"You Archibald?" a pudgy man said, walking into the coffee shop and spotting Jack.

"Yeah."

"I got your bagels. They're in my car."

"I'll check them out," Jack said, dropping a ten-dollar bill on his table as he followed the Bagel Man out of the coffee shop.

Bagel Man did not resemble anyone you would want to buy food from. He was short, fat and sloppy. His protruding belly poked out between his soiled slacks and tattered windbreaker.

Fortunately for Jack, no one was really talking bagels. (Truth be told, Jack hated bagels. He thought that eating a bagel was like swallowing your gum—repeatedly.)

As the two men approached Bagel Man's car, Jack just kept walking. "Pull around here," he said, gesturing for Bagel Man to pull around the coffee shop and into an alley. Bagel Man complied.

Parking his older SUV in the alley behind two large dumpsters, Bagel Man got out and opened the driver's side rear door. After checking to be certain that only Jack was around, Bagel Man slid his hand under a couple jackets and sweatshirts, pulled out a wrinkled brown paper bag, and tossed it on one of the jackets. He was careful not to raise it higher than the top of the rear seats.

He took half a step back, looked at Jack, then gestured with one hand toward the package, saying, "There it is, the bagels you ordered."

Jack said, "Open it up, I want to see it."

Bagel Man stepped up and opened the bag. He pulled out a small pistol, again cautious to conceal it.

Jack looked at it. Taking a handkerchief out of his pocket, he gripped the pistol, pushed the lever that restrained the cylinder, and snapped it open by jerking his wrist to the left. It was obvious that he was satisfied with the gun. With his thumb he then spun the cylinder, still careful to keep his handkerchief between his skin and the pistol. Then with a sudden snap of his wrist to the right, he flipped the cylinder back to its ready position.

Jack then removed a latex glove from his pocket but did not put it on. He just wrapped the glove around the suppressor to be sure it fit the pistol properly.

"Ammo?" Jack queried.

"Sure, it's in the bag."

"Show me," Jack demanded.

Bagel Man, looking a little disgusted, reached back into the bag and pulled out a full box of .22 caliber long rifle cartridges and a box of .380 ACP 80 grain cartridges.

"You idiot!" Jack snapped, sticking the .380s in his pocket, "I told you to get .22 longs, not long rifles! What the hell am I going to do with long rifles? You can't use them with that pistol. Damn it, I thought you knew what you were doing!"

"Keep your pants on!" Bagel Man snorted as he walked around to the front passenger door. He opened it and reached into the glove compartment. Fumbling around in it for a minute, he pulled out a tattered box of ammunition, examined it, and then tossed it onto the front seat. He pulled out another and another. Then he pulled out a fourth box, carefully read the label, opened it up, and slammed the glove compartment closed. He had found what he was looking for—half a tattered box of .22 longs. That he tossed over the back seat and onto the jacket with the pistol.

"There ya go, .22 longs."

"Load it," Jack said.

"Here, just take the whole box, or what's left, no extra charge," Bagel Man offered.

"Load the damn thing—four rounds only."

Now clearly disgusted, Bagel Man counted out four rounds from the box, picked up the pistol, and started to load it. This time, though, he was not so careful about raising the gun above the seat. Letting his frustration get the best of him, he rocked back and forth from one foot to the other. Perhaps it was just too hard for him to bend over anymore—he must have carried two hundred and eighty pounds on his wide but short five-foot-eight-inch frame.

"Damn it," Jack grunted, "you're gonna show it off to the whole damn world?"

Jack then slipped on the latex gloves and told Bagel Man to hand him the gun. He checked it over one last time. It was exactly what he had requested. He was certain that Bagel Man was too stupid to have had much to do with procuring the pistol. *All this joker did is write down what I told him and pick it up from a third party. This thing is probably traceable,* he concluded.

The fact that a firearm might have a history was not actually of significance to Jack, because he always disposed of his weapon after a hit. He did always make sure that he did not get busted in possession of such a firearm, and he never left fingerprints or DNA on one, so it would be impossible to trace it back to him.

Jack took a look over his left shoulder and feigned seeing someone approaching. "Quick, get in," he commanded, pushing Bagel Man into the rear seat, right on top of the jackets and the partial box of ammo. "We've got company."

Bagel Man reluctantly obeyed.

"My money. You owe me two grand," he said, holding out his hand as he clumsily landed on his side.

"Here you go," Jack said, raising the pistol to Bagel Man's temple and tossing a paper bag containing the cash on his lap at the same time. Just before he shoved Bagel Man, Jack had rotated the cylinder to an empty chamber. He then squeezed the trigger until the hammer slammed forward. Bagel Man was terrified.

"Now," Jack warned in his most ominous voice, "if I ever think that you have breathed a word about this to anyone, I'll look you up and kill you. ... Do you clearly understand what I am saying to you?"

Bagel Man, convulsing in fearful sobs, said nothing but did rapidly nod his head affirmatively.

Jack slammed the door, leaving Bagel Man too frightened to even look at him, much less speak. Jack then slid the revolver and ammunition back into the bag in which Bagel Man had transported it, tucked it into his jacket, and left.

Jack always preferred using a .22 caliber revolver. For one thing, unlike a semi-automatic, it did not spew out the empty cartridges. He always snickered when he watched hit men on television doing their job using a semi-automatic with a suppressor. "Someone didn't do his homework," he would mutter.

Another advantage with a .22 caliber revolver was muzzle velocity. A .22 long cartridge, shot from a four-inch barrel, would pierce any skull. And, because of the small entry wound, blood spatter and blowback would be minimal. Plus, a suppressor worked well on that particular pistol. He always requested Smith and Wesson.

He did carry with him a Walther .380 semi-automatic. He liked the Walther because it was reliable and easy to conceal. Thankfully, he had never fired it on a job. The .380 was intended for use only if the revolver failed, or should he need additional firepower to extricate himself from the scene of his hit. With scores of successful contracts, he never made a mistake that warranted its use.

As soon as he accepted a contract, he would start making arrangements to procure the kill weapon in the same city as the hit. That way he never had to transport it. As far as the Walther was concerned, he did transport it. But before getting on a plane, Jack would disassemble the .380 entirely, right down to every bolt and spring, and then pack the parts separately in his check-in luggage.

However, Jack never transported the ammunition for the .380. That he always procured along with the kill weapon.

Another thing Jack never did was load the pistol he intended to use with more than two rounds per victim—one for the head (or to the chest, if he were certain there was no body armor, and if a head shot were not feasible) and one to the brain stem. Jack's hits had always been clinical marvels. His plan was for this not to be an exception.

10:30 a.m., Friday, January 13

Jack had his checklist. Nothing was written down, of course—didn't need to be. Shouldn't be, in fact. The less clutter the better, Jack figured. Clutter, when it gets into the wrong hands, becomes evidence. And evidence can destroy.

"Judges don't send you to jail," Jack would frequently tell himself, "evidence sends you to jail."

Jack rehearsed in his mind what he needed to learn about his subject and just how he was to conduct his study.

Did his subject live alone? Was he married? Did he party? Did he know how to handle a firearm? Did he own one? Did he work out? Did he have a live-in lover? Was he gay? Did he have a dog? What sort of hours did he keep? What type of alarm system did he have? Did he even have one? And if he did, did he use it? What type of police response could be expected? And what were the best escape routes?

There were obviously dozens of other questions that Jack would have about an individual subject, but those were the big ones. Not always was he able to have all the answers he might like, but he knew that the more information he had, the better the job was likely to go.

Of course, there was no question about it—once he signed on to do a job, the subject was going to die. That was a given. Throughout his long career, every subject he had targeted died, and never did a client fail to pay him. Jack now collected no less than one hundred-fifty grand for a job—usually much more. And he never had a problem getting jobs.

The part that irked him most about this hit was that he was not being paid for it, at least not extra. He was supposed to receive several million from Reginald when his part of the assassination plot was consummated. Because of Reginald's untimely death, Jack received nothing. But even had he been paid, it would not have included the hit on Jerry and his wife.

He was executing the hit on Jerry mostly to make a point. Past and future clients had to know that he was not a person to be toyed with.

In every case, Jack tried to avoid the messy. That's where his memorized checklist came in.

Sometimes, mostly lately, his hits had been very clean. He would do his homework, study his subject thoroughly, and then execute a perfect kill. He never liked to spend more than one week in any given city. That was one of the things that made him feel uneasy about this hit—he had been in New York for over two weeks.

Only one other time in the past four years had he been in a subject's town for longer than a week, and that was because the subject was out of town visiting a sick mother when Jack arrived. When that subject returned, Jack hit him his first night back and then left town within hours.

Jack parked his rental car two houses down from where Jerry lived, and walked right up and rang the bell.

Carol, Jerry's trophy wife, answered the door: "What can I do for you?" she asked over the intercom, as she took a peek at him through a leaded glass panel beside the door.

"I'm sorry to bother you," Jack said in his most apologetic voice and with a very disarming smile, "I was walking my dog, and he slipped out of his collar." He then raised an empty leash and collar, showing it to Jerry's wife through the glass. He shrugged his shoulders and smiled broadly. "I thought perhaps he ran into your backyard to play with your dog."

Carol then unlocked and opened the door. Jack was struck with just how trusting Carol seemed to be and the fact that there was no chain on the door.

It was about eleven a.m. Jack knew Jerry would not be home, because he had arrived early enough to see Jerry leave. And he knew that Jerry would be spending the day in New York on business—business Jack had arranged to ensure Jerry's absence.

Jack observed that Carol did not have to disarm an alarm system and that she did not have a secondary security lock or deadbolts to dis-engage. This told Jack that his subject was not paranoid and actually fairly trusting. It seemed to Jack that Jerry was not concerned about safety, or he would have insisted his wife keep the alarm on even during the day. As he stepped in, he also noticed that there was an unusually thick weather strip installed on the door.

"I don't have a dog, but you're welcome to check the backyard, if you wish," Carol said. Then, turning around and looking toward the great room, called out, "Hey, Marion, my neighbor is here looking for his dog, have you seen anything?" Turning back to Jack, she said, "I'm sorry, but my cleaning lady hasn't seen any new dogs around. What's your dog look like?"

"He's a medium-sized Norwegian Elkhound, probably forty-five pounds. His name is Mister," Jack answered.

"What's a Norwegian Elkhound?" Carol asked. "No offense, please. I'm sorry, how rude of me. Please step inside and tell me about your dog, so I will know what to look for. I just never heard of that breed. Please come in."

Jack took the opportunity to step in and look around. He observed that there was an alarm system. There was a motion sensor—probably more than one—and a keypad by the front door. He also noticed that there was a drill-mounted hard-wired contact on the top of the front door. "Thanks," he said as he closed the door behind him.

Jack could be very disarming. He had a strikingly handsome and rugged face. While it was his green eyes that captured attention, it was his smile that melted hearts. And he smiled a lot, when he needed to.

He stood about five feet ten inches and weighed a very trim one hundred and seventy-five pounds. His upper body strength was obvi-ous.

No matter where he was or what he was doing, he always wore running shoes—expensive running shoes. On this day he was wearing, in addition to running shoes, a pair of loose-fitting but expensive jeans, a Yankees baseball jersey (which was not tucked in), and a Yankees warm-up jacket and baseball cap.

"Please, let me get you a beer. You should rest a moment before you go looking for your dog—your *Norwegian Elkhound*." She carefully articulated the name of the breed for Jack's benefit.

"A beer sounds great," Jack said. He knew he did not want to stay long, because he did not want to hang around, should company arrive. Already he had been surprised that the cleaning lady was there.

Carol returned to the foyer with a cold light beer and handed it to Jack. As she did, she noticed that her guest was wearing flesh-colored latex gloves.

"Don't they make your hands sweat?" she asked.

"They do, but I have to wear them because of a skin condition," Jack replied. His response was quick because he had been asked that question before—many times before.

Jack took a couple sips of his beer and then began to excuse himself. "I had better find Mister before he gets too far. Those Elkhounds are hunters by nature. He's probably chasing a squirrel or something. Thanks for the beer."

As he turned to leave, Jerry's wife asked him how she could reach him if she happened to spot his dog.

"Here," he said, reaching in his pocket, "just call my cell phone. I carry it with me all the time. I'm sure Mister will find me, once I get back outside. By the way, that beer really hit the spot. Do you mind if I take the rest of it with me?"

The phone number on the card was bogus.

"I don't mind at all if you want to look around. Good luck finding your dog."

"Thanks," Jack said as he smiled and closed the door behind him.

11:40 a.m., Friday, January 13

Jack felt a little uneasy carrying an opened can of beer to his car, so he dumped the remainder out as he walked to the rear of the house. He wanted to inspect the telephone interface—to find out whether they used a landline, VOIP (voice over IP), cell only, or a combination. He could not be sure without popping the cover on the interface, but he would do that when he came back. At least now, he knew where the interface was located.

As he got back into his car, he tossed the empty can in the back and started going over what he had learned. "I know that they have an alarm system, and that they don't use it during the day. I know his wife looks to be at least fifteen years younger than her husband, she is friendly, and very beautiful. I am quite sure he sleeps with her. And I know that there are no bedrooms on the main level—so they obviously sleep upstairs."

Experience had taught Jack that the easiest subject was a somewhat drunk middle-aged man after sex. Jack surmised that if he came back in the middle of the night, there was a good chance that Jerry and his wife would have been drinking and possibly screwing. *This just might be easier than most,* he concluded.

Jack had learned what he had hoped to learn. The stage was now almost set for the hit.

Jack returned to the area about six that evening. He knew that was about the time Jerry would be coming home, so he took up a position on the route he knew Jerry would be using. And, just as expected, he spotted Jerry's car approaching.

He followed at a safe distance to be sure that Jerry arrived at his house and parked the car in the garage. Jack waited until he was certain that Jerry had entered his home. He then set out to do the most dangerous part of the whole operation. Parking his car on the next block, Jack cut through the rear shrubbery (avoiding the mechanical gate in front of the house), scaled a six-foot fence, and made his way to the overhead garage door, which Jerry had opened to park his car.

Taking out a roll of transparent packing tape, he affixed it to the door, and onto the frame. Later he could use that tape to determine whether Jerry had left with his car.

At eleven o'clock that evening, Jack returned to the neighborhood, parking his rental car in front of a house several doors down, and across the street, from Jerry's house. He put a handicap permit on the dash and then grabbed a small shoulder bag from the back seat. He approached a medium-sized maple tree across the street from Jerry's front door, seized a small limb in his right hand, pulled himself up enough to snatch a similar limb in his left, and then pulled himself up into the branches. He waited there for a moment to see if he had been detected. Once confident no one had seen him, he continued up the tree until he found a relatively comfortable limb that afforded him a good view of the front of Jerry's home.

Jack had trained for this sort of thing for years. He had always been physically fit. He had never allowed the physical dexterity developed in the military to diminish. One of his favorite exercises was to climb a forty-foot rope using only his legs and right hand. And then he would switch hands, and come back down.

At one time he was a good friend of a man who ran a rock-climbing school, so he would frequently use his friend's equipment. But when his buddy's school went under, Jack decided to string a large rope from the upper limbs of a tree in his backyard and use it. He did not like going to gyms, because too many people asked questions.

Using binoculars, he spotted the bedroom Jerry and Carol slept in. "Just what I thought," he whispered to himself. "I can see them both in their bedroom, I don't even have to inspect the garage door."

Jack waited in the tree for nearly an hour—well after the last light went dark. Once he was confident that his subjects had settled in, he slid down the tree and returned to his car. He then drove away. He retired to his nearby motel (to which he had moved earlier that day), and waited until four in the morning. He figured that the bar crowd would all be home by then, so it would be a decent time to be on the roads. The cops would be finished testing for alcohol and would all be eating doughnuts. The only people on the streets at that time would be people headed to work.

This time he parked in front of Jerry's house. Taking the same bag (but with different contents) from off the rear seat, he scaled the fence and walked around to the back of the house.

Using his specialized tool, Jack removed the cover from the telephone interface and placed his lineman's butt set on the red and green terminals that were connected to the blue/white pair of telephone wires. He listened on the butt set for, and found, a dial tone. That told him Jerry most likely had a standard landline, and probably not VOIP. "A piece of cake," Jack mouthed, knowing that standard landlines are relatively easy to take out.

He then placed a small wire with alligator clips on each end across the red and green terminals, shorting them out. That would temporarily disable the telephone line and the standard communicator on the alarm system.

But that was not enough. Jack then had to deal with the possibility of a radio backup on the alarm system. To accomplish that, he removed two sophisticated looking devices—identical cell phone jammers. The difference between his units and the standard units used in certain commercial applications was that he had installed a twenty-watt linear amplifier to each of his. That made them capable of taking out all radio backups on any alarm system located within a hundred yards. He switched on the two devices and hung one on a tree limb at each end of Jerry's house.

After cutting the ground cable connected to the telephone interface and the telephone cable leading to the street, Jack then removed one end of the alligator clip jumper he had initially placed on the phone line terminals that connected to the house phones. Making sure that one end of that jumper was still connected to the house side of the surge protector, he attached the free end to the positive terminal of a very large electrolytic capacitor, fully charged. He then connected a second jumper to the other side of the surge protector. Finally, using a pair of insulated needle-nosed pliers, he touched the free alligator clip to the negative terminal on the capacitor.

When he did it, there was a very bright spark. "So much for their telephones *and* their alarm system," he said to himself. "That will have taken them both out."

To confirm his success, he then put his butt set on the green/white pair. Even though he did not detect a dial tone, he repeated the procedure he had used on the blue/white, using a second capacitor.

Finally, using wire cutters, he snipped all the cable connections. He knew that it was possible that Jerry had his alarm monitored through his cable Internet connection.

Knowing now that the alarm and the telephones were *most likely* totally disabled, along with any radio backup, he proceeded to make his entry.

He knew that the contact on the front door was on the top of the jamb and hard wired. He had determined that on his first trip. So he was prepared to cut a hole using a battery-powered hole saw and to disable the contact, should his earlier attempt at blowing the system with the capacitor have failed.

Happily, however, he was able to look in through the glass side panel and check out the status of the alarm keypad. Just as he had suspected, it was totally dark. He had successfully taken it out when he discharged the capacitor.

That meant all he had to do was open the door. No need to attack the contact.

Using a small flashlight, he looked into the crack where the door meets the jamb. While there was a deadbolt installed on the door, it was not engaged—just as it had not been engaged when he was at the house earlier that day.

Now all he had to do was get by the latch lock. Just for kicks, he pushed down on the thumb release, to see if perhaps they had left the door unlocked altogether. "No such luck," Jack muttered.

Recalling the thick weather strip from earlier, Jack gave a firm, sustained tug on the door. And just as he had hoped for, he heard the distinct clicking of the dead lock plunger sliding into the strike plate.

Jack smiled, because that little noise indicated all he would need to break in would be a screwdriver. Of course, he had one.

Sliding the thin tool into the crack, he painstakingly worked the latch until he got it to slide into the open position. He then quietly opened the door.

The rest was a piece of cake. He knew where their bedroom was. He strongly suspected they would be sound asleep. He set his bag inside the house and pushed the door closed but not latched. He slid the bag in front of the door to keep it from opening.

He then removed the .22 caliber revolver from the bag and walked up the stairs to where the couple was sleeping. He opened the door and walked over to Jerry. He could see him well enough to recognize him.

Beside him on the bed was beautiful Carol.

Just as Jack placed the muzzle of the suppressor a few inches from Jerry's temple, Carol turned over so that Jack got a good look at her peaceful face. *My God,* he thought. *She can't be more than ten years older than Kate.*

Jack reflected on all that he had been through over the previous two weeks in rescuing Kate—how Reginald had even made the ultimate sacrifice to save her.

Now Jack was looking into the face of another beautiful young woman. And this one was every bit as innocent as his Kate.

Never before had Jack ever hesitated when it came to squeezing the trigger. He prided himself on not allowing second thoughts.

But this time, looking into the sleeping face of an angel, he was questioning himself.

Darling, Jack thought, *this is the luckiest day of your life.*

Silently, Jack released the pressure from the trigger of his .22 revolver. He drew backward a step and prepared to leave.

But, just as he was about to turn around, Carol woke up.

Half sitting up beside Jerry, she grabbed her husband's shoulder and shook him. "Jerry," she said. "I think I heard something."

Now all options were gone. Jack extended his gun hand and fired a single shot through the left side of her forehead. The bullet entered the front of the left lobe and then the right. It shattered the back of her skull, pierced the headboard, and lodged into the wall.

Carol was dead.

Jack immediately fired a second round into the woman. This one struck her in the upper neck, severing her brain stem before striking the headboard.

The ruckus woke Jerry, and he turned to comfort his dead wife. Jack fired his third round through Jerry's left temple—also a fatal shot.

The bullet entered just above and in front of Jerry's left ear and passed through both sides of his brain. Jack knew that if he angled his shot slightly downward, the bullet would pass through the brain and exit from Jerry's lower temple. Jack did not want it to strike the hard skull on the opposite side of Jerry's head and possibly ricochet back in his direction.

And, just as Jack intended, the .22 caliber bullet delivered instant, paralyzing death to the target and ended up somewhere in the mattress.

He then held the pistol a few inches from Jerry's upper neck and put a round through his brain stem.

Jack then immediately prepared to leave. He went back down the stairs, placed the pistol in his bag, and walked out the door—this time closing it to the latched position.

He walked back to the side of the house, removed the radio jammer, and made sure he had left nothing incriminating by the telephone interface.

Then he made his way over to the other side of the house and removed the other jammer. In both cases, he made sure that they were turned off and their batteries were removed before placing them in his bag. He knew that there was a funny thing about linear amplifiers. Both HAM operators and the FCC took major exception to their being used for anything. If he were to forget and leave one on, eventually someone would find him out.

Once all his tools were properly accounted for, and the telephone interface closed up, Jack returned to his car and drove away.

"I don't know what the hell I was thinking," Jack mumbled, reflecting on his hesitation to consummate the hit. "*That* never happened before. Maybe it is time to hang it up."

This had been the toughest job he had ever done—given the death of his friend and the anxieties of his daughter's kidnapping. *At least this part of it's over,* Jack was relieved to think.

On his way back to his motel Jack stopped at a convenience store. There he bought half a dozen large bags of ice, a box of trash bags, and two large containers of table salt. As with every job he did, Jack wanted to quickly dispose of the pistol he had used, and these were the materials he used to do it.

Once back at his motel, he took the pistol apart as much as could be done and placed the parts on a towel on his bed. Then he placed two more towels on the bathroom floor and a garbage bag on top of them. On top of the trash bag he set a special oversized and plastic-lined briefcase and opened it. He lined the inside with another trash bag and then poured into that case two bags of the ice, then sprinkled one of the boxes of salt over the ice.

Next he placed the parts of the revolver used in the hit, along with the spent cartridges, on top of the ice. Then he sprinkled a little more salt over the ice and the revolver parts, followed by another layer of ice on top, making sure he would still be able to close the case. Finally, he poured the rest of the second box of salt over the ice.

He checked his watch. He left the case open for exactly two minutes, as the salt started working on the ice. Then he closed the case enough to allow excess water to drain out, and held it over the bathtub.

After ten or fifteen seconds, with the last of the water dripping out, he latched the case and dried off the outside. He then immediately left the motel, taking the case with him.

With the case securely stashed behind him in the car, he drove to his preselected spot accessing the East River. He got out of his car, taking the case with him.

Just as he had done so many times before, Jack unlatched the case just as he approached the river. He knew he needed to exercise caution when removing the ice from the case, for not to do so could result in severe frostbite. The salt, while melting off some of the ice, actually turned the remaining ice into a super cold block.

With one swift motion, he dumped the contents into the river, making certain to hang on to the trash bag lining his case. That he tucked into the case and latched it.

Immediately turning back, he headed briskly toward his car. *Let's see,* he thought, *it will take about forty-five minutes before the ice melts enough to drop the pistol. Given the current, that could be a quarter- to a half-mile. They'll have fun finding that gun—especially in this river. It might even reach the Atlantic.*

As Jack walked back, his mind wandered to a conversation he had had with Reginald regarding this job—that they both stood to earn millions from it.

To date, Jack had not received a penny for his work. Reg had presented him with the death mask, but he had passed it along to Roger. So, aside from the satisfaction that his effort (or lack thereof) saved the life of a US president, and that he now had a much closer relationship with his daughter Kate, these winter weeks in New York were a bust for Jack.

However, he did have that most curious puzzle he had found in Reg's pocket. *Someday,* Jack thought whenever he looked at it, *when I have more time, I'm going to sit down with that puzzle and see what I can make of it.*

Then his mind switched over to his fond memories of his friend. *Reg must be smiling right now,* Jack thought, as he approached his car.

Jack's tearless eyes were also smiling.

Appendix—The plotting of Allison's lair

As a former first lady, Allison abhorred the restrictions the Secret Service placed on her. Not only did she resent the loss of privacy, but she simply did not trust them. In fact, she did not trust anyone—at least not totally. But she was particularly suspicious of the Secret Service. If someone's paycheck was signed by any but her own hand, that person's loyalty could not belong totally to her.

Perhaps she learned too much from her husband, President Bob Fulbright, when they occupied the White House. His relationship to the Secret Service was possibly unique. To Bob, the Secret Service was just that—a service. Sometimes he used them a little like OJ used Al Cowlings, to spirit him around secretly.

She had heard that Bob would crawl under a blanket in the rear of an agent's personal car, and then be chauffeured around to private parties. Other times he used the Service to keep people away from him—friends and enemies.

Her husband was able to garner the loyalty of the Secret Service for a few good reasons. First of all, they feared him. But there was more to it than just fear. Bob rewarded them well for their service to him. Not only did he pay them handsomely under the table, but Bob's agents were well known around DC as the go-to guys for girls and drugs—all thanks to their relationship with him.

Allison did not share Bob's ability to use the Service in such a self-serving fashion. But after having left the White House she did develop her own method of working with and around the agents assigned to protect her.

For instance, when she was ready to venture out on her own, secretly, Allison would lock herself in her bedroom, leaving the Secret Service sitting outside. It was always understood that when she entered her bedroom, she was virtually entering her own private country, of which she was not only the president, but lone citizen as well. No one, other than herself, ever dared challenge her on that, and few ever even challenged the Secret Service agents assigned to protect the privacy of this former first lady.

Once inside the bedroom (which was actually more like a giant safe room than a bedroom, given the physical security employed in its construction), she would then enter a special walk-in closet. She had three closets, which were accessible only from her bedroom. They all looked the same, unless you were Allison. She knew that in the back of one of these closets was a secret door. It opened to reveal a small spiral staircase that led upward—upward to a secret apartment and to her secret life.

When using the staircase, she would always first take off her shoes. She had some very good reasons to go barefoot. First of all, the space inside the staircase was very tight—so tight, in fact, that it made her uneasy to use it. The last thing she wanted to do would be to stumble and injure herself. "These damn stairs," she frequently muttered, "I'm gonna kill myself on them one of these days. I don't know why the hell they could not have put in the elevator that I wanted. I can't imagine how I am going to do this in my old age. Guess I'm just going to have to move back into the White House."

With that comment, she would chuckle, sometimes out loud, other times through clenched teeth and a grin.

Actually, she was well aware why she was not allowed to have the secret elevator she wanted. For one thing, no elevator could ever be installed in the City of New York without a permit; not even for a former first lady. And permits meant there would be architectural drawings filed with the city.

Second, elevators had to be inspected periodically. That meant that the elevator she requested would not have been very secret.

But a spiral staircase, even a secret spiral staircase—that was a different matter. She merely waited until construction was finished and the inspectors had signed off on the project. Then she hired a different contractor to construct the staircase. That way she avoided having to take out permits and including it in the final architectural drawings. Of course, her little side project was illegal, but that didn't matter to Allison. All it took was a lot of money, and she had plenty of that.

Not only was it safer, she thought, to use the spiral staircase without shoes, but if she always removed her shoes before going up or down, she would never confuse herself with regard to wardrobe. She did, after all, maintain a totally different set of clothes in each apartment. And, not only was it a different set of clothes, elements of the wardrobes were stylistically distinctive from one another—totally so.

The third reason she never wore shoes on the spiral staircase was to avoid noise. She did not want to gamble on someone, such as an overly observant agent, hearing the hard soles of her shoes clanging on the steel staircase, then zealously investigating. No, Allison had no desire to advertise her secret. The spiral staircase, Allison believed, was the key to keeping her sanity—in her self-talk she referred to it as her "staircase to heaven."

During the renovation of her building, Allison had purchased the apartment directly above her apartment under a different name—Bernadette Lowery. Her status and connections allowed for that. Using her secret staircase, when she wanted to venture out on her own without the Secret Service tagging along, she would lock her "safe room" door, enter her special closet, and head up to the apartment above hers.

Interestingly, also during the renovation, she had the opportunity to buy the apartment beneath hers as well. Apparently, when the existing tenants discovered that a former first lady was moving into the building, several of them opted to move out, not wanting to deal with all the media attention and security personnel. Initially, she considered buying only the one above. That, she thought, would be ideal for the development of her secret persona. By placing Bernadette above her, she would be the only one able to hear noises passing through the floor. Actually, she was more concerned about the noticeable lack of noise emanating from above, because the only person ever to enter that apartment would be herself, disguised as Bernadette.

After giving it considerable thought, she decided to also purchase the apartment below hers for the Secret Service to use. While, technically, one agent always had to be stationed inside her living quarters, she knew that if they had a separate apartment it would provide her with a higher level of separation from them.

By far the most energetic aspect of the whole project involved the addition of new elevators. Initially, the eight-story building had only two—one used by the residents and their visitors, and a larger service elevator. The service elevator was used by residents only when moving in or out of the building and for deliveries of larger items. Workmen doing construction and the building's maintenance personnel also used it on occasion. But, generally speaking, it probably was not needed more than a couple times a week, if that.

Nevertheless, Allison insisted that there be three additional elevators incorporated in the renovation drawings. Initially, the architect objected, but soon he learned that once Allison had made up her mind, there would be no compromise.

She explained that the Secret Service needed its own elevator, and she needed hers; plus, she needed her own service elevator. She did not discuss this matter with the Secret Service, because she knew that they would insist on sharing the use of her elevator.

Her intention was to share the new service elevator, as well as her personal elevator, with the Secret Service. The third new elevator (the one she originally demanded for the Secret Service) she actually intended for the exclusive use of the occupant of apartment two—Bernadette Lowery. That way, when Allison was moving about as Bernadette, she would never have to come face to face with any other occupant of the building, at least not in the narrow confines of an elevator.

She was particularly concerned about Bernadette being stuck face to face with female Secret Service agents. She feared that no matter how good the disguise, another woman, particularly one familiar with her, would eventually see through it.

Another interesting aspect about the new elevators involved the way the elevator doors were controlled. All three of the new elevators could be accessed through the lobby, just as could the two existing elevators. But there was a second door on each of the three new ones. Allison's private elevator (the one she was planning to share with the Secret Service), the new service elevator, and the elevator she was intending for Bernadette's use, all could be accessed from a rear parking lot, where the Secret Service parked their cars.

The tenants always had to use the single doors on the passenger elevator and then walk around and through a secured door that led to the same parking lot. That did not change. Those residents (the ones not associated with Allison and the Secret Service) still had to follow the old procedure.

The original service elevator did, however, open from front and rear. That way deliveries could be made from the courtyard or through the lobby.

Access to all elevators could be gained at ground level through the use of proximity tags. In the cases of the two original elevators, tags had to be presented at a distance of eight inches or less. That feature had been added prior to Allison's renovations. Nothing changed for the original occupants in that regard either.

Of course, all the original elevators, and the new ones, could be accessed and used to go down to the ground level with the simple push of a button. Any other operation would not have met with the approval of the inspectors.

The three new elevators worked in a slightly different fashion. They all were equipped at ground level with a biometric reader, as well as the prox reader—at both the lobby and rear access points. That allowed Allison and the Secret Service to simply place their right hand on the reader and gain access to an elevator. So, if they did not want to present their tags, they could still use one of the new elevators.

Bernadette, however, never used the biometric reader. She always used only her tag.

The building was equipped with an inordinately large natural-gas-powered generator. This generator was added at the special request of Allison and the Secret Service. It was designed so that if the power to the building failed, even for an extended time, the elevators and emergency lights would still function. Of course, that emergency generator also backed up the power in Allison's, Bernadette's, and the Secret Service's apartments. The rest of the building's tenants did not enjoy this feature, nor did they even know about it.

However, even had they known they would not likely have cared much, because prior to Allison moving in, there was no generator at all. At least now the elevators functioned during a power outage.

Of course, there were emergency stairs. They could be accessed from the ground floor by using the same type of tag reader as was located at the front door, the courtyard (rear) door, and for all the elevators. That was a plus for everybody.

And then there were additional readers in this stairwell at three locations—those were the doors leading onto the floors housing Allison's entourage (her two apartments, and the one used by the Secret Service). In all three cases, Allison's apartments occupied an entire floor.

The lock on the ground-level door leading into the stairwell could also be accessed by a high-security key. The only people holding those keys were Allison, Bernadette, and the Secret Service. That means should the elevator fail altogether, all residents of the building could still access the stairs using their prox tags.

However, if the reader system failed as well, only Allison's people had keys to access the stairwell from the ground floor. Those same keys would access the doors leading onto Allison's floor and the Secret Service's floor. But only Allison's key would also access the emergency stairwell door leading onto Bernadette's floor. That meant that she, and only she, could ever access that floor from the stairwell.

On the stairwell side of each of the three special floors was a hidden color camera. There was a monitor just inside of each of those doors. They were there so that anyone desiring to enter the stairwell from any of those three floors would be able to see if someone was lying in wait.

There were, in fact, several very sophisticated closed-circuit color TV systems in place at her building. Again, Allison had designed much of it. From her apartment she was able to monitor the activities in all the common areas throughout her whole building and outside the building front and rear. The Secret Service, as well as Allison, could access that part of the system.

Of course, the cameras on Bernadette's floor and in Allison's safe room could be accessed only by Allison via monitors in her safe room and in Bernadette's apartment.

Access to Allison's private closed-circuit TV system was also bio-metrically controlled. But these readers were not like the ones that controlled the elevators. These were retina readers. They were more sophisticated than the others. She had considered employing retina readers at the new elevators but decided against it for hygienic reasons. Thinking that only she would ever be able even to attempt a retina read from within her private apartments seemed to justify that application in those instances.

There was one glaring exception made regarding ease of access to the CCTV system. Inside the stairwell that led from Allison's apartment to Bernadette's was a station where every camera inside and outside the whole building could be accessed without using any sort of biometric or card readers. Allison had set it up this way intentionally. Her thinking was that this stairwell, the one between her apartment and Bernadette's, would serve as a "safe room" within safe rooms.

In the event of an emergency, she could retreat to the secret stairwell and there wait until it was safe to leave—either through her apartment or through Bernadette's.

Therefore, she designed it so that all cameras could be accessed on the upper landing without any additional security precautions. All she would have to do, in such an emergency, would be to open a small access door, and it would reveal a monitor and a sophisticated digital switch.

Below the door that concealed the CCTV controls was another access door. That one, when opened, exposed a seven-day supply of food and water and necessary toiletries. It also contained an inflatable mattress just small enough to fit nicely on the landing when inflated.

Also, the door of that storage area had a fold-down cushioned seat, so that she could view the monitor for extended periods of time in relative comfort.

Allison had done a masterful job at designing every aspect of her secret life, and she took a lot of pride in it. "Imagine what I will do as president?" she often asked herself.

Allison kept her elevator tag in her purse. When she was on ground level, she merely had to hold her purse up to any reader, and that would activate the special prox reader, granting access at that particular point. However, when entering Bernadette's elevator, she would always remove an access card from her purse, just like the other residents of the building had to use.

As she expected, she had no problem having her plans approved by the City of New York and the Secret Service. No one ever wanted to do battle with Allison. Those who did were always severely punished.

At times it seemed as though she intentionally provoked fights, just so those around her could observe the futility of trying to stand up to her. Besides, it was always lucrative doing business with Allison.

The construction end of the project went as anticipated. And, just as she expected, the Secret Service insisted on sharing the use of Allison's elevator, seeming oblivious to the existence of Bernadette's private use of the elevator initially designated to them. Even Bob, Allison's quasi-estranged husband knew nothing about the existence of Bernadette's apartment.

Bob had for years viewed Allison as one of those proverbial "sleeping dogs." If Allison was not screaming at him or throwing things in his direction, he pretty much didn't get involved in her life. And he certainly made every effort not to antagonize her by involving himself in her affairs without invitation.

When Allison wanted to move about incognito, she would make certain that her keepers knew that she was retiring to her bedroom. Then, once she had secured her bedroom door behind her, she would access her special closet, enter the staircase, and make her way up to Bernadette's lair. That's where the transformation would take place. There she would don the Bernadette persona.

When Allison first began to develop the disguise, she had choices to make: would Bernadette be older or younger? Would she be a flirt or a tough broad? And if she were a flirt, would she be a straight or a gay flirt? Those were all decisions that had to be made before the wardrobe could be selected.

Allison decided that Bernadette would be a little on the younger side, and that she would be a bit more coquettish than was Allison. And that Bernadette would definitely be gay. Allison liked the idea of being able to be openly gay—something she could not get away with in the White House. Besides, as a lesbian, she would be permitted to maintain a higher level of anonymity, as that would help defend against guys hitting on her. In every respect, Allison liked Bernadette more than she liked herself.

Depending on how much time she had to work with, and where she was going, she would begin selecting what she would wear. Normally, when functioning as a former first lady, Allison always had attendants to help her with these mundane tasks. But upstairs, as Bernadette Lowery, she was totally on her own.

Initially, she had help putting the wardrobe together. But when it came to selecting a particular outfit and putting it on, there was no one to help her. She would have liked to have had someone she could trust enough to share this confidence. But there was just too much at stake. If she ever wanted to get back into the White House, every aspect of the plan must work perfectly. There could be no loose ends.

As Allison, she wore very little makeup, and she seemed to relish the more masculine outfits. That was the case partly because she had to perform in a masculine world, out-spitting and out-bragging even the big boys. She could handle that very well as Allison.

But Bernadette did not have to worry about such matters—Bernadette had a much softer side. She smiled more and flirted more. And, best of all, Bernadette got to wear sexier clothes—much sexier clothes.

Allison realized that her thighs were a little too stocky to do much with as far as showing leg, but she felt she could produce healthy cleavage. And that she did with amazing skill. While Allison was not shy about such things, Bernadette flaunted.

Then, of course, there was the alluring hairdo. She spent nearly twenty thousand dollars on that one, single piece of the puzzle that was Bernadette. She had researched it thoroughly. She knew that if the hair worked, the whole disguise could work.

Twenty grand was nothing compared to the millions she had spent renovating her three apartments. True, the Secret Service was provided to her compliments of the US government. However, she took it upon herself to construct an apartment for them.

It was not necessary to arrange for such an elaborate setup—the officers could have commuted. But she concluded that she could control them better by making their lives a bit more cushy. Plus, by so doing, she kept the Secret Service out of her hair, and out of Bernadette's wig.

Even though some people close to the former first lady did learn about the existence of Bernadette, no one outside Allison's inner circle had a clue.

What people are saying about the Jack Handler books

Top Shelf Murder Mystery—Riveting. Being a Murder-Mystery "JUNKIE" this book is definitely a keeper … can't put it down … read it again type of book … and it is very precise to the lifestyles in Upper Michigan. Very well researched. I am a resident of this area. His attention to detail is great. I have to rate this book in the same class or better than authors Michael Connelly, James Patterson, and Steve Hamilton. — Shelldrakeshores

Being a Michigan native, I was immediately drawn to this book. Michael Carrier is right in step with his contemporaries James Patterson and David Baldacci. I am anxious to read more of his work. I highly recommend this one! — J. Henningsen

A fast and interesting read. Michael ends each chapter with a hook that makes you want to keep reading. The relationship between father and daughter is compelling. Good book for those who like a quick moving detective story where the characters often break the "rules" for the greater good! I'm looking forward to reading the author's next book. — Flower Lady

Move over, Patterson, I now have a new favorite author, Jack and his daughter make a great tag team, great intrigue, and diversions. I have a cabin on Sugar Island and enjoyed the references to the locations. I met the author at Joey's (the real live Joey) coffee shop up on the hill, great writer, good stuff. I don't usually finish a book in the course of a week, but read this one in two sittings so it definitely had my attention. I am looking forward to the next installment. Bravo. — Northland Press

My husband is not a reader—he probably hasn't read a book since his last elementary school book report was due. But ... he took my copy of *Murder on Sugar Island* to deer camp and read the whole thing in two days. After he recommended the book to me, I read it—being the book snob that I am, I thought I had the whole plot figured out within the first few pages, but a few chapters later, I was mystified once again. After that surprise ending, we ordered the other two Getting to Know Jack books. — Erin W.

I enjoyed this book very much. It was very entertaining, and the story unfolded in a believable manner. Jack Handler is a likeable character. But you would not like to be on his wrong side. Handler made that very clear in *Jack and the New York Death Mask*. This book (Murder on Sugar Island) was the first book in the Getting to Know Jack series that I read. After I read *Death Mask*, I discovered just how tough Jack Handler really was.

I heard that Carrier is about to come out with another Jack Handler book—a sequel to *Superior Peril*. I will read it the day it becomes available. And I will undoubtedly finish it before I go to bed. If he could write them faster, I would be happy. — Deborah M.

I thoroughly enjoyed this book. I could not turn the pages fast enough. I am not sure it was plausible but I love the characters. I highly recommend this book and look forward to reading more by Michael Carrier. — Amazon Reader

An intense thrill ride!! — Mario

Michael Carrier has knocked it out of the park. — John

Left on the edge of my seat after the last book, I could not wait for the next chapter to unfold and Michael Carrier did not disappoint! I truly feel I know his characters better with each novel and I especially like the can-do/will-do attitude of Jack. Keep up the fine work, Michael, and may your pen never run dry! — SW

The Handlers are at it again, with the action starting on Sugar Island, I am really starting to enjoy the way the father/daughter and now Red are working through the mind of Michael Carrier. The entire family, plus a few more are becoming the reason for the new sheriff's increased body count and antacid intake. The twists and turns we have come to expect are all there and then some. I'm looking for the next installment already. — Northland Press

Finally, there is a new author who will challenge the likes of Michael Connelly and David Baldacci. — Island Books

If you like James Patterson and Michael Connelly, you'll love Michael Carrier. Carrier has proven that he can hang with the best of them. It has all of the great, edge-of-your-seat action and suspense that you'd expect in a good thriller, and it kept me guessing to the very end. Fantastic read with an awesome detective duo—I couldn't put it down! — Katie

Don't read Carrier at the beach or you are sure to get sunburned. I did. I loved the characters. It was so descriptive you feel like you know everyone. Lots of action—always something happening. I love the surprise twists. All my friends are reading it now because I wouldn't talk to them until I finished it so they knew it was good. Carrier is my new favorite author! — Sue

Thoroughly enjoyed this read—kept me turning page after page! Good character development and captivating plot. Had theories but couldn't quite solve the mystery without reading to the end. Highly recommended for readers of all ages. — Terry

Consider writing an Amazon Review?

If you like my books, please leave a short five-star review on Amazon. I would appreciate it! (Note: it is not necessary to have purchased the book from Amazon, only to have an Amazon account.)

This is how I approach writing reviews: When I consider a book I start with what I know about the author. Does he/she write on topics that are of interest to me? Is the book in a genre I like?

I then look inside the book on Amazon. If not dissuaded after having read a portion of it, I proceed.

Once finished, if I did not like the book well enough to give it at least 3 stars overall (with one 5-star element), then I pass on the whole thing. The reviews I write are always 5-star based on the 5-star element(s).

Why would I write a 5-star review of a book that might not in *every* respect be fully worthy of a Hemingway review? Because, I understand that no author becomes successful without a following, and no author obtains a following on the basis of reviews. All a positive review does is help a good author attract a one-time reader. What the author does with a reader from that point on is totally on his shoulders.

* * *

Here are the Amazon links to the seven books of
the "Getting to Know Jack" series:

Jack and the New York Death Mask (Jack):	http://amzn.to/MVpAEd
Murder on Sugar Island (Sugar):	http://amzn.to/1u66DBG
Superior Peril (Peril):	http://amzn.to/LAQnEU
Superior Intrigue (Intrigue):	http://amzn.to/1jvjNSi
Sugar Island Girl Missing in Paris (Missing):	http://amzn.to/1g5c66e
Wealthy Street Murders (Wealthy):	http://amzn.to/1mb6NQy
Murders in Strangmoor Bog (Strangmoor):	http://amzn.to/1IEUPxX

Made in the USA
San Bernardino, CA
02 August 2018